PENGUIN BOOKS

THE HISTORY MAN

Malcolm Bradbury was born in England in 1932. His first novel, *Eating People Is Wrong*, was published in 1959. *The History Man*, originally published in the U.S. in 1976, has long been unavailable. His most recent novel, *Rates of Exchange* (also available from Penguin), was shortlisted for the 1983 Booker McConnell Prize. Mr. Bradbury is married, with two children, and lives in Norwich, England, where he has been a Professor of American Studies at the University of East Anglia since 1970.

THE HISTORY MAN

a novel by
Malcolm Bradbury

PENGUIN BOOKS

PENGUIN BOOKS
Viking Penguin Inc., 40 West 23rd Street,
New York, New York 10010, U.S.A.
Penguin Books Ltd, Harmondsworth,
Middlesex, England
Penguin Books Australia Ltd, Ringwood,
Victoria, Australia
Penguin Books Canada Limited, 2801 John Street,
Markham, Ontario, Canada L3R 1B4
Penguin Books (N.Z.) Ltd, 182–190 Wairau Road,
Auckland 10, New Zealand

First published in Great Britain by Martin Secker &
Warburg Ltd 1975
First published in the United States of America by
Houghton Mifflin Company 1976
Published in Penguin Books 1985

LIBRARY OF CONGRESS CATALOGING IN PUBLICATION DATA
Bradbury, Malcolm, 1932–
    The history man.
    I. Title.
PR6052.R246H5 1985   823'.914   84-26392
ISBN 0 14 00.7630 1

Printed in the United States of America by
R. R. Donnelley & Sons Company, Harrisonburg, Virginia
Set in Baskerville

To Matthew and Dominic

AUTHOR'S NOTE

This fiction is for Beamish, whom, while en route for some conference or other, I last saw at Frankfurt airport, enquiring from desk to desk about his luggage, unhappily not loaded onto the same plane as he. It is a total invention with delusory approximations to historical reality, just as is history itself. Not only does the University of Watermouth, which appears here, bear no relation to the real University of Watermouth (which does not exist) or to any other university; the year 1972, which also appears, bears no relation to the real 1972, which was a fiction anyway; and so on. As for the characters, so-called, no one but the other characters in this book knows them, and they not well; they are pure inventions, as is the plot in which they more than participate. Nor did I fly to a conference the other day; and if I did, there was no one on the plane named Beamish, who certainly did not lose his luggage. The rest, of course, is true.

*   *   *

'Who's Hegel?'
'Someone who sentenced mankind to history.'
'Did he know a lot? Did he know everything?'

Günter Grass

I

Now it is the autumn again; the people are all coming back. The recess of summer is over, when holidays are taken, newspapers shrink, history itself seems momentarily to falter and stop. But the papers are thickening and filling again; things seem to be happening; back from Corfu and Sete, Positano and Leningrad, the people are parking their cars and campers in their drives, and opening their diaries, and calling up other people on the telephone. The deckchairs on the beach have been put away, and a weak sun shines on the promenade; there is fresh fighting in Vietnam, while McGovern campaigns ineffectually against Nixon. In the chemists' shops in town, they have removed the sunglasses and the insect-bite lotions, for the summer visitors have left, and have stocked up on sleeping tablets and Librium, the staples of the year-round trade; there is direct rule in Ulster, and a gun-battle has taken place in the Falls Road. The new autumn colours are in the boutiques; there is now on the market a fresh intra-uterine device, reckoned to be ninety-nine per cent safe. Everywhere there are new developments, new indignities; the intelligent people survey the autumn world, and liberal and radical hackles rise, and fresh faces are about, and the sun shines fitfully, and the telephones ring. So, sensing the climate, some people called the Kirks, a well-known couple, decide to have a party.

The Kirks have, in fact, had a party at just this time of the year—the turning-point when the new academic year starts, new styles are in, new faces about, new ideas busy—for the past three autumns; and, if it had been anyone else but the Kirks, you might have said it was a custom or tradition with them. But the Kirks are very fresh and spontaneous people, who invest in all their activities with high care and scruple, and do nothing just because it has been done before; indeed they are widely understood not to have such things as customs and traditions. If the Kirks happen to have thought of a party, well, they have thought of it innocently, afresh, and from a sense of need. Evolving time signals mysteriously to those who are true citizens of it; the Kirks are true citizens of the present, and they take their messages from the prevailing air, and answer them with an honest sense of duty. They are, after all, very busy people, with many causes and issues, many meetings and conspiracies, many affairs and associations to attend to; indeed they are very lucky to catch each other in like mind, very lucky to catch each other at the same time in the same house at all. But they do know a need when they see one, and here they are, together in their own kitchen, and the idea comes, it is not clear from whom, above all, in fact, from the force of the times. Their eyes brighten, as they always do when such news comes; they say yes to each other; they set to work at once on the who, what and how of it. Howard, because he is nearest, leaves their bright pine kitchen, and goes out into the hall, to fetch, from beside their busy telephone, their busy house diary, a crucial text and record for people like themselves. They put the book between them on the kitchen table, and open it; they inspect the long, predictive tale of doings and undoings it unfolds, the elaborate, contingent plot of the days ahead of them. 'When?' says Barbara. 'Soon,' says Howard. 'Are we free on the first day of term?' asks Barbara. It is improbable, but Howard turns the pages; there is the day, Monday 2 October, and the evening is a blank. It is almost an omen; and from his inside pocket Howard takes out, at once, his pen. He holds the diary open; he writes, in his neat little hand, as if writing the start of some new story, which in a sense is what it is, the word 'Party' in the small space of white on the crowded page.

The Kirks have had parties at this time of year before, they recall, and they know a lot of people will come; they are, after all, a very well-known couple. Howard is a sociologist, a radical sociologist, a small, bright, intense, active man, of whom you are likely to have heard, for he is much heard of. He is on television a good deal, and has written two well-known and disturbing books, urging new mores, a new deal for man; he has had a busy, literary summer, and a third book is on its way. He also writes articles in the papers, and he lectures at the local new university, a still expanding dream in white concrete, glass, and architectural free form, spreading on a hillside just to the west of, and just outside, the south-western sea-coast town in which they live. The university, having aspirations to relevance, has made much of sociology; and it would be hard to find anyone in the field with a greater sense of relevance than Howard. His course on Revolutions is a famous keystone, just as are, in a different way, his interventions in community relations, his part in the life of the town. For Howard is a well-known activist, a thorn in the flesh of the council, a terror to the selfish bourgeoisie, a pressing agent in the Claimants' Union, a focus of responsibility and concern. As for Barbara, well, she is at this minute just a person, as she puts it, trapped in the role of wife and mother, in the limited role of woman in our society; but of course she, too, is a radical person, and quite as active as Howard in her way. She is, amongst her many competences and qualifications, a *cordon bleu* cook, an expert in children's literature, a tireless promoter of new causes (Women for Peace, The Children's Crusade for Abortion, No More Sex for Repression). And she, too, is a familiar figure, in the streets, as she blocks them with others to show that traffic is not inevitable, and in the supermarkets, as she leads her daily deputation to the manager with comparative, up-to-the-minute lists showing how Fine Fare, on lard, is one pence up on Sainsbury's, or vice versa. She moves through playgroups and schools, surgeries and parks, in a constant indignation; she writes, when it is her turn, for the community newspaper. When you visit the Kirks, there is always a new kind of Viennese coffee-cake to eat, and a petition to sign. And, as for the Kirks together, the well-known couple, they are a familiar pair in the high-rise council flats, going up and down in the obscenity-scrawled Otis lifts, hunting out instances of deprivation to show the welfare people, of careless motherhood to take

3

to the family planning clinic; in the council offices, where they throw open doors behind which officials sit to thrust forward, in all their rebuking and total humanity, the fleshed-out statistic, the family that has not had its rights, not had just benefits, not been rehoused; and in the town in general, raising consciousness, raising instructive hell. The Kirks are active in the world as it is, in all its pathetic contingency; but they have higher hopes yet. They wake each morning and inspect the sky meticulously for dark hands, thunderbolts, white horsemen: evidence that the poor reality they so seriously tend has at least been wonderfully transformed, a new world, a new order, come overnight.

But in the meantime they go on, together and separately. They have been married now for twelve years, though you wouldn't think it, to look at them, to see them, to hear them in action. They have produced, by prophylaxis, two children, bright, modern creatures, both now of school age, of whom they are reasonably fond. They live together in a tall, thin, stuccoed Georgian house, which is in a slum-clearance area right in the middle of the town. It is an ideal situation for the Kirks, close to the real social problems, the beach, the radical bookshop, the family planning clinic, the macrobiotic food store, the welfare offices, the high-rise council flats, and the rapid ninety minute electric train service up to London, close, in short, to the stuff of ongoing life. From time to time, being passionate, liberated, consciousness-conscious people, they live apart, or with someone else, for a spell. But these always seem mature, well-thought interludes and infidelities, expressing their own separate individuality without disturbing their common Kirkness, and so somehow they always manage to be back together again within the month, and hence to seem, in the eyes of their friends, and presumably in their own eyes as well, a settled, but not an absurdly settled, couple. For the Kirks always generate excitement, curiosity. They are experimental people, intimates with change and liberation and history, and they are always busy and always going.

They look the way new people do look, this autumn. Howard, small, dark, and compact, has long hair, though not quite so long as it was last year, and a Zapata moustache; he wears neat white sweatshirts, with rousing symbols on the front, like

4

clenched fists, and hairy loose waistcoats, and pyjama-style blue jeans. Barbara, who is big and has frizzled yellow hair, wears green eyeshadow, and clown-white makeup, and long caftan dresses, and no bra, so that her stubby nipples show through the light cotton. Howard's two books being now staple radical documents in that expanding market, their jeans and caftans are rather more expensive than those of most of the people they know. But it is invisible expense, inconspicuous unconsumption, and it creates no distances and makes them no enemies, except for the enemies who were always their enemies. The Kirks are very attractive, very buoyant, very aggressive people, and, even if you dislike or distrust them, or are disturbed by them (and they mean to be disturbing), very good company.

After the instinct about the party comes to them, an instinct so harmonious that neither one of them can now remember which of the two of them thought of it first, the Kirks go down to Howard's study, which is in the basement of their Georgian terrace house, and pour themselves some wine, and start to work on what Howard calls 'the loose frame of reference surrounding this encounter'. There are two studies in the Kirk house, though it is a very unstructured house, the opposite of the kind of thing people call a home: Howard's, downstairs, where he writes books, and Barbara's, upstairs, where she means to. Howard's study is lined with bookshelves; the bookshelves are filled with sociology texts, books about encounter groups and interpersonal relations, new probes into radical experience by American visionaries, basic political manifestos. Under the window is a white desk, with a second telephone on it; on the desk lies a fluttering pile of paper, the typescript of the book—which is called *The Defeat of Privacy*—that Howard has been working on over the recess and withdrawal of the summer, the recess that is now ending. The grilled window over the desk looks out onto a basement yard, with an untended plant tub in it; you must look upwards to see the railings onto the street. Back through the grilled windows comes in the sun that has been shining all day, a weak, late-year sun that slants in and composes square shapes on the bookcases and the walls. On the walls, between the bookcases, there are African masks, faces in black and dark brown carved wood set against white emulsion. The Kirks, in their bright clothes, sit beneath the masks, in two low white canvas chairs. They each hold their glass of red wine, and they look at each other, and they begin to talk the party into existence. They name names, they plan food and drink.

After a while Barbara rises, and goes to the bottom of the stairs. 'Anne,' she shouts up into the hall, 'Howard and I are planning a party. I wonder if you'd give the children a bath?' 'Fine, Mrs Kirk,' shouts Anne Petty, the student who has been living with them over the summer, having fallen out so severely with her parents she cannot go home, 'I'll see to it.' 'I don't know how I'd manage without Anne,' says Barbara, sitting down in the canvas chair again. 'Beamishes,' says Howard, 'can we stand the Beamishes?' 'We've not seen them all summer,' says Barbara, 'We've not seen anyone all summer.' And that is true, for to the Kirks the summer represents the low point of the year, the phase of social neglect. Howard has finished his book—it flutters at them on the desktop—but creation is a lonely and introverted activity; he is in that flat state of literary post coitum that affects those who spend too much time with their own lonely structures and plots; he needs to be back into, to intervene in, the larger, grander, more splendid plots that are plotted by history. And Barbara has been domestic, and domesticity is an evasion to people like the Kirks; the self has bigger business to perform. But their party is a party for the world, too; they construct it solemnly. Howard is a theoretician of sociability; he debates about what he calls 'relevant forms of interaction', and the parameters of the encounter. Barbara performs the antithetical role, and thinks of persons and faces, not because men are abstract and women emotional—that is the sort of role-designation both of them would deny—but because someone has to keep abreast of who likes whom, and who can't be in the same room as whom, and who is bedding whom, and who ought sooner or later to bed whom, if you want to have really good parties. And the Kirks always do have good parties, have a talent for giving them. They are unstructured parties, frames for event, just as are Howard's seminars at the university, and his books, where urgent feeling breaks up traditional grammar, methodology and organization. But, as Howard always says, if you

6

want to have something that's genuinely unstructured, you have to plan it carefully. And that, then, is just what the Kirks do, as they sit in their study, and drink their wine.

The sunsquares on the wall fade; Howard switches on his desk lamp. The principle is creative mixture. So the Kirks are mixing people from the town with people from the university, and people from London with people from the town. They are mixing heteros with homos, painters with advanced theologians, scientists with historians, students with Hell's Angels, pop-stars with IRA supporters, Maoists with Trotskyites, family-planning doctors with dropouts who sleep under the pier. The Kirks have a wide intellectual constituency, an expansive acquaintance; there are so many forms and contexts of changing life to keep up with. After a while Howard gets up; he leans against the bookcase; he stays 'Stop there. I'm afraid it's hardening. If we say any more, it'll turn into the kind of bloody bourgeois party we'd refuse to go to.' 'Oh, you'd never refuse to go to a party,' says Barbara. 'I think we're losing spontaneity,' says Howard, 'we said an unpredictable encounter.' 'I just want to ask,' says Barbara, 'how many people we'll have at this unpredictable encounter. I'm thinking about the work.' 'We have to make it a real scene,' says Howard, 'a hundred, maybe more.' 'Your idea of a good party,' says Barbara, 'is to invite the universe. And then leave me to wash up after.' 'Oh, come on,' says Howard, 'we need this. *They* need it.' 'Your enthusiasm,' says Barbara, 'it never wears, does it?' 'Right,' says Howard, 'that's why I exist. Now I'm going to pick up the telephone and make twenty-five calls, and you're going to make twenty-five calls, and there's our party.' 'Martin's wet his pyjama trousers,' shouts Anne Petty from upstairs. 'Give him some more,' shouts Barbara, up the stairs. 'Roger, it's Howard,' says Howard, with the red telephone next to his ear. 'We're planning a bit of action. No, not that kind of action: a party.' There is a new book by R. D. Laing lying on the table next to Barbara's chair; she picks it up and thumbs through its pages. 'An accidental party,' says Howard, 'the kind where you might meet anyone and do anything.' 'Or meet anything and do anyone,' says Barbara. 'Barbara's fine, I'm fine,' says Howard, 'we're just ready to get started again.' 'Oh, yes, I'm fine,' says Barbara, 'fine fine fine.' 'No,' says Howard, 'it's just Barbara having schizophrenia in the background. See you on the second. And bring anyone you can predict will be unpredictable.'

'That's what we need,' says Howard, putting down the telephone, 'people.' 'You've had all the people you can eat,' says Barbara. 'We need some fresh ones,' says Howard, picking up the telephone again, 'who do we know that we don't know? Ah, Henry, we need you, Henry. Can you and Myra come to a party?' And so Howard talks on the telephone, and makes twenty-five calls, while Barbara sits in the canvas chair; and then Barbara talks on the telephone, and makes twenty-five calls, while Howard sits in the canvas chair. The Kirks are a modern couple, and believe in dividing all tasks equally down the middle, half for you, half for me, like splitting an orange, so that both get involved, and neither gets exploited. When they have finished on the telephone, they sit in the canvas chairs again, and Barbara says, 'You buy the drinks, I'll buy the food,' and the party is all ready. So they go upstairs, to the kitchen, and here, side by side, wearing similar butcher's aprons, they prepare the dinner. The children run in and out, in their pyjamas; Anne Petty comes in, and offers to make dessert. Then they all sit at the table and eat the meal they have prepared; Anne Petty puts the children to bed, and the Kirks sit down in the living-room with their coffee, and watch television. It is unusual for them to be so together; they dwell on their amazement. Later on they go upstairs to bed together and, standing on opposite sides of the bed, undress together. They turn down the duvet; they switch on the spotlight over the bed; they touch each other, and make love together. The faces and bodies they have invented to populate their party come into the bedroom with them and join in the fun. Afterwards the light shines down on them, and Barbara says to Howard, 'I'm just afraid I'm losing some of my enjoyment.' 'Of this?' asks Howard, pressing her. 'No,' says Barbara, 'parties. The swinging Kirk scene.' 'You couldn't,' says Howard. 'Maybe I'm getting old,' says Barbara, 'all I see in my mind are dirty glasses.' 'I'll make it interesting for you,' says Howard. 'Oh, sure,' says Barbara, 'you're a great magician of the feelings, aren't you, Howard?' 'I try,' says Howard. 'Howard Kirk,' says Barbara, 'what we have instead of faith.'

The days go by, and the telephones ring, and then it is the morning of Monday 2 October, when things are really starting again: the first day of term, the day of the party. The Kirks rise up, early and together. They pull on their clothes; they tidy the bed; they go downstairs. The kitchen is done out in pine. The rain washes down the window; the room is in wet half-light. In the kitchen Anne Petty stands by the stove in a candlewick dressing-gown, cooking an egg. 'What gets you up so early?' she says. 'We're going shopping,' says Barbara, 'for the party.' Howard goes to the toaster, and presses bread into it; Barbara takes a carton of eggs from the refrigerator. Howard pushes down the button on the toaster; Barbara cracks eggs and drops them into the frying-pan. The children come in, and sit down at the places Anne has already laid for them. 'Corn-flakes, yuk,' says Martin. 'Oh, Jesus,' says Barbara, looking in the sink, 'I didn't know we dirtied all those plates last night. How did we do that?' 'We ate,' says Howard, who sits down at the table, inspecting the outrages of the day in the morning's *Guardian*. Anne Petty looks up; she says, 'You want me to wash them up, Mrs Kirk?' 'Oh, would you really, Anne?' says Barbara, 'there's so much to do today.' 'Oh, yes, Mrs Kirk,' says Anne Petty. 'Eggs, again,' says Martin, as Barbara serves them, 'why do you always give us the same every day?' 'Because I'm busy,' says Barbara, 'and put your plates in the sink when you're through. Howard and I are going shopping.' 'But who's going to take us to school?' asks Celia. 'Oh, hell,' says Barbara, 'now what can we do about that?' 'Would you like me to take them to school?' asks Anne Petty, looking up. 'It would be marvellous,' says Barbara, 'but I hate to ask you. You're not here to do jobs. You're here because we like having you here.' 'Oh, I know that, Mrs Kirk,' says Anne, 'but I really do like helping you. I mean, you're both such busy people. I don't know how you do so much.' 'It takes a certain genius,' says Howard. 'I do hope you're staying on with us for a bit,' says Barbara. 'We'd love to have you, and I want to make one of my little shopping trips to London next weekend. So I'll need someone for the children.' 'Oh, I don't know,' says Anne Petty, looking embarrassed, 'next weekend?' 'She means no,' says Howard, looking up from the *Guardian*, 'the statement's equivocal, but the subtext says: "Lay off, you're exploiting me." '

Anne Petty looks at him; she says, 'Oh, Dr Kirk, Kirks don't exploit anybody. Not the Kirks. It's just that I really don't see how I can.' 'Oh, everybody exploits somebody,' says Howard, 'in this social order, it's part of the human lot. But some know it, some don't. When Barbara gets anxious, she starts handing out tasks to people. You're right to resist.' 'I hand out tasks,' says Barbara, 'because I have them to do.' 'Please, look,' says Anne Petty, 'no one's exploiting anyone. Really. I'd love to stay, but my friends are coming back to the flat, and I've paid part-rent.' Barbara says: 'Oh, you're right, Howard. Every-one exploits someone. Notably you me.' 'What did I do?' asks Howard, innocently. 'Oh, God,' says Barbara, 'how his heart bleeds for victims. And he finds them all over. The only ones he can't see are the people he victimizes himself.' 'I'm sorry, Mrs Kirk, I really am,' says Anne Petty. 'You mustn't blame Anne,' says Howard, 'she has her own scene.' 'I'm not blaming Anne,' says Barbara, 'I'm blaming you. You're trying to stop my trip to London. You don't want me to have a week-end in London.' 'You'll have your weekend,' says Howard, 'Leave it to me. I'll fix it. Someone will look after the kids.' 'Who?' asks Celia, 'Anyone nice?' 'Someone Howard likes,' says Barbara. 'Doesn't Howard like Anne?' asks Martin. 'Of course I do,' says Howard. 'Get your coat on. I'm going to fetch the van.' 'It's just I have to move back to the flat with these friends,' says Anne Petty, as Howard walks across the kitchen. 'Of course you do,' says Howard, in the doorway. 'Bring them to the party.' Howard goes out into the hall, and puts on a long leather coat from the peg, and a neat blue denim cap. The conversation continues behind him in the kitchen. He walks down the hall, opens the front door, and steps out. He stands in the wet light. The terrace is puddled, the rain pours down, the city is loud. He pulls the door to behind him, on the domestic social annex, which shrills behind him; he walks out onto the urban stage, the busy movingness of city life, the place where, as every good sociologist knows, the cake of custom crumbles, traditional role-ascriptions break, the bonds of kinship weaken, where the public life that determines the private one is led.

He walks along the terrace, with its cracked pavement stones, its scatter of broken glass; the rain soaks his hair, and begins to stipple the leather of his coat. The terrace curves around him; once an exact and elegant half-circle, the curious dentistry of demolition has attacked it, pulling out house after house from the curve as they have become empty. Most of those that still stand are unoccupied, with broken roofs and vacant, part-boarded windows, plastered with posters for political parties, pop groups, transcendental meditators, or rather surreptitiously occupied, for they are visited by a strange, secret, drifting population of transients. But, though there are few residents, the terrace has been metered for parking; the Kirks have to keep their minivan some streets away, in a square up the hill. A police car heehaws on the urban motorway being sliced through the demolition; buses grind below him, on the promenade. An air-force jet flies in off the sea, its line of flight an upward curve that brings it into sudden visibility over the jagged tops of the houses across the terrace from the Kirks' tall, thin house. He turns the corner; he walks up the hill. The long latticed metal of a construction crane swings into his eyeline, dangling a concrete beam. Up the hill he goes, past the remnants of the old order, the scraps of traditional Watermouth falling beneath the claims of the modern city. There are small shops—a newsagent with a window display of *The Naked Ape*, a greengrocer with a few crates of vegetables standing outside under a leaky canvas awning, a family butcher with a notice saying 'We keep our meat on ice in hot weather'. There are small back-to-back houses, whose doors open directly onto the street; the bulldozers soon will reach them. Higher on the hill grow the new concrete towers. Before he reaches them Howard turns to the left, into a square of small houses, mostly flats and private hotels. His old blue minivan stands in a line of cars beside the kerb, under a sodium streetlamp. He unlocks the driver's door; he gets in; he turns the ignition twice to fire the engine. He drives the van back and forth, to clear the space. Then he drives out of the square, down through the busy traffic of the hill, and back into the terrace.

On the pavement, outside their tall terrace house, set in its broken curve, Barbara is already standing, waiting for him to come. She wears a white, pinch-waist, full-length raincoat; she carries two red canvas bags, Swiss, from Habitat. He leans over to open the passenger door; she reaches into the van to put the bags into the back. 'You must be feeling very good,' she says, getting into the seat beside Howard, 'everything's starting for you, so you're feeling very good.' Howard lets out the clutch; he turns the van, back and forth, in the terrace. 'I'm fine,' says Howard, driving to the end of the terrace, turning up the hill. 'Shouldn't I be?' Barbara pulls on her seat-belt; she says, 'I can tell when you're feeling good because you always want to make me feel bad.' Howard follows the arrows and the directional marks, the lefts, the rights, the no entries, that lead him up the hill and towards the new shopping precinct. 'I don't want you to feel bad,' says Howard. There is a turn to the left, barred by a red arm; it is the entrance to the high multi-storey car park on the edge of the precinct. 'Well, I do feel bad,' says Barbara. Howard makes the turn; he stops the van in front of the arm; he takes a ticket from the automatic machine. 'You know what you need?' he says; the arm rises, and Howard drives forward. 'Yes,' says Barbara, 'I know exactly what I need. A weekend in London.' Howard drives up the ramp into the blank concrete of the place, through the flickers of light and dark, following the wet tyre-tracks. Howard says, 'You need a party.' The van spirals upward through the high, blank building. 'I don't need a party,' says Barbara, 'it's just another sodding domestic chore I have to clear up after.' Driving through the concrete and the metal, Howard sees, on the fifth floor, a space for the van to park; he drives into it. The garage is dark and grey; he pulls on the handbrake. 'You just had a very dull summer,' says Howard, 'now everything's happening again. Come on, let's go and shop.'

The car park is a low, cavernous place, devoid of people, a place for machines only; out through the unwindowed parapet, you can see the town spread out below. The Kirks get out of the van; they walk together, over the oily, roughened floor, to the blank metal door of the lift shaft. Barbara says: 'Your excitement fails to infect me.' Howard presses the button; the lift grinds in the shaft. The doors open; the Kirks get in. There are aerosoled scribbles on the lift walls: 'Agro', 'Boot boys', 'Gary is King'. They stand together and the lift descends. It stops and the Kirks walk out. A long tiled corridor leads towards the precinct; there is human excrement against the walls of the brightlit passage. They come out among the high buildings, into a formal square. The precinct has straight angles; it has won an architectural award. There are long glass façades, the fronts of supermarkets, delicatessens, boutiques, the familiar multiple stores, displaying the economy of abundance; there is a symmetry of tins and toilet rolls in the windows of Sainsbury's; spotlights and shade permute the colour range of sweaters and shirts, dresses and skirts, in the Life Again Boutique. In the open space in the middle are multicoloured paving stones; amid the stones, in some complex yet deducible code, are tiny new trees, fresh-planted, propped by wooden supports. A waterless fountain contains much litter. The Kirks divide their tasks, half to you, half for me. Barbara walks towards the automatic glass doors of Sainsbury's, which slide open mechanically as she approaches them, and close again as she passes inside; Howard goes on down the precinct, to the wine supermarket, which is called Your Wine Seller, and has very special offers at very special prices. He walks inside, under the bright spotlights; he stands under the anti-theft mirrors, and inspects the bottles of wine that have been tossed carelessly together in the wire bins. He goes to the small counter at the back of the store.

The assistant looks at him; he is young, with a beard, and wears a maroon jacket with a yellow Smile badge on the lapel; this leaves his face free to be very surly. Howard sees with gratification the indignation of the employed and oppressed, the token resistance. He gives his order, for five dozen litre-bottles of cheap red wine; he waits while the man goes into the storeroom, and wheels out, on a wire trolley, a stack of big cardboard cases. He asks for the loan of twelve dozen glasses; 'We don't lend them,' says the assistant. Howard delivers himself to the task of persuasion; he emanates concern, he invites the man to the party; he gets the glasses. The assistant stacks the boxes of glasses on another trolley. Howard takes the first trolley, and wheels it, across the open space of the precinct, over the coloured paving stones, past the empty fountain, through the tiled passage, to the lift; he ascends in the lift, and unpacks the cases into the back of the minivan. He returns with the empty trolley; he takes the second trolley of glasses up into the car park, and then back to the store. When he reaches the van again, Barbara has still not returned. He stands by the van, car keys hanging from one finger, in the empty, cavernous place, devoid of people, amid the shuttered concrete planes, the rough surfaces, the angular lines of air and space, light and darkness. He stares out, over the unwindowed parapet, at the topography of the town. There are torn spaces below, where the motorway and the new housing projects are being constructed; beyond are the rising shells of hotels, office blocks, flats. There are two Watermouths; the unreal holiday town around the harbour and the Norman castle, with luxury flats and expensive bars, gift shops and pinkwashed Georgian homes; and a real town of urban blight and renewal, social tensions, discrimination, landlord and tenant battles, where the Kirks live. To one side, he can see the blocks of luxury flats, complete but half-empty, with convenience kitchens and wall-to-wall carpeting and balconies pointed at the horizon; to the other side, on the hill, stand the towers of the high-rise council flats, superficially similar, stacked, like a social workers' handbook, with separated wives, unmarried mothers, latchkey children. It is a topography of the mind; and his mind makes an intellectual contrast out of it, an image of conflict and opposition. He stares down on the town; the keys dangle; he populates chaos, orders disorder, senses strain and change.

A Boeing 747 flies in off the coast heading for Heathrow; the engine noise booms in the cavernous building, sounds off the metal of the cars. In the corner of the concrete place, the lift-doors scrape back; someone walks out onto the sounding floor. It is Barbara, walking towards him, in her long white coat; she carries the two red bags, full. Her body is faint colour moving over grey cement. He watches her move through the planes of light and dark. She comes up to the van, and opens the back; into the interior, on top of the boxes, she pushes the bags, holding French loaves and cheeses. 'Enough?' she says. 'Of course, if there's five thousand, you'll be able to increase the quantity.' Howard opens the driver's door, and gets in; he opens the other door so that Barbara can come in to the passenger seat. She sits down; she fastens the seatbelt. Her face is dark in the shadowy place. He starts the engine, backs out of the space. Barbara says: 'Do you remember Rosemary?' Howard drives down the spiral ramp, with its code of arrows and lights; he says, 'The one who lives in the commune?'

'She was in Sainsbury's,' says Barbara. The van tilts down the ramps; it makes the sharp turns. 'So you asked her to the party,' says Howard. 'I did,' says Barbara. 'I asked her to the party.' They are on ground level now; Howard turns the van towards the exit, the bright wet daylight. 'Do you remember that boy she was living with?' asks Barbara. 'He had a tattoo on the back of his hand.' Through angular blocks of air and space, light and darkness, they move to the light square. 'I don't think so,' says Howard. 'You do,' says Barbara. 'He came to one of our parties. Just before the summer.' 'What about him?' asks Howard; the stubby red arm is down in front of him. 'He left a note for her on the table,' says Barbara. 'Then he went down the garden, to an old shed, and killed himself with a rope.' Howard reaches out of the window, and hands the ticket and a coin to the attendant, who sits opposite and above him, in a small glass box. 'I see,' says Howard, 'I see.' The attendant hands Howard change; the stubby arm rises in front of him. 'When?' asks Howard, moving the van forward. 'Two days ago,' says Barbara. 'Is she very upset?' asks Howard. 'She's thin and pale, and she cried,' says Barbara. Howard carefully eases the van out into the line of rush-hour traffic. 'Are you upset?' asks Howard. 'Yes,' says Barbara, 'it's upset me.'

The traffic line jams. 'You hardly knew him,' says Howard, turning to look at her. 'It was the note,' says Barbara. Howard sits behind the wheel, stuck in the line, and looks at the moving collage. 'What did it say?' he asks. 'It just said, "This is silly."' 'A taste for brevity,' says Howard, 'what was? The thing with Rosemary?' 'Rosemary says not,' says Barbara, 'she says they were going great together.' 'I can't really imagine going great with Rosemary,' says Howard. Barbara stares ahead, through the windscreen. She says: 'She says he found things absurd. He even found being happy absurd. It was life that was silly.' 'Life's not silly,' says Howard, 'it may be chaotic, but it's not silly.' Barbara stares at Howard; she says, 'You'd like to quarrel with him? He's dead.' Howard inches the van forward; he says, 'I'm not quarrelling with him. He had his own thing going.' 'He thought life was silly,' says Barbara. 'Christ, Barbara,' says Howard, 'the fact that he killed himself doesn't make it into a universal truth.' 'He wrote that,' says Barbara, 'then he killed himself.' 'I know,' says Howard, 'that was his view. That was his existential choice. He couldn't make sense of things, so he found them silly.' 'It's funny to be existential,' says Barbara, 'when you don't exist.' 'It's the fact that we stop existing that makes us existential choosers,' says Howard, 'that's what the word means.' 'Thanks,' says Barbara, 'thanks for the lesson.' 'What's the matter?' asks Howard, 'are you getting yourself seduced by this absurdist thing? It's a cop out.'

The traffic jam unstops. Howard lets out the clutch. Barbara stares ahead through the windscreen, down at the traffic movements on the hill. After a minute she says: 'Is that all?' 'All what?' asks Howard, moving forward through the peculiar private track that will take him through the traffic lanes and take him back to the terrace house. 'All you have to say,' says Barbara, 'all you can think.' 'What do you want me to think, that I'm not thinking?' asks Howard. 'Doesn't it worry you at all that so many of our friends feel that way now?' asks Barbara, 'do things like that now? That they seem tired and desperate? Is it our ages? Is it that the political excitement's gone? What's the matter?' 'He wasn't a friend,' says Howard, 'we hardly knew him.' 'He came to a party,' says Barbara. Howard, driving down the hill, turns and looks at her. 'Look,' he says, 'he came to a party. He was on drugs. He and Rosemary were getting into some crazy magical thing together, the kind of thing that hippies switch into when the trips turn sour. He never talked. We don't know what his problems were. We don't know what seemed absurd to him. We don't know where he and Rosemary were going.' 'Do you remember when our sort of people didn't think life was silly?' asks Barbara, 'when things were all wide open and free, and we were all doing something and the revolution was next week? And we were under thirty, and we could trust us?' 'It's still like that,' says Howard, 'people always dropped in and out.' 'Is it really like that?' asks Barbara, 'Don't you think people have got tired? Found a curse in what they were doing?' Howard says: 'A boy dies and you turn it into a metaphor for the times.' Barbara says: 'Howard, you have always turned everything into a metaphor for the times. You've always said that the times are where we are; there's no other place. You've lived off the flavours and fashions of the mind. So has this boy, who came to one of our parties, and had a blue tattoo, and

16

put a rope round his neck in a shed. Is he real, or isn't he?' 'Barbara, you're just feeling depressive,' says Howard, 'take a Valium.' 'Take a Valium. Have a party. Go on a demo. Shoot a soldier. Make a bang. Bed a friend. That's your problem-solving system.' says Barbara. 'Always a bright, radical solution. Revolt as therapy. But haven't we tried all that? And don't you find a certain gloom in the record?' Howard turns and looks at Barbara, inspecting this heresy. He says: 'There may be a fashion for failure and negation now. But we don't have to go along with it.' 'Why not?' asks Barbara, 'after all, you've gone along with every other fashion, Howard.' Howard takes the turn into the terrace; the bottles shake in the back of the van. He says: 'I don't understand your sourness, Barbara. You just need some action.' 'I'm sure you'll find a way of giving me that,' says Barbara, 'the trouble is, I've had most of the action I can take, from you.' Howard stops the van; he puts his hand on Barbara's thigh. He says: 'You just got switched off, kid. Everything's still happening. You'll feel good again, once it all starts.' 'I don't think you understand what I'm telling you,' says Barbara, 'I'm telling you that your gay belief in things happening doesn't make me feel better any more. Christ, Howard, how did we come to be like this?' 'Like which?' asked Howard. 'Depending on things happening, like this,' says Barbara, 'putting on shows like this.' 'I can explain,' says Howard. 'I'm sure you can,' says Barbara, 'but don't. Are you going straight off to the university?' 'I have to,' says Howard, 'to start the term.' 'To start the trouble,' says Barbara. 'To start the term,' says Howard. 'Well, I want you to help me unload all this stuff, before you go.' 'Of course,' says Howard, 'you take the food in. I'll bring the wine.' And so the Kirks get out, and go round to the back of the van, and unload what is there. They carry it, together, the bread, the cheese and the sausages, the glasses and the big red bottles in their cases, into the house, into the pine kitchen. They spread it on the table, an impressive array of commodities, ready and waiting for the party in the evening. 'I want you back by four, to help me with all this fun we're brewing,' says Barbara. 'Yes, I'll try,' says Howard. He looks at the wine; he goes out back to the van. Then he gets in, and drives off, through the town, towards the university.

II

The Kirks are, indeed, new people. But where some new people
are born new people, natural intimates of change and history,
the Kirks arrived at that condition the harder way, by effort,
mobility, and harsh experience; and, if you are interested in
how to know them, and feel about them, then this, as Howard
will explain to you, is a most important fact to possess about
them. The Kirks are now full citizens of life; they claim
historical rights; they have not always been in a position to
claim them. For they were not born into the bourgeoisie, with
its sense of access and command, and they did not grow up
here, in this bright sea-coast city, with its pier and beach, its
respectable residences and easy contact with London, its
contact with style and wealth. The Kirks, both of them,
grew up, in a grimmer, tighter north, in respectable upper
working-class cum lower middle-class backgrounds (Howard
will gloss this social location for you, and explain its essential
ambiguity); and, when they first met each other, and married,
some twelve years ago, they were very different people from
the Kirks of today: a timid, withdrawn pair, on whom life had
sat onerously. Howard was that conventional product of his
circumstances and his time, the fifties: the scholarship boy,
serious and severe, well-read in the grammar-school library,
bad at games and humanity, who had got in to Leeds University, in 1957, by pure academic effort—a draining effort
that had, in fact, left him for a time pallid in features and in

mind. Barbara was inherently brighter, as she had to be, since girls from that background were not pushed hard academically; and she made it to university from her girls' grammar school, not, like Howard, through strong motive, but through the encouragement and advice of a sympathetic, socialistic teacher of English, who had mocked her sentimental domestic ambitions. Even at university they had both remained timid people, unpolitical figures in an unpolitical, unaggressive setting. Howard's clothes then always managed to look old, even when they were new; he was very thin, very bleak, and had nothing to say. He was reading sociology, then still a far from popular or prestigious subject, indeed a subject most of the people he knew thought very weighty, Germanic, and dull. He had dark yellow nicotined fingers, from smoking Park Drives, his one indulgence or, as he called it then, with a word he has dropped, his vice; and his hair was cut, very short, when he went home, irregularly, at weekends.

Over this time he was interested in society only in theory. He rarely went out, or met people, or looked around him, or acquired anything other than an abstract grasp of the social forces about which he wrote his essays. He worked very hard, and ate his meals with the backstreet family with whom he had digs. He had never at that time been into a restaurant, and almost never into a pub; his family was Wesleyan and temperance. In the third year he met Barbara, or rather Barbara met him; after several weeks, with her taking the initiative, she started sleeping with him, at the flat she shared with three other girls; and she discovered, what she already suspected, that he had never been into a girl either. They grew attached to each other in that third year; though Howard was determined that personal matters should not interrupt his revision for finals. He sat at night with her in the flat, reading over texts, in extended silence, until at last they withdrew into the bedroom with a hot water bottle and a welcome cup of cocoa. 'All we did was huddle together for warmth,' says Howard, in subsequent explanation. 'It was never a relationship.' But, relationship or not, it was hard to break it. In the summer of 1960, they both graduated, Howard getting a first, and Barbara, who had not taken much interest in her English course, and spent more time over Howard's revision than her own, a lower second. Now their course was at an end, they found it hard to separate, to go their different ways. As a result they committed themselves to an institution which, as Howard nowadays explains, is society's technique for permanentizing the inherent contingency of relationships, in the interests of political stability: that is to say, they got married. It was a church wedding, or rather a chapel one, with many relatives and friends, a formal procedure designed to please both their families, to whom they both felt very attached. They had a honeymoon in Rhyl, taking the diesel train and staying in a boarding house; then they returned to Leeds, because Howard was to begin work on his thesis. He was now, on the strength of his good first, a research student, with an SSRC grant, which seemed ample to support them both. So he set to work on his project, a fairly routine sociology-of-religion study of Christadelphianism in Wakefield, a topic he had picked because when younger he had felt a spiritual fascination with the denomination, a fascination he now proceeded to convert into a sociological concern. As for Barbara, she became, of course, a housewife, or rather, as she put it, a flatwife.

For they now began living in a succession of bedsitters and small flats, with old high-level beds with heads and feet, and Victorian lavatories called 'Cascade', and moquette furniture, always looking out over rotting gardens. The gardens, the houses backing onto them, the back streets, the corner shop, the picture-house, the bus routes into the city centre, formed the main horizon and track of their lives, the limit and circumscription of their world. They took some pleasure in being married, because it gave them a sense of being 'responsible'; and they reported home, frequently, to both their families as a contented couple. But in fact, after the first few months together, when the sexual thrill, never very intense, had begun to wear off somewhat, and they looked around themselves, they rather quickly started to be irritated with one another, depressed by their circumstances, harassed by the simplest business of running their daily lives. It was hard to live in this drifting, ambiguous social position, this graduate student poverty, this little and friendless world; the problems of it ate into all the detail of their contacts and affections. Howard talked often at this time of 'maturity'—'maturity', he explained later, when he preferred other words, happened to be a key concept of the apolitical fifties—and spoke of it as a moral value he prized above all others. He was given to explaining their lives as very serious and mature, largely because they worried a lot about not upsetting each other and not spending money wastefully; this somehow made them the Lawrence and Frieda of backstreet Leeds. But the fact was, as they later came to agree, that neither of them was in the least culturally prepared to lead what Howard later started to call—when the word 'mature' had gone, outdated because of its heavy, Victorian plush, moral associations—'adult' lives. They were social and emotional infants, with grandfatherly solemnity; this was how he later came to portray them when he thought back, a stranger, into the curious early selves of that hasty matrimony. They were conventional nothings; they made heavy weather of the dullest of existences. Often Barbara, upset to be unable to buy more than one tin of beans or one bar of soap at a time, had sat down in their old red moquette armchair, and wept over money. Despite their air of virtuous poverty, she could not help feeling her mother's fondness for having 'things': a good three-piece suite for the lounge, a well-stocked kitchen cupboard, a white tablecloth to eat off on high days. As for Howard, though he talked about mature conduct, he applied this largely to a fondness for solemn conversations and to the arguments of books; he didn't cook, or do household chores, was too timid to like shopping, and he didn't notice any of Barbara's unease.

The Kirks, then, were hardly Kirks; they were very private people, with almost no friends, innocent and silent with each other. They did not discuss problems, mainly because they did not see themselves as the sort of people who had problems; problems were things less mature people had. Barbara spent most of her time alone in the flat, cleaning and tidying it to excess, doing a small amount of unorganized reading. Their sexual relations seemed to bind them in the ultimate intimacy, to tell them why they were married to each other, prove what an intensity this thing called marriage was; but in fact they were, as they later came to reflect, poor, unenterprising, a nominal pleasure, an act of detumescence, further strained by the fear they both had of Barbara's getting pregnant, for the only contraception they used was the Durex that Howard timidly acquired at the local barber's, as well as by something else—a bite of irritation they each felt with the other, but which each denied to himself or herself, and never spoke about. 'What we were doing,' Howard started explaining after all this, when they started seeing themselves, in Howard's word, 'properly', when this stage was all over and they began talking things out between themselves, and with their friends and their enlarging circle of acquaintances, 'was trapping each other in fixed personality roles. We couldn't permit personal adventure, personal growth. That would have been disaster. We couldn't let any new possibilities develop, could we, kid? And that's how people murder each other in slow motion. We weren't adult.' Being adult came much later; the Kirks went on in much the same way for three years, while Howard worked, very thoroughly and ploddingly, at the detail of his thesis, and Barbara stared at herself in the mirror in the bedsitters and the flats. But then they found themselves in their middle twenties, with Howard's thesis and his grant coming to an end, and the need to think about the next move. And around this time something did happen to them.

What happened? Well, their saliva began to flow faster; everything started to get a new taste. The walls of limitation they had been living inside suddenly began to give way; they both started to vibrate with new desires and expectations. Their timidity, their anger, their irritation slipped, bit by bit, off them, like their old clothes, the tired shiny suits for Howard, the dull blouses and skirts for Barbara, which they discarded. By themselves, and with other people, their manner, their style, their natures freshened. They laughed more, and challenged people more. They confessed things to each other, in extreme bouts of frankness, and embarked on ambitious new schemes of sexuality. In bed they lay endlessly talking about themselves, till three and four in the morning; in the bath, on the landing, in the kitchen, they began to tweak, probe, and inject each other with all sorts of new passions and sexual intents. And what was it that had done this to the Kirks? Well, to understand it, as Howard, always a keen explainer, always explains, you need to know a little Marx, a little Freud, and a little social history; admittedly, with Howard, you need to know all this to explain anything. You need to know the time, the place, the milieu, the substructure and the super-structure, the state of and the determinants of consciousness, and the human capacity of consciousness to expand and explode. And if you understand these things you will understand why it was that the old Kirks faded from sight and the new Kirks came into being.

For, let us remember, here were two people who had grown up, though in two different Northern towns, one in Yorkshire and one in Lancashire, in the same class and value background. That background was one of vestigial Christianity and in-herited social deference, the ideology, says Howard, of a society of sharply striated class distinctions and of great class-consciousness. They came, both of them, from well-conducted and more or less puritanical homes, located socially in that perplexing borderland between working-class anarchism and middle-class conformity. These were Chapel families, with high ethical standards and low social expectations; the result was an ethos in which ethics replaced politics, bringing about a mood of self-denial and deliberately chosen inhibition. Both of them, Howard and Barbara, had had their sights lifted by a grammar-school and university education, but they had retained toward that education the same attitude that their parents had held; it was an instrument, a virtuous one, for getting on, doing well, becoming even more respectable. In short, they had changed position without having changed values; and they had re-tained in detail the code of ethical constraint, decency and deference. They had been taught to be critical, but they had become critical only of each other, not of their environment or society; and they still retained in all their intimate values the reassuring, but self-limiting, standards of their families. They never asked, and they never received. And thus, says Howard, the nature of their psychological situation, and the con-sequential nature of their marriage, is all too clear and inevitable. They had married, it is quite evident in informed hindsight, in the adult modern vision, in order to reconstruct precisely that sort of family situation in which they had grown up. But they had done this in quite different historical cir-cumstances from those that had shaped the choices of their parents. If they had looked around them, they would have seen that the energies of social freedom had changed their world; they had only to start claiming a fuller historical citizenship. Access was not denied as much as they believed, not for people like themselves, who had been chosen for élite privilege, and who had the chance to open up privilege for others, turn it into total entitlement, And thus they were failing themselves and everyone else: 'We were a disaster,' says Howard now.

And so the Kirks' marriage had become a prison, its function to check growth, not open it. Barbara, her education over, had promptly closed out her opportunities and reverted to being standard woman, a pre-Reichian woman geared to nothing else but the running of a house. The result was a characteristic syndrome of relative frigidity, suppressed hysteria, bodily shame, and consequential physical and social self-loathing. As for Howard, his way had been to progress and work hard in order to please others, never doing anything radical, negative or personal. He retained this solemn and industrious pattern in order to please his social superiors, but also even his own wife. 'I'd come home,' he says now, 'and show her drafts of my thesis where my supervisor had written "This is a great improvement" and expect her to . . . do what? Buy me a bicycle for achievement?' But it could hardly go on; and it didn't. For the Kirks moved through a world in which their pallid acceptance was becoming absurd, where self-suppressive achievement was being seen for what it was, weak conformity, psychic suicide. Historical circumstances were changing; the whole world was in transformation, undergoing a revolution of rising expectations, asserting more, demanding more, liberating itself. 'Our change just had to happen,' says Howard. 'The constraints were weakening in all departments: class, sex, work-ethics, everything. And man explodes. He finally has to realize his own change.' 'And woman,' says Barbara. And indeed it was, as Howard will very honourably tell you, Barbara who first broke the frame, in that crucial summer, crucial for them, of 1963. It was a year of social movement; Howard can detail for you, if you can stay around after, the manifestations, in spheres as various as popular music, political scandals, third-world politics, and industrial wage-bargaining, that made it so. Trapped in the flat, unhappy, bewildered, taking private

24

snacks and therefore getting all too fat, she found the inherent contradiction first. 'She probed herself,' says Howard. 'That's not quite exactly it,' says Barbara frankly, 'I was probed.' 'That's true,' says Howard. 'At the purely external level, you got screwed.'

In fact what happened, at the purely external level, was that one afternoon a friend that the Kirks had made, a psychology student named Hamid, an Egyptian with big dark eyes and an obsessive devotion to Jung and Lawrence Durrell, had called at the flat, wanting to interest them in going to a jazz concert that evening. It was late in the afternoon, but Howard, who was—not by pure chance, says modern Howard—forgetful of the time, was still working away in the university library, busily reading other people's theses, and making notes on them, in order to write his own. Hamid had brought with him to the flat some photographs of Abu Simbel, and a box of Turkish Delight, and so somehow Barbara went to bed with him, in the high bed with the wooden head and foot, in the room overlooking the rotting garden. She had squeaked with a certain pleasure, though it was not anything more than a hasty fumble under the covers, by no means an exceptional moment for either party. But it left Barbara with a residue of severe guilt; it was, says Howard now, typical that her response to this was to drive it down and deny it, in the hope of suppressing the entire episode. However, Hamid had his own obscure moral imperatives to pursue; he insisted on staying for supper, and his purpose was, as it emerged, to tell Howard all about the moment on the high bed that afternoon, when, as he explained, Barbara and he had made some love. 'I think,' says Howard now, 'the purpose he had in mind, natural enough from his cultural standpoint, was to establish intimacy between the male parties. We have to recognize his culturally determined view of women.' 'My God,' says Barbara, 'he just liked me.' 'That's compatible,' says Howard. So Hamid, with his dark eyes, made his confession, comfortably awaiting Howard's response, while Howard sat, his jaws working on the supper, in a state of profound shock. 'My first thought was violence,' he says, 'not against Hamid, of course, against Barbara. I felt penetrated myself. The ethic of total possession of the woman you're married to runs very deep. Or did.' But he was calm, for he was

25

intelligent, and in any case he had been taught, overtaught, to control and exclude aggression.

And he did know a little Marx, a little Freud, and a little social history; he knew how quantitative change suddenly becomes qualitative change, and how reification occurs, and how sex is not simply genital interaction but an ultimate discharge of the libido, a psychic manifestation. He had known it all the time; now he realized it. For some time he had been feeling obscurely touched by and dispossessed by the way in which, in the onward transactions of the historical process, some new human rhythm, a new mode of consciousness, seemed to be emerging. He had felt it in the young people (at that time the young people were, to the Kirks, other people: they were the twenty-five-year-old old people) and in the revolts and the expressions of the American blacks, and in the Third World, the world Hamid came from. Now he felt stranded in historical foolishness, but he had a little sense of hope for himself. He sat over the sausages, and he listened to Hamid, who spoke in fatalistic terms ('It is what happens, Howard, because these things are willed to happen') and then to Barbara, who defended herself with a sudden new aggression ('I'm a person, Howard. I've been a person here all this time, stuck in this room, and he saw it, and you never have'). He poked a sausage; he recognized historical inevitability. The small revolution had come. 'I looked across the table at this person I had been calling a wife for the last few years, and her face suddenly switched on and turned real for me,' Howard says. 'Mine did?' asks Barbara. 'Mine?' 'That's right,' says Howard. 'And when one face becomes real, all faces become real.' 'Right,' says Barbara, 'especially the pretty ones.'

Barbara's tiny affair in the high bed had a powerful effect; it excited the Kirks with each other. And so they found themselves taken, for a time, with a hazy dream in front of them, a dream they talked out and out; it was a dream of expanded minds, equal dealings, high erotic satisfactions, a transcendence of what they had up to now taken to be reality. They now started transcending reality quite frequently, making love in parks, smoking pot at parties, going up on the moors past Adel and running with their clothes off through the wind, buying stereo equipment, taking trips to London, rubbing margarine

26

on each other in bed, going on demos. It was just after this affair of Barbara's that Howard's father died ('One inevitably recognizes the removal of the psychic focus of paternalist constraint,' says Howard, 'of course, I cared for him a lot'), and only a few days later Howard was asked to apply for a temporary assistant lectureship, right there at Leeds, in the department where he had been doing his research; a post he very quickly got. There were a few finishing touches to be given to the thesis, but he could set that more or less aside for a while; now the task was to prepare for teaching, get further into the ranges and depths of sociology. On the strength of the appointment, the Kirks got a bigger flat, with a smaller bed, and were able to install a new cooker, hire a television set, and have a few small parties. They made some new, and much more radical, friends, among other postgraduate students, and now as well among the faculty. The fact that he was no longer a man who was marked but a man who would mark pulled him out of the mental waste land of subservient achievement in which he had lived. The Kirks spent the summer in a state of continuous excitement; it was the most exciting summer of their lives.

Indeed things over those summer months began to get a little dangerous with them. They got up each morning feeling physically sated, excited with their own bodies and the other body that had excited them with their own. They talked a lot to each other about swinging, feeling good, getting high. They looked at each other and observed limitations, the obstructiveness of the other self, which was always so very there, always so very insistent, to the onward path they each had chosen; they each accused the other, from time to time, of closing the doors, killing the options, holding back, getting out. They quarrelled quite often; but these were no longer the mean little quarrels that their mean little selves, the selves of the old dispensation, before their consciousness revolution, had indulged in before, quarrels so low-keyed as to be almost invisible, while remaining deeply felt and unresolved. 'It was a politics of growth,' says Howard, 'an elaborate dialectic of self-statement. It was exactly what was needed.' 'But, How, you've got to remember,' says Barbara, 'there was still a deep bourgeois element.' 'Oh, right, there was indeed,' says Howard, 'it was inevitable.'

'And I remained in his eyes essentially property, still,' says Barbara. 'Of course it's an inevitable contradiction structured into the institution of marriage,' says Howard, 'and we came from the generation that focused on marriage.' 'Of course,' says Barbara, 'we're still in fact married.' 'But on our own terms,' adds Howard, 'we've redefined it internally.' 'I'll say,' says Barbara.

When the new academic year came around in the autumn, and Howard began teaching for the very first time, he found that the events of the summer had given him the gift for bringing a passionate fervour into the subject, making him want to teach it as it had never been taught before. He took his classes to the law courts, and lectured them in the corridors, until the noise became so great that he was asked to leave. He went with them and they all spent the night in a Salvation Army hostel, to know at first hand. He got into demography and social psychology, and took a Wright Mills reformist approach to the field. He found himself deeper into the academic sub-culture, the lifestyle of his fellow-lecturers and especially of his fellow-sociologists. He talked very seriously and solemnly about theoretical matters. He took to wearing the black leather jackets that most of his colleagues, for some reason, affected. There were many new beards in 1963; Howard's was one of them. Later he started selling *Red Mole* in the city centre on Saturdays, holding a copy high in his clenched fist in front of the faces of the market shoppers. Barbara no longer sat in the flat. She came to the university, went to lectures, attended political meetings, visited filmshows, and stapled provocative posters on boards when nobody was looking. She got into health foods and astrology, studying vitamin levels and cholesterol counts, and doing horoscopes of political opponents. She went to all the faculty parties, and became very outgoing and popular, standing in corners in lowcut dresses raising tendentious issues, and drinking a great deal. Altogether the Kirks became well known as a feature of the younger faculty, and one of the lively centres of the culture they had going.

They also both started having small affairs. Howard tried the wives of his friends, with what he thought of as the Hamid strategy, and was surprised to find how available many of them were, and how it improved his confidence in himself, and his social courage. Barbara began taking her pleasures at the parties they went to, slipping upstairs to the bedroom with someone around midnight, and then returning downstairs for the early-morning action, when dancing started or the pot started circulating, not wanting to miss a thing. They felt the strain, and some of the other relationships they formed seemed tempting, worth enlarging; they talked quite often about separating, feeling now that they were really bad for each other, and that the only real answer was a new start. None of their other relationships really became permanent, however. Once Barbara went and stayed for a week with some friends, the Beamishes, Henry Beamish being another young lecturer in the department; she took the television set with her, and began looking around in Leeds for a flat of her own. But their friends were all people who had psychological insights, and so they explained Howard's problems to Barbara, and Barbara's problems to Howard, and this made them seem quite interesting to each other again. So they ended up back together, at the end of the week, on a new alignment. This all had a rapid consequence; Barbara got pregnant. 'Oh, God, the primitive techniques we used then,' says Barbara, 'we were playing Russian roulette.' Barbara quite enjoyed the pregnancy, and she got massively fat. Her big peasant bosom swelled and she carried her enormous bump buoyantly in front of her. She went to natural childbirth classes, and Howard came along too; he did the exercises down on the floor along with her, sympathetically pushing when the nurse said push. When Barbara went into Leeds Infirmary, Howard insisted on being present. Indeed when the day came at last, he decided not to cancel his class, but to take the group along and see the birth, examining the problems of the National Health Service and the conditions of maternity care. The sister was strict and uncooperative, so the class waited out in the grounds, peering at windows, while Barbara delivered, by the Lamaze method, with Howard present, giving instructions and encouragement through a white mask. Then it was all over. Barbara sweated and the veins in her eyeballs stood out red, while Howard stared with intense and profound curiosity at the mystery of life, encapsulated there between his wife's legs, and contemplated the conditions and determinants, the Marx and the Freud, the history and the sex, that led to this most extraordinary of all outcomes.

Barbara had not at first welcomed the pregnancy, for she was enjoying things too much; but in the end it was a kind of victory for her. Howard had pushed sympathetically on the floor of the clinic, but in the end he had produced nothing; Barbara had made the ultimate statement, published in the ultimate way. Thereafter Howard had a lot of baby-minding to do, and he often slept in the day, in his chair in the room he had at the university, so as to be sure to be awake and aware for the two-o'clock feeds. He did his part, but all the same Barbara claimed to be struggling in the maternal yoke, which denied as well as satisfied, and so she made him pay her an economic salary for her useful social role as a wife and a mother, as proof that she was not second-class. But, after two months spent in the full-time company of the baby, she began to feel that it was time to realize herself as a fully-fledged economic unit. It was somehow only when an achievement was tested in the open, competitive market that it was a real achievement, a full mode of being, an existential act; she had started, in these matters, to acquire vocabulary from Howard. What she did was to get a neighbour to come in and mind the child, while she did part-time jobs on public opinion surveys and in market research, arguing with housewives in the Leeds back-to-backs about how important their views were on detergents and decimal currency, Rhodesia, abortion, and Coronation Street. She gradually became persuaded that market research was a community service, a form of grass-roots expressionism, of political action, and that she was very good at it. Altogether over this stage she became very bright and contented. Howard, correspondingly, came to feel very depressed. He was getting very tired, and doubted the rewards that were coming to him from his close, intense relationship with the small fleshly creature that was his baby. He liked the child, but not as much as he was being asked to; he actually suspected Barbara of neglect. But the trouble, for both of them, was that they had by now become busy people; there was so much for each of them to do. Now he acquired a bewildered expression, and a faint air of defeat. But he let his hair grow very long, and began to push people around intellectually at parties. He drank more, and looked sad. Gradually he found, to his surprise, that he was earning sympathy and regard; his recent troubles had impressed all the people he knew a good deal, and he was, with his accumulating reputation for having a vigorous and even dangerous wife, and an affair problem, and a baby problem, for the first time being considered as a very seriously interesting person.

It was at this time that the Kirks first started telling, to friends and acquaintances and utter strangers, their story. They presented it as the exemplary case of the Kirks, an instructive public matter, the tale of two bewildered people who had failed themselves and then suddenly grown. It was an attractive and popular story for the times, and it went through many refinements. The earlier tellings had concentrated on the liberation plot; the cramped lives, the affair, the running around naked on the moors, the explosion of consciousness and new political awareness. But after a while, there were certain elements of scepticism that needed to be introduced for probability's sake, not utterly disconfirming the tale of a couple moving buoyantly, self-realizingly, through the exploding consciousness of man in history, perhaps even complicating and improving it. For there were severe ambiguities and dark places in their relationship. The way Howard explained this, to himself and to a few others, was that they had moved from a consensus model of marriage, the usual model of marriage, which is generally taken as an ultimate consensus, wherein conflict is generated but ultimately reconciled with the famous kiss, to a conflict model, in which interests were starkly defined, and ultimate resolution must depend on violence or the defeat of one of the parties. What Howard was out to articulate was the suspicion, which could of course have been paranoid, that Barbara was out to destroy him. She of course denied this, when they talked about it; however, as Howard kept telling her, the question could not be posed at the conscious, but had to reckon with the unconscious, level. One thing was certainly true; Barbara, because she was using her mind more, was getting brighter. She had a shrewd, bitter intelligence, a strong nature, and more gift for feeling than he had. She also had the subtle arts of attack, and could use them on him well; there were times when Howard wondered whether he could survive them.

But by now Howard was Dr Kirk; he had finished off his thesis, and been awarded his PhD for his long labours. Now the focus of his attention could change; he had been at work on a book, an argumentative book, about cultural and sexual change, which urged, as you might expect, that there had been a total restructuring of sexual mores in Britain, that sexual roles had been totally reassigned, and that the use of the traditional concepts of 'man' and 'woman', to designate stable cultural entities, was irrelevant. 'We need new names for these genitally distinct types of persons,' it said. Howard wrote the book secretively, in his office, partly because it was yet another telling of the exemplary Kirk story, and so might bore Barbara if she read it, but even more he was, like Barbara with the baby, or a nation with a new energy-source, aware that he had possession of a powerful weapon in the power politics, the dialectics and strategies, of his marriage, his own home-made yet universal battlefield. But Barbara came into his office one day, while he was elsewhere in the building, teaching a class. She sat at his desk, read the letters that lay on it, the comments that he had written on the ends of his student essays, the typescript of the book. She began to penetrate it; by the time he came back from his class she had a view of it. 'Have you been writing this?' she asked. 'Why not?' asked Howard, looking at her as she sat in his desk chair, while he sat in the chair he put his students in for tutorials. 'It's us, isn't it?' said Barbara, 'it's also revealingly you.' 'How is it me?' asked Howard. 'Do you know what it says?' asked Barbara, 'it says you're a radical poseur. It tells how you've substituted trends for morals and commitments.' 'You've not read it properly,' said Howard, 'it's a committed book, a political book.' 'But what are you committed to?' asked Barbara, 'Do you remember how you used to say "maturity" all the time? And it never meant anything? Now it's "liberation" and "emancipation". But it doesn't mean any more than the other thing. Because there's nothing in you that really feels or trusts, no character.' 'You're jealous,' said Howard, 'I did something interesting, and you're jealous. Because I didn't even tell you.'

'No character,' said Barbara again, sitting in his chair.

'How do you define character?' asked Howard. 'How do you define a person? Except in a socio-psychological context. A particular type of relationship to the temporal and historical process, culturally conditioned and afforded; that's what human nature is. A particular performance within the available role-sets. But with the capacity to innovate through manipulating options among the role-sets.' 'I know,' said Barbara, 'you've said all that here. But what's it got to do with real people?' 'Who are these real people?' asked Howard. 'We need a new name for your genitally distinctive type of person,' said Barbara. 'You're a shit.' 'You're envious,' said Howard, 'I've made something without you.' 'It's a smart punishment for the baby,' said Barbara, 'but it's about us, and it's empty, so I don't like it.' 'It's about what we've experienced, but in its context,' said Howard, 'we wanted to change. We wanted to live with the movement, the times. We both wanted it. If that book's just trendy, then what are you?' 'I'm just living, the best way I can,' said Barbara, 'but you want to make it all into a grand plot. A big universal story. Something of major interest.' 'Well, that's exactly what commitment is, Barbara,' said Howard. 'I don't think so,' said Barbara, 'I just think I'm living, and you're simply theorizing. You're a kind of self-made fictional character who's got the whole story on his side, just because he happens to be writing it.' Howard had thought that he was living too, and when Barbara had gone he sat in front of the manuscript on his desk. Inspecting the end of it, he found that Barbara had written a comment she had copied from one of his own notes on the end of a student essay: 'This seems to me a reasonable theoretical statement on the subject, but it contains none of your real experience of life in it, as an aware person.' But he was an aware person, and he knew the book said so; the lesson was a lesson in jealousy.

So Howard went on with the book, with a new urgency, and he finished it off quickly. Then he sent it off, without telling Barbara; and almost at once he got a contract and a very good advance for it from a well-known left-wing publisher, who proposed to do both a hardback and a cheap paperback edition, with extensive publicity. He showed the letter to Barbara; despite herself, she was impressed. She had mentioned the book critically to a few friends; now she spoke warmly about it in a wider circle. The victory pleased him deeply. He felt the delicate balance of their relationship changing again; he had produced his baby. He knew he had better take the advantage while it was there, so he sat down again in his office one day and wrote off letters in answer to the advertisements in the professional journals, applying for posts in sociology in other universities. The subject was in a state of expansion; there was much movement in the profession, largely because of the impact of the new universities, many of which had made sociology a main part of their new academic structure. There was some advance publicity for the book out by now, and he had done an interview which had appeared in the *Observer*; all this seemed to help his chances. He was invited for interview at three of the universities to which he wrote; one of them was Watermouth, and that was the one that interested him most, for here was a new programme, with a chance for him to develop his own approach. Now he told Barbara what he had done. At first she was indignant, recognizing that it was an element in an obscure campaign against her. But then she became curious, and when he came down to Watermouth, taking the long train journey down from Leeds, to attend the interview, Barbara came down with him.

This was when the Kirks visited Watermouth for the first time. Howard was interviewed in the panelled Gaitskell Room of the Elizabethan hall which had been the original starting-place of the new university, before the towers and the pre-stressed concrete and the glass-framed buildings that were now beginning to spread across the site, the achievement of that notable Finnish architect Jop Kaakinen, had even been conceived. The interview was affable. The interdisciplinary programme of the university, and its novel teaching methods, excited Howard, after Leeds; he could see he was being taken seriously; the modernistic campus growing on the old estate pleased him, seemed in concord with his sense of transforming history. Meanwhile, down in the town, Barbara, who had left the baby in Leeds with friends, poked around in the radical bookshops, checked out the organic delicatessen, inspected the boutiques, and looked in on the family-planning clinic. She had never really been in the south of England before; it had an optimistic, exciting look to her; she thought she saw an amiable radicalism everywhere, a fighting modern style that seemed several light-years ahead of the grimmer, tighter world of Leeds. In this new place, she saw herself, saw both of them, claiming the remaining historical rights the old Kirks had denied themselves. She sat on a railed seat on the promenade and stared outwards at the sea, a novelty, a pleasure. There were two or three palm-trees flourishing in the promenade gardens, and a few oranges growing. She thought of the child playing down on the sandy beach; she thought of the swinging parties. There were hippies with backpacks leaning over the railings; there were people talking French; there were works by Marx and Trotsky on the railway station bookstall. She saw a chance for herself in this sunlight; when Howard came back from the interview, and she learned he had been offered the job, she was bright with excitement. 'You ought to take it,' she said, 'it's a good scene.' 'I already have,' said Howard, 'you're too late.' 'Oh, you shit,' she said, 'without consulting me'; but she was pleased, and they walked down on the beach, and skimmed stones together out at the sea. The stones bounced and it was not like Leeds. And that, more or less, give or take an element of self-interest here, a perceptual distortion or two there, a dark ambiguity in this place or that, is the exemplary and liberating story, as Howard explains, of how the little northern Kirks came to be down in Watermouth, with its high sunshine record and its palms and its piershow and its urban demolition, buying wine and cheese and bread, and giving parties; and, of course, growing some more—for the Kirks, whatever else they have done, have always gone right on growing.

III

So it was in just another such autumn, the autumn of 1967, when Vietnam was a big issue, and the tempers were fraying, but a year before *the* year, when self-revolutions like the Kirks' turned into a public matter, that the Kirks moved themselves, south and west, to Watermouth. They drove down from Leeds in the minivan, an item of possession they had just acquired; the new university of Watermouth had tempted him with two additional increments, and for the first time in their lives the Kirks found themselves with a little money to spare. In the van they sat side by side, watching motorway unroll, the landscape change. The baby chattered in its large basket in the back; on the rear window was a sticker saying 'I live in an effluent society'. In front the Kirks sat silent, as if each one of them was all ready to leap out, as soon as the van rolled to a stop at their destination, and tell his or her own story. It had been a busy summer; and there were stories to tell. For now it was coming to seem to Barbara that this was a false move, a victory for Howard, a defeat for her; passing through the Midlands, south of Birmingham, they crossed a line into error. One trouble was that, over the summer, despite the fact that she believed herself scientifically sealed inside against this sort of intrusion, she had found herself pregnant again; it was a matter of mystery and anger. She was also angry because she saw now that Howard was in the vastly stronger position over the move; he was coming to Watermouth with a reputation ahead of him.

It was, admittedly, a slightly shaky reputation, for popularizing innovation; but it really was a reputation. For, also over the summer, his book had come out, and done well. The publishers had changed a franker title to *The Coming of the New Sex*, which they thought would sell widely; and it was already clear that the book would be a commercial success. It had also been greeted, by the culturally attuned critics of the Sundays and the intelligent weeklies, as a work in consort with the times. Howard had not done a great deal of research on the book, and it was weak on fact and documentation; but what it lacked there it made up in argumentative energy, and a frank sense of participation in the permissive scene. As Barbara would tell people who came up to talk about it, at the many parties they were invited to in Watermouth that autumn: 'Oh, sex is Howard's field. I think you can say he's done a really big probe there.' But it had generally been found a committed, advanced book, on the right side; and it did sound quite sociological as you read it. So Howard, of course, arrived with an air of esteem already promised him, as well as a useful status as a sexual performer. Barbara, on the other hand, was coming pregnant, and part disabled, and with no reputation ahead of her, one way or the other, and brooding on this over the summer she had begun to resent the fact.

It was lucky that, on arrival, they were able to stay for a while with some old Leeds friends of theirs, the Beamishes, who had made the move down to Watermouth one year earlier, and had helped interest Howard in the place. Henry Beamish was a social psychologist, who had himself made quite a stir the year before by proving in a book that television socialized children much more effectively than their parents ever could. From this controversy he appeared to have done extremely well. Certainly the Beamishes, when the Kirks found them again, had changed. They had left the atmosphere of Leeds' radical bedsitterland, of beer parties and trips to watch City on Saturdays and demos outside the Town Hall, well behind them, and had found a new style for their new setting. These people who in Leeds had no money, and used to borrow kettles from their friends because they could not afford to buy one of their own, were now settled, outside Watermouth, in an architect-converted farmhouse, where they were deep into a world of Tolstoyan pastoral, scything grass and raising organic onions. Henry Beamish had grown a new beard of the naval type, heavily touched with grey. He looked very well, despite the pallor left by an unfortunate episode shortly before when he had been poisoned by a mushroom, gleaned at dawn off his own estate; he had even acquired a certain baffled, slightly elderly dignity. Myra now looked stouter, wore her hair in a tight Victorian bun, and smoked small brown cigars. It seemed to Howard that there were two accurate phrases for what they had become over the move, though he forbore to use them, for they were his friends, and they both involved the profoundest condemnation: but weren't they both middle-aged now, and middle-class? The Kirks stared, on their arrival, at the house, at their old friends; they spent much of the visit on their hands and knees with wet toilet paper, sponging out babysick from the good carpet in the smart guest bedroom. It was not an encouraging arrival; but, on the first night, as they sat in front of the opened-out brick fireplace, Henry, pouring homemade wine into Italian glasses, said: 'It's strange you should come today. I was just telling some friends of ours about you last night. About that time your marriage nearly broke up. And you came and stayed with us in the flat, Barbara, do you remember? You were carrying the television set and a saucepan.' 'Christ, yes, that's right,' said Barbara warmly, and immediately felt better, because she realized that she did come with a reputation ahead of her, after all.

The real truth about coming to Watermouth, Howard tells people now, with great frankness, is that their arrival unnerved them both. They had known how to live in Leeds, since it was a society that simply amended the one they had grown up in. But Watermouth, from the start, made them wonder what to become, how to build a nature. Leeds was working class, was built on work; Watermouth was bourgeois, built on tourism, property, retirement pensions, French chefs. As they inspected the Beamishes, it seemed to deny existence, to be a freak bazaar of styles; you could be anything here. Radical philosophy approved this, but here it was bourgeois indulgence. Admittedly, as Howard said, we are all performers, self-made actors on the social stage; all role is self- or other-assigned; yet, for a man who believed that reality didn't exist yet, he had to admit he found

Leeds more real. The Kirks, staring at Watermouth in the indulgent sunshine, discovered they did not know how to place themselves, house themselves. They drove around in the hilly inland behind the town, in Henry's little 4L Renault, looking at what Henry termed 'properties'. There were a lot of properties. Myra and Barbara sat in the back, the baby between them, a tight squeeze; friend to friend, they explored and analysed in high detail the latter-day ebb and flow of Kirk marital history. In the front seat, Howard sat next to Henry, peering through the windscreen, the visor down, an estate agents' map on his knee, noting with Northern radical scepticism the exotic social mixes through which they passed. From time to time, feeling the need to counter-balance the prejudiced narrative recorded in the back, he talked, victoriously, to Henry, in the sunlight, of his well-liked book, of the reviews, of the new commission and large advance the publisher had given him. Now and then Henry stopped the car, and they got out, and solemnly examined a property. Henry's taste in property had been transformed, become rural and bourgeois; he praised, mysteriously, 'advantages' like paddocks and stables. The Kirks stood and stared, peering through trees at hills. Never having encountered a property before, they had no idea how to behave in the presence of one; they knew their radical desires were being subtly threatened and impaired, even though Henry told them what was true, that they had more money now, that a mortgage was a good investment for the advance, that the time in their lives, with a second baby, was here when they should settle down. But down was not where they wanted to settle; a hideous deceit seemed to be being practised; Henry, having already destroyed himself, was seeking to inculpate them too. 'A property is theft,' Howard kept on saying, looking around at the endless wastes of unpopulated, orderly countryside that surrounded them, depressed them with its frightening timelessness, its unlocated look, its frank detachment from the places where history was happening, the world was going onward and on.

After two days of this, when Henry was about to take them into yet another estate agency in yet another commuterized small town, somewhere in the hinterland of Watermouth, its windows filled with announcements about retirement bungalows, Howard felt the need to speak true. 'Look, Henry,' he said, 'you're trying to impose some false image on us, aren't you? We're not like this, Barbara and me, remember?' 'It's a very sound residential area,' said Henry, 'you'd keep your re-sale value.' 'We'd go off our heads in one of these places,' said Howard, 'we couldn't live with these people, we couldn't live with ourselves.' 'I thought you wanted something nice,' said Henry. 'No, for Christ's sake, nothing nice,' said Howard, 'I don't come from anywhere like this. I don't accept its existence politically. You don't either, Henry. I don't know what you're doing here.' Henry stared at Howard with a slightly shamefaced, slightly baffled look. 'There comes a time,' he said, 'there comes a time when you realize, Howard. You might want change, well, we all want change. But there is an inheritance of worth-while life in this country, Howard. We all come to need a place where you can get down deeper into yourself and into, well, the real rhythms of living. That's what Myra and I are into now, Howard.' 'Here?' asked Howard. 'There's nothing here. You stop fighting.' 'Well, fighting,' said Henry, staring at little photographs of houses in the window, 'I'll do my bit for better-ment. But I'm divided. I'm not wild about all this violent radical zeal that's about now, all these explosive bursts of demand. They taste of a fashion. Punch a policeman this year. And I can't see what's wrong with a bit of separateness and withdrawal from the fray.' 'No?' asked Howard. 'That's because you're bourgeois now, Henry. You have the spirit of a bourgeois.' 'No, I don't,' said Henry, 'that's nasty. I'm trying to give my life a little dignity without robbing anyone else of theirs. I'm trying to define an intelligent, liveable, unharming culture, Howard.' 'Oh, Christ,' said Howard, 'evasive quietism.' 'You know, Henry, I'm sorry,' said Barbara, 'but if I lived like you, I'd die first.' 'Bourgeois, bourgeois,' said Howard the next day as, their things packed, the baby in the back of the van, they drove off from the farmhouse after an uncomfortable parting. 'Well,' said Barbara, trying to be kind to the kind, the people who had saved her when she was wandering loose with a television set, 'don't forget, they haven't had all our dis-advantages.'

They drove, over bridges, through chines, towards the town and the sea; they were escaping, back into Watermouth to get the feel of urban life again, to consort once more with staple reality. There were houses and dustbins and rubbish and crime. In the end, Howard resolved to visit the Social Security department in Watermouth; he needed to set his spirit right, to reassure himself that the place in which he was planting his destiny really did have a sociology—had social tensions, twilight areas, race issues, class-struggle, battles between council and community, alienated sectors, the stuff, in short, of true living. Leaving the van in the car park, with Barbara and the baby inside, he penetrated into the bleak offices, and was granted a stroke of luck. For here was working one of his own former students from Leeds, a girl called Ella, who wore granny spectacles, and denim jeans and top, and knew his radical temper, and, like any good student, shared it. An adult girl, Howard said to Barbara later, after she had left her desk in the office and got into the minivan with them, crouching in the back, next to the baby's basket, promising to show them the real Watermouth. She hunted out the areas of deprivation hidden between and behind the old private hotels, the new holiday flatlets; she probed the unexpected social mixes tucked behind the funfair and the holiday façade of the town; she showed them the acres of urban blight, the concrete of urban renewal. 'Of course it's a problem town,' said Ella. 'Oh, they'd like to pretend it isn't, that might discourage the tourists. But anywhere that brings in people for the holiday trade in the summer and then dumps them on unemployment pay in the winter is going to have problems, and they've got them.'

'Any radicals?' asked Barbara. 'Plenty,' said Ella. 'It's full of hippies and dropouts. All these places are. It's a town you can run to and disappear. There are empty houses. Visitors are soft touches. Lots of marginal work. No, it's a good place.' She gave some directions and brought them into the slum clearance area. 'Of course nobody wants to see this, but here's what they ought to rub their tourists' faces in,' she said, pushing her way into an empty old house where meths drinkers, drunks, addicts and runaways came, she said, to spend the night. You could see they did; the Kirks penetrated through the back door into the chaotic brokenness of the house; its stair-rails were snapped, and there was excrement in the corners, litter on the floor, bottles smashed in the bedroom, gaping holes where the glass had been knocked out from windows. Barbara stood in the bleak spaces, holding the baby on her shoulder; Howard wandered around. He said: 'We could get some permanent squatters into this.' 'Why not?' asked Ella, 'this one's going to be around for a long while yet. They've not got the cash to pull it down.' Barbara, sitting down on the bottom stair with the baby, said: 'Of course we could squat in it ourselves.' 'Well, we could,' said Howard. 'Maybe this sounds immoral,' said Ella, 'but you could even do it legally. I think I could fix it for you. I know all the people in the council to talk to.' 'It's a good scene,' said Barbara. 'You couldn't really call it a property,' said Howard.

So Ella and the Kirks walked out, through the broken back door; they stood and inspected the remnants of the curved terrace in which the house stood; they looked across to the castle and down toward the promenade. It was the debris of a good address. They drove back to the council offices, and Howard talked to people, and said he was going in there anyway, and he made an arrangement to rent the property, for a very small sum, promising to be out when it was all to be torn down, which would not be until two years' time. And so the Kirks ended up with an unpropertylike property after all. So, in that autumn, they rented a Willhire van. Howard drove the van, and Barbara tailed him in the minivan, and they moved all their stuff south and west down to Watermouth. When they came to load the van with their things, it was a surprise and mystery to them to see the amount of it; they believed they had almost no possessions, being free-floating people. But there was the cooker, the stereo system, the television set (for by now they had bought one), the blender, the wickerwork rocking chair, the Habitat crockery, the toys, the two filing cabinets and the door that Howard laid across them in order to construct his desk, the many books that he found he had accumulated, the papers in their files, the index cards, the Holorith system, the demographic graphs and charts that came from Howard's office at the university, the table-lamps, the rugs, the typewriter the boxes of notes.

They had an official key to the house in the curved terrace; they turned off the main road, parked in front of the terrace, opened the house, and unloaded. It all made a modest presence in the decrepitly fine rooms, with their filth and chaos. They spent three days just cleaning out. Then came the business of tidying, mending, reconstructing, a terrifying task; the house was badly damaged. But Howard now revealed a certain talent for fixing things, a handyman's skills he had not known he possessed, skills he had, he supposed, picked up from his father. They had all the windows fixed and the boards taken off the ones at the front. Of course, because the place was condemned, it was pointless to do anything major to the fabric. But the house was surprisingly sound. Water ran in through the roof beside the chimney stacks; someone got up there and stripped away all the lead flashing, not even before they had moved in, but a little after, one night when Barbara was there but Howard was away, up in London doing a television programme on the drugs problem on which he was taking a liberal line. The windows kept getting smashed, but Howard learned how to putty in new ones; and after a while this stopped, as if, by some massive consensus created between themselves and the unknown, their residence had at last been granted.

All through that first autumn term, the Kirks worked on their terrace house, trying at first to make it habitable, then more than habitable. Howard would dash back from the university in the minivan as soon as he was through with his seminars and tutorials—those instructive, passionate occasions where he was experimenting with new forms of teaching and relationship—in order to change clothes and set to work again on the rehabilitation. He got some help to fix things, like the lavatories, which were smashed when they came, and the stair-rail which he couldn't manage himself. But most of the work the Kirks did together. They spent two weeks stripping off all the brown paint that coated the interior woodwork, and then brushed seal into the natural colour of the wood. They bought saws and planks and rulers and replaced floorboards that had gone in. Singlehandedly Howard started painting, doing a lot of walls white and a lot of facing walls black, while Barbara borrowed a sewing machine and put up wide-weave curtains in yellow and orange at the windows. Since the place had to be rewired, they took out all the central lights from the ceilings and focused new lights off the walls at the ceilings and off the floor at the walls. Howard, as the term went on, got to know more and more students; they started to help. Four of them with a rented sander exposed, and then waxed yellow with a rented waxer, the good old wood of the floors. Another brought a sand-blaster and cleaned off the walls of the basement. They would stop in the middle of this to drink or eat or make love or have a party; they were making a free and liveable open space. At first the main furniture was the mattresses and the cushions that lay on the floor, but gradually the Kirks got around to going and buying things, mostly on trips up to London; what they bought was transient furniture, the kind that inflated, or folded up, or fitted this into that. They built desks with filing cabinets and doors, as they had in Leeds, and bookcases out of boards and bricks. What had started as a simple attempt to make space liveable in gradually turned into something stylish, attractive, but that was all right; it still remained for them an informal camp site, a pleasant but also a completely uncommitting and unshaped environment through which they could move and do their thing.

One of the results of this was that things became surprisingly better between the two of them. For the first time, they were giving shape to their lives, making a statement, and doing it out of their own skill and craftsmanship, working together. Watermouth began to please them more and more; they found shops where you could buy real yoghourt, and home-baked bread. They acquired a close, companionable tone with each other, partly because they had not made other friends yet, acquired other points of reference, partly because the people they did meet treated them as an interesting, attached couple. Towards Christmas, Howard got a large royalty cheque for his book, and put most of the money into the house, buying some white Indian rugs that would cover the downstairs floors. Barbara's was a smaller, more manageable pregnancy this time. Because they lived in a slum area, she got a good deal of treatment and, though it was a second baby, she was allowed forty-eight hours in hospital after the delivery. Howard was there, instructive in his white mask, as she produced the new child. It was a simple, routine delivery, she knew the rhythms perfectly: an elegant achievement, and one that, this time, seemed to offer no direct threat to Howard. He had not had time to get on with another book, but he was deep in pleasure with his new job; he had good students, and the courses he was working out were going well, amassing a considerable following. The house was now in good shape for the baby to come back to; it had its own room, as did the older child; the floors were clean, and there was a sound kitchen. The baby lay in its carrycot in its room; a lot of people came by; they spent a buoyant Christmas. 'I never wanted any possessions, never,' you could hear Barbara saying, as they stood in the house, during the parties they now started to give. 'I never wanted marriage; Howard and I just wanted to live together,' she said too, as they met more and more people. 'I never wanted a house, just a place to be in,' she also said, as they looked around at the bright clean walls and the clear wood floors, 'they can pull it down when they like now.' But the house was a perfect social space, and it was regularly filled with people; and as time went on and the place became a centre it seemed harder and harder to think that it ever could be.

As it turned out, there were a lot of people, and a lot of parties, in Watermouth. All through that autumn they had been going to them, in the gaps between working on the house: student parties, political parties, young faculty parties, parties given by vague, socially unlocated swingers who were in town for a while and then disappeared. There were even formal parties; once they were invited out by Howard's head of department, Professor Alan Marvin, that well-known anthropologist, author of a standard work entitled *The Bedouin Intelligentsia*. Marvin was one of the originators, the founding fathers, of the university at Watermouth; these were already a distinguishable breed, and, like most of the breed, the Marvins had chosen to live in a house of some dignity in the countryside on the further side of the university, in that bewildering world of paddocks and stables Henry had adopted. The Kirks had already made their mark with the young faculty, but they were instinctively at odds with the older ones; they had a clear-headed refusal to be charmed, or deceived by apparent or token innovation. They drove out in their minivan, self-consciously smelling of the turpentine they had used to get paint off themselves after an afternoon's work on the house, a smell that gave them the free-floating dignity of craftsmen. The Marvins' house turned out to be an old, white-washed converted farmhouse; there were Rovers and Mercedes parked in the drive when they arrived. Howard's colleagues had warned him that the Marvins

45

lived in a certain Oxbridge dignity, even though Marvin himself was, in the department, a shabby little man who always wore three pencils held by metal clips in his top pocket, as if research and accurate recording of data were never very far from his mind. And so it was; in an ostentatious gesture, lights had been strung in the trees of the big gardens that surrounded the house, and there were people in suits—the Kirks saw suits infrequently—on the lawn, where white wine, from bottles labelled 'Wine Society Niersteiner', were being served by quiet, recessive students. The Kirks, Howard in an old fur coat, Barbara in a big lace dress spacious enough to contain the bump of her pregnancy, felt themselves stark against this: intrusive figures in the scene. Marvin took them around, and introduced them, in the near dark, to many faces; only after a while did it dawn upon the Kirks that these were people in disguise, and that these faces he was meeting, above the suits, were the faces of his own colleagues, clad in the specialist wear they had acquired from marriages and funerals, supporting ceremony.

In the adjacent countryside, disturbed birds chattered, and sheep ran about heavily and snorted; Howard stared, and wondered at his place in all this. Barbara, who was cold, went inside, escorted by a punctilious Marvin, concerned about her pregnancy; Howard found himself detained in lengthy conversation by a middle-aged man with a benign, self-conscious charm, and the healthy, crack-seamed face of an Arctic explorer. Moths flew about them while they talked. Howard, in his fur coat, discoursed on a topic he had grown greatly interested in, the social benefits and purgative value of pornography in the cinema. 'I've always been a serious supporter of pornography, Dr Kirk,' said the man he was talking to, 'I have expressed my view in the public forum many times.' It dawned on Howard, from the tone of demotic regality in which he was being addressed, that he was talking to no other person than Millington Harsent, that radical educationalist, former political scientist, well-known Labour voter and mountain climber, who was Vice-Chancellor of the university of which Howard was now a part. He was a man of whom Howard had heard much; the radical aroma, the sense of educational freshness, that the colour supplements and professional journals had found in Watermouth were said to emanate from him. More locally, he had the reputation of suffering from building mania, or, as it was put, an Edifice Complex, and to have put many of his energies into dreaming up, along with Jop Kaakinen, the futuristic campus where Howard taught. It is hard to be a Vice-Chancellor, who must be all things to all men; Harsent had won the reputation for being this, but in reverse; he was thought by the conservatives to be an extreme radical, by the radicals to be an extreme conservative. But now this man, who was known for bonhomous democracy (he rode round the campus on a bicycle, and was said to have smoked pot occasionally at student parties), stood before Howard, and spoke to him warmly, and squeezed one of his shoulders, and congratulated the university on Howard's presence there, and discussed his book as if he knew what was in it; Howard warmed, and felt at ease. 'I can't tell you how pleased we are to have someone of your stature here,' said Harsent. 'You know,' said Howard, 'I'm quite pleased to be here.'

Harsent and Howard passed into the house together, in search of the source of the Niersteiner; Harsent pressed on Howard, out of a briefcase in the hall, a copy of the university's development plan, and a special brochure, an elegant document printed on dove-grey paper, and written five years earlier still, at the beginning of all these things, by Jop Kaakinen, whose inspired buildings were springing everywhere into existence on campus. 'That's Genesis,' said Harsent, 'I suppose you might say we're in Numbers now. And, I'm afraid, getting close to Job and Lamentations.' Harsent moved on to speak to other guests, doing his social duty; Howard stood with a glass of wine in Marvin's kitchen, with its Aga cooker and an old bread oven in the wall, and studied the brochure. It was called 'Creating a Community/Building a Dialogue', and on the cover was a drawing of five students, for some reason in that state of crotchless nudity beloved of the stylists of the early sixties, and talking to each other in a very energetic dialogue indeed. Inside Howard read, in facsimile handwriting: 'We are not alone making here the new buildings; we are creating too those new forms and spaces which are to be the new styles of human relationship. For an architecture is a society, and we are here making the society of the modern world of today.' Howard put down the brochure, and went out, under the low oak beams of the living-room, to survey his colleagues, chattering on the darkness of the lawn; he thought about the contrast between this rural place and the tall Kaakinen buildings that were transforming the ancient estate where the university stood. After a while, he looked around the house and found Barbara, lying on a sofa in an alcove, her head in the lap of a senior lecturer in Philosophy. 'Oh, boy,' said Barbara, 'you've made a good impression. The Vice-Chancellor came and found me, just to tell me how much he liked you.' 'He's trying to nullify you,' said the Philosophy man, 'steal your fire.' 'He couldn't,' said Barbara, 'Howard's too radical.' 'Watch it, they'll charm you,' said Barbara later, her foetal bump against the dashboard, as they drove home through the darkness into Watermouth. 'You'll become an establishment pet. A eunuch of the system.' 'Nobody buys me,' said Howard, 'but I really think there's something for me here. I think this is a place I can work with.'

But that was in the late autumn of 1967; and after 1967 there came, in the inevitable logic of chronicity, 1968, which was the radical year, the year when what the Kirks had been doing in their years of personal struggle suddenly seemed to matter for everybody. Everything seemed wide open; individual expectation coincided with historical drive; as the students massed in Paris in May, it seemed that all the forces for change were massing everywhere with them. The Kirks were very busy that year. On campus the Maoist and Marxist groups, whose main business up to now seemed to be internecine quarrel, found a mass of activist support; there was a sit-in in the administration building, and a student sat at the Vice-Chancellor's desk, while the Vice-Chancellor established his own office in the boiler-house and tried to defuse the tension. The Revolutionary Student Front went to see him, and asked him to declare the university a free state, a revolutionary institution aligned against outworn capitalism; the Vice-Chancellor, with great reasonableness, and a good deal of historical citation, explained his feelings of essential sympathy, but urged that the optimum conditions and date for total revolution were not yet here. They could probably be most realistically set some ten years away, he said; in the meantime, he suggested, they should go away, and come back then. This angered the revolutionaries, and they wrote 'Burn it down' and 'Revolution now' in black paint on the perfectly new concrete of the perfectly new theatre; a small hut was set on fire, and seventeen rakes totally destroyed. Hate and revolutionary zeal raged; people in the town poked students on the buses with umbrellas; there were demonstrations in the main square in town, and some windows were smashed in the largest department store. The faculty, as faculty do, divided, some supporting the radical students, some issuing statements recalling students to their duties. People stopped speaking to people, and offices and professors' rooms were broken into and files removed. A state of minor terror reigned, and minds were stretched and strained; ancient marriages broke up, as one party went with the left, the other with the right; all old tensions came to the surface. But Howard was not divided; he joined the sit-in, and his intense, small face was one of those that could be seen, by those locked out, peering forth from the windows, shouting, 'Free thought is at last established,' and 'Critical consciousness reigns,' or waving the latest slogans from Paris. In fact he was an inevitable focus, and was very active everywhere, radicalizing as many people as he could, leaving the sit-in to speak to workers' groups and trades union meetings. Their terrace house became a meeting place for all the radical students and faculty, town drop-outs, passionate working communists; there were posters in the windows that said 'Smash the System', 'Reality does not exist yet', 'Power to the people'. And as for the Kaakinen-plan university, and its pious modernismus and concrete mass, and the radical new education, the new states of mind and styles of heart, enshrined inside it, that all came to seem to Howard a hard institutional shell designed to restrain and block the onward flood of consciousness. Not radical enough. Nothing *was* radical enough for the Kirks that year. Howard stared at the campus from the sit-in and what he said was: 'I think this is a place I can work against.'

The summer realized the Kirks as they had never felt realized before. Time no longer seemed a contingent waste in which one passed out one's life; it was redeemable; the apocalypse stood at hand, the new world waited to be born. All present institutions and structures, the structures whose nature he had so carefully elaborated in his classes, now seemed to be masks and disguises, crude acts of imposition set over the true human reality, which came real around him. A massive, violent impatience overcame him; he looked around, and saw nothing but false and corrupt interests checking the passionate movement towards reality. But the times were his times; his beliefs were at last activated and made real. He found, too, that he was good at persuading people that this was so, that a new era of human fulfilment and creativity was at hand. He was busy at many meetings; and lots of people, on the edge of breakthrough, came to talk to him. He discussed with them their struggles with the vestigialities of the past, their breaking marriages. Barbara, large and yellow-haired, grew alive with expectation too; she began to push at the world. She felt herself on the front line again; the baby was old enough to leave. But now her old idea that she would go into social work, which meant a formal, institutional course, seemed just a compromise with the system; she wanted more, to act. She helped start a community newspaper. She led consumer protests. She shouted, 'Fuck,' in council meetings. She joined in with a group of Women's Libbers and led consciousness-raising sessions. She hurried women to clinics and welfare services, hoping to strain them to the point of collapse, so the people could see how they had been duped. She arranged sit-ins at doctors' surgeries and employment agencies. She helped get a Claimants' Union started. The sub-culture, the counter-culture, clustered around them, and the parties they went to, the parties they held, were now of a different kind: activist occasions, commemorating the anniversary of Sharpeville or the May struggle in Paris, and ending in a plan for a new campaign. The running motto was 'Don't trust anyone over thirty'; it was in the summer of 1968 that Howard was thirty, and Barbara thirty-one. But they did trust themselves, and they were trusted; they were on the side of the new.

But that was in 1968; now time has passed. Since then much has been going on with the Kirks, but the intimacy, warmth and consensus of that year, seems hard to recover. They look for it; they have a strong sense of something that was un-delivered then, and a hazy dream still shimmers ahead of them: a world of expanded minds, equal dealings, erotic satisfactions, beyond the frame of reality, beyond the limits of the senses. They remain in their terrace house, and they stand somehow still on the fulcrum between end and beginning, in a history where an old reality is going and a new one coming, living in a mixture of radiance and radical indignation, burning with sudden fondnesses, raging with sudden hates, waiting for a plot, the plot of historical inevitability, to come and fulfil the story they had begun in bed in Leeds after Hamid had slept with Barbara. They are busy people. Howard, with a group of students and a deep radical intent, has had a rehabilitation study done of the entire area where they live, part of a grass-roots exercise in local democracy. The local council, now impressed with Howard's urbanology, have accepted this scheme; this has the beneficial consequence that the Kirks will keep their house, while the surviving houses in the terrace will ultimately be restored. Beyond the windows of their house still stretches the waste, the transitional acres of devastation, the touches of reconstruction. Children have made playgrounds in the rubble, out of which, at a distance, prod grey, shuttered concrete tower blocks, new precincts, the terminus of the urban motorway. In the distance, across the mess, signs flash, saying 'Finefare', 'El Dorado', 'Life Again Boutique'. Jet fighters fly overhead; motorscooters whine in the streets round about; there are muggings in the spaces between the bright sodium lights. By day, adolescent bottle-breakers and five-minute fornicators inhabit the rubble around them. At night the Kirks can stand inside their house, fresh from *Wiener Schnitzel*, and see a flicker of small lights spurting in the derelict houses across the way: the meths drinkers and wandering hippies creep constantly into occupation, making an independent life-style, groaning in the darkness, sometimes setting fire to themselves. The Kirks respond each according to his competence: Barbara takes them Thermoses of coffee and blankets, and Howard counts them and, in the basement study he has now made—a guilty item in their now all too passable life—he writes up the results in indignant pieces for *New Society* and *Socialist Worker*.

The Kirks do not believe in property; but they look out upon this apocalyptic landscape of the times, these craters, this rubble, these clutches of willow-herb, these drifting migrants, with a sense of territoriality. It is the outside of the inside of their minds, their perfect vista; like landed squires having their portraits painted, they can be posed appropriately against it. Here is Howard, small and elegant, his Zapata moustache drooping around the corners of his mouth, the hair thinning slightly and therefore combed forward, the firm jaw jutting in an angry, thrusting look; beside him, his good wife Barbara, in her long caftan, large and light-haired, Thermos in hand, one fist slightly raised and clenched; behind them, in strong detail, a scatter of broken forms, a coming down and a going up, society and consciousness in transformation; the two central figures equal, their eyes alert, their limbs twitching, struggling to get out of the frame and on with the plot of history. The plot of history; it serves them, and it matters to them, but somehow it doesn't quite give them all now. For of course they are now in their middle thirties, and certain things have been achieved; that is part of the trouble, as Howard, who is frank in his own self-exposure, will tell you. As a famous radical at the university, Howard has a senior lectureship there, and has been put on a fair number of committees. He is still active in the town's radical causes, in a free school for underprivileged children, a rescue campaign called People In Trouble, and in the radical journals, where he writes often. He edits a sociology series for a paperback publisher, and has published a second book, *The Death of the Bourgeoisie*. The Kirks go to publishers' parties in Bloomsbury, and radical socialist parties in Hampstead, and parties for new boutiques in the King's Road. And of course they give good parties of their own, like the one they are giving tonight.

They are very busy people, with very full diaries; the days may lie contingently ahead of them, but the Kirks always have a plot of many events, an inferior plot to the one they have come to desire, but one that gives them much to do. And this is as well, for it means that they do not conflict with each other as directly as they might, for each in his or her own way distrusts the other, in some nameless, unexpressed dissatisfaction. Having bound themselves by marriage, they persist with it; but it is an adult, open marriage. They are both having affairs, though affairs now of a rather different kind. 'See a friend this weekend' say the advertisements at the railway station; Barbara does. She has met an actor called Leon, twenty-seven years old, who wears yak coats and does small parts at the Traverse and on television, on the train up to London one Friday. Now, every so often, she takes a weekend in London, and spends it at his flat, having first been careful to ensure that proper arrangements have been made about the children. These she calls her shopping trips, for she shops too: she makes avaricious love to Leon over the weekend, and then moves on to Biba, coming back home on the mid-morning train on Monday with a brighter look on her face and several dresses, each in their elegant, dark-brown plastic bags. Meanwhile, Howard is not idle. He has various desultory interludes; he has been having these for several years. But now he is spending a good deal of time with a colleague of his, a handsome big girl in her late thirties, whose name is Flora Beniform, a social psychologist who has worked with Laing and the Tavistock Clinic. Flora is formidable, and she likes going to bed with men who have troubled marriages; they have so much more to talk about, hot as they are from the intricate politics of families which are Flora's specialist field of study. Flora has a service apartment in a suburb of Watermouth, a clean and simple place, for she is often away. And here Howard and Flora lie in bed for hours, if they can spare long hours, fondling each other intimately, considerably satisfying each other, without too great commitment, but above all talking things over.

And there is much to talk over. 'What do you fear from her?' asks Flora, her big weight lying on top of Howard, her breasts before his face. 'I think,' says Howard, 'we compete too closely in the same area. It makes sense. Her role's still bound too tightly to mine; that traps her growth, so she feels compelled to undermine me. Destroy me from within.' 'Are you comfortable there?' says Flora, 'I'm not squashing you?' 'No,' says Howard. 'Destroy you how?' asks Flora. 'She has to find a weak core in me,' says Howard. 'She wants to convince herself that I'm false and fake.' 'You have a lovely chest, Howard,' says Flora. 'So do you, Flora,' says Howard. 'Are you false and fake?' asks Flora. 'I don't think so,' says Howard, 'not more than anyone else. I just have a passion to make things happen. To get some order into the chaos. Which she sees as a trendy radicalism.' 'Oh, Howard,' says Flora, 'she's cleverer than I thought. Is she having affairs?' 'I think so,' says Howard. 'Can you move, you're hurting me?' Flora tumbles off him and lies by his side; they rest there, faces upward toward the ceiling, in her white apartment. 'Don't you know?' asks Flora. 'Don't you bother to find out?' 'No,' says Howard. 'You have no proper curiosity,' says Flora. 'There's a living psychology there, and you're not interested. No wonder she wants to destroy you.' 'We believe in going our own way,' says Howard. 'Cover yourself up with the sheet,' says Flora, 'you're sweating. That's how people catch colds. Anyway, you stay together.' 'Yes, we stay together, but we distrust one another.' 'Ah, yes,' says Flora, turning on her side to look at him, so that her big right breast dips against his body, and wearing a puzzled expression on her face, 'but isn't that a definition of marriage?'

Flora has a comfortable room, a soft bed, a telephone beside it, and an ashtray, where a cigarette has burned away, while they have been busy. Howard looks at the ceiling; he says: 'You think we shouldn't be married? Did you come?' 'I always come,' says Flora. 'No, I didn't say that. It's an institution of multiple utility. I myself prefer unconditioned fornication, but that's just my particular choice within the options. Marriages can be very interesting. I think a lot of life gets worked out within that most improbable relationship.' 'I suppose Barbara and I really belong to the marriage generation, despite ourselves,' says Howard. 'If we'd been five years younger, we'd just have shacked up together. Taken the best of it, and then cut loose.' 'But why don't you cut loose?' asks Flora. 'Explain to me.' 'I'm not quite sure,' says Howard, 'I think we both still have expectations. We feel there's something yet to achieve. Somewhere else to go.' 'You've a spot on your back, Howard,' says Flora. 'Turn over and let me squeeze it. Where to go?' 'Your nails are sharp,' says Howard. 'I don't know. There's still a psychic tie.' 'You haven't quite finished defeating each other,' says Flora, 'is that it?' 'The battle means something,' says Howard, 'it keeps us alive. 'Well, you thrive,' says Flora. 'Does Barbara?' 'She's a bit depressed,' says Howard, 'but that's just the price of a dull summer. She needs a bit of action.' 'Oh, well,' says Flora, 'I'm sure you'll be able to fix that. Okay, Howard, out you get. Time to go home to matrimony.' Howard gets out of the big bed; he goes to the chair on which his clothes are neatly laid, picks up his shorts, and puts them on. He says: 'Shall I see you again soon?' For he is never quite sure of Flora, never quite sure whether he is having an affair with her, or a treatment, with inclusive intimacies, which could be

54

terminated abruptly at any moment, with the patient deemed fully recovered and fit to return to normal married life. 'Oh, well,' says Flora, reaching with a heave of her large naked self, to the bedside table, from which she picks up her diary, a pencil, and her glasses, 'I'm awfully busy just now, with the start of term. I hope it's going to be a quiet term for once.' 'Oh, Flora,' says Howard, 'where's your radical passion? What's life without confrontation?'

Flora puts on her glasses; she stares at Howard through them. 'I hope you're not brewing trouble for us, Howard,' she says. 'Would I?' asks Howard, innocently. 'I thought you just explained it was your way of keeping your marriage alive,' says Flora. 'That, and coming here.' 'When can I come here next?' asks Howard, pulling on his socks. Flora opens her diary; she flicks through the pages, as fully written over as the pages in that other diary which stands by the Kirks' telephone, in the hall that Howard must in a minute get back to. 'I'm sorry, Howard,' she says, looking at its busy pages, 'I'm afraid we'll just have to leave it open. I seem to be hopping about all over the place for a bit.' 'Oh, Flora,' says Howard, 'first things first.' 'That's what I'm doing,' says Flora. 'Never mind, Howard. It will give you a chance to make some things happen. And then you'll have something more interesting to tell me next time.' 'Well, there's one evening you've got to keep free,' says Howard. 'Next Monday. Come to a party.' 'That's the first day of term,' says Flora, looking in her diary. 'You do pick awkward days.' 'It's the perfect day,' says Howard. 'New starts all round. A beginning-again party.' 'You never learn, do you?' says Flora. 'There are very few new beginnings. Only more of the same.' 'I don't believe you,' says Howard, 'being a radical. There'll be plenty of interesting things happening there.' 'I'm sure,' says Flora. 'What time?' 'About eight,' says Howard. 'An informal party. If you see what I mean.' 'Oh, I think so,' says Flora. 'Well, I'll see, I may have to go to London. I'll come if I can, I won't if I can't. Can we leave it like that?' Howard puts on his jacket. 'Oh, come,' says Howard, 'however late. We'll be going on most of the night.' 'Well, I'll try,' says Flora, and, naked except for her glasses, she takes her little silver pencil, and writes, amid the scribble that fills the entry at the top of the page for the new and coming week, 'Party at

55

Howard's', and adds a question mark. Howard leans over Flora; he kisses her forehead; 'Thanks,' he says. Flora swings her big bulk off the bed; she says, 'I'm going to the bathroom. Can you find your own way out?' 'I always have,' says Howard. 'Now don't count on me,' says Flora. 'I do,' says Howard. 'Don't,' says Flora, 'I refuse to be counted on. We're not married, you know.' 'I know,' says Howard, 'but what kind of party will it be if you don't come?' 'Much the same,' says Flora, 'you'll find a way of making something happen to you, won't you?' 'You have a cynical view of me, Flora,' says Howard. 'I just know you,' says Flora, 'have a novel Monday.' Howard goes out of the bedroom, and across Flora's dark living-room, and down the stairs of the apartment block. The minivan is parked discreetly under the trees; he gets in, and drives down the marked roads into the city centre.

IV

But now here it is, the day of beginning again, the day that is written down in so many diaries, and it is raining, and dreary, and bleak. It rains on the shopping precinct, as the Kirks do their early-morning shopping; it rains on the terrace, as they unload the wine and the glasses, the bread, the cheese, the sausages; it rains even on the University of Watermouth, that bright place of glinting glass and high towers, the Kaakinen wonderland, as Howard drives up the long carriage drive that leads to the centre of the site, and parks in the car park. In the rain, busloads of students arrive from the station, descending and running for convenient shelter. In the rain, they unload their trunks and cases into the vestibules of the residence buildings, into the halls of Hobbes and Kant, Marx and Hegel, Toynbee and Spengler. In the rain, the faculty, scattered over the summer, park their cars in rows in the car park and rush, with their briefcases, toward the shapely buildings, ready, in the rain, to renew the onward march of intellect. In the rain, academic Howard, smart in his leather coat and denim cap, humping his briefcase, gets out of the van, and locks it; in the rain he walks, with his briefcase, through the permanent building site that is the university, past shuttered concrete, steel frame, glass wall; through underpasses, down random slopes, along walkways, beneath roofed arcades. He crosses the main concourse of the university, called for some reason the Piazza, where paths cross, crowds gather, mobs surge; he reaches the high glass tower of the Social Science Building. He goes up the shallow steps, and pushes open the glass doors. In the dry, he stops, shakes his hair, looks around. The building has a spacious foyer; its outer walls and doors are all of brown glass; beneath the glass, in one corner, trickles a small water-feature, a pool that passes under the wall and out into the world beyond—for Kaakinen, that visionary man, is a meta-physician, and for those with eyes to see, emblems of yin and yang, spirit and flesh, inner and outer, abound in his futurist city. The foyer contains much bustle; there are many tables here; at the tables sit students, representing various societies that contend, in considerable noise, for the attention of the arriving freshmen. Just inside the foyer Howard stands still, looking around; it is as if he is looking for someone, seeking something; there is a task to fulfil.

But he seems not to fulfil it; he walks on. At the tables, two groups, the Revolutionary Student Alliance and the Radical Student Coordinating Committee, have fallen out over a principle; they are busy throwing two lots of pamphlets, each labelled *Ulster: The Real Solution*, at each other. Howard ignores the altercation; he passes the tables; he goes on into an area of many notice-boards which, just like the tables, advertise much contention, contradiction, concern. Here are notices for all seasons. There are notices designed to stimulate self-awareness ('Women's Lib Nude Encounter Group') and self-definition ('Gaysoc Elizabethan Evening: With Madrigals'), reform ('Adopt an Elderly Person') and revolution ('Start the Armed Struggle Now?/Lunchtime Meeting Addressed by Dr Howard Kirk'). The invitations are rich, the temptations many; but even this does not seem to be what Howard is looking for. He passes on, towards the main part of the foyer, where the lift shaft is. There is much activity here too. Students crowd round the lift, going to their first meetings of the new academic year with their tutors, crowding in to their first seminars; there are members of faculty busily carrying papers, and registry persons carrying computer printouts, and signs pointing here, and others pointing there. Howard stops here; once again he looks seriously, purposefully around. There is a thing to do; but with whom might it be done? A figure emerges from the crowd; she wears a large wet raincoat; she carries a carrycot. It is one of Howard's colleagues, a girl called Moira Millikin, unorthodox economist and unmarried mother, notable for her emancipated custom of bringing her infant to class, where it gurgles and chunters as she explains the concept of gross national product to her solemn students. 'Hello, Howard,' she says, 'had a good summer?' 'Well, I finished a book, if that's good,' said Howard. 'What about you?' 'I got pregnant again, if that's good,' says Moira. 'We're a productive lot, aren't we?' says Howard. 'I'm glad I found you. I've a fascinating piece of news.' The bell pings above the doors of the lift, in front of which they stand; the doors open, and out walks a man in workclothes, pushing a wheelbarrow in front of him. 'They push those barrows so that no one can mistake them for students,' says Moira, 'that they'd hate.' 'Right,' says Howard, 'are you going up to Sociology?' 'Well, Economics,' says Moira, 'back to the grindstone.' 'Good,' says Howard; and they move forward with the surge, into the lift. He and Moira stand against the back wall, with the carrycot between them; the doors close, the lift rises.

'What were you going to tell me?' asks Moira, 'Is it an issue?' 'It is,' says Howard, looking around the lift, and leaning towards Moira, and speaking in a very low voice. 'There's a rumour that Mangel is coming here to speak.' 'A rumour that who is coming here to speak?' asks Moira. 'There's a rumour that Mangel is coming here to speak,' says Howard in a very loud voice; students turn and look at him, 'Mangel. Mangel the geneticist. Mangel the racist.' The metal box in which they stand creaks its way up the central tower of the building; bells keep pinging, the lift stops, and opens its doors, and disgorges persons, at floor after floor after floor. 'Oh, that Mangel,' says Moira, bouncing her baby, 'Christ, we can't have him here.' 'Well, that's precisely what I thought,' says Howard, 'we really can't.' 'It's an insult, an indignity,' says Moira. 'It's an outrage,' says Howard. 'But who invited him?' asks Moira, 'I don't remember our agreeing to invite him.' 'That's because we never did agree to invite him,' said Howard, 'someone must have acted over the summer, while we were all safely out of sight.' 'You mean Marvin?' asks Moira. 'I suppose,' says Howard. 'Well,' says Moira, 'we're not out of sight now. We all have a say. This passes for a democratic department.' 'Right,' says

Howard. 'I'll raise it at the departmental meeting tomorrow,' says Moira, 'I'm glad you told me.' 'Oh, will you?' asks Howard, 'I think someone ought to. I thought I might myself, but . . .' 'But you'd rather I did,' says Moira. 'Okay.' The liftbell pings; the doors open at the fourth floor; 'This is me,' says Moira. With the carrycot in front of her, she jostles through the crowds; she thrusts herself out of the lift; she turns, and stares back into the crowded interior. 'Howard,' she says over the heads, 'I'll fight. You can count on me.' 'Great,' says Howard, 'that's marvellous.'

The lift doors shut; Howard leans against the metal wall, looking like a man who is no longer looking for someone or something. The doors open again, at the fifth floor; Howard moves to the front, and steps out of the lift, into the stark concourse, for here, high in the building, is where Sociology is. Is, and yet in a sense is not; for no sociologist seriously interested in human interaction could have countenanced the Kaakinen concept at this point. From the lift shaft four straight corridors lead off, at right angles to each other, each identical, each containing nothing but rows of doors, giving or barring access to teaching rooms or faculty studies. There are buildings in the world which have corners, bends, recesses; where seats have been put, or paintings hung on the walls; Kaakinen, in his purity, has rejected all these delicacies. Along the corridors sit many students, waiting to see their advisers on this, the first day of the term. They sit on the tiled floors of the corridors, their backs against the wall, their knees up, their hands holding, or spilling, plastic cups of coffee, obtained from an automatic vending machine next to the lift shaft. The floors smell of tile polish; the corridors are lit only by artificial sodium light. Howard leaves the concourse, and walks along one of the corridors; the students scowl and clown and groan as he passes, and make cracking noises at him with the plastic of their cups. 'The only activity Kaakinen invented for people to do here, except teach or be taught,' Henry Beamish had once said, in the old days before the anguishes of 1968, when he was still witty, 'is a game called Fire. Where you ring the alarm, immobilize the lift, and file slowly down the fire escape with a wet jacket over your head.' Only Howard, who has a taste for the spare, finds it forgivable; there are merits in the alienation

60

it promotes. He walks on, down to the very end of the corridor;
here, at the most inconvenient point, is the departmental
office. He pushes open the glass door, and goes inside. Within
the big bare room, responsible for the endless documentation
that keeps the community humming, are two nice, neat
secretaries, Miss Pink from Streatham, Miss Minnehaha Ho,
from Taiwan; they sit in their miniskirts, opposite each other,
in front of typewriters, their knees just touching. They look
up as Howard comes in. 'Oh, Dr Kirk, what a very fine hat,'
says Miss Ho. 'Lovely to see your beautiful faces again,' says
Howard. 'Had a good summer?' 'You were on holiday,'
says Miss Pink, 'we worked.' 'It only looks like a holiday,' says
Howard, going over to the long rows of pigeon-holes, where the
faculty mail is deposited, 'that's when the real work of the mind
takes place. I come back full of new thoughts.' 'The trouble
with your thoughts,' says Miss Pink, 'is they end up as our
typing.' 'You're right,' says Howard, dropping most of the
correspondence addressed to him in a box marked 'For
Recycling'. 'Rebel. Fight back'. Through the wall can be
heard the sounds of intensive industry; the adjoining room is
the office of Professor Marvin, the heart of the operation.
Telephones click, buzzers buzz, the high voice speaks on the
telephone; there is much to be done. 'What's this?' asks
Howard, holding up a large grey envelope, one of the university's official envelopes for committee documents. 'That's
agenda for the departmental meeting,' says Miss Ho, 'very
good typing.' 'Oh, I'll read it with scruple,' says Howard, 'if
you've done it. You've had your hair styled. I like it.' 'He is
trying to find something out,' says Miss Ho to Miss Pink, 'he
always likes my hair when he is finding something out.' 'No, I
really like it,' says Howard, 'look, I'm just glancing at this
agenda; you haven't put Professor Mangel's name down on the
list of visiting speakers.' 'It wasn't on it,' says Miss Ho, 'that is
why.' 'It must be a mistake,' says Howard. 'You want me to
check with Professor Marvin?' asks Miss Ho. 'No,' says
Howard, 'leave it. I'll raise it with him myself. Can't you just
add it?' 'Oh, no, Dr Kirk,' says Miss Ho. 'Agenda approved.'
'Of course,' says Howard, 'well, type good.' He goes out of the
office; he walks back down the corridor. The squatting
students stare at him. Two builders on a ladder are removing

61

a ceiling panel, to gain access to the stark intestines of the premises; the whole tower is in an endless state of semi-completion. He stops in front of a dark brown door; on it is a panel, with his own name on it. He gets a key from his pocket; he unlocks the door; he walks inside.

The room is raw in the wet, dull light; it is a simple rectangle, with unpainted breeze-block walls, described in the architectural journals as proof of Kaakinen's frank honesty. The rooms at Watermouth are all like this, stark, simple, repetitious, each one an exemplary instance of all the others. The contents, standard, are as follows: one black-topped Conran desk; one grey gunmetal desk lamp; one plain glass ashtray; one Roneo-Vickers three-drawer filing cabinet; one red desk chair; one small grey easy chair; one gunmetal wastepaper basket; a stack of four (4) black plastic chairs, their seats moulded to the shape of some average universal buttock; six (6) wall-hung book-shelves. Howard, who likes economy, has amended it very little; the one mark of his presence is the poster of Che, sello-taped to the breeze-block wall above the Conran desk. There are big, bare windows; beyond the windows you can see, dead centre, the high phallus, eolipilic in shape, of the boilerhouse chimney, the absolute focus, the point of maximum archi-tectural eminence, of the entire university, its substitute for a tower or a spire or a campanile. Howard hangs up his coat on the hook behind the door, and puts his hat on top of it; he puts his briefcase down on the desk; he begins, after his absence over the summer, when the room has been in the hands of cleaners only, to re-establish occupancy. He sits down at the red desk chair in front of the black-topped Conran desk, switches on the gunmetal desk lamp, removes the agenda from its big grey envelope, opens the Roneo-Vickers three-drawer filing cabinet, and puts the agenda in a pocket file; scrumples up the big grey envelope, and tosses it into the gunmetal waste-paper basket. This work done, he rises, goes to the window, adjusts the plastic blind, and stares out at the rain, dropping very wetly over the Kaakinen concept that is spread out below, far below him. Down in the Piazza there is a scurrying of students; against the grand style of Kaakinen walk, in the wet, the small personal styles of the people, who always alter from autumn to autumn, in the changing rhythm of human

62

expression, which takes skirts higher or lower, gives faces more hair or less, alters posture and stance. These are matters of serious attention to true cultural inspectors, like Howard; he stands at his window, high in the glass tower, and examines the latest statements on the human prospect.

The university gets bigger, year by year; a new building, a new path, a new stretch of water, takes it inexorably towards its fuller realization. The place has been functioning for only ten years; but in those ten years it has done everything, indeed has enacted the entire industrializing process of the modern world. Ten years ago this stretch of land was a peaceful, pastoral Eden, a place of fields and cows, focused around the splendours of Watermouth Hall, the turreted Elizabethan mansion now screened from sight by the massive constructions that have grown on the pasture and the stubble. At Watermouth Hall, peacocks strutted; so did the very first students, pleasant, likeable, outrageous people, stylists of quite another kind from the present generation, inventors of societies and lectures and concerts, smart souls who, when the photographers from the Colour Supplements came down, as they did all the time in those days, photographed well, and reputedly had all the makings of a modern new intelligentsia. The sun shone regularly then, the same sun that had shone on Edwardian England; the students had their tutorials in the ancient library of the hall, surrounded by busts of Homer and Socrates, by leather-bound volumes scarcely disturbed since the onset of Romanticism, or, in summer, in the box maze, while gardeners clipped respectfully around them. The faculty met ceaselessly, innovating, planning, designing new courses, new futures, new reasons for trips to Italy; endless optimism reigned, and novelty was everywhere, and Kaakinen came, and stared at the grass, and dreamed dreams, while cows peered over the haha at his Porsche. A year later the box garden was gone; in its place was a building, the first of the modern new residences, called Hobbes, with round porthole windows scooping down to the floors, and transparent Finnish curtaining, and signs in lower-case lettering. The feudal era was ending; a year later it was gone for good, when teaching was shifted from Watermouth Hall, which became an office block, devoted to administration, into the bright new buildings, some high, some long, some square, some round, that began to spring up here and there all over the estate. There were two more residence halls, Kant and Hegel; the gardeners, their deference spurned, had gone to greener pastures, while men on brushbearing vehicles swept the new asphalt.

For now the university was beginning to secrete its history in clear annual stages, like a tree; and it was, in encapsulated form, the history of modern times. The bourgeoisie rose (Humanities and Natural Science opened their doors); the industrial revolution took place (the Business Building and the Engineering Building were opened); the era of the crowd and the factory arrived (the glass tower of Social Science came into use). The sun shone less often; the students appeared less and less in the newspapers, and looked different, and more confused. The new buildings all had toilets with strange modern symbols of man and woman on them, virtually indistinguishable; the new students came, and they stared at the doors, and at themselves, and at each other; they looked, and they asked questions like 'What is man, any more?' and so life went on. *Gemeinschaft* yielded to *Gesellschaft*; community was replaced by the fleeting, passing contacts of city life; people came into the university, and disappeared; psychiatric social workers were appointed, to lead them through the recesses of their angst. By 1967, when Howard came, it had been noticed that no given teacher could possibly remember the names and features of all the students he was teaching, nor master in face-to-face contact the number of colleagues he was teaching with. There were those who pined, and said more was worse, more people was worse life; but, as Howard told them, it was simply that the community was growing up. It grew and grew, up and up. In 1968, the year after Howard, full proletarian status was adopted; the students wore work-clothes, and said they were not an élite any more, and cried 'Destroy, destroy,' and modern citizenship was established. So it went on; in 1969, existential exposure, modern plight, the contemporary condition of pluralism and relativity, were officially accredited, with the opening of the multi-denominational chapel, named, to avoid offence, the Contemplation Centre; rabbis and gurus, ethical secularists and macrobiotic organicists presided at what was carefully not called its consecration. In 1970 the technotronic

64

age became official; the Computing Centre was put into use, and it began work by issuing a card with a number on it to everyone on campus, telling them who they were, an increasingly valuable piece of information.

And now the campus is massive, one of those dominant modern environments of multifunctionality that modern man creates: close it down as a university, a prospect that seemed to become increasingly possible, as the students came to hate the world and the world the university, and you could open it again as a factory, a prison, a shopping precinct. There is a dining-hall with a roof of perspex domes, looking like sun umbrellas, by the man-made lake; there is an Auditorium in the shape of a whale, its hinder parts hung out on an elegant device of metal ropes over the lake; the buildings poke and prod and shine in a landscape itself reconstituted, as hills are moved here and valleys there. Some eclecticism and tolerance prevails; at the Auditorium they perform that week a Marxist adaptation of *King Lear*, this week a capitalist adaptation of *The Good Woman of Setzuan*. But a zealous equality prevails in the air, and the place has become a little modern state, with the appropriate services, in all their inconsistency: a post office and a pub and a Mace supermarket and a newsagent stand side by side with the psychiatric service, the crèche, the telephone life-line for the drug addicts, the offices of the Securicor patrol. The sun rarely shines; the peacocks have gone; the students are not bright originals in the old style, but bleaker, starker performers in the modern play; and when they are photographed by the press, which is rather less often, they appear not in the glossy pages but in the news pages, and upside down, hanging between two policemen. The campus spreads; now and then Air Force planes swoop low over it, as if inspecting to make sure it is still in the nation's hands, before they sweep on to the woods and cornfields beyond. A plane flies over now, as Howard stares out of his window; down below, in the Piazza, the students criss and cross, this way and that, in elaborate, asymmetrical patterns, ants with serious yet unguessable purposes.

How are they this year? Well, no longer do they look like an intellectual élite; indeed, what they resemble this autumn is rather the winter retreat of Napoleon's army from Moscow. For in the new parade of styles, which undergoes subtle shifts year by year, like the campus itself, bits of military uniform, bedraggled scraps of garments, fur hats and forage caps and kepis, tank tops and denims and coats which have lost their buttons have become the norm; the crowds troop along raggedly, avoiding the paths which have been laid out for them, hairy human bundles fresh from some sinister experience. Like the faculty, the place itself, they look smaller and darker and more worn than they did ten years ago. There is little wonder; much anguish has visited the Kaakinen city. Plagues of boils have fallen upon it; the locusts have eaten at the old dream of a university life totally new, qualitatively fine. In the rain the buildings are black; the concrete has stained, the glass grown dirty, the services diminished. The graffiti experts have been at work, inscribing 'Stop Police Brutality' and 'IRA' and 'Spengler Bootboys' on concrete and steel; there has been a small fire in the library; rapes and muggings occur occasionally in the darker corners of this good society. From time to time the radical passions overwhelm, then subside again; right reason and divine anger, Apollo and Dionysus, contend ceaselessly; suddenly frenzies arise, mouths cry, eyes glare, features distort. There is a student divorce problem, a statistically significant suicide rate. In the Students' Union voices cry: 'Woe, woe, the great city.' As Howard says, the place has grown up. He stares from the window; he takes in its texture. But now, over the wet, futurist place, a strange sound arises. It is the silvery chime of the old stable clock at Watermouth Hall, an eighteenth-century perpetuum mobile marvel that will not be stopped, ringing out the hour of ten. The chimes foolishly chime; Howard turns; there is a knock at his door. 'Yes?' shouts Howard, moving away from his windows, 'Come on in.'

The door opens slowly; two students stand in the frame. They are girls, one neat and bra-less, the other fat and dressed in a long, Victorian-style dress. Howard has not taught them before, but they are both immediately recognizable as Watermouth types, bright and anxious looking, ringed under the eyes, entering rooms cautiously; Watermouth is notable for experimental forms of teaching that often resemble physical assault. 'Dr Kirk,' says the bra-less girl. 'We're minors,' says the fat girl. 'We're yours,' says the bra-less one. 'You're minors and you're mine,' says Howard. 'That's it,' says the fat girl. 'You want to do sociology,' says Howard. 'Well, we *have* to do sociology,' says the bra-less girl, 'to be frank.' 'Don't you want to?' asks Howard. 'Why do they make us?' asks the fat girl. Howard takes the girls across to the window; he shows them the glass and concrete view; he tells them about *Gemeinschaft* to *Gesellschaft*; he says, 'How else could you know why the world has become what it is?' 'Is that what it's about?' asks the bra-less girl. 'That's right,' says Howard. 'Well, that's everything, isn't it?' asks the bra-less girl. 'Exactly,' says Howard. 'Ooooo,' says the fat girl, standing on Howard's other side. 'What's that?' asks Howard. 'Over there,' says the fat girl, and she points her finger out over the gloomy campus, 'I can see where I live.' 'Where?' asks Howard. 'I'm in Hegel,' says the girl, 'but the roof leaks.' 'Dr Kirk, who was Hegel?' asks the bra-less girl. 'Ah,' says Howard, 'You see, you do need to study sociology.' 'Did he know a lot?' asks the bra-less girl. 'He did,' says Howard, 'but his roof leaks.' 'You know more,' says the fat girl. Howard laughs; he steps back into the centre of his room, and arranges two of his plastic chairs, so that they form a triangle with his own desk chair. In the plastic chairs he puts the girls; in his desk chair he puts himself; he talks to them, he tells them about their work for the term, he sets them some reading, he advises them on the purchase of books, he asks the fat girl to write him an essay for next week. The girls get up, and go. 'He didn't tell you who Hegel was,' says the fat girl, as they walk off down the corridor. 'Hey,' shouts Howard, after them, 'Come to a party, eight o'clock tonight at my house,' 'Ooooo,' says the fat girl.

And so the morning passes. At home, domestic Barbara unwraps cheeses, and cuts sausages, and tidies the house; in his rectangular room Howard sees students, old ones and new ones, sets essays, recommends courses, sets reading, asks for essays, invites them to his party. The stable clock chimes; the rain falls. At twelve-thirty there is no knock on his door; he takes his leather coat from the peg, and descends, down the lift, into the complexities of the campus. The student hordes pass, to and fro, across the Piazza; Howard walks through them, a contemporary stylist himself, and makes his way to the Students' Union building. There are many services for a Howard to perform in a modern society; he has now another duty. The Revolutionary Student Front, that vague, contentious coalition of Marxists and Maoists and Marxist-Leninists and Revolutionary Socialists, has its inaugural meeting of the term; Howard, busy in the world as well as in the mind, has agreed to address it, to help it recruit. In more plastic chairs, in a tiny room in the Union, a group of students sits. The rain splashes on the windows; a pop group rehearses in the next room. A student called Peter Madden, who, if this uncertain consortium believed in having a leader, would be it, leads him to the front of the group. Madden wears denims and hostile, one-directional sunglasses; he stands and says a few words, explaining the purpose of the group, its relevance and its ire, to the newcomers. There are not many there, for it is early for issues and political discovery, and they are solemn, like a class. Howard stands up; the faces look. He leans with one hand on the arm of a chair; he glances out of the window at the futurist city; he begins to speak. He offers a calm analysis of the socio-political situation in which, he says, we find ourselves. We are in a world of late capitalism, and capitalism is an over-ripe plum, ready to fall. It is cracking, bursting, from its inner contradictions; but who, from its fall, will benefit? How can the new world come?

He speaks on; he generates images of violence. The faces stare, as he talks of armed struggle, the need for unity, the claims of blood and force. The dark portrait builds up, to the room's consent. He stops speaking; he invites discussion; the minds contemplate the techniques of bloodshed, the degree of warfare, the bright new reality at the end of it all. Afterwards they go quietly from the room; the pop group raises the decibels in the next room. In the cafeteria, over a salad plate, Howard says to Peter Madden: 'Not too many there.' 'You don't radicalize people by talk,' says Peter Madden, 'you get them in by action.' 'That's right,' says Howard. A girl called Beck Pott, in denim, her fair hair done up in twists, says: 'Have you *got* some action?' 'I don't know,' says Howard, 'Moira Millikin told me this morning that Mangel might be coming here to speak.' 'You have to be joking,' says Beck Pott, 'everybody's so low-profile these days you can't get a fascist to perform a fascist action.' 'Why don't they repress us the way they used to?' asks Peter Madden. 'There's your problem,' says Howard, 'so

68

you have to go for the soft liberal underbelly. Find where they're tolerant and go for that. Mangel tempts them to tolerance.' 'But what makes you think they'll invite him?' asks Beck Pott. 'I expect they will,' says Howard. 'Well, great,' says Beck Pott. 'Buy me a beer, Howard. You've got more money than me.' 'Give her the money,' says Peter Madden, 'she can fetch it herself.' 'I'll get it, I'm going,' says Howard. 'Look, come to a party at my home tonight.' 'Okay,' says Beck Pott.

'Myra and I are looking forward very much to the party at your house tonight,' says Henry Beamish, a few minutes later, as they meet each other getting into the lift in the Social Science Building. 'We always look forward to your parties.' 'Well, good,' says Howard, 'it should be a lively evening. We've asked everybody.' 'You always do,' says Henry, standing inside the box, and pressing the wrong button; the lift begins to descend, irrevocably, into the basement of the building, where the rubbish is kept. 'Yours are the most interesting parties we go to.' The lift doors open; they stare at dustbins. 'How's Myra?' asks Howard, pressing the right button. 'Oh, well, you know,' says Henry. 'No,' says Howard, as they rise. 'She's all right,' says Henry. 'She's just bought a new Miele dishwasher. How's Barbara?' 'Ah, Barbara,' says Howard, 'she's fighting back.' 'A good girl,' says Henry. 'Ah, well, term again, thank the Lord, I don't have to do any more to my book.' 'You're writing a book, Henry?' says Howard, as the lift stops. 'That's good.' 'I thought I'd do a book,' says Henry, 'I've nothing to say, of course. Ah, here we are. Take care, old boy.' 'I will,' says Howard. 'Till tonight,' says Henry, disappearing down one of the corridors on the fifth floor. Howard walks along the facing corridor; he goes back to his room. And now there are more students to see, letters to write, memos to dictate to Miss Ho, who sits in the grey chair, and takes shorthand from him. After this he goes to the library; the computer issues him some books; he carries them back to his room, and packs his briefcase. Then, with a good start to the new term behind him, and the joy of the party ahead, he goes out to the car park. It is just before five o'clock, on the day that Flora, and so many others, have noted in their diaries, that he gets back to the house in the terrace, and walks through the cool hall into the kitchen at the back.

In the days when the Kirks had remodelled their house, they

had worked with particular dedication at the kitchen, since they both had to spend so much time there. They did it out in pine and rush; the long table is scrubbed pine, the shelves on the walls are pine, there are pine cabinets, and pine and rush chairs, and rush matting on the floors. Barbara stands amid this, in front of a vinyl wallpaper celebrating the bulbous lines of onions and garlics; she is wearing a striped butcher's apron, and making pâté. The children are here too, filling bowls with nuts and pretzels. 'I said come back about four,' says Barbara, as Howard kisses her lightly on the cheek. She wipes the cheek with the back of her hand; she looks at him. 'I've had a busy day,' says Howard. 'I'm sure,' says Barbara. 'Don't tell me about it. It's clearly set you up in a big way, and I'm not interested in other people's happy times right now.' 'You're late, Howard,' says Celia, 'that was naughty.' 'Well,' says Barbara, 'there are the following things to do. Wipe the glasses. Open all the bottles of wine; there'll not be time for doing that later. I should pour out a few dozen glasses full. Put out ashtrays; I'm not having dirty rugs, and for some reason students have started throwing cigarette-ends on the floor.' 'They always did,' says Howard, 'we didn't care, once.' 'Well, we do now,' says Barbara. 'And then arrange the house the way you want it, sociologically speaking, for all that there interaction you're always talking about. You also need a bath and a change. Especially if you propose to be intimate with anyone other than myself. I've had a wearying, infuriating day, Howard, I think you should know. I've had Rosemary on the telephone twice; I'm sure she's going crazy. I think my period's starting, too, isn't that great? And Anne has left.' 'She has?' asks Howard, wiping glasses with a cloth. 'Before she washed the dishes from last night, not after,' says Barbara. 'She's gone back to her flat.' 'I thought she'd help out today,' says Howard. 'Oh, you pushed her on her way this morning, didn't you?' asks Barbara. 'Everyone exploits somebody.' Howard begins to take out a row of bottles from one of the cardboard cases, and put them on the long table. 'No, not there, somewhere else,' says Barbara, 'I'm occupying that space.' She puts some long French loaves on the table, and begins slicing them neatly, putting the cut pieces into a rush basket. Howard stands by the kitchen cabinets; he takes the corkscrew from the pine drawer, and begins expertly opening bottles, one after another. The children run over, and begin to lick the pulled corks; the Kirks' party begins to take its shape.

After a while, Howard leaves the kitchen and begins to go around the house. He is a solemn party-giver, the creator of a serious social theatre. Now he goes about, putting out ashtrays and dishes, cushions and chairs. He moves furniture, to produce good conversation areas, open significant action spaces, create corners of privacy. The children run around with him. 'Who's coming, Howard?' asks Martin. 'A whole crowd of people,' says Howard. 'Who?' asks Martin. 'He doesn't know,' says Celia. Now he goes upstairs, to pull beds against the walls, adjust lights, shade shades, pull blinds, open doors. It is an important rule to have as little forbidden ground as possible, to make the house itself the total stage. And so he designs it, retaining only a few tiny areas of sanctity; he blocks, with chairs, the short corridor that leads to the children's rooms, and the steps that lead down to his basement study. Everywhere else the code is one of possibility, not denial. Chairs and cushions and beds suggest multiple forms of companionship. Thresholds are abolished; room leads into room. There are speakers for music, special angles for lighting, rooms for dancing and talking and smoking and sexualizing. The aim is to let the party happen rather than to make it happen, so that what takes place occurs apparently without hostly intervention, or rather with the intervention of that higher sociological host who governs the transactions of human encounter. He goes into the bathroom, to check there; Barbara lies, big and naked, in the bath, in a plastic showercap, reading Cohn's *The Pursuit of the Millennium*. She says: 'Howard, I want you to know this. I'm having my Biba weekend in London, Anne or no Anne. I know you'd like to fix that, but you won't.' 'Fix it?' says Howard in innocence. 'Of course you should go.' 'Then find me someone to replace Anne,' says Barbara, 'so I don't worry about the kids all the time.' 'No, you mustn't do that,' says Howard. 'But can I count on you? Will you really do it?' asks Barbara. 'Yes,' says Howard. 'I'm a fool,' says Barbara, 'I should find someone myself. Rosemary would come.' 'Magical Rosemary,' says Howard, 'fresh from the shed down the garden.' 'That's not funny,' says Barbara, heaving in the bath. 'I just meant there are better choices,' says Howard. 'I'll find someone.' 'Not too pretty,' says Barbara. 'Oh, no,' says Howard. 'I want to enjoy myself,' says Barbara, 'my God, after four weeks close to you, I need it. Mind, I want to come out now.' 'Oh, you look good,' says Howard, as Barbara steps from the bath. 'Don't touch,' says Barbara, 'get on getting ready.'

Howard goes on getting ready; later, he takes a bath himself. Afterwards, he walks back to the bedroom, a room that he has rearranged for the evening, and changes, putting on clean jeans, a purple vest shirt. Then he goes downstairs, and there is someone with Barbara in the kitchen. It is Myra Beamish, sitting at the pine table, slicing and breaking the long loaves of French bread. She looks up at him in the doorway; she is wearing a fluffy pink chiffon party dress, and her hair is neater and fresher and darker than usual; Howard realizes she is wearing a wig. 'Oh, Myra,' he says. 'Hello, Howard,' says Myra, 'I hope you don't mind, I came early. I knew Barbara would be glad of some advance help. She has so much to do.' 'That's good,' says Howard, 'how would you like a drink.' 'Oh, Howard,' says Myra, 'I would most certainly love a drink.' A row of glasses stands ready poured and waiting for the evening; Howard picks one up, and carries it over to Myra, who smiles at him, and says 'Ta.' 'Where's Henry?' asks Howard. 'Who knows?' says Myra. 'Who knows about Henry?' 'I thought you might,' says Howard, sitting down. 'Does Barbara know all and everything about you?' asks Myra. 'I don't,' says Barbara. 'Nothing.' 'Then why should I be expected to know about Henry?' 'Oh, you're not,' says Barbara. 'I haven't seen you since before the summer,' says Myra. 'What did you do over the summer? Did you go away?' 'No, we didn't,' says Barbara, 'we stayed right here, and Howard finished a book.' 'A book,' says Myra, 'Henry tried to write a book. A very profoundly solemn book. On charisma.' 'Fine,' says Howard, 'Henry needs another book.' 'Howard, Henry needs more than a book,' says Myra, cutting bread. 'I must say I like your books better.' 'You do?' asks Barbara. 'Especially the sex one,' says Myra. 'The only thing I never understand about that book is whether we could do all those perverse sex things now, or whether we had to wait until after the revolution.' 'Christ, Myra,' says Barbara, 'nothing in consenting sex is perverse.' 'What's more,' says

Howard, 'they are the revolution.' 'Oh boy,' says Myra, 'you have such terrific revolutions. You've really improved revolution's image.' 'I try,' says Howard.

Barbara gets up from the table. She says: 'Howard's books are very empty but they're always on the right side.' 'They're nice books,' says Myra, 'I can almost understand them. More than I can say of Henry's.' 'Perhaps that's what's wrong with them,' says Barbara. 'Of course, they sell very well.' 'What's the new book, Howard?' asks Myra. 'What are you abolishing now?' 'People,' says Barbara. 'Barbara doesn't understand this book,' says Howard. 'She's such an activist she thinks she can dispense with theory.' 'Howard's such a theoretician now he thinks he can dispense with action,' says Barbara. 'Why don't you tell Myra what's in the book? It's not often you meet someone who's really interested. You are really interested, aren't you, Myra?' 'Of course I am,' says Myra. 'It's called *The Defeat of Privacy*,' says Howard. 'It's about the fact that there are no more private selves, no more private corners in society, no more private properties, no more private acts.' 'No more private parts,' says Barbara. 'Mankind is making everything open and accessible.' 'Even me?' asks Myra. 'Oh, we know all about you,' says Howard. 'You see, sociological and psychological understanding is now giving us a total view of man, and democratic society is giving us total access to everything. There's nothing that's not confrontable. There are no concealments any longer, no mysterious dark places of the soul. We're all right there in front of the entire audience of the universe, in a state of exposure. We're all nude and available.' Myra looks up; she says, with a squeak, 'You mean there isn't a me any more?' 'You're there, you're present,' says Howard, 'but you happen to be a conjunction of known variables, cultural, psychological, genetic.' 'I think that's intellectual imperialism,' says Myra. 'I don't think I like your book, Howard.' Barbara says, 'But who is this me you're protecting? Isn't it just the old bourgeois personality cult, the idea that the individual just isn't accountable? Isn't that what the world's found the need to get away from?'

Myra casts her eyes, rather theatrically, around the kitchen, looking at the shelves with their Caso Pupo goblets, their French casseroles, their fish dishes, their dark brown pot labelled *Sel*;

she says, with some dryness: 'Well, it must be very nice to feel you've transcended bourgeois individualism. I can't say I have.' 'But tell us more about this self you've got in there,' says Howard. 'There's a busy, active agent, with will and motive and feeling and desire. But where does it all come from? Genes, culture, economic and social potential. It acts out of specified forces under specified conditions.' 'I thought you always reckoned we were free,' says Myra. 'I thought this was the big Kirk message.' 'Ah, the big Kirk message,' says Barbara. 'The point is, the self is in time, and it changes in time. The task is to realize our selves by changing the environment. To maximize historical potential to the uttermost.' 'By being nude and available,' says Myra. 'When history's inevitable,' says Howard, 'lie back and enjoy it.' Myra burst into laughter; she says, 'That's just what you are, Howard. An historical rapist. Prodding the future into everyone you can lay your hands on.' 'How true,' says Barbara. 'Oh, come on, Howard,' says Myra, 'of course there's a me. I'm in here, I know.' 'What's it like, Myra?' asks Howard. 'It's not you, and it's private, and it's self-conscious, and it's very bloody fascinating.' 'Oh, Myra,' says Howard. Myra suddenly puts down the knife; her laughter has gone. She says: 'There's a me, and I'm sick of it.' The Kirks look at her; they notice that a long streak of a tear has established itself on Myra's nose. Barbara sits down next to her; she says, 'What's up, Myra?' Myra reaches into the handbag she has brought, an old party handbag from the days when there were party handbags, black with cracked sequins sewn onto it. She takes out a green square of Kleenex and puts it to her nose. She says: 'Actually, Kirks, I didn't come here just to help you cut bread. I came because I want you to help me. I want to tell you something. Before Henry gets here. I'm separating from him.' Barbara says: 'You, Myra?' Myra sniffs. She says, 'I know I'm an old bourgeois individualist who's not supposed to freak out. But, God, I need help. And I knew just who to come to. I thought, the Kirks. They're such a great couple.' The Kirks, the great couple, stare at each other, and feel like a couple. 'Of course we'll help,' says Barbara, 'we'll do everything we can.'

V

The Kirks and Beamishes have known each other for a very long time, since the days in Leeds, in fact, where Howard and Henry were graduate students together. Over the years in Watermouth they have seen a good deal of each other; it is one of those relationships which, based on an old friendship, keeps on running its course, even though the subscribing parties to it have all changed and have little really to say to each other. The Beamishes have come to the Kirk parties; the Kirks go to the Beamishes; they talk a lot to one another, over the telephone and in person. There have even been closer intimacies. Once, in the days of 1968, when everything was unsettled, Howard went out to the farmhouse, after a telephone call from Myra. Henry was out teaching an evening class on Conflict in Modern Society, at an adult education centre in one of the nearby seaside towns; Myra was sitting on the sofa crying; Howard went to bed with her. It was a failed, unrepeated occasion; he remembers nothing about the event but the anxiety afterwards, with himself on his knees, naked, wiping all trace of his presence from the bedroom carpet, while Myra made the bed, hoovered the house, emptied the ashtrays and washed all the glasses, to make everything exactly and precisely as it was before. The space between them was growing wide then, and now seems immeasurable; today the Kirks have only to look at Myra, sitting there, a knife in her hand, in that old chiffon party dress no one else in their entire acquaintance would wear, to see how much they themselves have changed, developed, grown up with experience, since they first came to Watermouth. As for the Beamishes, they profess somehow to understand the Kirks, to be privileged intimates; what they do not understand is that the Kirks they understand are people of several protean distillations back, people they themselves cannot remember ever having been.

Meanwhile the Beamishes, like some extraordinary historical measuring rod, have managed to persist just as they were when the Kirks first found them in Watermouth. Enormities have torn through the world, tempers have altered; the Beamishes have become different only by their obstinacy in staying the same, living on in a strange cocoon of old experience which strains them without altering them. Or have they altered? The Kirks look at Myra, as she cries in their kitchen, her outrage stated. Howard remembers her tearful unease of years ago; he thinks, disconfirmingly, of Henry, and what he has become. For Henry has now grown fat; he has taken to talking in a loud, heavy voice; he has become noticeably lazy. In the department, in the common-room, when intellectual matters are discussed, he has acquired a manner of shifting conversation round to questions of manure and pasture and the state of nature in general. When Howard or others try to push him on sociological or political matters, he looks pained. Once, in Howard's study, as they had gone through finals marks together, he had begun to cry a little and accuse Howard of damaging his career, in ways he could not quite name; Howard, it seemed, by doing what Henry had always intended to do, had stopped Henry from doing it himself. 'That's foolish,' Howard had said; 'I've become foolish,' Henry had said. And Myra, too, has darkened and become stranger; she noticeably drinks more, and talks frenziedly at parties, as if there were nowhere else in the world to talk. 'Why?' he says to her. 'Why do you want to leave him?'

Myra's expression is blank but slightly mystified, as if she had not expected such a question; surely the Kirks have an instinctive comprehension of all marital disillusion. 'I suppose for the most obvious of all reasons,' she says, 'I want the chance to exist, which I've been denied. I'd like to assert my identity. That is, Howard, if you've left me with one.' 'Of course,' says Howard. 'Where is it, then?' asks Myra. Barbara says: 'Myra, has Henry done something to you?' 'No,' says Myra, picking up the knife, and starting slicing at the bread again, 'he never does anything to me. That's why he's so boring. If I were asked to define my condition, I'd say boredom. I'm bored because he never does anything to me, and nor does anyone or anything else. Am I making sense?' 'I think so, Myra,' says Barbara. 'Doesn't he sleep with you?' 'Oh, it's not that,' says Myra. 'He does, in his own trite way. But, contrary to prevailing opinion, that's no revelation. Someone should write a book on the boredom of orgasm. Why don't you, Howard?' 'Howard's not bored,' says Barbara. 'Look, have you tried anyone else?' Myra, her face a little red, looks down at the table. 'That's just not the issue,' says Myra. 'There's no one else.' 'You're not leaving him for anyone?' 'No,' says Myra, 'I'm leaving him for me.' 'What will you do?' asks Barbara. 'I don't know,' says Myra. 'It's push, not pull, that's driving me.' 'But what is the issue?' asks Howard. 'What is it you want that you don't have?' 'Well, obviously,' says Myra, with a little impatience, 'absence from Henry.'

The Kirks, compassionate instructors in the arts of separation, look at each other. 'I don't think you've told us much yet,' says Howard. 'You must have been thinking about this for a long time. You must know what it is your marriage isn't expressing.' 'It isn't expressing anything at all,' says Myra. 'You might say it was silent.' 'But you're not silent,' says Howard, 'you've something in yourself to be said.' 'Yes,' says Myra. 'Ouch.' 'And Henry?' asks Howard. 'Does he feel the same?' 'Howard,' says Myra, 'have you inspected Henry lately? Don't you find him banal? Don't you think really he's become ridiculous?' 'I've worried about Henry,' says Howard. 'I'm concerned for him.' 'Well, can't you imagine me wanting to be free of him?' 'But haven't you talked about it? A marriage is a thing in common; you have something to do with his nature,' says Barbara. 'I think that sounds a nasty question,' says Myra, 'as if I'm to blame. But he shapes me much more than I do him. The man shapes the woman. He has the advantages. He sets the pace.' 'But you've not talked,' says Howard. 'No,' says Myra, 'there's nothing to talk about. You always said marriage was an archaic institution. Now you seem to want me to stay with him.' 'Oh, no,' says Howard. 'Howard doesn't mean that,' says Barbara, 'he just wants to get into the question of where things went wrong.' Myra begins to cry again. She says: 'I thought you'd agree with me.' 'We're not trying to stop you leaving him,' says Barbara, 'we want you to understand what you're doing.' 'I think I do understand that,' says Myra, 'I'm quitting while the going's good.' 'Have you thought of asking what's wrong with Henry?' asks Barbara. 'Trying to help him?' 'I've been trying to help him ever since we married,' says Myra. 'You've been married as long as we have. It was the year after, wasn't it? You know what things are like.' Howard looks at Barbara; he says, 'Ah, but ours hasn't been one marriage. It's been several.'

Myra sits at the table, and contemplates this undoubted truth for a moment. She looks up at the Kirks, standing, one on each side of her, custodians of the coupled relationship, concerned, a striking pair. She says, 'Oh, you two. I don't know how you do it.' 'How we do what?' asks Barbara. 'Have such a good relationship,' Myra says warmly. 'I wouldn't exactly boast,' says Barbara. 'Do you remember when Howard and I split up in Leeds?' 'Of course,' says Myra, 'but you talked to each other and got back together again. You learned to deal with each other. We never will.' Howard says, 'Myra, everyone's life looks more successful from the outside. Ours has been a fight. We've had our disasters.' He takes Myra's glass, and pours some more wine into it. 'But you bounce back,' says Myra. 'Thanks a lot, love.' 'I suppose it's a question of being determined to keep up with every stage of life,' says Barbara, 'of never relaxing.' 'You've just been more mature about it than the rest of us,' says Myra. The word 'mature' rings pleasantly with the Kirks; they look at each other with some pleasure. 'I think yours is the only successful academic marriage I know,' says Myra. 'What's wrong with the others?' asks Howard. 'You know what's wrong,' says Myra. 'Look around you at all these sad pairs. How can they work? The man goes out to the university, his mind's alive, he's fresh with new ideas.' 'Sometimes it's the woman,' says Barbara. 'Even the women are men,' says Myra. 'He talks all day to pretty students who know all about structuralism, and have read Parsons and Dahrendorf, and can say "charisma" properly, and understand the work he's doing. Then he comes home to a wife who's been dusting and cleaning. He says "Parsons" and "Dahrendorf", and she says "Huh?" What can he do? He either gives her a tutorial, and thinks she's pretty B minus, or he shuts up and eats the ratatouille.' 'She should work,' says Barbara. 'Oh, fine,' says Myra, 'except she keeps getting older, and the students manage to stay eighteen. And then comes the bit where all your friends start separating and divorcing, because the husbands run off with the alpha students who can say "charisma".' 'Do you think Henry wants to run off with an alpha student?' asks Barbara. Myra looks at her. 'No,' she says, 'not Henry, he hasn't that much ambition. He might sort of stumble into walking off slowly with a beta student. Maybe I'd like him better if he did.'

Barbara says, 'You mean you blame him because he does stay at home.' 'That's right,' says Myra. 'Much more of this bloody connubial bliss, and I swear we'll kill each other, Henry and me.' Howard laughs; he says, 'Myra, you really don't make sense.' 'I'm not as clever as you,' says Myra, 'but I want to leave him. And I came to you so that you could tell me why and how. You're experts, aren't you?' There is car-noise outside in the terrace. 'Oh, Christ,' says Barbara, 'I must go and put on my dress.' Myra says suddenly, 'Look, you mustn't tell Henry I'm leaving him. I haven't told him myself yet.' 'We'll have to have a longer talk,' says Barbara. 'Tomorrow, call me.' 'I'll probably be gone by then,' says Myra. 'You won't,' says Howard. 'I mean it,' says Myra. 'Yes,' says Barbara. 'Go and let them in, Howard.' 'Is my face a mess?' asks Myra, as they hear Barbara's feet rushing up the stairs. 'You're fine,' says Howard. 'Do you remember when we slept together?' says Myra. 'Yes, we did once, didn't we?' says Howard. 'The only time,' says Myra, looking at him. 'The only bloody time I ever did it. I bet you find that extremely ridiculous.' 'No, I don't,' says Howard. 'I want to fix my face a bit,' says Myra, 'you go and welcome your guests. I hope I've not spoiled things.' 'Of course not, Myra,' says Howard, and he goes out of the kitchen and along the cool long hall to the front of the house, to open the door to arrivals.

He opens the door. Out over the town the sodium lights are lit, and they cast an artificial red tint into the air, illustrating the jagged shapes of the decrepit houses opposite, where no one lives. The bright lights from the windows of the Kirks' house fall out over the old, broken pavement stones of the terrace, which are drying now, for the rain has stopped. In the terrace a big black Daimler hearse, of rather old vintage, has come to a stop. There are artificial flowers stuck in its elegant silver flower-holders; on the etched glass of the long side window is a sticker, saying, 'Make Africa Black'. The rear window rises; out slide three young men, all in jeans; two more descend from the front, one wearing a floppy leather hat, the other carrying a guitar. They begin to walk towards Howard's front door. Now a reconstituted pre-war Standard Eight, in good condition, halts across the street. A thin young man in a black leather jacket gets out of the driving seat, and goes round to the passenger door to draw forth a very pregnant woman, in loose top and trousers. They too cross the street toward the Kirks' bright house. Behind Howard there is a bustle; Barbara comes hurrying down the stairs, her hair up in a social bun, her healthy peasant bosom thrusting through the lines of a pink velvet Biba dress she has brought back from her most recent trip to London, her face bright. She comes and stands beside Howard in the hall, her hand on his shoulder. 'First arrivals,' says Barbara. 'Come on in,' says Howard. They stand together, Barbara big and blonde, Howard neat in his turned down moustache. The students come in freely, saying 'Hi,' their unfitting shoes flapping on the sealed wood floor. The other couple, a sociologist from Howard's department, a new appointment, and his very round wife, are more nervous; they stand in hesitation on the threshold, each looking equally weighted by the heavy pregnancy. 'You must be the Kirks,' says the sociologist. 'My name's Macintosh.' 'Come inside,' says Howard, the manager of this social theatre, 'I'll bring some drinks.' 'This is nice,' says Macintosh, looking around, 'you really know how to live.' They go through into the living-room; Howard gives out drinks; the students sit in a circle on the floor, while the Macintoshes stand, he dour, she sharp with the divine anger of the bright wife.

Outside there are more arrivals; souped-up minis, beach-buggies, psychedelically painted wrecks are drawing into the terrace, the first of many that will park in the broken curve and then in the streets beyond. The people begin to come in; there are people in old suits that look new and new jeans that look old. There are students and youths in Afghan yak, loon-pants, combat-wear, wet-look plastic; bearded Jesuses, long-haired androgynes, girls with pouting plum-coloured mouths. There are somewhat older people, the young faculty, serious young men, bright young women, bearing babies in harnesses on their backs, or in carrycots, slung between them, that are subsequently disposed of in many corners of the house. The groups that began as separate and compartmentalized begin to merge and mix; the few becomes a crowd, and moves from room to room. The students begin to talk to the faculty, and both groups begin to talk to the third, the strangers: a civic leader from the local Pakistani community, a young man in dark sunglasses who owns the town's sex shop, which is called Easy Come, a Women's Lib polemicist from London in an Afro fright-wig, a radical Catholic priest and his Ouspenskyite mistress, the man with the Smile badge from the wine store, and, much later, when the performance is over, the entire cast and production staff of the nude touring production of *The Importance of Being Earnest*, in Watermouth this week. Howard is busy and protean, a knowing host, a master in the enterprise of sociability. Now he stands at the door or circulates carrying a bottle, negotiating contact and association. Now he disappears backstage, to shift a table, open a door, expose a bed, remove a strategic fuse from the fusebox in the hall, to advance the contingent but onward progress of the illusion that is taking place under his guidance. He watches social animation jerk into operation. He sees the dresses flutter, the clothes flash and, with precision, does all he can with light and sound and movement to stimulate the performance. Talk begins to rise in level, to fill all the aural spaces; conjugal loyalties begin to dissipate; peer-group affiliations start to shift; cathexis takes place; people talk to and touch and tease one another.

Now, in the Victorian conservatory at the back of the house, the lights have almost gone out, and rhythmic dancing has started. The group from the theatre arrive, talking very loudly. A local vigilante group, with signs saying 'Keep Britain Clothed', have picketed the theatre, and this has made them passionate and argumentative. They have also brought with them several bottles of spirits, which they pass liberally around.

Their arrival has the effect of increasing social particle-drift, the patterns of fission and fusion. The party has found new obstacles and options in new places. The collective appetite has struck, as food has been discovered; tables arranged with cheese and pâté have been suddenly cleared. Upstairs, Howard puts a record on a player; downstairs, from speakers in a bookcase, the voice of Joan Baez sounds. Momentarily, another of the impresarios appears; Barbara, in her long pink dress, passes around with olives and pretzels, saying, 'Eat, I'm a Jewish mother.' A small, podgy girl named Anita Dollfuss, in her second year, wearing long curled hair with an Indian headband, steel-frame spectacles and a patchwork skirt almost too long to walk in, has arrived dragging a small, brown terrier on a string. Mrs Macintosh, who, having made her timely appearance, has been sagging slowly downwards towards the floor all evening, is put to sleep on a daybed. The rumour has passed that there are drugs upstairs, which has spread the party upward through the house. Someone has gone to fetch a guru who was advertised to be in town, but who will never in fact arrive at the party. A German lectrice in a see-through blouse is being encouraged to take it off. Howard stands at the head of the stairs and surveys the spectacle. 'My wife and I have an arrangement,' says a man sitting on the top stair, to a girl. 'That's what all the married men say,' says the girl. 'This is different,' says the man, 'my wife doesn't know about it.' The downstairs of the house looks like a vast museum of costume, as if all the forms and styles of the past have been made synchronic and here, in Howard's own house, have converged, and blurred; performers from medieval mystery plays, historical romances, dramas of trench warfare, proletarian documentaries, Victorian drawing-room farces play simultaneously in one eclectic, post-modern collage that is a pure and open form, a self-generating happening.

Howard walks down the stairs in pleasure, feeling the dull and contingent reality of things mysteriously transformed. He looks at these people, instinct with the times, and feels their newness, their possibility. He goes from mouth to mouth in the crush, looks into eye after eye, hunting the contemporary passion. 'Would that be an authentic kind of guilt?' asks someone. 'That marvellous surrealistic sequence in colour towards the end,' says someone else. Downstairs Mrs Macintosh has some time back declared labour pains; there has been much fuss as she has been driven off to hospital in the Standard Eight. The divine anger of wives has sensed a case of suppression; anxious about her interrupted career in social work, which is being sacrificed for mere child-bearing, they are becoming neurotic about their own careers as well. Meanwhile her husband, Dr Macintosh, has returned to the party; he sits in the hall by the telephone, with his own bottle, an object of curiosity and contemplation. At the front door, Anita Dollfuss's small, brown, untrained terrier has bitten the ankle of a new arrival: the arrival is Henry Beamish, who has come on foot, looking dishevelled, wearing a big bush hat, and having the manner of one fresh from a dangerous safari. He is taken upstairs for antisepsis, his hat still on and tipped over one eye. 'Sit, Mao,' says Anita Dollfuss to the dog. In the living-room, faces and voices throw violent sound around; it is the noise of man, growing. 'Kant's version of the inextricable entanglements of perceptual phenomena,' says someone. 'I'm low because I'm high,' says someone else. By the wall Barbara is talking to a small, dark girl standing by herself, in a white hat and a dark-blue trouser suit. 'What kind of contraceptive do you use?' asks Barbara socially. 'What about you, Mrs Kirk?' says the girl, who has a mild Scots accent. 'Oh, I'm Pill,' says Barbara, 'I used to be Bung but now I'm Pill. What's your method?' 'It's called Brute Force,' says the girl. 'The devious workings of the totalitarian mind,' says someone. 'You're trying to confuse me and fuck up my head,' says someone else. Empty glasses prod at Howard, as he passes on his way to the kitchen to fetch more bottles.

In the crush, a hand plucks at his sleeve. He looks down into the face of a thin, dark-eyed girl; it is one of his students, called Felicity Phee. 'I have a problem, Dr Kirk,' she says. Howard pours some wine into her glass, and says, 'Hello, Felicity. What's wrong this time?' 'I always have a problem, don't I?' says Felicity. 'That's because you're so good at solving them.' 'What is it?' asks Howard. 'Am I a sexist?' 'I doubt it,' says Howard, 'with your radical record.' Felicity is well known for keeping advanced company; she appears now cleaner, now dirtier, now saner, now more psychotic, according to the group she happens currently to be running with. 'I'm in a hang-up,' says Felicity. 'I'm tired of being lesbian. I'd like to be with a man.' 'You were very anti-male last time we talked,' says Howard. 'Oh, last time we talked,' says Felicity, 'that was *last term*. I was coming to terms with my sexuality then. But now I've found that my sexuality isn't the one I've come to terms with, if you can see what I mean.' 'Oh, I can,' says Howard. 'Well, that shouldn't be a problem.' 'Oh, it is, Dr Kirk, Howard.' says Felicity Phee. 'You see, the girl I'm with, Maureen, says it's reactionary. She says I'm collapsing into a syndrome of subservience. She says I have a slave mentality.' 'She does,' says Howard. 'Yes,' says Felicity, 'and, I mean, I couldn't do something reactionary, could I?' 'Oh, no, Felicity,' says Howard. 'So what would you do?' says Felicity. 'I mean, if you were me, and belonged to an oppressed sex.' 'I'd do what, I wanted to,' says Howard. 'Maureen throws shoes at me. She says I'm an Uncle Tom. I had to talk to you. I said to myself, I have to talk to *him*.' 'Look, Felicity,' says Howard, 'there's only one rule. Follow the line of your own desires. Don't accept other people's versions, unless you believe them true. Isn't that right?' 'Oh Howard,' says Felicity, kissing him on the cheek, 'you're marvellous. You give such good advice.' Howard says: 'That's because it so closely resembles what people want to hear.' 'No, it's because you're wise,' says Felicity. 'Oh, boy, do I need a flat male chest for a change.'

He goes through into the kitchen. It is filled with people; a male human leg protrudes from under the table. A baby lies asleep in a carrycot on top of the refrigerator. 'Is it your view that there is a constant entity definable as virtue?' asks the Pakistani thought leader of the advanced priest, in front of the globular wallpaper. The record player roars; the booming decibels, the yelps of a youthful pop group on heat, bounce round the house. Howard takes some of the bottles of wine, dark red in the glass, and uncorks them. A stout, maternal girl comes into the kitchen and picks up a baby's bottle, which has been warming in a saucepan on the cooker. She tries the contents by squirting them delicately onto her brown arm. 'Oh, shit,' she says. 'Who's Hegel?' says a voice; Howard looks up, and it is the bra-less girl who had come to his office that morning. 'Someone who . . .' says Howard. 'It's Howard,' says Myra

Beamish, standing beside him, her wig tipped slightly to one side, laughing enormously. She has her arm around Dr Macintosh, who still holds his bottle. 'Oh, Howard, you give great parties,' she says. 'Is it going well?' asks Howard. 'Oh, great,' says Myra, 'they're playing "Who am I?" in the living-room. And "What are the students going to do next?" in the dining-room. And "I gave birth at three and at five I was up and typing my thesis" in the hall.' 'There's also a thing called "Was it good for you, too, baby?" in the guest bedroom,' says Macintosh. 'It sounds like the description of a reasonable kind of party,' says Howard. 'How does someone as beastly as you manage to make life so nice for us?' asks Myra. 'It's zap,' says Howard. 'It's zing,' says Myra. 'It's zoom,' says Macintosh.

Howard picks up the new bottle, and returns to the living-room. He bears the libation about, hoping for transfiguration to follow. 'Is his vasectomy reversible or not?' asks someone. 'Tell him you're coming to Mexico with me,' says someone. A fat girl with chopped-down hair, lying on the floor, looks up at Howard and says: 'Hey, Howard, you're beautiful.' 'I know,' says Howard. Across the room Barbara is ministering with nuts and pretzels. 'All right?' asks Howard, approaching her. 'Good,' says Barbara. He carries the bottle over to a corner of the room, where, in a cluster, stands a group of bearded Jesuses and dark, sunglassed faces, students from the Revolutionary Student Front. They look aggressive and they stand in a rather tight circle; 'We only want to destroy them,' Peter Madden is saying in a loud voice. 'It's not personal.' Somewhere in the middle of the circle is a human figure, smaller than the others. It wears a white hat. 'Can I ask you just one wee question?' asks the figure in the middle, in a female, faintly Scots voice. 'Don't you think that politics is really just about the lowest form of human knowledge? Lesser than morals, or religion, or aesthetics, or philosophy. Or anything that's concerned with real human density?' 'Christ, look,' says Peter Madden, who stands there in his gunmetal sunglasses, 'all forms of knowledge are ideological. That means they are politics.' 'Are reducible to politics,' says the female voice. 'Can be rendered down, like soup.' Beck Pott is there, in a combat uniform with a 'Rocket Commander' patch sewn onto the shoulder, and with a white silver peace symbol hanging on a chain around her neck; she turns and finds Howard behind her, coming with the bottle. 'Who is this crazy doll?' she asks. 'She says we don't need a revolution.' 'There are people who think like that,' says Howard. 'I don't understand them,' says Beck Pott. 'There have to be,' says Howard; 'if there weren't, we wouldn't need a revolution.' 'You're right there, Howard,' says Beck Pott, 'right.' Howard offers the bottle to the girl in the middle of all this; she wears a blue trouser suit and a neat scarf, and is much too formal for the party. 'A wee drop,' says the girl. 'If you're not the solution,' says Peter Madden, 'you're part of the problem.' 'It would be terribly arrogant of me to believe I was the solution to anything,' says the girl. 'Or you, too, for that matter.'

Howard turns, with his bottle, and goes back through the house, to the gaunt, flowerless Victorian conservatory at the back of it. The pink sodium lights of Watermouth shine in through its glass roof; this is now the only illumination. The place booms with violent sound. Dancers sway their bodies; a baby, high up in a papoose-rig, jogs on the back of a noisy daddy. The German girl in the see-through blouse has started, in a corner, with a group of men around her, to take it off. She lifts it upward, over her head, and it whirls in the air above them for a moment. It is hard to get through the crowd. 'Who's Hegel?' says someone. It is impossible now quite to tell who are faculty, who students, who strangers, who friends. The social mix has remixed itself. The music thumps in the half-dark; bodies gyrate, and minds are sacrificed to beat. The Catholic priest's Ouspenskyite companion is close by him, on the floor, demonstrating bodily positions from an exercise she has recently learned. The German girl has joined the dancing, and is gyrating in front of him, her big breasts bouncing, a mobile Aryan sculpture of the New Woman. 'This is heuristic, *ja?*' she says to Howard. '*Ja,*' says Howard. '*Gesundheit.*' Howard looks at the moving spectacle; as he watches, he sees the silvery twirl of a glass as it spins from a hand and crashes to the floor. The fragments disappear under the busy feet. 'Are all these persons intellectuals?' asks the Pakistani thought leader of the Catholic priest. 'The orgy is replacing the mass as the prime sacrament,' says the priest. 'Is this an orgy?' asks the

Pakistani. 'There are better,' says the priest. But not for Howard; what he sees in front of him is man free, free of economic timidity, sexual fear, prescriptive social norms, man cocky with the goodness of his own being. Now food, drink, and Barbara all seem to have disappeared, but no matter. The party is now totally self-governing, feeding on its own being.

He walks back through the house. The party is busy everywhere; everywhere, it seems, but by the wall in the living-room, where a large circle of space has cleared around the dark girl in the trouser suit and the white hat, who stands, one leg crossed over the other, holding up a veined marble egg that is part of the mantelpiece decor, and inspecting it with a fastidious expression. Her air is that of a figure in a Victorian painting, portraying, in rococo fashion, innocence. Her clothes have a formality which makes it impossible to judge her age, and therefore guess whether she is a teacher or a student. Howard takes the bottle over to her, and puts it to her glass. 'Just a very, very tiny drop,' says the girl. 'Enough.' 'Come along and meet some people,' says Howard; he puts his hand on her arm. The arm, surprisingly, resists. 'I've met some,' says the girl, 'now I'm digesting them.' 'Are you enjoying yourself?' asks Howard. 'I'm enjoying myself fine,' says the girl. 'I'm enjoying some of the other people as well.' 'But not all of them,' says Howard. 'I'm very discriminating,' says the girl. 'What's your name?' asks Howard. 'Oh, I'm invited,' says the girl. 'Everyone's invited,' says Howard. 'Oh, that's good,' says the girl, 'because I wasn't invited. I was brought by someone who's gone.' 'Who's that?' asks Howard. 'He's a novelist,' says the girl. 'He's gone home to write notes on it all. Were you invited?' 'I invite,' says Howard, 'I'm the host.' 'Och,' says the girl, 'you're Dr Kirk. Well, I'm Miss Callendar. I've just joined the English Department. I'm their new Renaissance man. Of course I'm a woman.' 'Of course,' says Howard. 'That's good, because I like women.' 'Aye, I've heard about that,' says Miss Callendar, 'I hope you're not wasting any of your valuable time trying to get after me.' 'No,' says Howard. 'Good,' says Miss Callendar, holding up the marble egg, and looking at it. 'I just love small objects like this, I could hold it for hours. Am I keeping you from your party?'

The party booms around them. Howard stares at Miss

87

Callendar, who is somehow outside it. She leans against the mantelpiece, her white hat shading solemn, dark brown eyes that look back at him. Behind her, over the mantelpiece, is a domed, round mirror; Howard sees that they are both reflected in it, on the tilt, portrayed at a foreshortened angle, as in some conscientious modern film. There is her dark head, capped with its white decorated hat, the nape of her neck, her tapering long blue back; there is himself, facing her in the adversary position, his economical, fierce-eyed features staring; beyond them both is a realm of space, and then the moving manikins of the party. 'You were in a fight with the revolutionaries,' says Howard. 'That's my trouble at parties,' says Miss Callendar, 'I get into fights.' 'Of course,' says Howard, 'for perfectly good reasons these kids don't trust anyone over thirty.' 'How old do you think I am?' asks Miss Callendar. 'I don't know,' says Howard, 'you're disguised by your clothes.' 'I'm twenty-four,' she says. 'Then you ought to be one of them,' says Howard. 'How old are you?' asks Miss Callendar. 'I'm thirty-four,' says Howard. 'Oh, Dr Kirk,' says Miss Callendar, 'then you oughtn't.' 'Oh,' says Howard, 'there's also the question of right and wrong, good and bad. I choose them. They're on the side of justice.' 'Well, I can understand that,' says Miss Callendar. 'Like so many middle-aged people, you're naturally envious. All this youth charms you. I'm sure you'd allow it anything.' Howard laughs; Miss Callendar says, 'I hope you don't think I'm rude.' 'Oh, no,' says Howard. 'For the same reason, I'd allow you anything.' In the corner of his eye, Howard sees the movements of the party; hands are touching breasts, partners are transacting, couples are disappearing. 'You would?' says Miss Callendar. 'I thought you were trying to make a rebel out of me.' 'I am,' says Howard. 'But what could I rebel about?' 'Everything,' says Howard. 'There's repression and social injustice everywhere.'

'Ah,' says Miss Callendar, 'but that's what everyone's rebelling about. Isn't there anything new?' 'You have no social conscience,' says Howard. 'I have a conscience,' says Miss Callendar. 'I use it a lot. I think it's a sort of moral conscience. I'm very old-fashioned.' 'We must modernize you,' says Howard. 'There,' says Miss Callendar, 'you *won't* allow me anything.' 'No,' says Howard. 'Why don't you let me save you from yourself?' 'Och,' says Miss Callendar, 'I think I know just how you'd go about that. No, I'm afraid you're too old for me. I never trust anyone over thirty.' 'What about men under thirty?' asks Howard. 'Oh, you're prepared to vary, if necessary,' says Miss Callendar. 'Well, I don't trust many under it, either.' 'That doesn't leave you much room for manoeuvre,' says Howard. 'Well, I don't manoeuvre much, anyway,' says Miss Callendar. 'Then you're missing out,' says Howard. 'What are you frightened of?' 'Ah,' says Miss Callendar, 'the new man, but the old techniques. Well, it's been very nice talking to you. But you've got a lot of people here to look after. You mustn't waste your time talking to me.' Miss Callendar puts the marble egg back in the basket on the mantelpiece. 'They're looking after themselves,' says Howard. 'I'm entitled to find my own enjoyment.' 'Oh, I could hardly claim to be that,' says Miss Callendar, 'you'd do much better elsewhere.' 'I also ought to save you from your false principles,' says Howard. 'I may need it one day,' says Miss Callendar, 'and if I do, I'll promise to let you know.' 'You need me,' says Howard. 'Well, thank you,' says Miss Callendar, 'I take your offer of help very kindly. And Mrs Kirk's offer to take me to the family-planning clinic. You all offer a real welcome at Watermouth.' 'We do,' says Howard. 'An entire service. Don't forget.'

Howard walks back into the party; Miss Callendar remains standing by the mantelpiece. Someone has gone out and found more to drink; there is a more subdued air now, a softer sexual excitement. He passes through the bodies, face to face, rump to rump. He inspects the scene for Flora Beniform; there are many faces, but none of them hers. Later on, he is up in his own bedroom. There is deep and utter silence here, except for the sound of an Indian raga, playing on a record player in the corner. The curtains are pulled shut. The spotlight over the bed has been moved from its usual downfacing position, and made to shine upwards at the ceiling; some coloured material, the pink of what is probably a blouse, has been wrapped around it. The bed, with its striped madras cover, has been pushed away from its central place, and is in a corner of the room, under the window. Around the room in the quiet, a circle of people are sitting or lying, touching or holding each other, listening to the rhythm and movements of the music.

They are a group of formless shapes, with heads jutting, hands reaching out, held together by arms that thread from one shape to the next. Joints are passed from hand to hand; they light with a red glow as someone draws, and then they fade. Howard takes in the wordless words of the music; he lets his own room grow stranger and stranger to him. Barbara's housecoat and her caftan, hanging on the hook behind the door, change colour and transpose into pure form. The shine of the misshapen handles on the old chest of drawers, bought in a junk shop when they were furnishing the house, become a focus of colour, a bright, mysterious knot. The wine and the pot make rings inside his head. There are faces that take shape and dissolve in the watery light: the faces of a girl with freaked green eye-rings and white powdered cheeks, of a boy with a skin that is the shade of wet olive. A hand waves idly near him, at him; he takes the joint; retains the hand, turns to kiss the unsexed face. His mind relishes ideas, which rise like smoke, take shape as a statement. The walls shift and open. He gets up and goes, past hands and bodies and legs and hips and breasts, onto the landing.

He opens the door of the toilet. There is a run of water, and a voice that says: 'Who's Hegel?' He shuts it again. The house is quieter now, the party dissipated from its noisy social centre into numerous peripheries. He goes down the stairs. Macintosh sits there, and next to him Anita Dollfuss and her little dog. 'The baby,' says Howard. 'It hasn't started yet,' says Macintosh, 'they think it was all some kind of false alarm.' 'But there is a baby in there?' 'Oh, yes,' says Macintosh, 'there's one there all right.' 'There's a rumour that Mangel's coming here to lecture,' says Howard. 'Good,' says Macintosh, 'I'd like to hear what he's got to say.' 'That's right,' says Howard. In the living-room the faces have all changed; none of them does he recognize. A six-foot woman lies asleep under a five-foot-six coffee table. A man comes up and says: 'I was talking to John Stuart Mill the other day. He's gone off liberty.' Another man says: 'I was talking to Rainer Maria Rilke the other day. He's gone off angels.' Howard says, 'Flora Beniform?' 'Who?' asks one of the men. There is a space by the mantelpiece where the girl stood: Miss Callendar. Myra Beamish comes out of the kitchen, her hair tipped yet further over. 'You didn't tell

Henry,' she says. 'I didn't tell anyone,' says Howard. 'It's our secret,' says Myra, 'yours and mine and Sigmund Freud's.' 'He won't tell either,' says Howard. 'I was talking to Sigmund Freud, the other day,' says a man. 'He's gone off sex.' 'Mmmm,' says Myra Beamish, kissing Howard. 'Mmmmmm.' 'Why don't you write a book about it, and shut up?' says someone. 'Howard, do you think it's really true that fully satisfying orgasm can alter our consciousness, as Wilhelm Reich says?' asks Myra. 'I've got to play host,' says Howard. He leaves the living-room. He moves the chair that blocks the staircase down to his study, and goes down the steps.

Above him he can hear the feet of the party pounding. He has had a thought about his book. The book begins: 'The attempt to privatize life, to suppose that it is within single, self-achieving individuals that lie the infinite recesses of being and morality that shape and define life, is a phenomenon of narrow historical significance. It belongs to a particular, and a brief, phase in the evolution of bourgeois capitalism, and is the derivative of peculiar, and temporary, economic arrangements. All the signs are that this conviction about man will soon have passed away.' He opens the door of the study; the glow of the sodium streetlighting falls crazily over the walls, the book-shelves, the African masks, sliced through with lines of shadow from the basement railings. The light is off; he realizes, sud-denly, that someone is in the room, sitting in the canvas chair in the further corner. He puts on the light. Half-sitting, half-lying in the chair, her dress awry, the manuscript of the book on the floor around her, is Felicity Phee. He says: 'How did you get here?' 'I knew you had a study down here,' she says, 'I wanted to find it. I thought you were busy with the party.' Howard stares at her: at her anxious white face, at the mottle of spots above her breasts, visible where her dress falls forward as she leans towards him, at her tight-knuckled hands and bitten nails. He says: 'Why? What were you after?' 'I wanted to know what you were like when I don't see you,' she says, 'I wanted to look at your books. See your things.' 'You shouldn't,' says Howard, 'you just get caught.' 'Yes,' says Felicity, 'Is this your next book? I've been reading it.' 'You'd no business to do that,' says Howard, 'it's not quite finished. It's private.' 'The attempt to privatize life is a phenomenon of narrow historical

significance,' says Felicity. 'Why are you doing this?' asks
Howard. 'I've made you my subject of research,' says Felicity,
'my special option.' 'I see,' says Howard. 'You're my tutor,
Howard,' says Felicity Phee, her face screwed up, 'I'm in
trouble, I'm not right. You have to help me.'

Howard walks across to his desk, and reaches across it, to
draw the curtains. He looks out onto the railings, the area wall,
the gaunt outlines of the houses opposite outlined against the
pink urban sky. Someone is leaving the house. The figure
comes directly in front of the window, by the railings, and looks
down into the basement. It is alone, it wears a white hat and a
blue trouser suit. Miss Callendar, who looks immensely tall
when seen from below, unlocks from the railings and carefully
detaches a high, elderly, black bicycle. Her cheeks look flushed,
and she appears to be beaming a private smile to herself. She
offers a small wave of recognition to Howard; then she tugs
her white hat straight, slides a leg across the bicycle, and sits
up on the high saddle. She pushes forward and pedals off, in
furious motion, a frenzy of uncoordinated forms, back stiff,
knees jostling, her legs going up and down, as she disappears
through the dereliction towards wherever she lives. 'Who's
that?' asks Felicity. 'She's someone new in English,' says
Howard. 'You were talking to her at the party,' says Felicity.
'You like her.' 'Were you watching me upstairs too?' asks
Howard. 'Yes,' says Felicity. Howard draws the curtain across.
He says: 'What's the matter with you, Felicity?' 'You must
help me, help me,' says Felicity. 'What's wrong?' asks Howard,
sitting in the other canvas chair. 'How am I ever going to get
out of this screwed-up, stinking, shitty, uptight me?' asks
Felicity. 'Why am I stuck in this beastliness of self?' 'Aren't we
all?' asks Howard. 'No,' says Felicity, 'most people get out.
They have other people to get them out.' 'Don't you?' asks
Howard. 'Maureen?' asks Felicity. 'She's a thug.' 'I thought
you were going to find a man.' 'Yes,' says Felicity, 'I meant, of
course, you.' 'You did?' says Howard. 'As you knew,' says
Felicity. 'No,' says Howard.

'Christ,' says Felicity, 'you showed much more curiosity
about that girl there than you show about me.' 'Which girl?'
asks Howard. 'The one who went.' 'I hadn't really thought
about her,' says Howard. 'Have you really thought about me?'

asks Felicity. 'Thought what about you?' 'Well, my curiosity in you. My coming to see you so much. All the unhappy things I've told you about. Didn't those things affect you?' 'Of course,' says Howard, 'as a tutor and a teacher.' 'Those are just roles to play,' says Felicity, 'I've been asking for something better than that. For a year I have. I've concerned myself with you. I've not just been watching you to write an article. I want you to concern yourself with me.' 'Let's go upstairs,' says Howard, 'there's a party.' Suddenly Felicity pushes herself forward out of her chair, and is on the floor beside him. Her face is distorted and her mouth open. 'No,' says Felicity, 'you're my tutor. You're responsible for me.' 'I think you're mistaking how far the responsibility goes,' says Howard. 'Are you frightened of me?' asks Felicity. 'Not a bit,' says Howard, 'you're just offering too much.' 'Aren't you lucky?' asks Felicity. 'Won't you take it?' 'I get a lot of offers,' says Howard. 'You remember what you told me,' says Felicity. 'Follow the line of your own desire. Do what you want.' 'But your desire has to connect with other people's desire,' says Howard. 'Can't you make it?' asks Felicity. 'Can't you try and make it?' 'I ought to see what's happening upstairs,' says Howard. Felicity pushes her hand in between his legs. 'Forget what's happening upstairs,' she says, 'do something for me. Help me, help me, help me. It's a work of charity.'

What is happening upstairs is something that Howard will hear about only the following day. A window smashes in one of the small bedrooms, along a corridor where silence reigns; the cause is Henry Beamish, who has put his left arm through and down, and slashed it savagely on the glass. Only a few people hear this, and most are heavily occupied; but someone is curious enough to look into the little bedroom where he is, and see him, and lift him from the debris around him, and call others. Someone else, the girl who thinks about Hegel, sets off to look for the host of the evening. Someone else, Rosemary, sets off to look for Barbara. But they are neither of them to be found, and nor, for that matter, is Felicity Phee, or young Dr Macintosh. It is lucky that there is someone to take charge; it is Flora Beniform, who has arrived at the party, the date of which she has inscribed in her diary, very late. Indeed a day late; for she has come back on the midnight train from London, where she has been listening to a new paper on female schizophrenia at a seminar at the Tavistock Clinic. But she is an able and reassuring woman, and everyone feels that she is the one to cope: she manages a tourniquet; she sends someone to ring for an ambulance. 'We've had people looking all over the house,' says a thin faculty wife, sensible and sober because it is her turn this time to drive the car home through the police traps of early-morning Watermouth. 'No one can find Howard or Barbara anywhere.' 'I've no doubt they have their own fish to fry,' says Flora. 'Well, you can't hold the hosts responsible for everything that happens at a party like this. It might have been better to look for Myra.' 'I think she's down in the kitchen,' says the faculty wife. 'Find her,' says Flora, 'but look at her first, and don't bring her up here unless she's sober and rational.' 'Is it serious?' asks the faculty wife. 'Fairly,' says Flora. A solemn student has found a broom and a dustpan, and he sweeps away the broken glass under the window, and around Henry. 'Steady,' says Flora. 'Oh, God, I'm ridiculous,' says Henry, on the floor. Myra comes in, clutching her sequinned handbag, her coiffure now very tipsy, and looks at Henry, at Flora. She says: 'I hear Henry's done something else silly.'

'He's hurt himself quite badly,' says Flora. 'I don't know how, I wasn't here. He'll have to go to the casualty department and have this stitched.' 'I expect he was trying to make me feel sorry for him,' says Myra. 'I'm not sure we're interested in your response at this moment,' says Flora. 'You're over-acting, it's a nuisance.' 'What are you doing, Henry?' says Myra. 'Go away, Myra,' says Flora, 'I'll take Henry to the hospital. I've been there many times. Why don't you go back home and wait for him?' 'I might,' says Myra, 'I might.' The ambulance arrives, with a flashing blue light, and so a lot of people help in the task of carrying Henry, who keeps groaning, down the staircase. Their feet thump heavily on the woodwork, and down in the basement study Howard hears the thunder of noise. The flashing light is shining bluely in through the curtains, casting strange shapes across the bookcases and the masks. But Howard, who is busy, does not properly see it, or interpret it. 'They seem to be enjoying themselves,' he whispers into the ear of Felicity Phee. Felicity, underneath him, whispers, 'I am too.' 'Good,' says Howard. 'And you?' 'Yes,' says Howard. 'Not very much,' says Felicity, 'but I'm glad to have what you find you can give me.' 'It's the very usual thing,' says Howard. 'No,' says Felicity. The ambulance klaxon sounds out in the terrace as it drives off. 'Drugs squad,' says Howard. 'No, lie still, stay there,' says Felicity. 'I thought something had happened, I should have been around,' Howard will say in the morning, when Flora tells him what it was that had happened. But Flora will also explain what is clearly true: that, at parties, everyone has his own affairs to attend to, and should be presumed to be attending to them, just as Henry, in his way, also was. For people are people, and parties are parties; especially when they happen to be at the Kirks'.

VI

It is four in the morning when the party comes to its end. The last guests stand in the hall, some of them needing the support of the wall; they say their goodbyes; they venture through the door into the quietness of early-morning Watermouth. The Kirks, that hospitable couple, usher them forth, and then they go upstairs to their disorderly bedroom, which smells sharply of pot, and push the bed back into position, and take the ashtrays off it, and undress, and get under the duvet. They say nothing, being tired people; they do not touch each other, having no need; Barbara, in her black nightdress, folds her body into Howard's, her buttocks on his knees, and they are quickly asleep. And then it is the morning, and the Habitat alarm clock rings on the bedside table, and they wake again, back into the life of ordinary things. Consciousness returns, and feels heavy with use; Howard presses his eyelids open, jerks towards being, regresses, tries again. Traffic thumps on the creases of the urban motorway; a diesel commuter train hoots on the viaduct; the graders are revving on the construction sites. The bed vibrates and bounces; Barbara is getting up. The Habitat alarm clock says it is v to VIII. Barbara pads across to the door, and takes her housecoat from the hook; she goes across to the window and pulls back the curtain to admit dull wet daylight. The room appears in its unmitigated thinginess, flavoured with the dusty smell of cigarette smoke, the sweet aftersmell of pot. A thrown-off dress, gutted by its long zip, hangs askew on the door. On the junkshop chest of drawers, its grain surface rough, one handle gone, two handles broken, are some plates, three full ashtrays, and many empty wine glasses from the supermarket. The lavatory flushes along the landing. Outside black rainclouds move in off the sea and over the tops of the luxury flats; the rain pours and smudges and blackens the brickwork of the shattered houses opposite, dripping violently in the Kirks' unstable guttering. In Howard's head is the dry image of a person: Felicity Phee, a mottling of spots above her breasts. He activates muscular mechanisms; he gets out of bed and walks, through the party detritus and the unredeemed daylight, to the bathroom. He urinates into the bowl; he takes his razor from the medicine cabinet, and unravels the cord. He plugs the razor into two black holes under the white globe of the light.

He pulls the string of the switch. Light and razor, glare and noise, both come on. His face rises into visibility in the fingermarked glass of the mirror. In the cool urban sheen of the morning, he inspects the Condition of Man. His bleak, beaky features, the moustache worn like a glower, stare out at him as he stares back in at them. 'Christ,' he says, 'you again.' His fingers come up and touch and shape this strange flesh into position. He runs the razor over it, shaping and ordering the construct before him, sculpting neatly round the edge of the moustache, clipping at the line of the sideboards. He stops the razor; from downstairs, he can hear the barbaric yawp of his children. The features he has been designing hang pallidly, abstractly, before him in the mirror; he pokes at them, hoping to urge into them that primordial glow which is actual and real livingness. There is no response. He picks up a bottle of aftershave lotion with a machismo label, and slaps some into his cheeks. He switches off the light above the mirror; the face fades. A family row of toothbrushes are prodded into a metal rack above the washbasin; he takes one, and scrubs up a foam inside his mouth. The rain splashes in the gutters. A female cooing sounds in the acoustical complexities of the staircase; he is being called to breakfast and his domestic duties, for it is his turn to take the children to school. He combs his hair, and drops a fuzz of haircombings into the yellow waters of the lavatory bowl. He presses the handle, and flushes it. He returns to the bedroom and reaches into the wardrobe, selecting some clothes, his cultural identity. He puts on jeans and a sweater; he straps on his watch. He goes toward the domestic arena. On the landing, on the stairs, there are empty glasses and plates, cups and ashtrays, bottles. Anita Dollfuss's dog has left its traces, and there are strange dark drips of something along the length of the hall. A silvery dress lies on the floor. He goes through into the pine décor of the kitchen, where chaos is total. Many empty bottles stand on the pine counters; many dirty plates are scattered everywhere. The stench of old parties prevails. In an endless sequence of little explosions, rain plumps on the glass roof of the Victorian conservatory, where the children are playing. The electric kettle fuzzes a thin line of steam around Barbara, who stands in her housecoat, in front of the cooker, her hair untidy.

'My God, just look at it,' says Barabara, putting eggs into a pan. 'Go on, just look at it.' Howard puts bread into the toaster; obliging, he looks around. 'It's a mess,' he says. 'Which you undertook to help me clear up,' says Barbara. 'That's right,' says Howard, 'I will.' 'Can you advise me when?' 'Well, I'm teaching this morning,' says Howard. 'And there's a departmental meeting this afternoon, which will go on very late.' 'It wouldn't,' says Barbara, 'if you didn't argue so much.' 'I exist to argue,' says Howard. 'I just want to be clear,' says Barbara. 'I am not doing this by myself.' 'Of course not,' says Howard, picking up the *Guardian* from the kitchen table. The headlines advise him of many indignities and wrongs. There is a new anti-pornography drive, a trial of a group of anarchist bombers, an equivocal constitutional meeting in Ulster, a fudging Labour Party Conference in Blackpool. Liberties are sliding; his radical ire thickens, and he begins to feel some of the bitterness that is part of the sensation of living self. 'I am not going to be that person,' says Barbara. 'Did you find me somebody?' 'Not yet,' says Howard, 'I'll find someone though.' 'I could fix it with Rosemary,' says Barbara. 'She was in good shape last night. She went home with your friend from the sex shop.' 'You see how quickly these agonies pass?' says Howard. 'No, Barbara; please not Rosemary.' 'In the meantime, the mess,' says Barbara. 'We'll do it tonight,' says Howard. 'I'm going out tonight.' The toaster pops; Howard takes out the warmed bread. 'Where?' he asks. 'I've signed up for an evening class at the library,' says Barbara. 'It starts today, and I mean to be there. Okay?' 'Of course okay,' says Howard. 'What's it on?' 'Commercial French,' says Barbara. *'Acceptez, cher monsieur, l'assurance de mes solicitations les plus distinguées,'* says Howard. 'What do you need it for?' 'It's something new,' says Barbara. 'Don't they have car mechanics?' asks Howard. 'I want to read Simone de Beauvoir in the original.' 'In commercial French?' 'Yes,' says Barbara, 'that was all the French they had.' 'Well, it should bend your mind,' says Howard. 'Don't patronize me,' says Barbara, 'I'm not Myra Beamish.' 'Did she leave him?' asks Howard. 'I don't know,' says Barbara, 'I lost sight of that particular little drama, Myra making it into the now scene. There were so many.' 'A good party,' says Howard. 'A mess,' says Barbara, switching on the radio.

The radio trills, and there is a newsbreak. The noise of the radio draws the children, Martin and Celia, fresh, separate, critical beings, in their clothes from the manikin boutiques, into the kitchen; they sit down at the table, in front of coloured enamel bowls from Yugoslavia. *'Bonjour, mes amis,'* says Howard. 'Did the party make you drunk, Howard?' asks Martin. 'Who left her bra in the plantpot of the living-room geranium?' asks Celia. 'Not me,' says Howard. 'You have the messiest friends in the whole world,' says Celia. 'One of them broke a window,' says Martin, 'in the guest bedroom.' 'You've checked around, have you?' asks Howard. 'Anything else I should advise the insurance company about?' 'I think someone jumped out,' says Martin, 'there's all blood in there. Shall I go and look outside?' 'Nobody jumped out,' says Barbara. 'You sit there and eat your cornflakes.' 'Cornflakes, yuk,' says Martin. 'My compliments to the cook, and tell her "yuk",' says Howard. 'I expect this person jumped out because he couldn't stand the noise,' says Celia. 'You say *we're* noisy, but that was terrible.' 'Is there really some blood, Celia?' asks Barbara. 'Yes,' says Celia. 'Why does it always have to be cornflakes?' asks Martin. 'You can't say all that much for the human lot, as we bumble around in the Platonic cave,' says Howard, 'but sometimes there are glimpses of the eternals beyond. Like cornflakes.' 'No metaphysics, Howard,' says Barbara. 'Let's all just eat our cornflakes.' 'Are you opposed to metaphysics?' asks Celia, not eating her cornflakes. 'She's a British empiricist,' says Howard. 'Look,' says Barbara, 'these kids leave for school in fifteen minutes, right? I know it's against your principles, which are dedicated to driving me insane. But could you exercise a bit of parental authority here, and get them to eat their sodding cornflakes?' 'Are you going to eat your sodding cornflakes?' asks Howard of the children. 'Or do you want me to throw them out of the window?' 'I want you to throw them out of the window,' says Martin. 'Christ,' says Barbara, 'here's a man with professional training in social psychology. And he can't get a child to eat a cornflake.' 'The human will has a natural resistance to coercion,' says Howard. 'It will not be repressed.' 'By cornflake fascism,' says Celia.

Barbara stares at Howard. 'Oh, you're a great operator,' she says. 'Why don't you give them wider options? Set them free?' asks Howard, 'Weetabix? Rice Krispies?' 'Why don't you keep out of it?' asks Barbara, 'I feed this lot. They're not asking for different food. They're asking for my endless sodding attention.' 'We are asking for different food,' says Martin. 'We'd like the endless sodding attention too,' says Celia. 'Eat,' says Barbara. 'If you don't you'll die.' 'Oh, marvellous,' says Howard. 'And if you don't eat fast, you'll be late for school as well,' says Barbara. 'Okay?' 'They don't want you at school if you're dead,' says Martin. 'They give your crayons to another person.' 'Shut up, Martin,' says Barbara. 'If you speak again, I'll drop this egg on your head.' 'Speak,' says Celia. 'Resist tyranny.' 'You've built this one up,' says Barbara to Howard. Howard inspects the *Guardian*; the radio trills; the rain drips. After a minute, Celia says: 'I hope Miss Birdsall doesn't make me stand outside the classroom again today.' Howard recognizes a situation designed for his attention; he looks up from the *Guardian*; he says, 'Why did she do that?' 'Because I said "penis",' says Celia. 'Honestly,' says Barbara, 'that woman.' 'It's a proper word, isn't it?' asks Celia, pleased with the development of the situation. 'I told her you said I could use it.' 'Of course it's a proper word,' says Howard, 'I'm going to call the Education Committee. I want an enquiry into that sick, nasty woman.' 'Is she sick and nasty?' asks Barbara. 'Maybe she's just overstrained.' 'You're identifying,' says Howard, 'Miss Birdbrain needs a good kick up her protestant ethic.' This creates delight in the constituency; the children shout, 'Miss Birdbrain, Miss Birdbrain,' and Martin knocks over his egg. It performs an elegant arc, and smashes on the rush matting. Howard watches as the yellow yolk oozes out and forms a coagulating pool. He says: 'Take care, Martin.' Barbara tears paper off the kitchen roll; she bends over, in her housecoat, her face red, and begins to wipe up the mess. When she has finished, she looks at Howard. 'You wanted that to happen,' she says.

'No,' says Howard. 'You built it up,' says Barbara. 'I was just radicalizing the children a little,' says Howard. 'To fix me,' says Barbara. 'You see plots everywhere,' says Howard. 'As you often say,' says Barbara, 'the reason people have conspiracy theories is that people conspire.' 'I think Miss Birdbrain's a marvellous name for her,' says Celia. 'She's just a nasty old penis.' 'And you told her that?' says Barbara. 'Yes,' says Celia. 'So she sent you out of the room,' says Barbara. 'Yes,' says Celia. 'You'd better explain that when you call the Education Committee,' says Barbara. 'Maybe I won't call the Education Committee,' says Howard. 'No,' says Barbara, 'save your radical indignation for higher things.' 'How come the male organ is now a term of abuse?' asks Howard. 'It's just us second-class citizens getting our own back,' says Barbara, 'thanks to reading Simone de Beauvoir in the original.' Out in the hall the telephone rings; Barbara goes out to answer it. Celia says, 'Who's Simone de Beauvoir?' 'Who's Hegel?' asks Howard. 'You should answer a question directly when I ask one,' says Celia. 'She's a woman women read,' says Howard, 'she's on the right side.' 'Why do women read her?' asks Celia. 'They're angry at men,' says Howard. 'At you?' asks Celia. 'Oh, not me,' says Howard, 'I'm with them in their fight.' 'Is Barbara glad?' asks Celia. 'I'll never eat another cornflake in the whole of my life,' says Martin. The phone goes down in the hall; Barbara walks back into the kitchen, and Howard sees that her face is strange. 'What in hell happened at our party?' she asks. 'A good time all round,' says Howard. 'Who was it?' 'Myra,' says Barbara. 'Aha,' says Howard, 'where is she?' 'Home,' says Barbara. 'I knew she'd stay,' says Howard, smiling, 'she was playing.' 'There was an accident at our party,' says Barbara. 'I told you that,' says Celia. 'An accident?' asks Howard. 'Is the guest-room window really broken, Martin?' asks Barbara. 'I'll show you, come on,' says Martin. 'It was Henry,' says Barbara, 'he cut himself on it. He had to go to hospital and have twenty-seven stitches.' 'Henry?' asks Howard, 'When was this?' 'Didn't you know?' asks Barbara. 'Weren't you there? Wasn't there a host at this party?' 'Where were you, baby?' asks Howard. Barbara says, 'Get your coats on, you kids. Nearly time for school.'

When the children have run out into the hall, the Kirks sit and look at each other. 'Another one,' says Barbara, 'Rosemary's boy, and Henry.' 'You said an accident,' says Howard. 'Well, was it?' asks Barbara. 'You think Myra told him she was leaving?' asks Howard. 'Isn't that one explanation?' asks Barbara. 'People cry out like that.' 'Some people might,' says Howard, 'Henry wouldn't.' 'It makes me feel sick,' says Barbara. 'Henry already had one accident last night,' says Howard, 'A dog bit him. Anyway, Myra didn't leave him. She's at home.' 'Yes,' says Barbara. 'Did *she* tell you what happened?' asks Howard. 'She didn't really explain anything,' says Barbara. 'She didn't want to talk. Just to apologize for ruining our party. I told her it didn't.' 'Was she disappointed?' asks Howard. 'Is it funny?' asks Barbara. 'It's just Henry,' says Howard, 'even in his big drama he makes a mess of things.' 'Shouldn't you go and see him?' asks Barbara. 'My bet is he'll bounce right back. Turn up at the departmental meeting this afternoon. Voting with the reactionaries.' 'You wouldn't have pushed him, would you? Just to fix the vote?' 'I'm more subtle,' says Howard. 'Besides, I *want* Henry's reactionary vote.' 'I had a sick feeling about that party,' says Barbara. Howard eases the last curve of egg out of the shell; he puts down the spoon. 'Everyone else enjoyed it,' he says, and goes out of the kitchen to get ready for departure. The children are waiting in the hall; he goes toward his study. A chair still stands in place at the top of the stairs; he moves it, and goes down the steps. In the study, the curtains are still drawn in place; he opens them, and lets daylight in. Two cushions lie on the floor, between the desk and the wall; he picks them up, fluffs them, replaces them in the canvas chairs. The creased pages of the typescript of his book lie scattered everywhere. Carefully he picks them up, flattens them, sorts them, remakes the neat stack, and puts it by the typewriter on his desk. Doing this, he sees again the blue light that had flashed over the room, over the two bodies on the floor; he hears the footsteps on the stairs and in the hall. He moves around, pulling books off shelves, picking up marked essays, lecture notes, committee papers, thinking of Henry and Felicity. He puts all these things in his leather briefcase, and hurries upstairs.

Barbara comes out into the hall as he puts on his coat; she says, 'I'm really going to London. You'll get me someone.' 'Yes,' says Howard, 'I'll do it'; and he bends down and picks up two wet letters that lie deposited under the letterbox. He tears them open, glances through them: one is a circular from a radical publisher, announcing new books on Marxism; the other is a letter from a group of modern churchmen in London, inviting him to speak to them on the topic of the changing fabric of morality, a topic on which, says the letter, 'you are a recognized authority'. A recognized authority, he goes back into the kitchen to find the children. Barbara has a cup of coffee in her hand; she says, 'How late are you going to be tonight?' 'Who knows?' says Howard, 'a departmental meeting.' 'I'm leaving at seven fifteen for my class. I'm going whether you're here or not. If you're not, there's no Anne Petty, so we don't have a babysitter. I leave you to sort that out in your own way.' 'Okay,' says Howard, 'are you out late? Supposing I have to find a babysitter?' 'Pretty late,' says Barbara, 'people usually go to a pub and have a drink after an evening class.' 'I suppose so,' says Howard. 'So I'll see you when I see you,' says Barbara. 'Right,' says Howard, 'come on, kids, be ready and waiting. I'm going to fetch the van.' He picks up his briefcase, and goes along the hall to the front door. He steps out of his domestic interior into the day and the pouring rain. The city world takes him in again; the puddles shimmer on the terrace. The morning begins; the edge of nameless melancholy with which he started the day begins faintly to lift. He walks round the corner, adapts to the anonymous world, watches the traffic lights glint, the umbrellas move in the street, the yellow bulldozers churning the mud of demolition. Up the hill he goes, to the square; he finds the van, and starts it. He drives back down to the terrace, and the front door opens to his hoot. Barbara stands on the steps; she ushers out two huddled, miniature figures in red wet-look raincoats. They run through the rain, and pull open the passenger door, arguing about who will sit in front, who in the back. On the step, Barbara waves; the children climb in; Howard starts the van, and turns it in the terrace, and drives, past his long, thin house to the business of the main road up the hill.

The route to the children's school is a track of familiar lanes, arrows and pointers, lines and halts, a routed semiology. Tail lights give out red reflections onto the wet road; the rain-stipple accumulates on the windows, and the wiper-arms swing in a steady beat back and forth in front of his eyes. An expert performer, he plays the gears, releasing and checking energy with his feet, swinging from this lane to that, gaining, steadily, maximum advantage in the traffic. The sealed metal and glass box round him is an object he uses well; the surrounding city is a structure he can master, by special routes and short cuts. But now the traffic jams; they come to rest in the line. Rear-lights shine back at them. Music wells out of a boutique; there is a chiming of the townhall clock. Shoppers and pedestrians press along the pavements; the buses disgorge crowds. In front of the van, a man crosses. He has long yellow hair, pulled together at the back with a band, a tie-dyed shirt split down to the navel, leather suede-fringed trousers, a bedroll on his back. He stops in the space between the van and the car in front; he puts one hand on the front of the van, the other on the boot of the other car, and swings between them for a moment. Then he goes on, through the traffic, to the other side of the street. 'Hey, why did he do that?' asks Martin. 'He feels free,' says Howard. The traffic moves again. Howard pushes the gear lever in; he turns down sidestreets and back ways until he reaches the red-brick enormity that is the children's school. Many middle-class mothers are parked in a row down the narrow street, releasing themselves from their children for the day. Howard uneasily joins the line, pulling up near the school entrance, and pulling open the van door to let Martin and Celia out. They run to join the woman who guards them across the road. He watches their wet figures across the street. Then he starts the van again, and drives back into the central traffic jam. The town is busy; there are crowds moving to work around the park and the cathedral, the Town Hall and Woolworth's. He is heading towards the university, which lies beyond the western side of the city, reached through a rundown residential area of Victorian terraces, dirty, carelessly maintained, marked with all the signs of transience. Down these streets the students who do not live in Spengler and Hegel, Marx and Toynbee, Kant and Hobbes, have flats and lodgings; at this time in the morning they flood, from the flats and bedsitters, onto the main road, lined with builders' yards, garages for used cars, stonemasons' premises with sample gravestones. Here they stand, waiting for buses and thumbing lifts.

Howard sits behind the wheel, inspecting faces, looking for one he knows. Shortly he sees one: standing at a bus-stop, over-arched by a large maroon umbrella, is a girl in a dark grey dress. He waves on the following traffic; he stops, a little way beyond the stop; he hoots the horn. But the girl clearly knows a pickup when she sees one; she glances at the minivan with a very cool curiosity, and then stares back down the main road, investigating the traffic for a sight of the bus she is dedicated to catching. Howard hoots again; finally he opens the door of the van and gets out, pressing against the door to avoid the rushing traffic. He shouts: 'Miss Callendar, Miss Callendar.' In the queue, Miss Callendar turns again and stares; then there is a shock of recognition. 'Och,' she says, 'it's Dr Kirk beckoning me.' 'Come on,' says Howard, 'I'll give you a lift to the university.' Miss Callendar stands for a moment, giving this due consideration; then she detaches herself from the line of waiting students, and walks toward the van. 'Well, it's extremely kind of you,' she says, stopping on the passenger side, 'on such a poor day.' 'A pleasure,' says Howard, 'get in.' Miss Callendar reefs in her umbrella, securing its maroon folds to its silver stalk; then she opens the van door and begins to climb inside. 'I thought you marched in every day under a banner,' she says as she twists her long legs to fit them into place, putting her brief-case on the floor, her umbrella upright between her knees, 'I'd no idea you drove about in motorized luxury.' Howard lets out the clutch; he says, 'It will save you your busfare.' 'That's right,' says Miss Callendar, 'a real consideration, these days.' The van pulls out into the traffic lane, and it joins the row of cars that every weekday morning, just before nine, makes its way out from Watermouth toward the university.

From Miss Callendar comes the scent of a healthy shampoo. Her umbrella is elegantly capped with a glass knob, into which a flower is set, like some Victorian antique; her white hands curl around it. She turns toward Howard and says, as if confessing a guilty secret, 'Actually, I'm almost late for a class. I just couldn't stir myself out of bed.' 'You know why?' says Howard, 'too much partying.' 'It doesn't do, does it?' asks Miss Callendar. 'What time did you finish?' 'Oh, late,' says Howard, 'long after you left. About four.' 'I don't know how you do it,' says Miss Callendar, 'it was an awfully demanding party.' 'All parties are demanding,' says Howard, 'if you take a real interest.' 'Ah,' says Miss Callendar, 'I do agree. The last thing they should be is fun. That demeans them into something trivial.' Howard laughs, and says: 'But did you take an interest?' 'Oh, I did,' says Miss Callendar, 'in my own way. You see, I'm a stranger, and I have to find out what you're all up to.' 'Did you?' asks Howard. 'I'm not sure,' says Miss Callendar, 'I think you're very interesting characters, but I haven't discovered the plot.' 'Oh, that's simple,' says Howard, 'it's the plot of history.' 'Oh, of course,' says Miss Callendar, 'you're a history man.' 'That's right,' says Howard, 'and that's why you have to trust us all. Like those kids last night. They're on the side of history.' 'Well, I trust everyone,' says Miss Callendar, 'but no one especially over everyone else. I suppose I don't believe in group virtue. It seems to me such an individual achievement. Which, I imagine, is why you teach sociology and I teach literature.' 'Ah, yes,' says Howard, 'but how do you teach it?' 'Do you mean am I a structuralist or a Leavisite or a psycho-linguistician or a formalist or a Christian existentialist or a phenomenologist?' 'Yes,' says Howard. 'Ah,' says Miss Callendar, 'well, I'm none of them.' 'What do you do, then?' asks Howard. 'I read books and talk to people about them.' 'Without a method?' asks Howard. 'That's right,' says Miss Callendar. 'It doesn't sound very convincing,' says Howard. 'No,' says Miss Callendar, 'I have a taste for remaining a little elusive.' 'You can't,' says Howard. 'With every word you utter, you state your world view.' 'I know,' says Miss Callendar, 'I'm trying to find a way round that.' 'There isn't one,' says Howard, 'you have to know what you are.' 'I'm a nineteenth-century liberal,' says Miss Callendar. 'You can't be,' says Howard, 'this is the twentieth century, near the end of it. There are no resources.' 'I know,' says Miss Callendar, 'that's why I am one.'

Howard looks across at Miss Callendar. She is looking back at him, with cool eyes, her mouth a little open, her manner serene. Her white face and dark hair and grey-dressed body fill the little van. He remembers her leaving his house last night, standing above the study, looking in; 'You showed much more curiosity about that girl there than you do about me,' Felicity Phee had said. The road now leaves the suburban belt and is running into the scrap of countryside that lies between town and university. The thirty mile limit finishes now; on the dual carriageway Howard picks up speed. There are a few high elms, a few chopped-down hedges, a converted cottage or two by the roadside. He looks again at Miss Callendar, who provokes him. He says, 'Where do you live?' 'I have a flat,' says Miss Callendar, 'a very convenient flat. It has a bathroom; that's convenient. And a bedroom with a bed. And a tin-opener with a tin. And a very pleasant living-room.' 'Do you do a lot of pleasant living?' asks Howard. 'Not a lot,' says Miss Callendar, 'one hardly has the time. Being in the twentieth century, very near the end of it.' 'Where is this flat?' asks Howard. Miss Callendar turns her head and looks at him. She says, 'It's very hard to find.' 'Oh, yes,' says Howard, 'why is that?' 'Mainly because I don't tell anyone where it is,' says Miss Callendar. 'Tell me,' says Howard, 'you must tell me.' 'Why?' asks Miss Callendar curiously. 'I hope to come there sometime,' says Howard. 'I see,' says Miss Callendar, 'well, it's just that kind of casual, arbitrary visiting I'm trying to stop.' 'Oh, you shouldn't,' says Howard. 'Oh, yes,' says Miss Callendar, 'otherwise any old structuralist or Leavisite or Christian existentialist who happened to be passing would be there. Knocking at the door, ringing the bell, wanting to fit you up with a contraceptive or get you into history. How is your wife, Dr Kirk?'

The entrance sign of the university, done in the distinctive modern lettering which is, along with the Jop Kaakinen cutlery (now mostly stolen) and the Mary Quant robes for congregation, part of its contemporary stylistic mannerism, appears on the right side of the road. Howard moves into the outer lane to be ready for the turn; there is a sudden screech of brakes behind him. 'Screw you,' says Howard. 'Why, Dr Kirk,' says Miss Callendar, 'I do believe you want to do that to everybody.' 'I meant the man behind,' says Howard, pulling into position in the long line of cars waiting to make the turn into the campus. 'Of course, I'd like to.' 'You'd like to what?' asks Miss Callendar. 'Screw you,' says Howard. 'Would you?' says Miss Callendar, her eyes staring ahead, her hands holding tight to the umbrella. 'Oh, now, why would you want to do a thing like that, Dr Kirk?' The van makes the turn into the carriage drive that leads through the university site, the drive that led once to the Elizabethan splendours of Watermouth Hall. Loud bangs thump on the van roof, a fusillade of rain-drops falling from the chestnut trees that line one side; those on the other side have been removed, to widen the road, and have been replaced by a row of saplings that, in the course of time, if there is a course of time, will hopefully acquire the old dignity. 'I think you're attractive,' says Howard, 'I think you need serious attention.' 'I gathered you'd been researching in the sexual field,' says Miss Callendar, 'you're still working at it, are you?' 'Oh, that's all finished and published,' says Howard, 'no, this would be purely for pleasure.' 'Oh, pleasure,' says Miss Callendar, 'but what would be the pleasure? My own lovely self, of course. That goes without saying. But I'm sure you have grander motives.' 'I like you physically,' says Howard, 'and you're a serious challenge. You haven't been made over.' 'Oh, I see,' says Miss Callendar. 'You're a provocation,' says Howard. 'I'm sorry,' says Miss Callendar, 'were you being provoked last night?' 'Last night,' says Howard. 'When I left the party,' says Miss Callendar. 'Oh, that was part of my tutorial duties,' says Howard. 'One has many obligations.' 'But I'm not an obligation, I'm a pleasure.' 'That's right,' says Howard, 'come out to dinner with me.'

'Dinner,' says Miss Callendar. 'We ought to get to know each other,' says Howard. They are passing, one on either side of the drive, two of the Kaakinen residences, Toynbee and Spengler; from them, in the pouring rain, comes a bedraggled procession of students, carrying cases and books, on their way to nine o'clock classes. 'Why, Dr Kirk,' says Miss Callendar, 'I don't think it would do.' 'Why not?' asks Howard. 'You go out to dinner and eat scampi and seduce nineteenth-century liberals,' says Miss Callendar, 'and meanwhile your wife sits at home and sews. Do you honestly think this is right?' 'My wife can't sew,' says Howard, 'and she goes her own way. She has wicked weekends in London.' 'And you sit home and sew?' says Miss Callendar. 'No,' says Howard, 'we get little time for sewing.' 'I can imagine,' says Miss Callendar, 'well, it's very kind of you to invite me, but I really don't think I can accept.' A sign says P, and points: Howard turns the van towards the car park. Now the main buildings of the university are in sight, up and down, high and low, glass and cement. 'Why not?' asks Howard, 'Am I too old? Too fast? Too married?' 'I don't think I belong in your company,' says Miss Callendar, sitting beside him, holding her umbrella. 'Mightn't it do you good?' asks Howard. 'It's the good I'm suspicious of,' says Miss Callendar, 'I think I know what your interest is in me. I think you regard me as a small, unmodernized, country property, ripe for development to fit contemporary tastes. You want to claim me for that splendid historical transcendence in which you feel you stand.' 'That's right,' says Howard, 'you're repressed, you're uptight, you haven't begun to reveal yourself yet. I want to reveal you.' In the car park, a student in a Rover 2000 backs out of one of the spaces; Howard drives neatly into the vacated space. 'Don't think I don't appreciate it,' says Miss Callendar, 'some people would just want to lay you and forget it. You provide redemption as well, a full course in reality. But I do have an idea of reality already. Only it's not quite the same as yours.'

Howard stops the engine; he turns to face Miss Callendar. She is sitting, looking forward towards a row of concrete bollards, with a very cool look on her face, her hands still around the handle of the umbrella. He puts his hand on top of her hands. He says, 'Tomorrow night, yes?' 'Tomorrow night, no,' says Miss Callendar. 'I'm sorry,' says Howard, 'I'm really after you. You know what Blake says.' 'Yes,' says Miss Callendar, 'I know very well what Blake says.' ' "Better murder an infant in its cradle than to nurse unacted desires," ' says Howard. 'Of course you would say that,' says Miss Callendar, 'actually what he said was that it was better to nurse unacted desires than murder an infant in its cradle.' 'I think I have it right,' says Howard. 'It's my field,' says Miss Callendar, opening the car

door. 'Many thanks for the lift. It saved me seven new pence.'
'I'm delighted to have supported your economy,' says Howard,
'what about my invitation?' 'Maybe one day,' says Miss
Callendar, angling herself out of the car and rising up beside it
to her full height, 'when I'm hungry.' Standing in the wet lake
of the car park, she erects her maroon umbrella. Then, as
Howard watches, she pushes it up in the air and walks off across
the lake, her briefcase swinging beside her knee, towards the
Humanities Building. Howard gets out of the van too, locks it,
and, with his briefcase, walks off in the other direction,
towards Social Sciences. He walks past posters advertising
theatrical productions, the forthcoming visit of many Maha-
rishis, some new anti-Vietnam demonstrations, lectures on
picketing, drugs, and the development of Byzantine art; he
walks under cranes and welders; he crosses the Piazza. A large
figure under a transparent domed umbrella is crossing the
Piazza from the other direction; it is Flora Beniform, swinging
her briefcase, wearing a big black fur-collared coat. They meet
just under the portico of the Social Sciences Building, outside
the glass doors; they stop and smile at each other.

'Hello, Howard,' says Flora, 'how's Barbara?' 'I can't tell
whether she loves me or she hates me,' says Howard. 'Of course
you can't,' says Flora, shaking out her umbrella, 'she can't
either.' Howard pushes open the glass door to let Flora go
through. 'Thank you,' she says, 'you look tired, Howard.'
Howard takes off his wet cap and shakes it. 'You missed a good
party last night,' he says. 'Oh, no,' says Flora, 'that's where
you're wrong. The guests were present. It was the hosts who
were absent.' 'You came?' asks Howard. 'I did,' says Flora,
'and then I went.' 'I wanted to see you,' says Howard. 'I'm
sure you did,' says Flora, 'but in default you saw someone else.
It was perfectly sensible of you.' 'You must have come late,'
says Howard. 'I did,' says Flora, 'I went up to London first to
catch a seminar at the Tavistock Clinic.' 'I hope,' says Howard,
as they walk across the foyer, 'it was worth missing me for?'
'Yes, it was,' says Flora, 'the paper had a very narrow concept
of normative behaviour and they all seem very clitorally
centred these days. But the question period was very challenging and provocative.' 'You mean you were,' says Howard.
'I did say some interesting things,' says Flora, 'did anyone say

anything very interesting at your party?' 'Flora,' says Howard, 'you're a scholar and a gentleman. No, they didn't. But interesting things were done, though.' They reach the lift in the centre of the foyer, and stop and wait there, surrounded by a large crowd of waiting students. Flora turns to Howard. 'I know,' she says, 'they were doing them when I got there.' 'Did I miss the best of it?' asks Howard. 'I think you did, Howard,' says Flora, 'I must say I feel very suspicious about a sociologist who is absent from the tensions of his own party.' The lift doors open in front of them; Howard follows Flora, in her fur-collared coat and her big leather boots, for Flora is always well and strikingly dressed, inside. A faint smell of perfume comes off her; her body is big against Howard's. 'What happened?' asks Howard. 'Don't you know, don't you really?' asks Flora. 'I heard something about a misfortune occurring to Henry Beamish,' says Howard.

'Yes, indeed,' says Flora. 'What happened?' asks Howard, 'Were you there?' 'Of course I was,' says Flora, 'I'm always there.' 'Tell me about it.' 'I think not here, I'll come to your study, if you've time.' 'I have,' says Howard. 'By the way, this new man Macintosh was telling me last night there's a rumour that Mangel is coming here to speak.' 'Now isn't that funny?' says Flora. 'I met Mangel at the Tavvy last night. And he obviously knew nothing about it at all. Macintosh did mention it at your party, actually. He said the rumour came from you.' 'Word of mouth is a curious system,' says Howard. 'I'm sure you're trying to be interesting,' says Flora, 'is this us?' 'That's it,' says Howard, and they both get out at the fifth floor; they walk along the corridor, with its artificial lighting, towards the department office. They go inside the office; the secretaries, Miss Pink, Miss Ho, have just arrived, and taken off their boots, and are at their first serious duty of the day, watering the potted plants. Through the breeze-block wall comes the sound of switches switching, buzzers buzzing; Marvin, who always rises at five and drives through the steaming rural mists of early morning into the university, is well into his work, calling foreign countries, advising governments, planning the afternoon meeting, getting his car fixed. 'A student just came in to look for you,' says Minnehaha Ho. 'Well, I'm here now,' says Howard, 'what's all this?' In the pigeon-holes, in the distinctive large grey envelopes, is, for all the faculty, yet another agenda, the supplementary agenda, for the afternoon's meeting; one agenda is never enough. Flora and Howard pick up their mail, sift quickly through it, side by side, and then walk back, side by side, to Howard's rectangular and regulation room. Here Flora, by some automatically assumed right of precedence, seats herself at Howard's red desk chair, leaving him to sit in the grey chair placed there for his students; she puts her umbrella beside the chair; she unbuttons the raincoat with the fur collar, to reveal a black skirt and a white blouse that stretches tightly across her large breasts. Then she turns to Howard, and tells him of Henry and the window, and Myra and her strange behaviour, and then of Henry, at the casualty ward, saying 'Don't tell Howard, will you? We mustn't spoil his party.'

VII

'Well,' says Howard, sitting in the wet light of his room, over-looking the boilerhouse chimney, after Flora has stopped speaking, 'it's a very interesting story.' 'The trouble is,' says Flora, picking up her handbag, and feeling into its interior, 'I'm not sure it is. Isn't a story usually a tale with causes and motives? All I've told you is what happened.' 'Perhaps it's a very modern story,' says Howard, 'a chapter of accidents.' Flora takes from her handbag her cigarettes and a lighter; she says, 'The trouble with our profession is, we still believe in motives and causes. We tell old-fashioned stories.' 'But aren't there times when just what happened is just what happened?' asks Howard. 'I mean, didn't Henry just have an accident?' 'Oh, Howard,' says Flora, lighting her cigarette, 'what is this thing called an accident?' 'An accident is a happening,' says Howard, 'a chance or a contingent event. Nobody has imposed meaning or purpose on it. It arises out of a set of unpredictable features coming into interaction.' 'Oh, I see,' says Flora, 'Like your parties. And you think Henry had one of those? 'That's what you said,' says Howard, 'a Henry and a window came into chance collision.' 'That's not what I said at all,' says Flora. 'You said he went into the guest bedroom, fell, and cut himself.' 'That's interesting,' says Flora, 'because I didn't say that. I portrayed a consciousness, with an unconscious. He went into the bedroom. His arm went through the window, and he was cut. That's what I said.' Howard gets up; he goes to the window, and looks through it down into the Piazza, where the wind beats, the rain falls. He says: 'Is there some reason for thinking it wasn't an accident?' 'You worry me, Howard,' says Flora. 'Why do you need to believe it was an accident? Or that accidents are like that?' 'I thought most events were accidents until proved otherwise,' says Howard. 'You're trying to make something interesting that probably wasn't. Of course you have a great gift for it.' 'No, I don't,' says Flora, 'I have a gift for not making it sound dull. And for asking the questions you chose, from some need, not to ask. I don't understand it. It's not like you at all.'

Howard laughs, and touches Flora's hair. He says, 'Well, you see, I *know* Henry. And for me Henry and accidents naturally go together.' 'Like love and marriage, horse and carriage,' says Flora. 'But *why* do they?' 'Did I ever tell you the story of the first time I saw Henry?' asks Howard. 'No,' says Flora, 'I don't think I ever knew Henry meant anything to you.' 'Oh, yes,' says Howard, 'I'm quite attached to Henry. I've known him for ages. We were research students at Leeds together.' 'I've noticed your hostility towards him,' says Flora, 'I ought to have guessed you were friends.' 'I'd seen his face around the department. He was doing something with termites, because they wouldn't let him use people. But my first real encounter with him was one day when I was walking down a back street, quite near the university. I saw this person in front of me, lying in the middle of the pavement, flat on his face. He'd got a big rucksack, stuffed with notes, on his back. Flat in the street near the Express Dairy. His nose was bleeding, and the rucksack was holding him down. My first real sight of Henry.' Flora laughs and says: 'It's a very interesting story. And how had he got there?' 'He'd been knocked down by a football. A football had come over the fence from the playing fields, next to the path, and hit him in the middle of the back. The football was next to Henry in the road. A purely contingent football. No one had thrown it purposely at him.' 'Not even you, Howard?' asks Flora. 'As I say, I hardly knew him then,' says Howard. 'No, a boy had kicked it high in the air, and it had come down, as footballs do, and under the trajectory of its descent there happened to be Henry, who was knocked over by it. So, you see, Henry has accidents.'

'Well, it's true, of course,' says Flora, 'Henry has accidents.

He's a man on whom footballs fall. But why do footballs fall on Henry, and not you, and me? Haven't you ever asked yourself that?' 'Well, he's careless and clumsy and uncoordinated,' says Howard, 'and he has an instinct for disaster. If Henry came to two paths, one labelled safe and one labelled dangerous, he'd confuse the signs and take the dangerous one.' 'Exactly,' says Flora, 'he colludes with misfortune.' 'But he can only collude so far,' says Howard. 'If a branch were rotten and going to fall, it would wait to fall until Henry passed under it. How does he get the message to the tree? There has to be a higher plotter, the God of accident.' 'I never knew you were such a mystic, Howard,' says Flora, knocking out ash into Howard's grey-glass ashtray, 'you're making me very suspicious. Now why do you need a theory like that?' 'Because it seems to me true to experience,' says Howard. 'It also explains innovation.' 'But all your theories depend on the great historical purpose working itself out,' says Flora, 'it's hardly consistent. No, you're covering something up. You're denying Henry his psychological rights. In this, I should add, you aren't alone. Myra has a version too.' 'What's Myra's?' asks Howard. 'Well, she at least granted Henry a motive,' says Flora, 'she looked at him, bleeding away on the floor, and decided it was all an appeal for her sympathy, which she didn't feel like giving.' 'Myra was very drunk last night,' says Howard, 'and upset herself.' 'My God,' says Flora, 'you're turning into a great simpleton of life, aren't you, Howard? Myra's behaviour last night was fascinating. I was the one who took Henry to hospital; Myra stayed on at your party. For all she knew, he might have been dying. He had twenty-seven stitches, and they had to give him blood. They should have kept him in hospital, of course, but, no, he had to get back to Myra. So I got my car, and shipped him home. And Myra wasn't even back. She turned up ten minutes later; she'd got your friend Macintosh, the one who told you things he couldn't possibly know, to drive her home. And as soon as she saw us she went and locked herself in the bathroom. I had to roar at her through the door for half an hour before she'd come out. Then she scarcely glanced at the poor man; just shouted at him for spoiling her lovely evening. If that's normal behaviour, then I'm crazy. Of course you'd explain it all as a typical drunken performance.'

'What's your explanation?' asks Howard. 'Well, obviously,' says Flora, 'she wished to state that she was rejecting all possible appeals he could make. I think she was disappointed he hadn't done the job properly. A fascinating vignette into family life.' 'It's true,' says Howard, 'there's stress there, in that marriage. But that's not to say it wasn't an accident.' 'My God, Howard,' says Flora, 'what *are* you hiding?' 'Nothing,' says Howard, 'I suppose you think with Barbara that I pushed him through the window. I didn't.' 'The thought never crossed my mind,' says Flora. 'Is that what Barbara thinks? I thought she knew you better.' 'Ah, Flora,' says Howard, 'what a vote of confidence in me.' 'Well, I have been to bed with you, Howard,' says Flora, 'and so I know how your aggression operates. If you wanted someone through a window, you wouldn't push him yourself. You'd get someone else to do it. Or persuade the man he should do it himself, in his own best interests.' 'You don't think he was pushed, then,' says Howard. 'God, no,' says Flora, 'it's not that kind of story. But he could be pushed emotionally. You'd grant that was possible.' 'I might,' says Howard. 'But you'd rather it was all a little act of chance, a happening,' says Flora. 'Part of the fun of your party.' 'It's not what I want it to be,' says Howard, 'it's what I think it is.' 'I wonder why you're evading this,' says Flora, 'I really wonder why.' 'Perhaps I'm worried about my insurance responsibility,' says Howard. 'That would be a good bourgeois reaction.' 'You have more of those than you think,' says Flora. 'No, I think there's a better reason. You weren't there, you see. You were busy. So you'd like as ordinary an explanation as possible.' 'Whereas you were there,' says Howard, 'and so you'd like an extraordinary one.' 'It's true, though, isn't it?' asks Flora. 'You'd hate to admit that something really interesting happened at your party, when you were absent. As with Myra. The only significant occurrences are the ones that happened to you. What did happen to you, Howard?' 'Ah,' says Howard, 'so that's what you're after. You've been trying to find out who I was with.' 'Now you're getting uneasy,' says Flora. 'I'm right, aren't I?' 'You sound jealous,' says Howard. 'I don't suffer from female complaints,' says Flora, pulling her coat up over her shoulders, and stubbing out her cigarette in the regulation ashtray, 'Well, you tuck the whole thing away, Howard. Let's say that nothing at all happened.'

And Flora gets to her feet, and picks up her umbrella from beside the chair.

'Oh, don't go, Flora,' says Howard, 'you haven't told me anything yet.' 'You've not told me anything,' says Flora. 'You know more than you say. You're not sharing. I think you want to keep Henry for yourself. You want to fathom him in your own way. Redeem him with your own instruments.' 'No, sit down, Flora,' says Howard, 'I really do admit it. The more one thinks, the more it seems not like one of Henry's usual accidents.' Flora smiles, and sits down in the chair again; she flicks her lighter, and lights another cigarette. 'Not at all like,' says Flora. 'You know, I'm sure Henry acted.' Howard looks out of the window; he can see the shuttered concrete of Kaakinen's inspiration, which in its pure whiteness is intended to induce the sense of unadulterated form, and hence belongs really in some distant, Utopian landscape of sun and shadow, in New Mexico, perhaps, or on the Cap d'Agde; here the teeming rain stains it all a dark and dirty grey. 'Acted?' says Howard. 'One doesn't just slip and procure that kind of wound,' says Flora. 'He pressed down into that glass. I think it was a minimal suicide attempt. An act of anger and despair. An appeal.' 'Did Henry tell you that it was?' asks Howard, turning. Flora laughs, and says, 'If only he had. Then we could have brought our superior wisdom to bear, and proved him wrong. No, Henry said nothing at all about it. All he could say was "Don't tell Howard". Which shows a real sweetness of nature.' 'Oh, come, Flora,' says Howard, 'there must be a deeper meaning than that.' Flora laughs; she says, 'I'm sure I'm right.' 'The trouble is I can't see it,' says Howard. 'You could convince me about almost anyone except Henry. You say he acted. But Henry doesn't act. All action leads to suffering, someone else's, or one's own. That's why Henry disapproves of it.' 'And that, of course, is why you do approve of it,' says Flora, 'I think you favour the suffering more than the action. But anyway, suicide is the traditional way of nullifying oneself as an actor. You know Hamlet.'

'Honestly, Flora,' says Howard, 'this is getting all too grand for Henry. Henry's not capable of that kind of bargain with the universe. He's not capable of that kind and degree of misery.' 'No, not like you,' says Flora. 'The trouble is, you can't take him seriously. He's on the fringes of your life, so you see him as a buffoon, an accident machine. I don't think you've ever really seen Henry.' 'I've known him a very long time,' says Howard. 'Yes,' says Flora, 'he's become part of your life's furniture. So you can use him and dismiss him. Hence your football story. A story about the fact that one doesn't need to take Henry seriously.' 'You take him too seriously,' says Howard. 'No,' says Flora, 'I just give him his due. You see, to see Henry plain, you have to feel love. And you've never felt love.' 'You're wrong,' says Howard, 'but in any case, when people attempt suicide, they make an accusation. And the accusation is perfectly clear. But there's no sign that Henry's accusing anyone.' 'Well, I'm sure Henry would try to manage even suicide without causing anyone fuss or trouble,' says Flora, 'but I did say a *minimal* suicide attempt. A gesture to say, look at me, think of me. The trouble is, we're busy people, none of us have the time.' 'Oh, what are we doing now?' asks Howard. 'But, anyway, a radical gesture against the self, but not an absolute one. When a man who publishes, like Henry, chooses his left arm, you can be sure he has hopes of going on writing with his right.' Howard laughs, and says: 'Flora, you're marvellous.' 'So Henry stays alive,' says Flora, 'and we're left free, without guilt, to pursue the gesture and its meaning. And interfere in his life in a well-intentioned way. As I'm sure we shall.' 'You're sure Henry is right-handed?' asks Howard. 'Well, you're his friend; is he?' asks Flora. 'I don't know,' says Howard. 'Well, he is, actually,' says Flora, 'I checked. A kind of love.' Howard says, 'All right, we must look at Henry. But what would you say the meaning was?' 'Well, some of it we've said,' says Flora, 'Henry is caught in an auto-destructive cycle. He doesn't believe in his own being. His aggression is inward, turned against himself. He despises himself, and feels himself despised. He can't make living values or living feelings, and he reaches sudden despair. Last night, in your guest-room. Aren't I right? Isn't that a portrait of Henry?'

Howard sits down in his chair. 'Yes,' he says, 'right as far as it goes. But I think we can go further.' 'Oh, yes?' says Flora, smiling. 'You're seeing simply a purely psychological problem,' says Howard. 'Inevitably, that's your training. Of course I see something else.' 'I've always said the most interesting thing about anyone's misfortune is the way it's adopted by the surrounding parties,' says Flora, 'I suppose you've got a political version.' 'Well,' says Howard, 'a socio-cultural one.' 'So that really to understand Henry,' says Flora, 'we'll need, naturally, a little Marx, a little Freud, and a little social history.' 'How right you are,' says Howard. 'Poor Henry,' says Flora, 'caught in the web of so much concern. I knew, when we got into it, you'd really want him for yourself.' 'It's not a question of that,' says Howard, 'what Henry needs is understanding. And I think I can claim to have some understanding of Henry. After all, we grew up in the same class, same background, same part of the country. His father was a railway clerk, mine worked in a bakery, but the differences of milieu were minimal. And then we went to university at just about the same time, got our first jobs together, and married within a year of each other. So I saw all the choices he made, the paths he took.' 'You observed,' says Flora, 'his failure to be as intelligent as you.' 'I saw him falsify himself,' says Howard. 'It wasn't a wise marriage. Myra was his social superior, she had all the bourgeois ambitions; and this was in the fifties, when everyone wanted to have it so good. Before he knew where he was he was into goods and chattels. He stopped thinking, he got caught up in this fancy, pseudo-bourgeois rural life-style, he lost his social conscience. He became repressed and a repressor. As Marx says, the more you have, the less you are. Henry's got, and he isn't. And since he's a serious person, he feels guilt. He knows he's in a context of no value, but he just can't break out. Isn't that the statement he was making?' 'Ah,' says Flora, 'so it wasn't just an accident?' 'No,' says Howard, 'it wasn't an accident at all. It's been coming for years.'

Flora laughs. 'You're easily convinced,' she says. 'Ah,' says Howard, 'but not in your way. The awful thing is, though, I ought to have known, last night. I ought to have been there. It was so predictable.' 'We managed perfectly well without you,' says Flora. 'No,' says Howard, 'I have a conscience about Henry.' 'It's hardly necessary,' says Flora, 'Henry was attended to in a competent manner. And you did have your own affairs to occupy you.' 'They weren't important,' says Howard. 'They would have done some other time.' Flora puts her head back, and laughs again. She says, 'My dear Howard, you really are an awful rogue. A moment ago it was all an accident, poor Henry, and no one could think any different. Now you have a theory. And of course what you've spotted is that Henry must have been in that happily unhappy condition where you might have influenced him. Never mind, he's not dead. You still can. I'm sure you'll do lots for Henry. Put him on a course of redemptive, contemporary sex. Get Myra hanging on pulleys from the bedroom ceiling.' 'Well,' says Howard, 'I do have some reason for thinking my interpretation significant.' 'Oh, yes?' asks Flora, 'what's that?' 'He did choose my window,' says Howard, 'not your window.' 'I see,' says Flora, 'a clearcut preference for Marx and Reich over Freud.' 'It could hardly have been accidental,' says Howard. 'You really do want him,' says Flora. 'I have a curious regard for Henry, believe it or not,' says Howard. 'Oh, I know,' says Flora, 'it's called friendship, and it means you can despise him.' 'No,' says Howard, 'I ought to have sensed something would go wrong last night. I have a sense of having betrayed him.' 'You have an elegant conscience, when it suits you,' says Flora. 'Actually, of course, when people so strongly deplore what they didn't do, they're usually expressing dissatisfaction with what they did do. You're just having regrets at the way you spent your evening. I'm sorry she disappointed you. Whoever she was. Who was she?'

Just then there is a knock at Howard's door. 'Come in,' he shouts. The door opens and a figure hovers uncertainly in the frame, doubtful whether to enter or to go away. It is Felicity Phee, looking very dark-eyed and untidy. 'Can I talk to you, Howard?' she says, 'I've been trying to catch you for ages.' 'Look, I'll go,' says Flora, picking up her umbrella and her handbag from the desk, and pulling her coat round her shoulders, 'We'd finished talking anyway.' 'No, there is something else,' says Howard, 'Would you mind waiting outside there a minute or two, Felicity? I shan't be long.' 'Well,' says Felicity, 'it's an important thing, and I've got a class at ten.' 'I know,' says Howard, 'I'm teaching it.' 'All right, Howard,' says Felicity, and goes out again. Flora looks at the closing door. She sits back in her chair. She says: 'Who's she?' 'She's just one of my students,' says Howard, 'I expect she's got an essay to give me.' 'Do all your students call you by your Christian name?' asks Flora. 'A lot of them,' says Howard.

'The ones I've been teaching for some time. Don't yours?'
'No,' says Flora, 'I don't think any of them ever have.' 'Ah,
well, you're more frightening than I am,' says Howard.
'Felicity who?' asks Flora. 'Felicity Phee,' says Howard.
'Uummm,' says Flora, getting up, 'well, there's nothing I like
better than talking to my colleagues about my other colleagues,
but I'd better go and see some students too.'

Howard says: 'Flora, can I come and see you sometime?'
'I'm not sure,' says Flora, 'I really only want someone who tells
me the truth. You still haven't told me anything.' 'I will,' says
Howard. Flora stands by the door, not quite touching the
handle; she pauses; she reaches in her bag, and takes out her
diary. 'I'm awfully busy,' says Flora. Howard reaches in his
pocket and pulls out his; they stand there, two busy professional people, and flip the pages. 'Next Monday?' asks
Howard. 'No good,' says Flora, 'that's my period. Friday
evening, I've a free space then.' 'Barbara's away and we've not
fixed the child arrangements,' says Howard. 'Any chance of
Thursday?' 'I have a review to get into the post on Thursday,'
says Flora. 'That's right out, I'm afraid.' 'Can I come tonight?'
asks Howard. 'Oh, tonight,' says Flora. 'I'll tell you a thing
about Myra,' says Howard. 'Well,' says Flora, 'I could manage
from about half-past seven till nine.' 'I'll have to get a sitter,'
says Howard, 'Barbara's starting an evening class.' 'Oh, is she?'
asks Flora. 'What's she doing?' 'A course in commercial
French,' says Howard. 'It sounds like an age-old statement of
boredom,' says Flora, 'you ought to watch Barbara.' 'She
wants to read Simone de Beauvoir in the original,' says
Howard. 'So does that,' says Flora, and lifts up her diary, and
says, 'Well, provisionally, Howard.' She writes these words in
the diary; Howard makes a note in his. They stand there for a
moment, looking at each other. Howard says: 'I shouldn't
have any trouble finding someone to sit. One of the students.'
'Ask that one,' says Flora, pointing her pencil at the door. 'I
might,' says Howard. Flora puts her diary away in her bag.
Howard says: 'I'll confirm at the departmental meeting this
afternoon. Goodbye, Flora.'

Flora puts her hand on the doorknob; then she stops. She
says: 'Isn't that strange? You never asked me what Barbara
was doing last night.' 'No, I didn't,' says Howard, 'so perhaps I

know.' 'Alternatively, perhaps you don't care,' says Flora. 'In any case, if you knew, and I didn't, would you tell me?' asks Howard. 'I probably wouldn't,' says Flora, 'but you might have asked.' 'I doubt if you know,' says Howard, 'I think you're just trying to find out.' Flora laughs; she says, 'Oh, Howard, interpersonal relations, why *do* we bother? There's never any rest, any end to it. Except what Henry tried.' 'That's a bleak view,' says Howard, 'In any case, what else is there?' 'That's right,' says Flora, 'God, there's paradise awaiting the Beamishes, if they listen to you, and follow your path.' 'It could help,' says Howard. 'Well,' says Flora, 'I may see you tonight. Byebye now.' She opens the door. The figure of Felicity Phee comes into view, standing just beyond the doorframe. 'I'm going now,' says Flora. 'Have a nice time at the party?' 'Yes,' says Felicity, 'very nice.' 'Good,' says Flora. 'Sorry to keep you waiting.' 'And who's she?' asks Felicity, when Flora's big bulk has gone away down the corridor, and the door is shut, 'I never saw her at your party.' 'She was there,' says Howard. 'She came late. What's it about, Felicity?' Felicity steps forward, deeper into the room. 'Can I sit down?' she asks. 'Of course,' says Howard. Felicity lowers herself into his grey chair. She is wearing a light tie-dyed shirt, with a scooped-out neckline, threaded through with a draw-string, and a long blue skirt reaching down to the ground. She has rings under her eyes, and nothing on her feet, which are dirty, and she has a drained and saddened look. 'I've got to find out how we stand,' she says. 'How do we stand, Howard?' 'Is something wrong?' asks Howard. 'I went home last night and told Maureen,' says Felicity, 'about what we did. She hit me with a shoe. She's turning me out. I came to see if you're going to do anything for me.' 'What should I do for you?' asks Howard, 'You can always get a room in the residences.' 'Maureen says I'm a dirty fink,' says Felicity. 'I told you to forget what Maureen says,' says Howard. 'Oh, yes,' says Felicity, 'but you told me an awful lot last night that seems to get forgotten pretty fast in the morning.' 'What did I tell you?' asks Howard. 'There's telling and telling,' says Felicity, 'I thought you told me, in a sense, you wanted me.' 'I made love to you, largely because you wanted me to, and in a mood we both understand. I think you're now trying to convert it into something else.'

'Oh, great, I see,' says Felicity, 'it was a purely neutral event. No further significance. Like having a tooth out on the National Health, right. Lie still, I'm just going to do this to you. Then off you go, make another appointment with the receptionist if you want one. Impersonal social welfare, good hygienic conditions, one quick visit, next patient please. Is that it?' Felicity stretches out her body in the chair; she looks woefully sad. She says: 'Christ, Howard, how do I get through to you? Hasn't anything happened, hasn't our relationship changed?' 'You've always been through to me,' says Howard, 'I have a concern for you. It's my job.' Felicity stares; she says, 'Your job? Laying me's part of your terms of service?' Howard asks: 'What are you playing at, Felicity?' Felicity looks down; she draws her bare toes across Howard's floor, and watches them. She says, 'I told you, I want to make me matter to you.' Howard looks at his watch. 'Look,' he says, 'we can't talk about this now. The class is in five minutes, and I've a job to do in the department office. We'll have to meet another time.' Howard gets out his diary. 'Oh, yes?' says Felicity, 'when's another time?' 'I've a meeting all afternoon,' says Howard. 'Tomorrow morning.' 'No,' says Felicity, 'see me tonight.' 'I'm going out tonight,' says Howard. 'Well,' says Felicity, 'I'm not getting out of this chair. You can go to your class and leave me here if you want. The humanity here just refuses to budge.' 'That's ridiculous,' says Howard. 'It's a standpoint you ought to recognize,' says Felicity, 'it's a traditional radical gesture.' 'All right,' says Howard, 'just wait here for a moment. I'll do my job and come back.' Howard goes along the corridor, and into the department office; it is the secretaries' coffee-time, when they go over to the Union, so he dictates a message onto the dictaphone. He returns along the corridor to the oblong room; Felicity Phee still sits in the grey chair, but there is disorder among the papers on his desk, and the filing-cabinet drawer is open; Felicity has a file from the drawer out on her knee and is reading its contents. 'This is interesting,' says Felicity. 'Of course,' says Howard, 'as soon as I got along the corridor, I realized you'd do that. Give it back.' Felicity hands over the file, a very dull file about admissions statistics, from one of Howard's committees; he slips it back into the cabinet and shuts it. 'What are you up to, Felicity?' he asks. 'I told you,

Howard,' says Felicity, 'I take an interest in you. I think about you all the time. Look at me. I can help you.'

Howard sits down in his desk chair. 'You can help me, Felicity?' he asks, 'How can you do that?' 'I didn't sleep at all last night,' says Felicity, 'I just thought about you. Do you know what I thought? I thought, if that man only really knew himself. He thinks he's free. He talks about liberation, openness, all the time. And what is he? An institutional man. That stuffy job he does. That stuffy desk he sits at. That stuffy academic manner he has, that he thinks is so equal, so matey. He hasn't started on himself yet. He's in a mess of inconsistencies. I know it's hard for you to admit it. But isn't it just true?' 'And you have a means for freeing me from this disaster?' asks Howard. Felicity leans forward. 'Oh, Howard,' she says, 'why don't we just go?' 'Go where?' asks Howard. 'Just walk out of here with me,' says Felicity. 'Let's take off. Let's stop being teacher and student, let's go somewhere and be us.' 'Did you have somewhere in mind?' asks Howard. 'Somewhere cheap,' says Felicity, 'The South of France.' 'To do what?' asks Howard. 'You can write books, get mixed up with the French radicals,' says Felicity. 'I'll cook French food, I'm a good cook. And we'll swing.' Howard looks at her. He says: 'Felicity, are you really a good cook?' 'Not very,' says Felicity. 'And the South of France isn't cheap.' 'It doesn't have to be the South of France,' says Felicity. 'And I'm not trapped that way,' says Howard, 'I'm very free.' 'You're not,' says Felicity, 'you just think you are.' 'Felicity,' says Howard, 'this is one of your fantasies. You're a fantasy-maker.' 'You don't see, do you?' asks Felicity. 'You don't see what you could be. I think I've thought about you more than you ever have yourself.' 'Nobody has ever thought about anybody more than they have themselves,' says Howard. 'So nobody can teach anybody anything?' asks Felicity. 'You don't believe that.' 'Of course people teach other people things,' says Howard, 'it's the critical education.' 'But you're so smart you only do it to others,' says Felicity. 'No one can teach you a thing about you. Aren't you lucky? But you want to see yourself from outside. It looks different then.'

Howard looks at Felicity. He says, 'You're determined to wriggle into my life. You track me, you spy on me. Then you start accusing me of flaws that only you can solve. It's a game to hook me with. But what for, Felicity?' 'You ought to know,' says Felicity, a tear in her eye, 'it's what some people call love.' 'Love's a strange business,' says Howard, 'an activity that needs very close examination.' 'Oh, God,' says Felicity, 'aren't you stuffy? Aren't you what I said?' 'You say you want to free me,' says Howard, 'but what you mean is you want to own me. And you'll never develop a relationship like that. With me, or anyone else.' The old stable clock at Watermouth Hall rings out its ten o'clock, in high, absurd notes, over the campus. Felicity's tear runs down her nose. 'You're cheating me,' says Felicity. 'Come on, Felicity,' says Howard, 'come on to class.' 'Have you got some tissue?' says Felicity. Howard reaches in his desk drawer and hands Felicity a white Kleenex. 'I expect you need that all the time,' says Felicity, 'for the rows and rows of us.' 'No,' says Howard, 'get up.' 'You win by being older,' says Felicity, 'but that's how you lose, too.' 'All right?' asks Howard, and opens the door. Felicity throws the Kleenex into the wastepaper basket; she crosses the room and goes out into the corridor; she stands slackly, waiting while Howard picks up books and notes, and then steps out of his room and locks the door. They begin walking down the corridor, under the sodium lights. Felicity says, sniffing, 'When will you see me again?' 'We can talk again tomorrow,' says Howard. 'Are you really going out tonight?' asks Felicity. 'Yes,' says Howard, 'I am.' 'Who are you seeing?' 'I have a professional meeting,' says Howard. 'Do you have a sitter?' asks Felicity, 'can I come?' Howard stops and looks at Felicity; her face is innocence.

A pair of buttocks suddenly emerge from a door to the right of the corridor, and collide with Howard; they belong to a colleague of his, a young man of radical persuasion called Roger Fundy, who is dragging a slide-projector forth from a classroom. He stands upright; he stares briefly at Felicity's wet face, but students at Watermouth, with its rigorous teaching, cry so often that his attention is not detained. 'Howard,' he says, 'have you heard all this talk about Mangel?' 'What's that?' asks Howard. 'He's supposed to be coming to speak,' says Fundy. 'You ought to stop it,' says Howard. 'I'm a good babysitter,' says Felicity, as they walk on, 'I like kids.' 'But if you came, you'd pry,' says Howard, 'it wouldn't work, would it?' They come towards the end of the corridor; in front of them, around the lift shaft, a crowd of students mills, leaving classes that have just ended, going to classes that are about to begin. 'If I didn't?' says Felicity. 'If I reformed?' 'But can you?' asks Howard. They stop on the fringe of the crowd, waiting for the lift to come. 'I cheated,' says Felicity, 'I know you didn't take me seriously last night. I know you were just being kind.' The bell pings; the lift doors open; they move in with the crowd. 'The trouble is it's hard to know you're little,' says Felicity, 'people like to make themselves matter.' The lift descends one floor, and then they get out again. They are standing in another service area identical to the one they have just left; a similar pattern of corridors leads off it. 'I can face reality,' says Felicity, 'it's just that I remember how you told us reality doesn't exist yet, it's up to us to make it.' They move into the corridor to the right; Felicity pads at Howard's side down the long bright passage. 'I'm afraid what happened in my study was just a fragment of what was happening in my house last night,' says Howard, 'you weren't the only one to get hurt.' 'Someone got hurt?' asked Felicity. 'Only really hurt,' says Howard. The vacant doors line the corridor walls; they move towards their classroom at the end. 'Wow,' says Felicity, 'what happened?' 'I wasn't there,' says Howard, 'it was while we were downstairs. You remember the blue light? That was the ambulance.' 'Oh, Christ,' says Felicity, 'you mean it was a real accident?'

VIII

The seminar room where Howard meets this weekly class, Socsci 4.17, is an interior room without windows, lit by artificial light. The room is a small one; on three of its walls are pinned large charts, illustrating global poverty, while the fourth wall is occupied by a large green chalkboard, on which someone has written, as people are always writing, 'Workers unite'. The room contains a number of tables with gunmetal legs and bright yellow tops; these have been pushed together in the centre to form one large table, where some previous tutor has been holding a formal class. In the room stand three students, positioned somewhere indeterminate between the tables and the walls; it does not do, at Watermouth, to take it for granted that a room arrangement that suits one teacher will ever suit another. Classes at Watermouth are not simply occasions for the one-directional transmission of knowledge; no, they are events, moments of communal interaction, or, like Howard's party, happenings. There are students from Watermouth who, visiting some other university, where traditional teaching prevails, stare in amazement, as if confronted by some remarkable and exciting innovation; their classes are not like that. For Watermouth does not only educate its students; it teaches its teachers. Teams of educational specialists, psychologists, experts in group dynamics, haunt the place; they film seminars, and discuss them, and, unimpressed by anything as thin as a manifestation of pure intellectual distinction, demonstrate how student C has got through the class without speaking, or student F is expressing boredom by picking his nose, or student H has never, during an hour-long class, had eye-contact with the teacher once. They have sample classes, where the faculty teach each other, sessions in which permanent enmities are founded, and clothes get torn, and elderly professors of international reputation burst into tears. So Howard comes into the room, and he looks around it, and he inspects the arrangement of the tables. 'I'm afraid this is what Goffman would call a bad eye-to-eye ecological huddle,' he says. 'We don't want these tables here like this, do we?'

'No, Dr Kirk,' says one of the students standing in the room, a big-boned girl named Merion Scoule, in a nervous way. Watermouth makes students nervous; you never know quite what to expect. There are classes where you have, on arrival, to eat something, or touch each other, or recount last night's dreams, or undress, in order to induce that strange secular community that is, in Watermouth terms, the essence of a good class, a class that is interesting. There are others where you have to sit and listen to tutors in self-therapy, talking about their problems or their wives or their need to relate; there are other classes where almost the reverse happens, and the students become objects of therapy, problem-bearers, and where an apparently casual remark about one's schoolboy stamp collection, or a literary reference to the metaphoric significance of colour, will lead to a sudden psychic foray from a teacher who will dive down into your unconscious with three shrewd enquiries and come up clutching something in you called 'bourgeois materialism' or 'racism'. Howard's classes are especially famous for being punitive in this way. Altogether, caution and courage are necessary, and a protean nature; there are so many roles for a student to perform. There are classes where the teacher, not wanting to direct the movement of mind unduly, will remain silent throughout the class, awaiting spontaneous explosions of intelligence from his students; there are classes, indeed, where the silence never gets broken. There are other classes where the teacher never appears in person at all, but materializes suddenly into existence on a screen in the corner of the room, beamed there from the audio-visual centre, mouthing sound that can be turned up, or down, or off, according to the dedication and whim of the class, while he is off lecturing for the British Council in Brazil. Anything can happen, except the normal, save that the very idea of innovation becomes customary; to experienced Watermouth students, like these, it is conventional for Howard to come into the room, as now, and make the students form pairs—Merion Scoule and Michael Bennard; Felicity Phee and Hashmi Sadeok, from Morocco, who, older than the others, is better at carrying tables—and hump the furniture out into the corridors.

When they have moved the tables, Howard has the students arrange their chairs in a neat little circle, near to but not at the precise centre of the room. 'Right,' he says, dragging his own chair into the circle, 'that should improve interaction. We can't see you properly, Hashmi. Move your chair forward about two feet.' Hashmi stares. 'A metre and a half,' says Michael Bennard. Hashmi smiles; the group, shapely now, relaxes. Felicity and Merion sit side by side, an anguished Watermouth pair, Felicity in her shirt and long skirt, Merion in incredible thicknesses of garment, including a skin waistcoat and a crocheted long cardigan. Michael Bennard is next to Felicity; he has a large black beard, and wears a frock coat and jeans. Hashmi is next to Merion; he has a fine splayed-out hairdo, and platform shoes. 'There's something wrong,' says Howard. 'Well, we're not all here,' says Merion. 'No,' says Howard, 'who's missing?' 'George,' says Michael, 'he's starting discussion.' 'Has anyone seen him?' asks Howard. 'He's always late,' says Hashmi. 'His congenital disease,' says Howard, 'just as it's mine to eliminate him from memory. I wonder what that signifies.' The class laughs. Howard says, 'Did he show up this term?' 'Well,' says Merion, 'he's not the kind of person we associate with.' 'He'll come,' says Michael Bennard, 'he always comes.' 'We could start without him,' says Merion, 'I expect we've all read the stuff.' 'No,' says Howard, 'I really think we ought to hear George exercise himself on the topic of social change. It should be quite an occasion.'

At this moment the door is jogged, and then it opens. In the aperture stands a student; he carries a large stack of books, which reach from the level of his crotch to just under his chin. His chin holds the pile unevenly steady. From two of the fingers of his hands, which are clasped underneath the books, there dangles a shiny new briefcase. The established circle inspects the stranger, who appears confident. 'I'm sorry I'm late, sir,' he says, 'I've been working all night on my paper. Just this minute finished.' 'Get a chair,' says Howard, 'bring it into the circle.' 'Hold my books,' says the student, who is very neat, to Merion; he brings a chair, inserts it into the group, causing much scraping of the floor; 'Is that all right, sir?' he asks, 'can everyone see my face from this position?' 'Enough of it,' says Howard. 'Look, I asked you to prepare this class over the summer, not leave it until last night.' 'I wanted to be fresh,' says the student. 'Besides, I was shooting in the summer.' 'Who were you shooting?' asks Howard. 'I was shooting film in Scotland,' says the student. 'Bag any?' asks Michael Bennard. 'Come on,' says Howard, 'I want to get started. Theories of social change.' 'If you could just give me half a minute,' says the student, 'I just have to sort these books out. Would you mind if I had a table? There are some outside in the corridor.' 'We've just taken them out,' says Howard, 'and what is all this stuff, George?' The student has begun to arrange the large pile of books around his chair; each of the books has little bits of toilet paper protruding from its pages, no doubt to mark significant references. 'I've tried to be as scholarly as possible,' says the student, 'I wouldn't want to go off at a tangent with a crucial issue like this. Social change, sir.' 'It doesn't seem necessary to me,' says Howard, 'but we'll start off by giving you the benefit of the doubt. Now are you ready?' 'One more tiny moment?' says the student; he reaches into his shiny leather briefcase, and brings forth a blue cardboard file. From the file he removes a fat document, written in very cramped, close handwriting, places it on his knee, and looks up. 'Ready to go now, sir,' he says.

The student's name is George Carmody; he has the reputation of being appalling. The group stare at him, question whether they can contain him; their tolerance is not easily strained, but something in Carmody strains it. They have been meeting together weekly, now, for two whole years; they have shared many experiences, been through dark purgatories of insight, together; they have acquired a cohesion, a closeness. They have changed together, passing through those utter transformations of personality which at Watermouth are an ongoing spiritual necessity: students here will suddenly acquire new modes of being, so that not only does dress, hairstyle, appearance alter utterly, but somehow the entire physiology and physicality. A neat, respectful public schoolboy has become irritable, proletarian Michael Bennard; a frail, bright teenager has become dark-eyed Felicity Phee. But to these transactions of spirit and belief Carmody has remained a stranger; he has changed most, and changed by not changing at all. Here he sits, in his chair, looking beamingly around; as he does so, he shines forth unreality. He is a glimpse from another era; a kind of historical offence. In the era of hair, his face is perfectly clean-shaven, so shaven that the fuzz of peach-hair on his upper features looks gross against the raw epidermis on his cheeks and chin, where the razor has been. The razor has also been round the back of his neck, to give him a close, neat haircut. From some mysterious source, unknown and in any case alien to all other students, he has managed to acquire a university blazer, with a badge, and a university tie; these he wears with a white shirt, and a pair of pressed grey flannels. His shoes are brightly polished; so, as if to match, is his briefcase. He is an item, preserved in some extraordinary historical pickle, from the nineteen-fifties or before; he comes out of some strange fold in time. He has always been like this, and at first his style was a credit; wasn't it just a mock-style to go with all the other mock-styles in the social parody? But this is the third year; he has been out of sight for months, and here he is again, and he has renewed the commitment; the terrible truth seems clear. It is no joke; Carmody wants to be what he says he is.

Now he looks at Howard, with bright eyes; he says, 'You asked me to look at theories about the workings of social change in the works of Mill, Marx and Weber. I hope this is a justifiable interpretation.' Howard looks at the intolerable figure; he says, 'I hope it is.' Carmody now dips his head, and draws the fat document from its folder; he begins to read the first sentence from the handwritten page. 'Wait a minute,' says Howard, 'are you proposing to read all that?' 'Yes, sir,' says Carmody. 'I'm not "sir",' says Howard, 'I don't want your deference. Now, what did I ask you to do?' 'You asked me to look at Mill, Marx and Weber, and make a report,' says Carmody. 'I asked you to go away and read their works, over the vacation,' says Howard, 'and then to make a spontaneous verbal statement to this class, summing up your impressions. I didn't ask you to produce a written paper, and then sit here with your head hanging over it, presenting formalized and finished thoughts. What kind of group experience is that?' 'You did say that, sir,' says Carmody, 'but I thought I could do something more developed. I've put in so much time on this.' 'I don't want it developed,' says Howard, 'I want development to occur in discussion.' 'I'm sorry, Dr Kirk,' says Carmody, 'but I felt this was better. I mean, I felt I could sum this stuff up and get it out of the way so we didn't need to spend a lot of time going over and over it.' 'I want us to go over it,' said Howard, 'it's called discussion. Now put that script away, take it outside, and then tell us what impressions you've got from the reading I asked you to do.' 'You think I haven't done the reading, sir?' asks Carmody. 'I don't think that at all,' says Howard, 'I think you've made a heavy, anal job of this, because you're a heavy, anal type, and I want you to risk your mind in the insecurity of discussion.' 'Well, I'm sorry, sir, but I can't,' says Carmody. 'Of course you can,' says Howard. 'No,' says Carmody, 'I just don't think like that, work like that. I am an anal type, you're right. It's not all easy. If you like, I'll go over to Counselling Service and get them to write me a note to that effect. *They* know I can't think like that. They know I have a linear mind, Dr Kirk, I'm afraid.' 'A linear mind,' says Howard, 'is that what they told you?' 'Yes, sir,' says Carmody, 'it's a mental condition.'

'I'm sure it is,' says Howard, 'I'm trying to cure it.' 'Oh, they wouldn't like that, Dr Kirk,' says Carmody, 'I'm under treatment for it. Please let me read my paper.' 'Well,' says Howard, 'it's up to the rest of the class. I'm not going to accept anything like this from them. But it's a democratic class. We'll vote on it, and you'll have to accept their decision. Right, Mr Carmody wants to submit a written paper; those who are prepared to hear it?' 'How long is the paper?' asks Merion Scoule. 'No discussion, just vote,' says Howard. 'In favour?' Three hands go up. 'Against?' Two go up, one of them Howard's. 'Well,' says Howard, 'you've got the consent of these tolerant people. Go ahead and read your formal paper.' Carmody casts a fast, uneasy glance at Howard, as if mystified by his good luck. Then he coughs, ducks his head down, and begins to read again, in the same careful voice. It is dull, dogged stuff, an old scheme of words, a weak little plot, a culling of obvious quotations surrounded by obvious comments, untouched with sympathy or that note of radical fire that, in Howard's eyes, has so much to do with true intellectual awareness. Occasionally Carmody picks up the books from beside his chair, and reads from them; occasionally he tries a rhetorical flourish; occasionally he glances, uneasily, up and around. The clock, on the wall above the greenboard, ticks and turns; the circle of people is bored; Michael Bennard, that irritable Marxist, draws large black crosses on a notepad, and Merion Scoule is blank-eyed, withdrawn into thoughts that take her elsewhere. Felicity is looking expectantly at Howard, awaiting his anger, his interruption. But Howard does not interrupt. The paper is like an overripe plum, collapsing and softening from its own inner entropy, ready to fall. It is the epitome of false consciousness; its ideas are fictions or pretences, self-serving, without active awareness; it moves towards its inevitable fate. Now the class follows Carmody's eyes as he tracks through his writing, moves towards the bottom of a page. He knows this; he fumbles the turnover, lifting two pages instead of one. He sees this, pauses, turns back one sheet. Merion Scoule says, 'Can I ask a question?'

Carmody looks up, his neat cropped head staring at her. He says, in a precise, judicious manner: 'If it's a point of detail. I'd prefer general issues to wait to the end, when the argument is clear.' 'It is a general issue,' says Merion. Howard says, impersonally: 'I think a little discussion would clear the air.' 'Well,' says Merion, leaning forward, 'I just want George to explain the methodology of this paper. So that I can understand it.' Carmody says, 'Isn't it evident? It's an objective summary of my findings.' 'But it doesn't have any ideology, does it?' asks Merion. 'It's filled with it,' says Michael Bennard, 'The ideology of bourgeois self-justification.' 'I meant ideological self-awareness,' says Merion. 'Oh, I realize it doesn't agree with your politics,' says Carmody, 'but I think someone ought to stand back and look critically at these critics of society for a change.' 'It doesn't even agree with life,' says Michael Bennard. 'You're seeing a society as a consensus which bad people from outside set out to upset, by wanting change. But people desire and need

change; it's their only hope, not some paranoid little deviance.'
'That's pure politics,' says Carmody, 'may I get on with my
paper?' 'It won't do, George,' says Howard, intervening, 'I'm
afraid this is an anal, repressed paper in every way. Your
model of society is static, as Michael says. It's an entity with
no internal momentum and no internal conflict. In short, it's
not sociologically valid.' A redness comes up Carmody's neck,
and reaches his lower face. He says, insistently, 'I think it's a
possible point of view, sir.' 'It may be in conservative circles,'
says Howard, 'it isn't in sociological ones.' Carmody stares at
Howard; some of the polite finish begins to come off him. 'Isn't
that debatable, Dr Kirk?' he asks, 'I mean, are you sociology?'
'Yes,' says Howard, 'for the present purpose, I am.' There is
discomfort in the room; Merion Scoule, humanely trying to
soften the atmosphere, says, 'I think you're just a little hung up,
George. I mean, you're too much involved; you're not standing
outside society and looking at it.' Carmody ignores her; he
looks at Howard; he says, 'Nothing I say could ever please you,
could it?' 'You'd certainly have to try harder than you do,'
says Howard. 'I see,' says Carmody, 'Do I have to agree with
you, Dr Kirk, do I have to vote the way you do, and march
down the street with you, and sign your petitions, and hit
policemen on your demos, before I can pass your course?'
There is a pause in the class, a tiny, uneasy movement of
furniture. Then Howard says: 'It's not required, George. But
it might help you see some of the problems inside this society
you keep sentimentalizing about.' 'I think, George,' says
Merion, 'the trouble is that you don't have a conflict model of
society.' 'Don't let him off the hook,' says Howard, punitive.
'There's a lot more missing than that. All of sociology and all
of humanity as well.' Carmody's entire face is red now; his eyes
glare. He pushes his paper savagely back into his shiny briefcase,
and says, 'Of course you all *do* have a conflict model. Everyone's
interest conflicts with everyone else's. But better not conflict
with Dr Kirk. Oh, no, it's not a consensus model for his classes
all right. I mean, we're democratic, and we vote, but no dirty
old conservative standpoints here. Sociology's revolutionary,
and we'd better agree.' 'I'm going to have to cool this down,'
says Howard, 'I don't think you're in a state to understand
anything that's being said to you. We'll forget the paper, and

start in on this Mill, Marx, Weber topic from the beginning.'
'Do what you like,' says Carmody, 'I've had enough.' He gets
off his chair and kneels on the floor, picking up his pile of
books. His hurt, angry face looks up at Howard as he does this.
Then he stands, captures his briefcase with his fingers, and
walks out of the circle, towards the door. The door is difficult
to open, with his burden of books, but he manages it; he hooks
a foot round it to bring it slamming to as he leaves. The circle
of people stare after him; but to these habitués of the seminar
as an event, this is a fairly modest outrage, a simple pettish
hysteria, not at all as fancy as many of the intense psycho-
dramas that develop in class. The door bangs, and they turn
inward again, and resume their eye-to-eye ecological huddle.
Howard leads them through a discussion of the issues that, in
Carmody's gloss of nineteenth-century thought and society, had
not existed: the compelling machine of industrialism, the fetish
of commodity, the protestant ethic, the repression of the worker,
the revolutionary energies. Carmody wanders somewhere else,
forgotten; the class generates its rightful work and then its
excitement, for Howard is a busy, compelling teacher, a man
of passion. The faces wake, the hour turns in no time at all.

And then the stable clock chimes; the class gets up, and
carries the tables back from the corridor into the room again.
It is Howard's custom to take his class for coffee afterwards,
and now he leads them, a little group, down in the lift, across
the foyer, through the Piazza. They go into the coffee bar in the
Students' Union, overlooking the lake. The noise level is high;
in a corner a pin-table pings on different notes, in serial
composition; people sit at table arguing, or reading. They find
a booth by the wall, littered with cups and cigarette packets,
and sit down, squeezing into the circular bench; Merion and
Michael go off to join the queue at the counter to bring back
coffee. 'Wow,' says Felicity, pushing in next to Howard, and
resting her knee against his leg, and looking up into his face,
'I hope you never decide to destroy me like that.' 'Like what?'
asks Howard. 'The way you did George,' says Felicity, 'If he
wasn't such a reactionary, I'd feel sorry for him.' 'It mystifies
me,' says Howard. 'It's as if he invites it, as if he's set himself up
as masochist to my sadist.' 'But you don't give him a chance,'
says Felicity. 'No chances for people like that,' says Hashmi,

'he's an imperialist fascist.' 'But you are a sadist,' says Felicity. 'The trouble with George,' says Howard, 'is that he's the perfect teaching aid. The enemy personified. He almost seems to have chosen the role. I don't even know whether he's serious.' 'He is,' says Felicity. The others join them, with the coffee. 'Coffee, coffee, what they here call coffee,' says Hashmi. 'Oh, Hashmi,' says Howard, 'Roger Fundy tells me Mangel's coming here to lecture. The man who did that work on race.' 'But you can't have him,' says Hashmi, 'I shall tell this to the Afro-Asian Society. This is worse than Carmody.' 'It is,' says Howard. He drinks his coffee, quickly, and gets up to go. As he leaves the table, squeezing over Felicity, she says, 'What time shall I come tonight, Howard?' 'Where?' asks Howard. 'I'm baby-sitting for you,' says Felicity. 'Oh,' says Howard, 'can you get there just before seven-fifteen?' 'Fine,' says Felicity, 'I'll come straight there. You won't even have to pick me up.' 'Good,' says Howard.

He goes back to the Social Science Building; getting out of the lift, at the fifth floor, he can distantly see a figure waiting outside the door of his study. From this standpoint, Carmody looks like a creature at the end of a long historical corridor, back in dark time; Howard stands, in the brightness of the emanci-pating present, at the other. Carmody has shed his books; he carries only his shiny briefcase; he has a dejected, saddened look. As Howard gets nearer, he glances up, and sees him; his demeanour stiffens. 'I think I ought to have a talk with you, sir,' he says to Howard, 'can you give me some time?' 'A minute or two,' says Howard, unlocking his door. 'Come in.' Carmody follows Howard through the doorway and then, just inside the room, he stops, his big body ungainly, holding his briefcase. 'Sit down, George,' says Howard, placing himself in the red desk chair, 'What's this about?' 'I want to discuss my work,' says Carmody, not moving from his position, 'I mean, a really frank discussion.' 'All right,' says Howard. 'I think I'm in trouble,' says Carmody, 'and I think you've got me into it.' 'What does that mean?' asks Howard. 'Well, this is my third year in your course,' says Carmody. 'I've written about twenty essays for you. They're here, in my bag. I wonder if you'd go over them with me.' 'We've been over them,' says Howard. 'I wonder if we could look at the marks,' says Carmody, 'it's a

136

question of the marks.' 'What about them?' asks Howard. 'Well, sir, they're not very good marks,' says Carmody. 'No,' says Howard. 'They're mostly fails,' says Carmody. 'Yes,' says Howard. 'I mean, I could fail this course,' says Carmody. 'It rather looks as though you might,' says Howard. 'And that's all right with you?' 'It's the inevitable consequence of doing bad work.' 'And if I fail your course I fail my degree,' says Carmody, 'because if you don't pass in your subsidiary subject you can't get a degree.' 'That's right,' says Howard. 'You think that could happen?' asks Carmody. 'I do.' 'Well, in that case,' says Carmody, 'I have to ask you to look at these marks again, and see if you think they're fair.'

Howard examines Carmody's expression; it is civil, serious, rather nervous. 'Of course they're fair,' says Howard. 'Are you telling me I don't mark fairly?' 'Not exactly,' says Carmody, 'I don't think they're consistent.' 'Of course they are,' says Howard, 'Consistently bad. They're about the most consistent marks I've ever given.' 'Not consistent with my marks in other subjects,' says Carmody. 'My major's English; I get As and high Bs in that. I have to do Social History; I get mostly Bs there. And then there's Sociology, and that's all Ds and Fs.' 'Isn't the obvious deduction that you're working seriously in English and History, and not in Sociology?' 'I admit I'm not attracted to Sociology,' says Carmody, 'especially the way it's taught here. But I do work. I work hard. You admit that in your comments on the essays. I mean, you say there's too much work and not enough analysis. But we know what that means, don't we?' 'Do we?' asks Howard. 'It means I don't see it your way,' says Carmody. 'Yes,' says Howard, 'you don't see it sociologically.' 'Not what you call sociologically,' says Carmody. 'You have a better sociology?' asks Howard, 'this Anglo-Catholic classicist-royalist stuff you import from English and want to call sociology?' 'It's an accepted form of cultural analysis,' says Carmody. 'I don't accept it,' says Howard. 'It's an arty-farty construct that isn't sociology, because it happens to exclude everything that makes up the real face of society. By which I mean poverty, racialism, inequality, sexism, imperialism, and repression, the things I expect you to consider and account for. But whatever I do, whatever topic I set you, I get this same old stuff rolled out.' 'In that case,' says Carmody, 'isn't it fairest to accept that we disagree? And perhaps move me to another sociology teacher, one who might accept that there is something in this approach?' There is sweat standing out on Carmody's brow. 'Ah, I see,' says Howard, 'you think you could get better marks from someone else. You can't con me, but you might swing it with someone else.' 'Look, Dr Kirk,' says Carmody, 'I can't ever satisfy you, I can't ever be radical enough to suit you. I have beliefs and convictions, like you. Why can't you give me a chance?'

'And what are these beliefs and convictions?' asks Howard. 'I happen to believe in individualism, not collectivism. I hate this cost-accountancy, Marxist view of man as a unit in the chain of production. I believe the superstructure is a damned sight more important than the substructure. I think culture's a value, not an inert descriptive term.' 'Beliefs, in short, incompatible with sociological analysis,' says Howard. 'I'm not moving you. You either accept some sociological principles, or you fail, and that's your choice.' Carmody's head ducks; and in the light coming into the room from behind Howard it is suddenly apparent that there is a dangerous wetness in Carmody's eyes. He reaches his hand into the pocket of his pressed trousers, takes out a very neat handkerchief, unfolds it, shakes it, and blows his nose into it. When he has done this, he looks at Howard. He says, 'Dr Kirk, you're not being either frank or fair. You know you don't like me. I don't hold the right opinions, I don't come from the right background or the right school, I don't look right for you, so you persecute me. I'm your victim in that class. You've appointed me that. And you turn everyone there against me.' Howard swings in the red chair. He says: 'No, you're self-appointed, George. Look at the way you behave. You always come in late. You never do quite what you've been asked to do. You break up the spontaneity and style of the class. If I ask you to discuss, you read; if I ask you to read, you discuss. You bore people and offend them. There's a chill round you. Why do seminars with you in them grind away into the dust? Have you ever asked why?' 'Oh, you get me every way, don't you?' asks Carmody, leaning his back against the door, 'I fit in, or I fail. And if I try to fight back, and preserve myself, well, you're my teacher, you can tear me to pieces in public, and mark my essays down in private. Can't I exist as well?' 'You can,' says Howard, 'if you're capable of changing. Of learning some human sympathy, some contact with others, some concern, some sociology.' 'You see,' says Carmody, 'it's not my work, it's me. You're marking *me*. F for fail. Why won't you say it? You just don't like me?' 'What I think of you isn't the issue,' says Howard, 'I can dislike someone's work without disliking them.' 'But it's both with me,' says Carmody, 'so why won't you let me have someone else's judgment? Someone who doesn't dislike me like this? A different teacher?' 'For the obvious reason,' says Howard, 'because I don't admit your charge. That my marking of you is unfair. That is your charge, isn't it?'

Carmody puts his head down. He says, 'I didn't come for that. You're making me say what I don't want to.' Howard gets up and looks out of the window. He asks, 'What did you come for, George?' 'I came because I've got a new tutor in English, and she looked back over all my marks and saw I was failing. I didn't know. And she told me to come and talk to you about it.' 'I presume she didn't suggest you make these accusations?' 'No,' says Carmody, 'she thought you'd help me. She doesn't know you very well, does she?' 'I don't think you do, George,' says Howard. Carmody steps forward, and puts his hands on the back of the grey chair. 'I know more about you than you think,' he says. Howard turns and looks at Carmody. 'What does that mean?' he asks. 'All right,' says Carmody, 'you're making me say this. But what do you think people outside universities would say if they knew the kinds of things you do?' 'What things?' 'Teaching politics in your classes,' says Carmody. 'Getting all the radical students to your parties, and feeling them up, and getting them involved in causes and demos, and then giving them good grades. But the ones who won't play your game, the ones like me, you give them bad grades. I've got my essays here, in my bag. I've got the things you've scribbled all over them, "pure fascism", "reactionary crap". I want to know if it's right to treat me like that, treat anyone like that.' 'You've made it quite clear now, haven't you?' says Howard, 'You *are* accusing me. Let's be explicit.' 'I don't want to,' says Carmody, 'I just want fairness.' Howard sits on his desk and looks at Carmody. He says, 'There are many things you fail to understand, George. One of them is the right to intellectual freedom.' 'I don't know how you can say that,' says Carmody, red with anger, 'doesn't that include me? Don't I get any? That's all I'm asking you for.' 'No, you're not,' says Howard, 'you're accusing me of political bias in my marking, and threatening me with exposure if I don't improve your marks. Aren't you?' Carmody stares. He says, 'Look, give me a chance. That's all I want.' 'No,' says Howard, 'you're blackmailing me. I never want to see you in my classes again.' Carmody's eyes fill with tears. 'I'm not blackmailing you,' he says quietly. 'Of course you are,' says Howard, 'I've given your work the marks it's worth, you can't accept the judgment, so you come to me, and accuse me, and threaten me, and question my fairness and competence in every possible way. We call that blackmail.'

Carmody's hands clutch on the back of the grey chair. He says: 'I was just asking for a chance. If you won't give it me, I'll have to ask Professor Marvin for it. I want someone else to read these essays, and see if these marks and comments are right and fair. That's all I want.' 'Well, you go to Professor Marvin,' says Howard. 'Make your complaint, and I'll make mine, and advise him about this blackmail attempt, and we'll see how it all comes out.' 'Christ,' says Carmody, 'I don't *want* to complain about you. You've pushed me this way.' 'But I do want to complain about you,' says Howard. Carmody bends down and picks up his briefcase. He says, 'You're crazy. This'll look just as bad for you as it does for me.' 'I don't think so,' says Howard. 'Now get out. And don't ever come to a class of mine again.' 'I think you're obscene,' says Carmody, turning and opening the door. 'George,' says Howard, 'who is your tutor in English? I'll have to advise her you're not getting any more sociology, and therefore have presumably already failed your degree.' 'You're destroying me,' says Carmody. 'I need her name,' says Howard. 'It's Miss Callendar,' says Carmody. 'Thank you,' says Howard. 'Don't bang the door when you shut it.' Carmody drags himself out of the room; the door, predictably, bangs behind him. Howard gets up off the desk, and walks to the window. After a moment he goes back to the desk chair and sits down, pulling open the second left-hand drawer of the desk, and taking out a slim book. He opens the book, finds an entry that says 'Callendar, Miss A', and opposite it a telephone number. He pulls the handset towards him, and begins to dial the number; but then a thought crosses his mind, for he stops, replaces the receiver, and gets up from the chair again. He crosses the room to his bookshelves, and finds, among the routine paperbacks on sociology, a slim Penguin. He takes it to the desk, thumbs through its pages for a while. Then he picks up the receiver, and dials Miss Callendar's number.

The telephone rings along the line; 'Callendar,' says a sharp voice at the other end. 'Hello, Callendar,' says Howard, 'Kirk.' 'Och, yes, Kirk,' says Miss Callendar, sounding very Scots, 'I've got a class in my room. I can't engage in casual conversation.' 'Oh, it's not casual,' says Howard, 'it's a serious matter of university business.' 'I see,' says Miss Callendar, cautiously, 'Of an urgent kind?' 'Very,' says Howard, 'A serious problem has arisen with one of your advisory students.' 'Could you ring me again after lunch?' asks Miss Callendar. 'I presume you take your responsibility to your students seriously?' says Howard. 'I do,' says Miss Callendar. 'I think we ought to deal with it now, then,' says Howard. 'Just a minute,' says Miss Callendar, 'I'll ask my class to step outside.' There is a small babble at the other end of the wire; then Miss Callendar returns onto the line. 'I hope this isn't part of your seductive campaign,' says Miss Callendar, 'we were right in the middle of *The Faerie Queen*.' 'I think you'll see this is serious,' says Howard. 'You have an advisee called George Carmody.' 'A big, fairhaired boy who wears a blazer?' says Miss Callendar. 'An unmistakable boy,' says Howard, 'the only student in this university with a trouser press.' 'I know him,' says Miss Callendar, with a giggle. 'You sent him to see me,' says Howard. 'I did,' says Miss Callendar, 'I saw him yesterday, for the first time, I looked through his marks, and found he was failing your course. I'm afraid he'd not seen his situation. I told him to come and talk to you. I said you'd assist him in every way possible.' 'Well, he came,' says Howard, 'and he tried to blackmail me.' 'My goodness,' says Miss Callendar, 'he wants you to leave some money in a phonebox?' 'I hope you're taking this seriously,' says Howard, 'it is serious.' 'Of course,' says Miss Callendar. 'What did he do?'

'He claimed that he was failing because I marked with a political bias,' says Howard. 'He didn't!' says Miss Callendar,

'I'm afraid that's very rude of him. I'll urge him to apologize to you.' 'That's no use,' says Howard, 'it's gone much further than that. I, of course, refused to reconsider his marks. So he proposes to see my head of department and complain.' 'I'm afraid we live in an age of dreary legalism,' says Miss Callendar. 'Isn't the best thing for us all to sit down and talk it over?' 'Oh, no,' says Howard, 'I want him to complain. I want the man to expose himself. I want him out of this university.' 'Oh, Dr Kirk,' says Miss Callendar, 'isn't that a bit harsh? Aren't we all making a mountain out of a molehill?' 'You say you don't know this man very well?' asks Howard. 'I don't,' says Miss Callendar, 'I'm new here.' 'I think I do,' says Howard. 'He's a juvenile fascist. He's both incapable and dishonest. I mark his work for what it is, totally devoid of merit; he then tries to solve his problems by accusing me of being corrupt. I think we need to make the real corruption here quite visible. It's the classic syndrome; arrogant privilege trying to preserve itself by any means once it's threatened.' 'Is it like that?' asks Miss Callendar, 'Isn't he just being rather pathetic and desperate?' 'I hope you're not excusing him,' says Howard. 'After all, he's just gone to see my professor and challenge my professional integrity.' 'Yes,' says Miss Callendar, 'but who'll believe him?' 'Oh, many would like to,' says Howard. 'Of course they daren't. He wants to destroy me; in fact he's already destroyed himself. He'll get no more sociology teaching, so he won't get a degree. And I think our regulations permit us to get rid of him.' 'You make me feel sorry for him,' says Miss Callendar. 'I thought you might feel sorry for me,' says Howard. 'Here's a student of yours putting my career at risk. I have the rights of the victim.' 'I'm sorry for both,' says Miss Callendar. 'I've been looking at his file while you're talking. His father died. He had a period of depression and psychiatric counselling. He's kept up his work well. His tutors in English and History give him quite favourable reports.' 'He said he'd been getting As and Bs in English,' says Howard, 'I find it hard to believe.' 'Well, Bs and As,' says Miss Callendar. 'He's said to have a good critical intelligence. There's a person here, and a background. Oughtn't we to go into it?'

'I don't think I want to go into it,' says Howard. 'But you do take your responsibility to your students seriously?' asks Miss

Callendar. 'What are you proposing?' asks Howard. 'Can't we talk about it?' asks Miss Callendar. 'I don't know,' says Howard. 'When?' 'I could come to your room this afternoon, or one afternoon this week,' says Miss Callendar. 'I've a department meeting today,' says Howard, 'and a very full diary.' 'Isn't there any other time?' asks Miss Callendar. 'I did ask you to have dinner with me,' says Howard, 'we could discuss it then.' 'Oh,' says Miss Callendar, 'I hope this isn't a scheme.' 'Oh, Miss Callendar,' says Howard, 'can we make it Thursday night?' 'All right,' says Miss Callendar. 'Try and be hungry,' says Howard. 'Oh, can I just check a literary reference with you?' 'My class is rioting outside,' says Miss Callendar. 'It won't take a second,' says Howard, 'I'm looking at the Penguin Poets *William Blake*, page 98, "Proverbs of Heaven and Hell". Here's a quotation from the Proverbs of Hell: "Sooner murder an infant in its cradle than nurse unacted desires".' 'Yes,' says Miss Callendar, 'what's your question?' 'How you came to reverse it when we talked this morning?' 'Ah,' says Miss Callendar, 'I did it via the instrument of literary criticism.' 'This is your good critical intelligence,' says Howard. 'That's it,' says Miss Callendar, 'you see, I was offering a paraphrase of its implicit as opposed to its surface meaning. You see, read the lines carefully, and you'll find the fulcrum is a pun around the words "infant" and "nurse". The infant and the desires are the same. So it doesn't mean kill babies if you really have to. It means it's better to kill desires than nourish ones you can never satisfy.' 'I see,' says Howard, 'so that's what you people do over there in English. I've often wondered.' 'I'm only saying it's not the seducer's charter you took it for,' says Miss Callendar, 'and as for an interest in the substructure, I don't think that's confined to English.' 'It's hardly the same substructure,' says Howard. 'We're concerned with exposing the true reality, not with compounding ambiguity.' 'It must be nice to think there is a true reality,' says Miss Callendar, 'I've always found reality a matter of great debate.' 'Well, we obviously disagree,' says Howard, 'you keep your Blake, and I'll keep mine. You may find mine has something to offer.' 'I doubt it,' says Miss Callendar, 'but to quote again from the same source, "Opposition is true Friendship". Goodbye, Dr Kirk.'

Howard hears the telephone click at the other end; he puts

down the receiver. He gets out his diary, and makes a note in it; Miss Callendar, Thursday, dinner. As soon as he has finished doing this, the telephone rings again. 'It's Minnehaha Ho,' says the voice, 'Professor Marvin for you, Howard.' The equipment clicks; there are mumblings; another voice says 'Howard?' 'Hello, Professor Marvin,' says Howard. 'Ah,' says Marvin, 'are you, er, alone?' 'I am,' says Howard. 'Good,' says Marvin, 'I've got here a matter of exceptional delicacy.' 'Oh, yes?' says Howard. 'A student of yours has just been to see me,' says Marvin, 'I've just had a very tearful session with him.' 'I take it the tears were his?' asks Howard. 'Oh, yes,' says Marvin. 'His name is Carmody.' 'Ah,' says Howard, 'I was just going to ring you about him. To lodge a formal complaint.' 'Oh, dear, dear,' says Marvin. 'He was complaining about you, you see. He thinks you've marked him rather harshly.' 'Did he tell you he'd attempted to blackmail me?' asks Howard. 'No,' says Marvin, 'he didn't say that. He did say that you and he didn't get on, and that he'd like to be taught by someone else.' 'He doesn't seem to have told you very much at all,' says Howard. 'He's failing, of course, and he wanted his marks raised. His way of trying to obtain this was not by doing passing work, the way of most of our students. No, he was going to expose the political bias of my teaching, unless I cooperated. He visited you because I didn't.' 'Oh,' says Marvin. 'Um, um.' 'I hope you kicked him out,' says Howard. 'No, I didn't kick him out,' says Marvin, 'I gave him a glass of sherry.' 'I see,' says Howard. 'He told you he wasn't satisfied with my marking, so you sat him down and gave him sherry.' 'Yes,' says Marvin. 'As head of department, I think I have a duty to do him the fairness of listening.' 'To unfair nonsense,' says Howard. 'He came with a sense of injustice,' says Marvin, 'I felt it my duty to explain to him how we work here. The concept of academic disinterestedness.' 'I hope that impressed him,' says Howard. 'If so, it would be the first concept he'd ever grasped.'

'Can you kindly tell me how this situation has got this far?' asks Marvin, 'He tells me you refuse to teach him.' 'I do,' says Howard, 'I don't teach blackmailers.' 'Oh, look, Howard,' says Marvin, 'can't we resolve this as between gentlemen?' 'How do you think we should do that?' asks Howard. 'He accepts his grades,' says Marvin, 'you take him back, and do all you can to bring his work up to passing level.' 'You may be a gentleman,' says Howard, 'but he isn't, and in another sense nor am I. I come with a sense of injustice too. He made a corrupt accusation, and I won't teach him.' 'Then I'll have to move him to someone else,' says Marvin. 'Oh, no,' says Howard, 'I can't accept that either.' 'I don't understand,' says Marvin, 'someone has to teach him.' 'No,' says Howard, 'I want him banned from the department. I want him disciplined.' 'Howard,' says Marvin, 'I hoped we could cope with this informally. You're forcing an issue.' 'Yes,' says Howard, 'it is an issue.' 'There are two sides to every case,' says Marvin, 'I shall have to listen to his.' 'But there aren't two sides to every case,' says Howard, 'you'll just sink into your liberal mess, if you accept that.' 'I have to accept it,' says Marvin, 'I shall need both your complaints in writing, please. And then I shall have to read those disputed essays.' 'That won't help,' says Howard. 'I think it might,' says Marvin. 'No,' says Howard, 'why should your judgment be better than mine? In any case, the marks aren't just for what he's written. We try to take everything into account here, don't we? Isn't it our ideal to judge the man in as many ways as possible?' 'I agree we try in marking to take some account of seminar performance,' says Marvin, 'I shall take that into consideration. But I have to read those essays. Unless, of course, you think there's still an informal solution?' 'Oh, no,' says Howard, 'by all means, let's have an issue.' 'That doesn't delight me,' says Marvin, 'it can only open many doors better kept shut.' 'I'd like them open,' says Howard. 'I've never understood your taste for confrontation,' says Marvin. 'As Blake says,' says Howard, ' "Opposition is true friendship".' 'I haven't noticed the note of friendship,' says Marvin, 'but so be it.' The telephone goes down at the other end. Howard replaces his receiver; then he walks to the window, and looks out, with pleased regard, on the wet campus.

IX

'It's a very serious issue,' says Roger Fundy, excavating into a jacketed baked potato filled with false cream, 'it's the ultimate test of whether sociology is a relevant subject.' 'Ah, what's that?' asks Dr Zachery, the micro-sociologist, a small man who works on small problems, approaching the table in his wool hat, carrying his tray, 'I've been looking for such a test for a very long time.' 'You're a reactionary, you wouldn't know an issue if you saw one,' says Fundy, 'I'm talking about the visit of Mangel.' 'The visit of Mangel?' says Zachery, sitting down and taking off his hat. 'There's no visit of Mangel.' 'A departmental memo just came round to say that Mangel's coming here to speak,' says Moira Millikin, at the further end of the table, peering down into her baby's carrycot, which lies in the aisle where the students pass back and forth. 'You know, I already had four food contacts today already,' says Melissa Todoroff, a strong-minded American lady who is at Watermouth on a year's leave from Hunter College, here to study English women, 'can anyone do me a quick calory count on this hunk of steak-and-kidney pie?' 'Mangel the geneticist?' asks Howard Kirk, sitting in the precise middle of the table, and looking about with innocent curiosity. 'Mangel the racist,' says Fundy. 'He studies the genetics of race,' says Flora Beniform, at the end of the table, 'I don't think that makes him a racist.' 'I thought we'd driven biological explanation right out of sociology,' says Moira Millikin, 'I thought we were through with all that shit.'

'Hey, any of you kids into *I Ching* yet?' asks Melissa Todoroff. 'You've also driven sin and evil right out of sociology,' says Flora Beniform, 'which doesn't prove there's no sin.' 'I'm all for making the subject as economical as possible,' says Dr Macintosh, 'it does mean less work.' 'A serious and well-known scholar,' says Zachery, 'very distinguished work.' 'It's obscene,' says Moira Millikin. 'Jesus Christ was a Capricorn,' says Melissa Todoroff, 'what's your sign, honey?' 'I'm a little bewildered, I think,' says Zachery, 'we believe in differentiation by class, and promote those for the tension they create. Yet not the racial ones. Now, how is that?' 'Class is cultural, race is genetic,' says Moira Millikin. 'I don't believe in astral influence,' says Dr Macintosh, 'in any case it gives an advantage to people whose mothers have good memories.' 'Of course, Flora,' says Howard, 'you know Mangel. You worked with him at the Tavvy at one time, didn't you?' 'Yes, I did, Howard,' says Flora, 'I worked in social anthropology with him. He's a fat, ugly man, he smells of borscht, he's serious and liberal, he believes we have a biology, which most of us here actually do, like it or not, and he's certainly not a racist.' 'It's all been exposed by the radical press,' says Moira Millikin, 'all that tradition. Jensen, Eysenck, Mangel. It's all been shown to be racist.' 'Don't you believe in *anything*, honey?' asks Melissa Todoroff. 'We can't have him, we've got to stop him,' says Roger Fundy.

The sociologists are sitting at a large plastic table, taking lunch, under the domed plexiglass and flexiglass of Kaakinen's university cafeteria. Students talk, girls yelp, babies squall. The great fancy room towers above them, a thing here of stark places, there of wild Scandinavian frenzies. Such is the detail of design that the very food they eat seems converted into artefact: Jackson Pollock hash, Mondrian fried eggs, Graham Sutherland chicken leg are followed by David Hockney ice cream and Norman Rockwell apple pie. The sociologists eat off their trays; as they eat, they examine, with formal solemnity, the agendas for their coming meeting, turning over the stencilled pages, lifting a bean or a sausage, passing from main agenda to supplementary agenda to document A and document L and document Y, moving from egg to yoghurt. At the time when he conceived the refectory facilities at Watermouth,

Kaakinen was taken by a great, democratic dream; deeply mindful of the social symbolism of eating, he was determined at a stroke to remove those distinctions between senior and junior common-room which privatize the essential communion of food, and so have the formal effect of separating, in some root way, the student from his teacher. Instead, therefore, Kaakinen invented prandial community; he made rooms, and corners of rooms, where, under one roof, in democratic babble, every sort of social mixture might occur. Thus, as the fancy takes you, you might sit over there, among rubber plants, with a view through thick leaves straight out over the artificial lake, and eat in some grandeur, at some expense; or you might sit over here, in a place of purity and simple functionalism, where, with specially designed plastic forks that look like spoons, and knives that look like forks, you may, having waited in the cafeteria line, practise contemporary eating of contemporary, plastic-wrapped food at a most modest cost. This of course, has the informal effect of separating the student from his teacher; it is the faculty who sit among the rubber plants, eating *oeufs en plat* and *pommes frites à la chef*; the students sit at the plastic tables, with their plastic implements, eating their egg and chips.

But in these matters the sociologists, in so many things the exception, are the exception. The sociology students eat in the expensive section, in order to express indignation; the sociology faculty eat in the cheap one, in order to maintain the egalitarian spirit, and save a penny or two at the same time. And today, because it is the day of the departmental meeting, there are many of them, along the long table which is somehow, historically, *their* table; they consume, simultaneously, the food and the agenda; they examine both with critical expressions. For, over time, the food has grown less, in quantity and quality, as economic rot sets in; meanwhile the agenda has grown longer, as bureaucratic growth occurs. They eat with dislike; they read with rue. There are two kinds of rue. There are some of them who inspect the documents as a diary of necessary or even unnecessary boredom, a poor way to spend an afternoon, a routine plod through matters of budgets and parties, SSRC research grants and examinations; there are some with higher criticism to offer, who read the agenda with an energetic scepticism, as one would read a contract from a hire-purchase company, looking in the fine print for errors, enormities, evasions, the entire sphere of the unsaid.

'I think some of us are missing the entire point,' says Roger Fundy to the table. 'The point is that genetics isn't an innocuous science. It's a highly charged area, with deep social implications, and you have to protect your conclusions from having racialist overtones.' 'Oh, yes?' asks Dr Zachery. 'Even if that means falsifying the results?' 'If necessary, yes,' says Moira Millikin. 'Extraordinary,' says Dr Zachery. 'I think this is meant for me,' says Flora. 'Look, Roger, have you ever known me think that anything was innocuous? It's against my nature. But I know Mangel. He knows the dangers as well as you do. He happens to be a serious scientist. He's never over-stated his conclusions, and I don't agree that any results should ever be falsified. He'd like them to come out your way as much as I would, but when they come out they come out.' 'Why do you think all the radical press is attacking him? They know what they're doing,' says Moira Millikin. 'I'm sure of that,' says Dr Zachery, 'but they're not doing what we should be doing, protecting disinterested research.' 'There was a pregnant woman on the bus today,' says Dr Macintosh, 'funny how once your wife's pregnant you see them everywhere.' 'We're all responsible for our conclusions,' says Roger Fundy, 'because all mental organizations are ideological in significance. Which means that it is we who organize the results, not science.' 'I got up to offer her my seat,' says Dr Macintosh, 'and then I suddenly realized that in this radical climate there's no way to address her. Finally I said: "Excuse me, person, would you like to sit down?".' 'But even that's patronage,' says Melissa Todoroff, 'why shouldn't she stand up like anyone else?' 'Which item on the agenda does Mangel come under?' asks Flora Beniform. 'I'd burn mine,' says Melissa Todoroff, 'you could say I have, symbolically. But I jiggle and hurt whenever I run upstairs.' 'Item 17,' says Moira Millikin, 'visiting speakers. That's when the fun should start.'

A very loud crash comes from the direction of the self-service line. The sociologists' heads all turn; in the line, someone, a bandaged person, has dropped an entire tray and its contents. 'Oh, God,' says Flora, 'it's Henry.' Henry Beamish stands transfixed in the line, with yoghurt all over his trousers;

a skilful student blocks with his feet a rolling roll. 'My God,'
says Howard, 'he's come.' Flora rises wearily from her chair:
'I'll go and collect him some more food,' she says. 'Of course
Henry would elect to carry a tray when he had only one
available hand.' 'What's happened to Henry?' asks Moira
Millikin. 'Didn't you know?' asks Dr Macintosh, 'he gashed his
arm on a window last night. At Howard's.' 'Oh, did he?' says
Moira Millikin. 'Jesus, it's terrible,' says Melissa Todoroff, 'I
lost my IUD someplace, and ten whole weeks of term still to
go.' 'God, I can't bear to look,' says Moira Millikin, for Henry,
apparently acting under Flora's orders, has made his way to
the end of the self-service line, where there is a turnstile, to keep
count of consumers, and he is now attempting to push through
it, moving steadfastly in the wrong direction. 'He shouldn't be
here,' says Macintosh, 'what's he coming in for a meeting like
this for?' 'No doubt he's sensed that great issues are at stake,'
says Dr Zachery drily. 'Isn't that nice of Flora?' says Henry,
coming up to the end of the table, where he stands, his arm in a
white sling, beaming at his colleagues, with his usual pointless
congeniality and air of detachment. 'Everyone's so kind.'
'Ah, Henry,' says Howard, rising, so that his chair catches
Henry's foot. 'I could have managed, of course,' says Henry, 'I
was balancing well, but someone turned and caught my tray
with a flutecase.' 'How are you?' asks Howard. 'I'm pretty
well, Howard,' says Henry, 'it was just a cut, you know. I'm
terribly sorry about that window. And the fuss, too. I hope you
got my message?' 'You look very pale,' says Howard, 'you
shouldn't have come in.' 'Oh, I couldn't miss a departmental
meeting,' says Henry, 'not a departmental meeting. There are
some things on this agenda which are of serious concern to me.'
'It's excessive devotion, Henry,' says Flora, coming up with
a tray, 'and I can't believe your presence will make much
difference on an occasion like this. I'll put your tray here.' 'Oh,
Flora,' says Henry, 'Myra and I both want to say thank you
very much indeed. You were marvellous last night. She was
marvellous.' Henry bends over Flora a little; he says, in a loud
quiet voice, 'Myra had drunk rather a lot, and wasn't at her
best. So she really appreciates the way you stepped in and saw
to things.' 'She should,' says Flora. 'Yes,' says Henry, and leans
over Dr Macintosh, 'and she wanted me to thank you for

bringing her home. How's the wife?' 'Not delivered yet,' says Macintosh. 'They think now it's a false labour. It could go on for weeks.' 'Oh, they'll induce,' says Moira Millikin. 'It's an awful pest for you,' says Henry, 'if we can do anything . . .' 'The best thing you can do, Henry,' says Flora, 'is sit down and eat.' Henry draws out a chair, next to Howard's; he seats himself unevenly on it. 'Whoops,' he says. 'Oh, they're just some psychiatric friends of mine who live in Washington,' says Melissa Todoroff. 'He was her analyst until they got married, but now she's being analysed by her ex-husband.' Henry leans over to Howard and says, 'I see there's a note to say that Mangel's coming to lecture. That's good, isn't it? Marvellous man.' 'Except that he's a fascist,' says Roger Fundy. 'A who?' asks Henry. 'Oh, it's some great big apartment block called Watergate,' says Melissa. 'I don't know where it is, somewhere around, it's in the book.' 'Look, Howard,' says Henry, 'I wonder whether we could have a little talk, after the meeting. Let me buy you a drink.' 'Of course, Henry,' says Howard. 'Something to discuss,' says Henry, 'didn't see much of you last night.' 'Yes, fine,' says Howard. 'I'll pick you up after,' says Henry. 'Who else could have asked him?' asks Roger Fundy. 'It has to be Marvin.'

'Unfortunately I remember I've no car,' says Henry. 'We'll go in mine,' says Howard. 'I'll have to leave around six thirty,' says Henry, 'Myra's cooking steak. I think there's a bus.' 'I'll drive you home,' says Howard. 'How did you get in?' 'You see, I can't drive with this sling on,' says Henry, 'and Myra has a headache. Get in? I hitchhiked in a lorry.' 'Sure he'll be elected,' says Melissa Todoroff, 'these are hard times for America, they call for special talents.' 'I'm sorry I couldn't stop to the end last night,' says Henry. 'What time did you finish?' 'Yeah, we need a special kind of little twisted guy, with no talents or values, who doesn't trust anyone and nobody trusts. He'll get in.' 'About four,' says Howard. 'I don't know how you manage it,' says Henry, admiringly. 'It's the politics of Parkinson's Law,' says Melissa Todoroff, 'shit spreads to cover the area of the stable floor.' 'It would tire me out,' says Henry, 'you can't keep up the pace when you get to my age.' 'Your age is exactly my age,' says Howard. Henry, digging with a plastic fork in one hand into something gelatinous on his plate, looks at Howard: 'I suppose it is,' he says. 'How's your caucus, Roger?' asks Melissa Todoroff. 'I think we've fixed him on item 17,' says Roger. 'Come on, it's nearly two o'clock.' The sociologists push back their chairs, and begin to rise, except for Henry. 'Bring it with you, Henry,' says Howard. 'Oh, I couldn't,' says Henry, getting unevenly up. They walk, a small procession, out of the cafeteria, and across the Piazza, as students watch them: Moira leads with her carrycot, and Henry brings up the rear, with his sling. With that air of special seriousness a meeting confers, they enter the lift in the Social Science Building, and rise up in it to the very top of the construction. At the top, in penthouse style, and with distractingly good views over and beyond the campus to the fields and the sea, is the place of the afternoon's encounter, the Durkheim Room.

It is a long, thin chamber preserved only for conference purposes; as a result a certain dignity, a spacious seriousness, has been attempted. On two sides there are long glass windows, giving onto the distractingly good views; to prevent these being distracting, white slatted Venetian blinds have been hung, and these are dropped now, and will clatter ceaselessly throughout the afternoon's deliberations. The other two walls are pure and white and undecorated, conscious aids to contemplation, save that in one spot a large abstract painting, conceived by a nakedly frantic sensibility, opens a large, obsessive hole into inner chaos. The architect and his design consultant, a man of many awards, have exercised themselves considerably in conceiving and predicating the meetings that would come to be held here. For the long central space of the room, they have chosen an elaborate, table-like construct which has a bright orange top and many thin, brushed-chrome legs; they have surrounded this with a splendid vista of forty white vinyl high-backed chairs. Three more chairs with somewhat higher backs and the university's crest embossed into the vinyl designate the head of the table. On the floor is a serious, undistracting brown carpet; on the ceiling, an elaborate acoustical muffle. Minnehaha Ho, Professor Marvin's secretary, has been diligent during the morning; she has put before every place a large, leather-edged blotter, a notepad, and copies of the department's prospectus and the university's calendar and regulations, their covers all backed out in the official design colours of the university, which are indigo and puce. In the original masterplan, Danish grey-glass ashtrays had been provided for each place; but the room has seen a fair incidence of sit-ins, and the ashtrays have been stolen, and replaced by many one-ounce Player's Whiskey tobacco tins, retrieved from the wastepaper basket of Dr Zachery. Someone has sprayed the room with scented deodorant, and emptied these ashtrays. All stands in its committee dignity; the meeting, then, is ready to begin.

When the party from the cafeteria arrives, Professor Marvin, who is always early, is there already, in the central high chair, his back to one of the windows. A row of pens is in his top pocket; an annotated agenda lies between his two hairy hands on the blotter before him. To the left of his left hand is a stack of files, the record of all recent past meetings, bound in hard-loop bindings; to the right of his right hand is a small carafe of water. On his left sits Minnehaha Ho, who will take the minutes; on his right sits his administrative assistant, Benita Pream, who has before her many more files, and a small alarm clock. At the top of the long row of chairs where the faculty sit there is, on Marvin's left, Professor Debison, a man rarely seen, except in meetings such as this. His field is Overseas Studies, and overseas is where he most often is, as the fresh BOAC and SAS tags on his worn brown briefcase, laid on the table before him, indicate. Dr Zachery, by custom, takes the place opposite; he goes up the long room and sits down. It is his boast that on one such occasion he read the entirety of Talcott Parsons' *The Social System*, no mean feat; he has now prepared for the afternoon by placing here a backfile of bound volumes of the *British Journal of Sociology*; he is head-down at once, flicking over pages with practised hand and putting in slips to mark articles relevant to his micro-sociological scheme of things. Beside him, resting informally across a chair, there is already present one of the six student representatives, who always sit together as a caucus; he passes time usefully by inspecting photographs of female crotches in a magazine. The room fills up; the sociologists and social psychologists, sophisticates of meetings, readers of Goffman who all know intimately the difference between a group and an encounter, who are expert in the dynamics of interaction, come in and pick their places with care, examining existing relationships, angles of vision, even the cast of the light. Finally the elaborate social construct is ready. Marvin sits at the head of the table, in that curious state of suspended animation appropriate to the moment before the start of a meeting. Outside, pile-drivers thump, and dumper-trucks roar; inside is a severe, expectant curiosity.

Then the alarm clock of Benita Pream, the administrative assistant, pings; Professor Marvin coughs very loudly and waves his arms. He looks up and down the long table, and says:'Can we now come to order, gentlemen?' Immediately the silence breaks; many arms go up, all round the table; there is a jabber of voices. 'May I point out, Mr Chairperson, that of the persons in this room you are addressing as "gentlemen", seven are women?' says Melissa Todoroff. 'May I suggest the formulation "Can we come to order, persons?" or perhaps "Can we come to order, colleagues?" ' 'Doesn't the phrase itself suggest we're somehow normally in a state of *dis*order?' asks Roger Fundy. 'Can I ask whether under Standing Orders of Senate we are bound to terminate this meeting in three and a half hours? And, if so, whether the Chairman thinks an agenda of thirty-four items can be seriously discussed under those limitations, especially since my colleagues will presumably want to take tea?' 'On a point of information, Mr Chairman, may I point out that the tea interval is not included within the three and a half hour limitation, and also draw Dr Petworth's attention to the fact that we have concluded discussion of longer agendas in shorter times?' 'Here?' asks someone. 'May I ask if it is the wish of this meeting that we should have a window open?' The meeting has started; and it is always so. It has often been remarked, by Benita Pream, who services several such departmental meetings, that those in History are distinguished by their high rate of absenteeism, those in English by the amount of wine consumed afterwards, and those in Sociology by their contentiousness. The pile-drivers thump outside; the arguments within continue. The sociologists, having read Goffman, know there is a role of Chairman, and a role of Argumentative Person, and a role of Silent Person; they know how situations are made, and how they can be leaked, and how dysphoria can be induced; they put their knowledge to the test in such situations as this. Benita Pream's alarm has pinged at 14.00

hours, according to her own notes; it is 14.20 before the meeting has decided how long it is to continue, and whether it is quorate, and if it should have the window open, and 14.30 before Professor Marvin has managed to sign the minutes of the last meeting, so that they can begin on item 1 of the agenda of this one, which concerns the appointment of external examiners for finals: 'An uncontentious item, I think,' says Professor Marvin.

It is 15.05 before the uncontentious item is resolved. Nobody likes the two names proposed by Professor Marvin. But their dissents are founded on such radically different premises that no two other names can be proposed from the meeting and agreed upon. A working party is suggested, to bring names to the next meeting; no one can agree on the membership of the working party. A select committee of the department is proposed, to suggest names for the members of the working party; no one can agree on the membership of the select committee. A recommendation that Senate be asked to nominate the members of the select committee who will nominate the members of the working party who will make proposals for nominations so that the departmental meeting can nominate the external examiners is defeated, on the grounds that this would be external interference from Senate in the affairs of the department: even though, as the chair points out, the department cannot in any case nominate external examiners, but only recommend names to Senate, who will nominate them. A motion that the names of the two external examiners originally recommended be put again is put, and accepted. The names are put again, and rejected. A motion that there be no external examiners is put, and rejected. Two ladies in blue overalls come in with cups of tea and a plate of biscuits, and place cups in front of all the people present. A proposal that, since the agenda is moving slowly, discussion continue during tea is put and accepted, with one abstainer, who takes his cup of tea outside and drinks it there. The fact that tea has come without an item settled appears to have some effect: a motion that Professor Marvin be allowed to make his own choice of external examiners, acting on behalf of the department, is put and accepted. Professor Marvin promptly indicates that he will recommend to Senate the two names originally mentioned, an hour before; and then he moves onto the next item.

155

'A rather contentious item,' he says, introducing a proposal that the number of student representatives be increased from six to eight. The six students already there, most of them in sweatshirts, breathe hard, look fierce, lean their heads together; they separate to discover that there has been no discussion, and that the item, presumably in weariness, has been passed immediately. The tea-ladies come in to remove the cups. Trading on success, the student representatives propose that membership of the department meeting be further expanded, to include representatives from the tea-ladies. The motion is put and passed. Benita Pream, the administrative assistant, intervenes here, whispering first in Marvin's ear, then addressing the meeting; she states that under regulations the tea-ladies are not entitled to membership of department meetings. The meeting passes a recommendation urging Senate to change regulations in order to permit tea-ladies to serve on department meetings. The resolution and the preceding one are both ruled out of order from the chair, on the ground that neither refers to any item on the agenda of the meeting. A resolution that items not on the agenda of the meeting be allowed is proposed, but is ruled out of order on the grounds that it is not on the agenda of the meeting. A resolution that the chair be held out of order because it has allowed two motions to come to the vote which are not, according to standing orders, on the agenda of the meeting is refused from the chair, on the grounds that the chair cannot allow motions to come to the vote which are not, according to standing orders, on the agenda of the meeting. Outside it rains a great deal, and the level of the lake rises considerably.

'Are all your meetings this boring?' asks Melissa Todoroff, who will later be discovered not to be entitled to be in the meeting at all, since she is only a visitor, and will be asked to leave, and will do so, shouting. 'Don't worry,' whispers Howard, 'this is just a preliminary skirmish. It will warm up later.' It warms up, in fact, shortly after 17.05, when it is beginning to go dark, and when Professor Marvin reaches item 17, which is concerned with Visiting Speakers. 'A noncontroversial item, I think,' says Professor Marvin. 'A few proposed names here, I think we can accept them.' Roger Fundy raises his hand and says, 'Can I ask the chair under

whose auspices the invitation to Professor Mangel was issued?'
The chair looks bewildered: it says, 'Professor Mangel? As far
as I know, Dr Fundy, no invitation has been issued to Professor
Mangel.' 'Can I draw the chair's attention to the departmental
memo, circulated this very morning, which states that Professor
Mangel has been asked here to give a lecture?' 'I sent out no
such departmental memo,' says the chair. 'I have here a copy
of the departmental memo which the chair says it did not send
out,' says Roger Fundy. 'Perhaps the chair would like to see it.'
The chair would; it inspects the memo, and turns to Minnehaha
Ho. 'It was on the dictaphone,' says Miss Ho, with wide
oriental eyes, 'so I sent it out.' 'It was on the dictaphone so
you sent it out?' murmurs Professor Marvin, 'I didn't put it on
the dictaphone.' 'Can I ask the Chairperson,' says Melissa
Todoroff, 'if that person is aware that this invitation will be
seen by all non-Caucasians and women on this campus as a
deliberate insult to their genetic origins?' 'This is trouble,
man,' says one of the student representatives, 'he's a racist and
a sexist.' Professor Marvin looks around in some mystification.
'Professor Mangel is to my knowledge neither a racist nor a
sexist, but a very well-qualified geneticist,' he says. 'However,
since we have not invited him here the question seems scarcely
to arise on this agenda.' 'In view of the opinion of the chair
that Mangel is neither a racist nor a sexist,' says Howard, 'would
that mean that the Chair would be prepared to invite him to
this campus, if his name were proposed?' 'It isn't proposed,'
says Marvin. 'The point is that Professor Mangel's work is
fascist, and we've no business to confirm that by inviting him
here,' says Moira Millikin. 'I had always thought the dis-
tinguishing mark of fascism was its refusal to tolerate free
enquiry, Dr Millikin,' says Marvin, 'but the question needs no
discussion, since there's no proposal to invite this man. I doubt if
we could ever agree on such an invitation. It would be an issue.'
    'May I ask why?' asks Dr Zachery, the *British Journal of
Sociology* forgotten. 'Why?' asks Fundy. 'Do you know what the
consequences of inviting that man would be? One doesn't
tolerate . . .' 'But that is just what one does,' says Dr Zachery.
'One tolerates. May I propose, and I think this is in order,
since the agenda permits us to make suggestions for visiting
speakers, that we issue a formal invitation from this department

to Professor Mangel, to come and speak to this department?'
There is much noise around the table; Howard sits silent, so
silent that Flora Beniform leans over to him and murmurs,
'Don't I see a hand at work here?' 'Ssshh,' says Howard, 'this
is a serious issue.' 'You wish to put that as a motion?' asks
Marvin, looking at Zachery. 'I do,' says Zachery, 'and I
should like to speak to my motion. I observe, among some of
my younger colleagues, perhaps less experienced in recent
history than some of us, a real ignorance of the state of affairs
we are discussing. Professor Mangel and myself have a background in common; we are both Jewish, and both grew up in
Nazi Germany, and fled here from the rise of fascism. I think
we know the meaning of this term. Fascism, and the associated
genocide, arose because a climate developed in Germany in
which it was held that all intellectual activity conform with an
accepted, approved ideology. To make this happen, it was
necessary to make a climate in which it became virtually
impossible to think, or exist, outside the dominant ideological
construct. Those who did were isolated, as now some of our
colleagues seek to isolate Professor Mangel.' There are many
murmurs round the table from the sociologists, all of whom are
deeply conscious of having definitions of fascism they too could
give, if asked. 'May I continue?' asks Zachery. 'Fascism is
therefore an elegant sociological construct, a one-system world.
Its opposite is contingency or pluralism or liberalism. That
means a chaos of opinion and ideology; there are people who
find that hard to endure. But in the interests of it, I think we
must ask Professor Mangel to come here and lecture.'
'Then you'll get your chaos all right, if he does,' says Fundy.
'You know what the radical feeling is about this. You know
what uproar and violent protest there always is when someone
like Jensen or Eysenck is invited to lecture at a university. The
same will happen with Mangel.' 'Justified violence and protest,'
says Moira Millikin. 'I'm extremely disturbed, Mr Chairman,'
says Dr Macintosh, 'to see so many of my colleagues stopping
us from inviting someone we haven't even invited.' But now
there is much shouting across the table, and Professor Marvin
has to stand, and bang his wodge of files down hard onto the
desk in front of him, before something like silence returns.
'Gentlemen!' he shouts. 'Persons!' 'Oh, Howard, Howard,

is this you?' whispers Flora. 'Flora,' whispers back Howard. 'Stop taking the plane to bits once it's left the ground.' 'You're playing games,' whispers Flora. 'I've not spoken,' says Howard. Professor Marvin, now, has resumed his seat. He waits for full quietness, and then he says: 'Well, Dr Zachery has proposed a motion, which is now on the table, that we in this department of Social Studies issue an invitation to Professor Mangel to come and lecture here. Does that motion have a seconder?' 'Go on, Flora,' whispers Howard; Flora puts her hand up. 'Oh,' says Marvin, 'well, let me briefly note that this issue could become a bone of severe contention, and remind the department of the experience of other universities who have ventured in this unduly charged area, before I put the motion to the vote. Let us be cautious in our actions, cautious but just. Now may we vote. Those in favour?' The hands go up around the table; Benita Pream rises to count them. 'And those against?' Another group of hands, some waving violently, go up; Benita Pream rises once more to count these. She writes the results down on a piece of paper, and slips this over the table top to Marvin, who looks at it. 'Well,' he says, 'this motion has been carried. By eleven votes to ten. I'm sure that's just, but I'm afraid we've committed ourselves to a real bone of contention.' There is uproar at the table. 'Castrate all sexists,' shouts Melissa Todoroff; and it is now that, on a point of order from Dr Petworth, a constitutional spirit dedicated to such precisions as points of order, it is discovered that Miss Todoroff is not, as a visitor, formally a member of this meeting at all, and therefore has been voting without entitlement, and so she is taken from the room, shouting, 'Sisters, rebel,' and, 'Off the pigs'. The table settles; Howard's hand goes up; 'Mr Chairman,' he says, 'may I point out that the vote just taken—and passed by only one vote—is now clearly invalid, since Miss Todoroff's should not have been cast.' 'I had seen that constitutional point, Dr Kirk,' says Marvin. 'I'm afraid it leaves us in a very difficult position. You see, that applies not only to the last vote, but to all the votes taken throughout the meeting. Unless we can see a way round it, we may have to start this entire meeting from the beginning again.'

There are groans and shouts; Benita Pream, meanwhile, has been fumbling through papers; now she whispers a brief

something into the ear of the chair. The chair says: 'Oh, good.'
There is still much noise in the room, so Marvin taps the table.
'I feel quite sure,' he says, 'my colleagues will bear with me if I
say that it is undesirable to re-run this entire meeting. It now
appears that this is the only motion today which was passed on
a margin of one vote. With the consent of the meeting, I will
assume all other votes satisfactory. Do I have that?' The
sociologists, weary from the fray, agree. 'Now our last vote,' says
Marvin. 'As your chairman, I have to consider the position here
very carefully. Do we happen to know the way Dr Todoroff
voted?' 'It seemed to me rather obvious,' says Dr Zachery,
'from her comments on leaving.' 'That's injustice,' says Moira
Millikin, 'a ballot should be secret. When one individual's
vote can be singled out in this way, the system's wrong.' 'I
think there may be another way to answer this,' says Marvin,
looking at another note from Benita Pream. 'I think I've
resolved it, I hope to the satisfaction of this meeting.' The
meeting looks about itself; it does not have the air of a group
easily satisfied. 'If Dr Todoroff had voted against the motion,'
says Marvin, 'and we simply subtracted her vote, that would
leave the voting as eleven to nine, with the motion carried.
Do we agree?' The meeting agrees. 'If, on the other hand, she
had voted for the motion, and her vote was subtracted, that
would give us a tie, at ten ten. But in the event of such a tie,
I as chairman would have had to use my casting vote. In the
circumstances, and only because of the circumstances, as a
pure matter of procedure and not of preference, I would have
had to vote for the motion. Either way, therefore, the motion
may be presumed to be carried.'

There is once again much uproar. 'Wishy-washy liberal
equivocation,' shouts Moira Millikin, while her baby squawks
by her chair. 'A crime against mankind,' says Roger Fundy.
'I can only tell you, Dr Fundy,' says Marvin, 'that I do
not myself greatly relish the idea of Mangel visiting this
campus. Not because what has been said about him seems to
me true, but because we as a department do much better
without these contentious situations. But this has been forced
on me, and there was no other way procedurally for justice to
be done.' 'A reactionary reason,' says Moira Millikin. 'Justice!'
cried Roger Fundy. 'Democratic justice is clear injustice.'

'You always seem to find it convenient when it is in your favour,' says Marvin. This generates much more uproar, through which come many shouts for the vote to be retaken, and the level of the lake outside continues to rise, and the darkness increases beyond the big windows with their rattling blinds. The dumper-trucks have stopped; the pile-drivers have been put away; but, high in the dark, the lights of the Durkheim Room shine bright. The meeting goes on, and then, at 17.30, there is a loud ping of Benita Pream's alarm clock, and it is over. Or almost over, for even now they have to consider a proposal that, since there has been no tea interval, a notional time should be set for the actual consumption of the tea and the biscuits; it is this spot of notional time that is finally used to justify the fact that the meeting has gone on a few minutes longer in order to consider whether it should go on a few minutes longer. The sociologists rise and disperse; Professor Debison, who has not spoken at all, hurries off to his taxi, which will take him straight to Heathrow; in the corridor outside the Durkheim Room, caucuses huddle and discuss coming upheaval. 'You were very quiet,' says Flora Beniform to Howard, as they leave the room. 'Well,' says Howard, 'some of these bones of contention are very hard to resolve.' 'You've never had that trouble before,' says Flora. 'You want Mangel. You want a fight.'

'Who, me?' asks Howard, innocently, as they get into the lift. They stand there, waiting for the doors to close. 'I've got a babysitter,' says Howard. 'I see,' says Flora, and reaches in her bag, and gets out her diary, and deletes from the page marked with a thread a word that says: 'Provisionally'. 'Secret assignation?' asks Henry Beamish, getting into the lift, his arm sticking out stiffly before him, 'Well, Howard, that was very enjoyable. I'm glad I took the trouble to come. There were some issues there that greatly concerned me.' 'Were there, Henry?' asks Flora. 'What were those?' 'The question of the grant for research into senile delinquency,' says Henry. 'We can really move forward on that one now.' 'Did we discuss that?' asks Flora. 'Flora, you weren't attending,' says Henry, 'it was one of the most important items. I thought we'd have a battle over it, but it went straight through without discussion. I suppose people see its importance. A very uncontentious meeting, I thought.' 'Were you attending?' asks Flora, 'I noticed a certain flurry round the matter of Mangel.' 'I found that terribly predictable,' says Henry. 'The trouble with sociologists is that they usually fail to take genetics seriously. They talk about the balance of nature and nurture, but when it comes down to it they're all on the side of nurture, because they can interfere with that. They can't realize how much we're genetically predetermined.' 'But it is, as the chair says, a bone of contention,' says Flora. 'It'll blow over,' says Henry. 'Will it, Howard?' asks Flora. 'I doubt it,' says Howard. 'There's a lot of passion on this.' 'Oh, God,' says Flora, 'I must admit I was really hoping for just one quiet term. Without an issue, without a sit-in. I know it sounds terribly reactionary. But even though permanent revolution may have its claims, I really think before I die I'd like the peace to write one decent book.' 'But we won't let you,' says Howard. 'No,' says Flora, 'so I see.'

The lift stops at the fifth floor, and they get out, back into Sociology. 'Funny how it came up,' says Henry, 'it was all a bit of an accident.' 'Henry,' says Flora, wearily, 'there are no accidents.' Henry turns and looks at her, puzzled. 'Of course there are,' he says. 'I don't think Howard agrees with you,' says Flora. 'I must go home and work. Take care of yourself, Henry.' 'Of course,' says Henry. The three of them separate, going along three of the four corridors that lead away from the lift, to collect up the briefcases and the books and the new essays and the new department memos, the accumulated intellectual deposit of the day, which will now need fresh attention. 'Grand girl, Flora,' says Henry, a few minutes later, when Howard comes to the door of his room, to remind him of their appointment. Henry's room, like all the rooms, is a matching version of Howard's own, with the Conran desk, the Roneo-Vickers filing cabinet, the gunmetal waste-paper basket, the red desk chair, all in approximately similar places in the rectangle. The difference is that Henry has domesticated the space, and filled it with potted plants, and a bust of Gladstone, and a modernistic silver-frame mirror, and a loose-weave Norwegian rug for the floor, and a machine called a Teasmaid, which links a teapot to a clock, and throws out an intense smell of tea-leaves. 'Are you ready, Henry?' asks Howard. 'I've got a somewhat busy evening. And I've

162

got to take you home for your steak.' 'I think that's about it,' says Henry, 'I shan't get much work done tonight like this. I wonder, Howard, if you could give me a hand to get my raincoat on? The problem is to fit this arm of mine in some-where.' 'Let's put it over your shoulders,' says Howard, 'and I'll button it up for you at the neck.' They stand in Henry's domestic room, Henry with his chin up, as Howard attends to his coat. Then they pick up their briefcases and walk down the empty corridor towards the lift.

The lift comes quickly, and they get inside. 'I do hope you're not angry with me,' says Henry, as they descend. 'Why should I be?' asks Howard. 'I mean, over the Mangel question,' says Henry, 'I had to vote for him, of course, on principle. It was quite clear to me, though I respect the other point of view. I suppose you voted against.' 'I abstained, actually,' says Howard. 'But I know what you must have thought,' said Henry. 'If only Henry had done the sensible thing, and stayed at home, and then the vote would have gone the other way.' 'Nonsense,' says Howard, 'if you'd stayed at home, we wouldn't have had an issue. Now there'll be trouble, and it will radicalize everyone, and we shall have a good term.' 'Well, I don't think we agree on that,' says Henry. The lift doors open, and they step out into the empty foyer. The Kaakinen waterfall has been turned off for the night; many of the lights are out; the floors are being cleaned by a cleaner with a cleaner. 'No,' says Henry, 'I'm like Flora. I cry for peace. My political days are good and over. I'm not sure I was ever really very far in. In any case, politics were fair, in the fifties.' 'That was why nothing got done,' says Howard, 'and there is no peace.' They go out, through the glass doors, into the darkening campus. 'Well, that's my point of view,' says Henry, 'though of course I do respect the other one.' 'Yes,' says Howard, as they stop and stand in the rain, 'well, where shall we go for our drink?' 'Ah,' says Henry, brightening, 'that's what I call a really serious issue. Where do you think?'

X

There is a pub on campus, the Town and Gown, a modernistic place done out in oiled pinewood; here students meet
students, and faculty faculty, and faculty students, and students
faculty, and they sit at very littered tables, in the crush, with
the noise of reggae music from the jukebox loud in their ears,
and discuss very open and discussable affairs, such as term-
papers, union politics, theses, colleagues, abortions, demonstrations, and sexual and matrimonial difficulties. But for matters
of a more confidential or a more furtive kind, for caucuses,
small liaisons, large conspiracies, or the resolution of serious
methodological questions, it is customary to go off campus;
and there are, nearby, two familiar and well-known pubs with
a straightforward atmosphere and a number of convenient
corners. Howard names one of these pubs; but Henry, it
seems, has other ideas. 'Look,' he says, 'why don't we go to
my local?' 'You have a local?' asks Howard. 'Well, I always
pop into the Duke of Wellington for a drink on my way
home,' says Henry, 'it's a good place for a serious talk.' The
good place for a serious talk is down in the city; it smells of
warm scampi and has a natty clientele dressed by Austin Reed
and Howard has never entered it. 'Very well, Henry,' says
Howard, 'let's go to my car.' The rain blows over them as
they enter the exposure of the car park, flapping Henry's
bandages. They get in the minivan and drive off, with Henry's
arm stiffly out ahead of him. As they go down the long approach

164

road, Howard can look back, in the mirror, and see the campus behind him, a massive urban construct, lit with spots and flashes, throwing out beams and rays in the half-light, the image of an intellectual factory of high production and a twenty-four hour schedule. To each side of them, behind the wet trees, are the round porthole lights of Spengler and Toynbee, each window with its own diaphanous, indeed transparent, blind, each one in a different and pure colour, each presenting to the eye a penetrable circular blob, one found of great fascination by many citizens of Watermouth, who can walk a dog by night and see, focused in these elegant, composed circles, as in the lens of a camera, the shimmering image of a student, undressing. At the end of the drive, Howard turns the van left, on the main road, and drives them towards the town centre.

It was at 17.30 that Benita Pream's alarm clock pinged, to announce the end of the department meeting. It is just striking six, on the brass-faced grandfather clock that stands in the hall, as they enter the Duke of Wellington. 'I think you'll find this a nice ambience, Howard,' says Henry, as they go into the Gaslight Room, brightly lit by electricity and done out in camp Victorian detail. 'Well, well, well,' says the barmaid, who has somehow been persuaded into wearing a long Victorian dress with a lace neck, 'you've been in the wars, haven't you, Mr Beamish?' 'Two pints of bitter,' says Henry, standing at the counter, his raincoat fastened Napoleonically under his chin, his white bandaged arm sticking out stiffly below. 'Have I?' 'Looks as though you've been in a real punch-up,' says the barmaid, 'tankards or glasses?' 'Tankards, I think,' says Henry. 'No, I'm fine. I just had a bit of an accident.' Behind Chloë is a large mirror; in the mirror are etched, for the solace of contemporary man, the firm, delicate lines of Paxton's building for the Crystal Palace Exhibition of 1851, upon which is imposed the reflection of the plushy room. 'It looks quite a lot of an accident to me,' says Chloë, pulling the handle, and beaming at Howard, 'lucky you've got a friend here to look after you.' 'Oh, this is Mr Kirk,' says Henry, 'yes, he's looking after me.' 'There we are, then,' says Chloë, 'two pints, anything else?' 'I think we might have a packet of cheese and onion crisps,' says Henry. 'I wonder,

Howard, would you be good enough to reach into my left-hand trouser pocket and get out my money? I've put it on the wrong side of me, for some reason.' 'You be careful,' says Chloë, 'you'll get your friend arrested.' 'Never mind, I'll get it,' says Howard. 'I protest,' says Henry, 'I invited you here as my guest.' 'You get the next one,' says Howard. 'Shall we sit down?' asks Henry, attempting to lift up the two pint tankards from the bar in his single hand, and spilling a considerable quantity of the beer down his trousers. 'Let me,' says Howard. 'Do you want the evening paper tonight, Mr Beamish?' asks Chloë, as they move away from the bar. 'I always read the paper here,' says Henry to Howard. 'Not tonight, I think, Chloë. I've some important business to discuss.' 'I see they went and hijacked another,' says Chloë, 'I don't know what it's all coming to.'

'Ah, the world, the world,' says Henry vaguely, putting the packet of crisps between his teeth, 'if only people could learn to live together.' 'That's right, Mr Beamish,' says Chloë, 'not what it was, is it? Except for the sex. That's improved, definitely.' 'And the surgery,' says Henry, through clenched teeth, starting to move unsteadily across the room with his glass, 'there are real advances in surgery.' 'Well,' says Chloë with a laugh, 'I'm afraid you look as though you need them, Mr Beamish, tonight.' 'Grand girl, Chloë,' says Henry, as they sit down in a lush plush booth across the room, overhung with an aspidistra, 'they know me here, you see.' 'Yes,' says Howard. 'Nice place,' says Henry, 'the landlord's an old military man. I suppose it's not your sort of thing really.' 'Not exactly,' says Howard, 'what did you want to talk to me about?' 'Oh,' says Henry, 'yes. Well, Howard, I wanted to have a little word with you about last night.' 'The party,' says Howard. 'Yes,' says Henry, 'the party. I wonder, Howard, would you mind, I can't open this packet of crisps.' 'There we are,' says Howard. 'Rather a chapter of accidents for me, I'm afraid,' says Henry, 'I got there late, then I got bitten, and then I broke your window. I'm extremely sorry.' 'You needn't worry,' says Howard, 'things break at parties.' 'I'm afraid Myra was rather drunk too,' says Henry, 'not our evening, all round.' 'People drink at parties, too,' says Howard, 'but was there something wrong last night?' 'I wouldn't say wrong,' says Henry, 'but it's not like us, is it?'

'I suppose not, Henry,' says Howard. 'Anyway,' says Henry, 'the main thing I wanted to ask you is this. Would you let me pay for that window to be mended?' 'Yes,' says Howard. 'Good,' says Henry, looking brighter, 'well, that's settled, then. The lavatories are through that door over there, if you want them.'

'Henry,' says Howard, 'what happened to you last night?' 'I had twenty-seven stitches,' says Henry, 'very nice Indian doctor. Quite good English.' 'But how did it happen that you cut yourself like that?' 'Aha,' says Henry, 'now there's a question. I've been thinking about that a lot. I slipped, you see, and put out my arm to save myself, and shoved it through your window. But it can't have been as simple as that.' 'No,' says Howard. 'No,' says Henry, 'I think there was a piece of ice. I think someone must have had ice in his drink, and dropped it on the floor, and I stepped on it. I don't mean dropped it deliberately. I mean, I was to blame, of course. Of course I was a bit unsteady, after the dogbite.' 'You didn't mean to fall through the window?' Henry stares at Howard; he says, 'No, heavens, no. Why should I do that?' 'You do have a lot of accidents,' says Howard, 'doesn't it worry you?' 'I'm a very clumsy person, Howard. I'm big and a bit top-heavy. I blame it on not playing games at school. They wouldn't let me, you know, after the beri-beri.' 'You had beri-beri?' 'Haven't I told you?' asks Henry, 'Oh, yes. A nasty attack.' 'Where was this?' asks Howard. 'Huddersfield,' says Henry. 'But, look, as a professional social psychologist, haven't you ever wondered how you got into this accident pattern?' 'Well, it's not my line, really, is it?' says Henry, 'I'm more a social control and delinquency man. I admit there's an inexplicable statistical frequency.' 'Two last night,' says Howard. 'Yes,' says Henry, 'it makes you think. I suppose you're asking me if I'm drinking too much, or on drugs. The answer's no. I didn't touch drugs last night, I don't get on with them. And I didn't get much to drink, either. If you remember I got to the party very late. When I walked home from the university to drive Myra back to the party, I found she'd already gone in the car. So of course I had to walk back all the way into town again, took me more than an hour. Then the dog bit me as soon as I got there, and I was ages in the bathroom, soaking my leg in antiseptic.

And then I can't have had more than two glasses of wine at the most, Howard, before I went into the guest bedroom, to change my socks, and I thought I'd open the window, and I put my arm through it. So it's not that. Have a crisp?' 'No, thank you,' says Howard.

'It doesn't give way to analysis, does it?' asks Henry. 'It was funny. It didn't hurt at first, but then I realized you could die from a cut like that, so I thought I'd better yell for help. And then Flora turned up; wasn't she marvellous? Well, I suppose things like that happen at parties, as you say. We like to read something into it, that's our line, but nothing stands up. It really was just a bit of an accident.' 'Henry, you weren't upset last night?' asks Howard, looking at Henry's bland face. 'I was shaken by the dogbite,' says Henry, 'but not especially.' 'I think I'm more worried about you than you are by yourself,' says Howard. 'Well, that's very nice of you, Howard,' says Henry, 'but I shouldn't bother.' 'Well, that could have been fatal,' says Howard. 'You've got plenty going on yourself to worry about,' says Henry, 'from all I hear.' 'I have known you for a long time,' says Howard, 'I remember when I first met you.' 'My God, yes,' says Henry, 'yes. Some boys had just knocked me down with a football. I'd told them to get off the university playing fields, because they were private property, and they flung a football at me. You picked me up.' 'You had accidents even then,' says Howard. 'Look,' says Henry, 'I don't like you being so worried about me. Do you think I did it on purpose?' 'What's purpose?' asks Howard. 'I think you might have had good reason to be distressed.' 'What reason?' asks Henry. 'Wasn't there a reason, last night?' asks Howard. 'Look,' says Henry, 'I want to know just what you're getting at.' 'You don't know what I'm getting at?' 'No,' says Henry, 'stop being so bloody mysterious.' 'Well,' says Howard, 'when you went home, and Myra wasn't there, did you know where she'd gone?' 'Of course,' says Henry, 'she left me a note, she always leaves me a note. On the mantelpiece. She'd gone to you.' 'Do you know why?' 'Yes,' says Henry, 'it said in the note. To give Barbara a hand. She worries about how much Barbara has on her plate. We both do. Didn't she come?' 'Oh, yes,' says Howard. 'There we are, then,' says Henry, 'what's all that got to do with it?'

'We thought she was upset,' says Howard. 'Grand girl, Myra,' says Henry. 'She's had a bad summer of it, actually. This book of mine has decidedly not gone well. I've had what they call writer's block. The words won't come. Of course, charisma's a difficult concept. And I'm perhaps a bit out of touch with new developments. You get that way, at our age. Lose the spark, go a bit dead. You know what I mean. Did she talk about that at all?' Howard looks at Henry's face, which has acquired a small moustache of froth from the beer, but seems free of all calculation, and says: 'Yes, she did.' 'I'm sure it helps her to chat,' says Henry, 'she needs someone to take an interest. Not that I don't. But she's exhausted me. And to be frank I'm under the weather, rather, Howard. Not at my best. Did she say I was under the weather?' 'Yes,' says Howard. 'I see,' says Henry. 'You had quite a talk then.' 'Yes,' says Howard. 'Oh, well,' says Henry, 'is that why you wondered about me last night?' 'Yes,' says Howard. 'Did she say anything else about me?' asks Henry. 'She said that your marriage wasn't going too well,' says Howard. 'Did she?' says Henry. 'Well, as I say, it's not been a good summer. And the book hasn't helped. Books make you withdrawn. But it's nothing serious.' 'She thought it was,' says Howard. 'Isn't she thinking of leaving you?' 'Is she?' asks Henry. 'Didn't she tell you?' asks Howard. 'Don't you know?' 'No,' says Henry. 'Is that what she told you?' 'Would it be a surprise?' asks Howard. 'Not entirely,' says Henry, 'Myra's unhappy, you have to understand that. I'm not entirely good with her. I don't give her all she needs from life. She gets unhappy, and telephones people. Talks to them about us. Sometimes she goes out and buys a new thing, a new Miele dishwasher or something. Because all the girls, what she calls the girls, in her set round the village are buying Miele dishwashers. Sometimes she talks of separating. Because all the girls at the uni, what she calls the uni, in her set talk about separating. It's a kind of fashionable female preoccupation. The wives all seem to be doing it. They want a lot, and we can't give it them, the kind of sex and attention they're after. I'll have to go soon. Have you got time for a quick one before we take off, Howard?'

'All right,' says Howard. 'Get the money out of my pocket,' says Henry. 'Never mind,' says Howard. 'Have it, Howard,' says Henry, reaching across himself, and pulling the contents of his left-hand pocket out over the bench and the floor. 'There we are.' Howard picks up some coins and goes over to the bar, where Chloë stands in her Victoriana. 'Another two pints,' he says. 'One of my best, Mr Beamish,' says Chloë, pulling on the handle, 'in here every night. Fit as a fiddle, yesterday, he was.' Howard lifts the drinks and carries them back across the room; when he gets back to the red plush seat, Henry, picking up his coins, raises his face, and Howard notices that, tucked into the indentation at the corner of his nose, there resides a small tear. 'Thank you,' says Henry. 'All right?' asks Howard. 'You must excuse me for responding to the situation we've described with my usual inadequacy,' says Henry. 'Of course, she is upset. Or she wouldn't have come to you. I mean, you're in it professionally, aren't you, the separation business. Myra always talks about how Barbara left you in Leeds. An act of heroism, she says.' 'She did mention that,' says Howard. 'She discussed it all then, did she?' asks Henry, 'I think that's a very bad sign.' 'She seems very unhappy,' says Howard. 'I know,' says Henry, 'I can see it from her point of view. What's the matter with Myra is me.' 'Not exactly,' says Howard, 'it's both of you. Myra's just beginning to realize what you've both chosen to miss.' 'Oh, yes,' says Henry, 'and what's that?' 'Well, Myra can see it,' says Howard. 'You've withdrawn too far. You've closed in on yourselves, you've lost touch with everything, you've no outside contacts, and so when anything goes wrong you blame it on each other. What you're doing is trapping each other in fixed personality roles. You can't grow, you can't expand, you can't let each other develop. You're stuck out there, in your little nest, out of time, out of history, and you're missing out on possibility.'

'I see,' says Henry. 'Is that what you told Myra?' 'There wasn't much time to tell Myra anything,' says Howard, 'the party started. But it's what Myra sees.' 'Yes, it's what she expects you to tell her,' says Henry. 'Find someone else, try new positions, start swinging.' 'Myra's growing up,' says Howard. 'Is that growing up?' asks Henry. 'Look, Howard, we're in different worlds now, you and I. I don't agree with you. I don't see things like that, I'm at odds with it.' 'I don't think Myra is,' says Howard. Henry looks at Howard. He says: 'No. That's why it's such a betrayal for her to come and talk to you.'

'But perhaps talking to me is the only way she can talk to you,' says Howard. 'To say what?' asks Henry. 'If Myra wants to talk to me, I'm there. We sit across the dinner table from each other every evening. We lie in bed together every night.' 'Most beds aren't as intimate as people think they are,' says Howard. 'You've always seemed to like them,' says Henry. 'I don't understand it. Is she leaving me, or isn't she?' 'I think she was, last night,' says Howard. 'Isn't it usual, in these things, to indicate one's intentions to the partner one leaves behind? I mean, leave a note on the mantelpiece or something?' 'Perhaps talking to us was the note on the mantelpiece,' says Howard. 'But she's back there at the farmhouse, cooking steak,' says Henry. 'I think she is.' 'Things have happened, since then,' says Howard. 'Ah, I see,' says Henry, 'you think she was leaving me last night, and my accident changed her mind. If it was an accident.' 'That's right,' says Howard. 'So it's a temporary stay of execution.' 'Unless you stop her, talk to her,' says Howard. 'I suppose,' says Henry, 'I could go and have another accident.' 'You know,' says Howard, 'I thought this was what you wanted to talk to me about this evening.' 'Oh, no,' says Henry, 'you don't understand. You're the last person I'd want to talk to about this. It's nothing personal, I grant you your point of view. I just don't believe in your solutions.'

'But you believe in the problems,' says Howard. 'God,' says Henry, 'the Kirk consultancy parlour. I'm out of all that now. I had enough of it in Leeds. I've stopped wanting to stand up and forge history with my penis. And I'm rather sick of the great secular dominion of liberation and equality we were on about then, which reduces, when you think about it, to putting system over people and producing large piles of corpses. I think Ireland's really done the trick for me, turned me sour on all those words like "anti-fascism" and "anti-imperialism" we always used. I don't want to blame anybody now, or take anything off anyone. The only thing that matters for me is attachment to other knowable people, and the gentleness of relationship.' 'Well, that's what we all want, isn't it?' asks Howard, 'sweetness and light and plenty of Mozart. But we can't have it, and you can hardly sit back and rest on your own record. If that's life, Henry, you're not very good at it, are you?' 'No,' says Henry, 'that's the whole sad little comedy. The personal, which is what I believe in, I can't bloody well manage. I'm stuck. And that's why it's no use your worrying about me. I don't want my soul saved. I don't want to be grist to the historical mill.' 'But what about Myra?' asks Howard. 'Right,' says Henry. 'Myra is the optimum point of suffering that arises. I'm a disaster for her. I know it. I look at her, and the feeling I count on doesn't come: the love, the enormity of otherness, I'm after and can't get. There are occasional cheap sparks: some student with nice legs comes alive in the chair in front of me, or the nagging caring about Myra, which is a sort of love. I wish the funds were there, I'd like to spend them on her, but they're not. Well, it's not hard to provide a psychological profile or a political explanation for all this. Actually I can probably do it nearly as well as you can, Howard. Or could, if we were talking about someone else. But in this case it's me., And there's not much help for being that, thanks, Howard. I do appreciate your thinking about me.' 'You mean you'll let Myra go,' says Howard. 'Isn't that what you'd advise her to do, anyway?' asks Henry. 'And me to find someone else?' 'I suppose so,' says Howard.

Just then Henry looks up, and stares, and says: 'My God, look at the time. I promised Myra I'd be home at seven to eat her steak. I can't tell you the row there'll be if I'm late.' There is an old railway station clock over the bar, which says that the time is six forty-five. 'I've got a busy evening too,' says Howard, 'we'd better rush.' 'Howard, would you mind doing up my top button again?' says Henry, and Howard fastens the button, and helps Henry up from the bench. 'Goodnight, Chloë,' calls Henry, as they hurry out of the Gaslight Room. 'Night night, Mr Beamish,' calls Chloë. 'Take care, don't have another accident.' They go through the cold car park to the van, and get in, and Howard drives them out onto the main road and out toward the countryside. They go at speed through the rurality of Henry's kingdom, down narrow lanes, covered in big wet leaves, through fords, over small bridges, down rutted tracks. Dark creaking branches lean over the van; the wheels slip and skid; small animals appear under the wheels and force them to swerve. The cart-track to the farmhouse is on a high bank, but they reach it safely. Stopping the van, Howard can see that, in the kitchen, where he had eaten cheese and biscuits with Myra on the evening when Henry was out, there is a light. 'Come inside a minute and have a word with Myra,' says Henry, getting out of the van, his briefcase clutched in his good hand. 'She seems to be in.' And surely enough the back door opens, and there is Myra, in an apron, standing on the steps; she waves to Howard. 'Tell her I'd have liked to,' says Howard, 'but I'm late myself, I have to rush.' 'Well, look, Howard,' says Henry, leaning his head in through the van window, 'I just want to say that I really do appreciate it. Our talk, and the lift. And don't forget to send me the bill for the window.' 'I won't,' says Howard, 'Can you just see me back to turn?' 'You've got two feet,' says Henry, going behind the van. 'Come on, come on.' It is fortunately not a bad bump, and Henry is only slightly grazed on his good hand, the hand that he has put out to save himself as he falls forward onto the gravel as the van topples him. Happily there is Myra to pick him up, and dust him down. 'He's all right,' she says in through the van window, 'Christ, would you believe it.' Turning the van, Howard sees them, momentarily, inside the kitchen, apparently in a quarrel, as he sets his wheels on the high bank.

The busy evening lies ahead; he drives down the rutted tracks, over the small bridges, through fords, down narrow lanes, covered in big wet leaves. It was just on seven when he reached the farmhouse; it is just on seven fifteen as, following the street markings, responding to the red and green lights, he pulls the van into the decrepit terrace. He parks, and hurries indoors. In the kitchen is a domestic scene. Felicity Phee has come, and 'I don't know how all those dirty glasses got there in the sink,' is what Barbara is saying to her. 'You want me to wash them, Mrs Kirk,' says Felicity. 'Well, it would be marvellous if you could, after you've got the kids in bed. It's usually a bath night for them,' says Barbara. 'You want me to bath them, Mrs Kirk,' says Felicity. 'Would you like to?' asks Barbara. 'You're all set up, I see,' says Howard. 'I'm sorry I'm late. I had to take Henry home. He came without a car.' 'The selfless service you perform,' says Barbara, 'it never ceases to astound. I gather you're right off out again.' 'I have to go to a meeting,' says Howard, 'a psychological meeting. Everything all right, Felicity?' 'Yes,' says Felicity, 'I got here early, and Mrs Kirk and I got everything sorted out. It's really great to be in a real house. I just love it.' 'Fine,' says Howard, 'can I give you a lift to your class, Barbara?' 'No,' says Barbara, pulling on her coat, 'I'll find my own way. Well, well, a psychological meeting.' 'A physiological meeting might have been a truer description,' says Flora Beniform, her naked body raised above him, her dark brown hair down over her face, her strong features staring down at his face on the pillow, while the clock in her white bedroom records the time as seven forty-five, 'but it's a familiar type of displacement syndrome.' 'I like to think it's a psychological meeting as well,' says Howard, looking up at her. 'So do I, Howard, so do I,' says Flora, 'but I begin to wonder about you. I think you enjoy deceptions, and I don't.' 'I just try to make things interesting,' says Howard. 'Oh, you're heavy.' 'Too fat?' asks Flora. 'No,' says Howard, 'I like it.'

Around them is Flora's white bedroom, which has long, deep windows and fitted wardrobes, and one picture, a large, steel-framed print of a Modigliani nude, and two small chairs, on which their two piles of clothes have been neatly stacked; they have hastened into the bed, but Flora maintains in all these things a certain orderliness. And now on the bed they lie, dipping and jogging in a steady rhythm; Flora's big bed is fitted with a motorized health vibrator, her one great opulence. 'Mangel,' says Flora, moving about him, above him, 'I'm disgusted about Mangel.' 'Don't talk, Flora,' says Howard. 'There's no hurry,' says Flora, 'you've got until nine o'clock. Besides, you don't come to my bed just for the fun of it. You have to give a reckoning.' 'No, Flora,' says Howard, 'do that more. It's marvellous. You're marvellous, Flora.' 'You lied to me,' says Flora, looking down at him fiercely from her eminence, 'didn't you?' 'When?' 'This morning in your room,' says Flora. 'How?' asks Howard. 'By not telling me what you knew. By not giving me all the truth.' 'There's so much truth to tell,' says Howard brightly. 'I don't know why I let you come this evening,' says Flora. 'You *haven't* let me come,' says Howard. Flora giggles, and says, 'Come to see me.' 'You did it because you wanted to find out the rest,' says Howard. 'Which is, of course, why I didn't *tell* you the rest.' 'Oh, yes?' says Flora, 'well tell me one thing . . .' 'Sssshhhhh,' says Howard. 'At a really good psychological meeting, the main business comes first, and then the question period afterward.' 'All right,

Howard,' says Flora. 'All right, Howard.' And she weaves
above him, her breasts dipping, her ribcage tight. Her body is
there once and then twice, three times, because shadowed high
on the wall and the curtains and the ceiling, in shapes thrown
by the two small lights on the tables at either side of the bed.
The shapes, the formidable body and its shadows, move
rhythmically, as the bed does; the pulses of self in Howard's
body beat hard; and time, at seven fifty-two, on Tuesday
3 October, pings like Benita Pream's alarm clock, comes to a
point, distils, explodes; and then spreads and diffuses, becomes
flaccid and ordinary and contingent time again, as Flora's head
drops forward onto Howard's chest, and her body collapses
over him, and the clock ticks emptily away on the table next
to his sweating head.

The bed moves slowly, lazily under them. After a while,
Flora's body slides off his, and comes to rest at his side, tucked
in, delicately connected. Their sweat is ceasing, their pulses are
slowing, the shadows are still. They lie there together. There is
Flora, with Howard's left hand on her large right breast, her
body long and solid, with dark hair, Flora with her doctorate
from Heidelberg, and her famous little book on the growth of
affection in the young child. And there is Howard, with Flora's
right hand on his left inner thigh, his body neat and wiry, his
Zapata moustache black on his skin; Howard with his radical
reputation, and his two well-known books on modern mores,
and his many television appearances. They lie there in the
master bedroom of Flora's compact, modern service flat, with
its good-sized living-room, well-fitted galley kitchen, its second
bedroom that doubles as study, its bathroom with bath and
fitted shower, in the elegant block in the landscaped grounds
in the leafy suburb, all described by the letting agents as perfect
for modern living, and ideal for the professional single person.
They lie, and then Flora moves, turning slightly, lifting her
head. She has a deep, serious, thoughtful face; it comes up and
looks into his. He opens his eyes, he closes them, he opens them
again. 'Good,' he says lazily. 'Very good. A perfect psychological
meeting.' Flora runs a fingernail down the centre of his chest;
his hand comes out, and strokes her hair. Her thoughtful face
still looks at him. 'Yes, it was,' she says, and adds, 'Howard?'
'Yes?' says Howard. 'Howard,' she says, 'how's the family?'

XI

There are people who ask the question 'How's the family?' and, receiving the answer 'Fine' are perfectly satisfied; there are other people, the real professionals, who expect the answer in a very different realm. Families are Flora's business; all over the world there are families, nuclear and extended, patriarchal and matriarchal, families cooked and families raw, which pause, rigid, in their work of raising children, bartering daughters, tabooing incest, practising wife-exchange, performing rites of circumcision, potlatching, as Flora enters their clearing or their longhouse or their living-room and asks, notebook in hand, 'How's the family?' It is a serious and searching question about the universe; and Flora is seeking a universal answer. For Flora is famous for questions. When she is not in her service flat in the leafy suburb, or out in the world on fieldwork, she is to be found at meetings and congresses, in small halls in London or Zurich; here she habitually sits in a left-hand aisle seat near the front and, the paper over, rises first, a pencil held high for attention, to ask the initial and most devastating question ('I'd hoped to bring evidence to show the entire inadequacy of this approach. Happily the speaker has, presumably unconsciously, performed the task for me in the paper itself. As for my question . . .'). Flora, it is widely known, wherever she goes, is formidable, with her dark serious eyes, her firm manner, her big, intimidating body. And as for her more intimate relationships, well, it sometimes seems to Howard, when he lies, on the happy occasions when the privilege has been granted to him, on her moving bed in her large white bedroom, that Flora has reinvested fornication, an occupation at which she is in fact extremely skilled and able, with new purpose and significance. She has conceived of it as a tactical advance on the traditional psychiatrist's couch; permitting more revelation, more intimacies, it therefore leads, inevitably, to better questions. So he looks up at her serious face, peering at him over his bent arm; he considers; he says, 'Well, of course, it's the old story.'

'Oh, Howard,' says Flora, 'I want a new story. Which old story?' 'Well, when I'm up, Barbara's down,' says Howard, 'and vice versa.' 'When you're up who, Barbara's down on whom?' asks Flora. 'Flora, you're coarse,' says Howard. 'No, not really,' says Flora. 'And Barbara's down now?' 'Well, I'm up,' says Howard. 'Things are happening to me.' 'You ought to watch Barbara,' says Flora. 'Oh, it's the usual things,' says Howard. 'We battle on, emissaries of the male and female cause. Barbara says: "Pass the salt." And then, if I pass it, she smirks. Another win for the sisters over the brothers.' 'Marriage,' says Flora, 'the most advanced form of warfare in the modern world. But of course you usually pass the pepper.' Howard laughs and says: 'I do.' 'By accident,' says Flora. 'Oh, Flora,' says Howard, 'you should have married. You'd be so good at it.' The bed heaves; Flora pushes herself up from her place against Howard, and sits in the bed with her knees up, her hair loose, the bedside lights glowing on her flesh and casting sharp shadow. 'Isn't it amazing?' she says, reaching across to the table at her side, and picking up a packet of cigarettes and a lighter, 'Why is it that married people always say "Come in" when everything they do says "Get out"? They talk about their miseries and then ask you why you're unmarried. No, Howard, I prefer to stand on the sidelines and watch. I really find it much safer.' Howard laughs; he reaches out, and runs his hand round the curve of Flora's breast. 'It has its compensations,' says Howard. 'You're never lonely.' 'I know you aren't, Howard,' says Flora, 'but it seems to me that you've demonstrated that the main compensation of marriage is that you can commit adultery. A somewhat perverse argument.'

Flora bends her head, and lights her cigarette; she looks down slyly at Howard. 'Well, have you found out?' she asks. 'Found

out what?' asks Howard. 'Who Barbara was with last night?'
'I don't know that she was with anybody,' says Howard. 'I've
told you,' says Flora, 'you ought to take an interest in Barbara.'
'Have *you* found out?' asks Howard. 'No, I've not had time,'
says Flora, 'but I think I can make an inspired guess.' 'Your
guesses are always inspired,' says Howard. 'It's not serious,'
says Flora, 'just something interesting. You mustn't try her
with it.' 'I won't,' says Howard. 'You know, I sometimes
wonder whether you have anything else to think about besides
the fornications of your friends.' 'I pay attention,' says Flora,
'but, after all, it's my research. Sex and families.' 'An interesting
field,' says Howard, 'rather better than Christadelphianism in
Wakefield.' 'Look,' says Flora, 'do you want to know my guess?'
'Yes, please,' says Howard, flat on his back. 'Dr Macintosh,'
says Flora. 'A man gets very competitive when his wife's having
a baby.' Howard stares at her face, lit with amusement; he says,
'That's marvellous, Flora. Though actually his wife seems *not*
to be having a baby.' 'Oh, she's tantalizing him with it, she'll
have one in the end,' says Flora. 'But I mean, what else can a
man do at a time like that, except go to bed with the hostess of
the party she's so wilfully chosen to leave?' 'Of course, nothing,'
says Howard. 'It's a very interesting speculation.' 'Not to be
used or quoted, of course,' says Flora. 'I didn't say it was *true*.
Barbara was probably out of sight having a bath or something.'
'I must say,' says Howard, 'you're very good at making life
sound interesting.' 'Well, we both are, aren't we?' asks Flora.
'Presumably for fear it may not be.' 'Oh, it is,' says Howard.
'There's always something or someone to do.' 'But don't you
ever find it too much work, Howard?' asks Flora, 'All this
dressing and undressing, all these undistinguished climaxes, all
this chasing for more of the same, is it really, really, worth the
effort?' 'Of course,' says Howard. 'Well, you, Howard,' says
Flora, 'who did you screw last night?'

Howard laughs and says, 'Well, Flora, it's awfully personal.'
Flora turns her face toward him: she says, 'My God, what kind
of an answer is that? Where would the state of modern psychological knowledge be if Dora had said to Freud: "I'm sorry,
Sigmund, it's awfully personal." ' 'Oh, Freud deduced,' says
Howard. 'Ah, well, so did I, of course,' says Flora. 'It was that
student, wasn't it?' 'Which student?' asks Howard. 'Oh,

Howard, come on,' says Flora, puffing at the cigarette, 'Felicity someone, the one with spots. The one who came into your room this morning for morning-after recompense.' 'Another inspired guess,' says Howard. 'No,' says Flora, 'this one was absolutely bloody obvious. I never saw two people who looked more as if they'd just jumped off each other. She felt entitled to a new role, you felt compelled to resist it.' 'Flora,' says Howard, 'you're jealous.' 'My God,' says Flora, flicking ash into an ashtray, 'I don't suffer from these female diseases. Why do you need me to be jealous? So that you can believe I care for you much more than I do?' Howard laughs and says, 'You do care for me, Flora. And you sounded jealous.' 'Oh, no,' says Flora, 'I sounded disgusted. You drift off and screw that scrawny, undistinguished girl, whom you could have had at any time, day or night, just when all those interesting things were going on. It shows a shameful lack of concern in the human lot.' 'She had her problems, too,' says Howard. 'Well, of course, she'd have to have,' says Flora, 'but what were her problems, compared to the kind of problems you'd got at your party last night? How did you get on with Henry?' 'Get on with Henry when?' asks Howard. 'You know,' says Flora, 'when you grabbed him and took him off, after the meeting, so you could get to him before I did. Just now.' 'So-so,' says Howard. 'He took me to his local. It's got a barmaid in a bustle. Henry goes there every night to gird his loins before going home to the marital fray.' 'That's sensible enough,' says Flora, 'but did he tell you what happened last night?' 'He said it was an accident,' says Howard. 'He said he'd slipped on a piece of ice someone dropped from a drink.' 'I didn't see any ice at your party.' 'No,' says Howard, 'there wasn't any.' Flora laughs, and looks satisfied. She says, 'Oh, Howard, how sad. It's the typical story of those who show a true concern for others. You try to convince them that there are serious psychological factors at work in their situation, and all they can do is talk about chances and accidents.'

Howard looks up at Flora, her elbows on her knees, her face staring ahead at the windows, blowing smoke. 'Well,' he says, 'he did begin to agree with me, with us, later.' 'Oh, did he?' asks Flora, glancing at him. 'Yes,' says Howard, 'after I told him that Myra wanted to leave him.' Flora's big naked body heaves and moves; the bed bounces; her face appears above his, staring down into his eyes. 'After you told him *what*?' she cries. 'After I told him Myra had come to us last night and talked about a separation,' says Howard. 'Oh, you shit, you shit, you shit,' says Flora, shaking Howard's arms with her hands, '*That's* the essential item you were suppressing this morning. That's what you wouldn't tell me. Why not, Howard?' 'Flora, Flora,' says Howard, 'I was saving it for you. Something interesting.' 'Something interesting!' says Flora, 'it's the piece I've been looking for. And you knew last night?' 'Myra came to us before the party, and asked our advice,' says Howard. 'My God,' says Flora, 'and you still went off and bedded that spotty student, when all that was going on in your house? I call that a grave dereliction of duty. No wonder you wanted it to be an accident.' 'Don't you think it's interesting?' asks Howard. Flora lets go of him, and drops her hair into his face, and laughs. 'Yes,' she says. 'Of course it's all clear now. Myra leaving, Henry desperate, there's a convenient and tempting window. Smash, you perform the classic appeal. My blood's on your hands, darling.' 'It's not all clear,' says Howard, 'which is why I wasn't alert. Myra didn't tell Henry she was leaving him. He didn't know until I talked to him just now.' 'Oh, there's tell and tell,' says Flora. 'They didn't even see much of each other,' says Howard. 'Henry was late and spent most of the evening attending to his dogbite.' Flora giggles; she says, 'Did he have a dogbite?' 'Yes,' says Howard, 'he got bitten on the threshold by a student's dog. Do you think it was an accident?' 'Oh, Christ,' says Flora, 'shut up. I'm trying to take him seriously. Anyway, you told him, naturally. What did he say then?' 'He admitted the marriage was collapsing,' says Howard. 'That should cheer you,' says Flora. 'You'll be able to hand out radical deliverance to both of them now. One at the front door, and one at the back.'

'Henry appears not to appreciate my explanation,' says Howard. 'Ahh,' says Flora, 'what a shame. I had no idea he was so sensible.' 'I knew that would please you,' says Howard. 'Of course it leaves him in a situation which is in every sense absurd. He doesn't exist, he can't feel, he can't love Myra, he can't even lay his students.' 'It must have been hard for him to confess all that,' says Flora, 'talking to a man who can do all those things.' 'But he was able to tell me he has a belief that sustains him,' says Howard. 'Does he?' asks Flora. 'What's that?' 'He believes in personal relations,' says Howard, looking at Flora, who begins, her breasts bouncing, to giggle. 'Oh, no, Howard,' she says, 'did he tell you that? Solemnly?' 'He did,' says Howard. 'Poor Henry,' says Flora. 'If anyone in the world should be banned from personal relations, it's Henry. He's lost all self-conviction. And he's not only in a classic auto-destructive cycle himself; he's also sweeping in everything and everyone around him. Of course this is what Myra can see. Hence her frenzies and extraordinary performances. She's afraid of being sucked in. Brought under the football with Henry.' 'Oh, that reminds me,' says Howard, 'the football. It turns out that the football wasn't an accident. A boy Henry had told off threw it at him, and knocked him down with it.' Flora's body, which has been shaking with laughter, becomes weak; it collapses and falls across Howard. 'Oh, God, we shouldn't laugh,' she says. She pushes up her head, so that her mouth meets Howard's; she kisses him. 'My dear man,' she says, 'it's terrible, but for that I forgive you everything. You're a crook and a harm to your friends, but that is just so good.' Howard strokes Flora's back. 'Something interesting?' he asks. 'Something interesting,' says Flora, 'you really earned your place in my bed tonight. Time's up, though, boy, out you get.'

'It's early,' says Howard, putting his hands out to her. Flora kneels up and switches off the bed vibrator; then she pushes at Howard's body. 'Come on, Howard, some of us have got work to do,' she says, rolling him off the bed, 'there's some Kleenex there for you on the bedside table.' 'You think of everything,' says Howard, getting up and wiping himself. 'Throw me my pants, will you?' says Flora, sitting on the other side of the bed. 'So the Beamishes are breaking up.' 'That's right,' says Howard, 'catch.' Flora stands up and, one on each side of the bed, they both begin to dress themselves. 'What did you say to Myra when she came?' asks Flora, pulling her white pants up her legs and drawing them over her dark crotch, 'did you tell her to leave him?' 'Not exactly,' says Howard, stepping into his shorts. 'I'm amazed,' says Flora, 'no doubt you will in time. Chuck my tights across, please.' 'We were too busy trying to find out her reasons,' says Howard, pulling on his sweatshirt. 'Well, those are pretty obvious,' says Flora, fitting her toes into the light, stretchable mesh of the tights, 'she's a classic female type, who clearly had a good relationship with father, and expects male domination, and sought a direct transference to Henry. Who presumably had an overdominant father and a weak mum, so he wanted a mother surrogate. So both are looking for a parent and neither's looking for a spouse.' 'Many marriages work like that,' says Howard, pulling on a sock. 'Fine,' says Flora, 'my bra. So long as nobody starts growing up.' 'Is Myra growing up?' asks Howard, pulling on the other sock, 'No, I doubt it,' says Flora, fastening her bra at the back, 'she still can't remember to put out the milk bottles. And as for Henry, well, you can get Henry by reading his book. A plea for television to take over all parental authority, so that Henry won't have to exercise any. A silly book, even yours is better.' 'Well, thank you,' says Howard, drawing up his jeans and buckling them. 'A pleasure,' says Flora, pushing her arm into a white blouse, 'it's all of a piece. An inert, compromise, undemanding marriage. They have no kids. They're probably sexually almost dormant. Unlike most of their colleagues, they don't have affairs. But they look around and feel uneasy.' 'Henry doesn't have affairs,' says Howard, clothing himself in the splendour of his neat leather jacket. 'Does Myra?' asks Flora, dropping a black skirt over her head, and catching it at the waist. 'She did once,' says Howard, pushing his feet into his shoes, 'on one single occasion.' 'I see,' says Flora, pushing her feet into her shoes. 'I've hung up a towel behind the bathroom door for you, if you want a wash.'

Howard leaves the lighted bedroom, and goes through Flora's long darkened living-room to her bathroom. It is a neat, spare room. On the shelf above the bowl is just one small bottle of perfume, a toothbrush, and a tube of fluoride toothpaste. Howard washes his hands and face, looking into the mirror and seeing his wilted, questioning, pleased expression. He reaches for the towel behind the door, and sees on the adjoining peg an unexpected item, a black silk negligée, a new view of Flora. There is a tap on the door, and Flora comes in. 'Do you mind?' she says, sitting on the side of the bath, fully dressed, her social self restored, her splendid secrets hidden, 'You didn't tell me who Myra had her little affair with.' 'Guess,' says Howard, wiping his face with the towel. 'Of course,' says Flora, 'if Myra in her entire existence managed just one little extramarital venture, one tiny infidelity, it would of course have to be with you. They ought to award medals for that kind of service, Howard.' Howard laughs and pecks Flora on the cheek; he says, 'She hasn't got your touch, Flora.' 'Of course not,' says Flora, 'I've nothing to fear. Myra must have had everything. But you wouldn't notice.' 'It's true she put all her energy not into the event itself but into tidying the place up again afterwards,' says Howard. 'Well, well,' says Flora, 'now we know why she came to talk to you. She'd like to make a better job of it next time.' 'Oh, God,' says Howard. 'Well, she'll be back,' says Flora, 'once Henry is a little better. And of course you must give her all the help you can, all the help she needs. You see how everyone counts on you.' 'You think she intends to leave Henry for me?' asks Howard. 'Of course she intends to leave him,' says Flora, 'you don't go and see the Kirks if you intend to remain together. That's like going to the Family Planning for advice on maintaining celibacy. And of course it's obvious there'd be advantages to her in a separation, as you're bound to tell her. I've no doubt at all that Henry's acting extremely destructively on her. And you must look a fascinating alternative.' Howard hangs up the towel; he says, 'Flora, you're terrifying me.' Flora, perched on the side of the bath, laughs. 'Oh, Howard,' she says, 'are your chickens coming home to roost?' 'That's hardly a matter for delight,' says Howard. 'Ah,' says Flora, 'never mind. If you want my honest opinion, she'll play with the idea, and chase you and drink your whisky, but in the end she'll find she can't really desert Henry.' 'You think she cares for him?' asks Howard, 'Not much,' says Flora, getting up off the bath, 'but she's got as much invested in that unhappy ménage as he has.' 'That's one thing I hadn't thought of,' says Howard. 'It's obvious,' says Flora, 'you'll have to go in a minute. Come and have a quick drink before I rush you off. You look as if you need it.'

Flora's living-room is long and dark, with a white Indian rug and a few scattered furnishings. In her white blouse and black skirt, she goes around, switching on table lamps and spotlights. The lights reveal the straight lines of plain modern furniture, and the texture of unpatterned fabric. Flora's room is a room of shapes and colours, rather than of things, though there are few things that, carefully chosen, do stand out: a blue Aalto chair by the bookcase, a Hockney print on the wall, an Epstein bust on the teak coffee table. The galley kitchen is a construct in oiled wood at the end of the room, and looks straight out into it; Flora can see Howard from here as she goes and begins opening wall cupboards. 'I don't have very much drink in stock,' she says, 'I'm not here enough to build up a collection. What would you like? There's whisky and gin and . . . whisky.' 'I'll have whisky,' says Howard, standing in the room. 'Teacher's or Teacher's?' asks Flora. 'Yes, please,' says Howard. Flora stands in the galley and pours whisky from the bottle into two squat, thick, Swedish glasses. The spotlight in the ceiling shines on her; she is a splendid, formidable figure. She comes round and hands one of the glasses to Howard. 'It's all right,' she says, 'sit down for a minute.' Howard sits in the bulb shape of the Aalto chair; Flora, in her black and white, seats herself on the plain grey straightback modern sofa. 'Well, here's to you, Howard,' she says, 'and your work in the world.' 'Cheers,' says Howard. 'You know, I often think there's something rather noble about the likes of us,' says Flora, 'meeting together like this, and giving so much of our attention and concern to the fate of others, when we could just have been concentrating on having fun by ourselves.' 'Yes,' says Howard, 'it is a peculiarly selfless activity.' 'Of course there is some pleasure in what we do for them,' says Flora, 'there must be, or we wouldn't want to keep our victims to ourselves.' 'Oh, do we?' asks Howard. 'Well, you didn't really want to tell me about Myra's visit to you last night.' 'The sanctity of the confessional, the privacy of the consulting room,' says Howard. 'But you don't believe in privacy,' says Flora, 'you'd tell anything if it suited you. You wanted them for yourself.' 'No,' says Howard, 'I wanted you, Flora.' 'So you held back so I'd ask you into bed,' says Flora. 'Exactly,' says Howard. 'You didn't need to,' says Flora, 'I would have asked you anyway.' 'You would?' asks Howard. 'Why?' 'A terrible reason,' says Flora, 'a terrible, terrible reason.' 'Tell it to me,' says Howard. 'I hardly can,' says Flora, 'you see, I like it with you.' 'It's the nicest thing you've ever said to me,' says Howard. 'Or to anybody,' says Flora. 'So you'll ask me again,' says Howard.

Flora sits on the sofa and looks at him. 'No, I'm not sure I shall,' says Flora. 'But you must,' says Howard. 'I've admitted I'd like to,' says Flora, 'but duty does call.' 'What duty?' asks Howard. 'Isn't it obvious?' asks Flora, 'I really ought to get Henry to come to bed with me.' 'That's absurd,' says Howard. 'Why is it?' asks Flora. 'We both just agreed that Henry's virtually sexless.' 'I'm sure it's true,' says Flora, 'but one doesn't do these things simply for the pleasure.' 'You mean you're now going to prefer Henry to me?' 'Prefer only in a sense,' says Flora, 'I think he has more need.' 'Oh, Christ, Flora,' says Howard, 'it's ridiculous.' 'You're jealous, Howard,' says Flora. 'Well, I'm prepared, unlike you, to admit it,' says Howard, 'I am.' 'I'm not trying to take him from you,' says Flora. 'We can share him.' 'Not jealous like that,' says Howard, 'I want you.' 'We'll see each other around,' says Flora, 'well, it's nine thirty, out you go. I've got some work to do. Can you find your way down?' Howard rises from the Aalto chair; he puts his glass on the teak coffee table; he walks towards the door. 'Well, goodnight, Flora,' he says. 'Goodnight, Howard, my dear,' says Flora, 'here, give me a kiss.' Flora steps towards him; they embrace in the doorway. 'Howard,' she says. 'Yes?' asks Howard. 'Do let me know if you find out anything very interesting,' says Flora. 'Yes, I will,' says Howard, 'will that change your mind?' 'We'll have to see,' says Flora, 'it depends how interesting it is.' Howard goes out onto the landing. 'Goodnight, love,' says Flora, shutting her door.

Flora's flat is on the fourth floor of this five-storey block; Howard walks down, from landing to landing, on the mosaic concrete, past the closed doors of other flats. He goes out through the lobby, past the letterboxes of the residents, and out into the carefully landscaped private gardens. A private drive wends up from the road; on it, among the Rovers and the Datsuns, he has parked his minivan. The estate is charming, with beeches and cedars; under the trees he can see a night-walker strolling, looking up at the neat modern building. He looks up too, and identifies the flat he has just left: the lighted living-room and, with its fainter lights, the bedroom. And now

Flora's big shadow comes up on the bedroom curtains; he watches as it passes across the room, to the point where the bedhead is, close to the spot where he has lately been lying. One of the lights douses; then Flora switches off the other, and the window disappears into the general darkness. After a moment her figure reappears against the plain curtains of the living-room. Then it passes from view, to reappear once more as the lights go on in a new room, the tiny little room at the end of the flat which is Flora's study. The room is uncurtained; he can see Flora sitting down at a desk by the window, in front of a typewriter, and beginning work, her face bent forward and down, her dark hair visible in the glow of a desk lamp. He gets into the van, starts the engine, and drives down the drive, and out into the leafy suburban road, and turns towards the town. He parks the van in the square where he leaves it overnight, walks down the hill, under the sodium lamps, past the failing shops, to the terrace. He unlocks his front door and lets himself into the hall.

There is a light in the pine kitchen, and a great business. He opens the door and sees at once that all the glasses from the party have been collected, and put in neat rows on the central table; the dirty plates have been stacked in a pile on the kitchen cabinets; the empty wine bottles stand in a neat row against the wall. At the sink, a very active figure, stands Felicity Phee. She has put on, over the vest-top and the long skirt, one of the two butcher's aprons that hang behind the kitchen door; the one, in fact, that is Howard's own, for the stripes on Barbara's run, for easy identification, the other way. Cupboards are open, to put things away; many of the glasses are already washed, and stand against the cardboard boxes from the wine supermarket, waiting to be put back in. The kitchen smells, as it has rarely smelled, of the sudsy smell of washing-up liquid. Howard stares at this scene of cleanliness and domestic efficiency; he says, 'Good God, Felicity, what have you been doing?' Felicity has apparently not heard him come in; she looks up, shows surprise, and says, 'Oh, Howard, you're back. How was your meeting?' 'Very good,' says Howard. Felicity takes down a towel from the wall and dries her hands on it; she says, 'Would you like me to fix you a drink?' 'What is all this?' asks Howard. 'I've been using some of those domestic skills you told me this morning I didn't have,' said Felicity, 'Barbara asked if I'd tidy up a bit after the party.' 'I hope she's not exploiting you,' says Howard. 'Of course she's not exploiting me,' says Felicity, 'I wouldn't do it if I didn't want to. I like being in your house. I like being indispensable.' 'Did you get the children to bed?' asks Howard. 'Aren't they lovely children?' cries Felicity, 'I bathed them and read them stories, and we had a long talk. I promised to take them to the fun-fair on Saturday.' 'What's happening on Saturday?' asks Howard. 'Didn't you know?' asks Felicity, 'Barbara's asked me to come and stay here over the weekend, and look after the children while she goes to London.' 'I see,' says Howard. 'Is Barbara in?' 'No,' says Felicity, 'she said that you shouldn't bother to wait up for her. She thought she might be quite late. She says these evening classes often go on a long time.' 'Well,' says Howard, 'you seem to have made a hit. Are you ready now? I'll drive you back to your flat.' 'There's no need,' says Felicity, 'I'm staying. Barbara asked me to. She told me to make a bed up in the guest bedroom.' 'The window's broken in the guest bedroom,' says Howard. 'I know,' says Felicity, 'I've fixed it with cardboard and tacks.' 'Are you staying right through to the weekend?' asks Howard. 'No,' says Felicity, 'I'll have to go back to the flat, and sort out my stuff, and tell Maureen. She'll be raging crazy. But I just feel so happy in this house. You don't mind, do you?'

'I'm not sure it's a wildly good idea,' says Howard. 'Don't worry,' says Felicity, 'I shan't expect anything of you. I'll just be about, if you ever want anything of me. I'm feeling very sensible at the moment.' 'I see,' says Howard, 'are there any more surprises you ought to tell me about?' 'I don't think so,' says Felicity. 'Oh, there was a message. Professor Marvin rang. I told him you were at a psychological meeting, and he asked if you'd ring him back when you got in.' 'I'll do it now,' says Howard. 'Let me get you a drink first,' says Felicity. 'No,' says Howard. He goes out of the kitchen, into the darkened hall; then he goes down the stairs into the basement study. The curtains are undrawn; the town light shines in. He switches on the overhead light and sees that Felicity, despite her enormous domestic activity upstairs, has found time to come down here and visit, for the typescript of his book, which he had tidied up

187

and put in a neat pile on his desk before he left the house this morning, now lies scattered once again in a disorderly mess around the canvas chair. He can hear Felicity moving about upstairs, and the pots clashing in the sink, as he sits down at his desk chair, reaches for the telephone, and dials a number. Outside, through the grilled window, he can see the familiar shapes opposite, the stark railings, the jagged houselines, lit in sodium glare. The telephone trills; the receiver is lifted at the other end. 'Kirk,' says Howard, 'I've been asked to ring you.' 'Your babysitter's very efficient,' says Marvin's voice at the other end, 'I gather she's one of our students.' 'Yes,' says Howard. 'I'm sorry to drag you to the telephone after you've been out at a wearisome meeting,' says Marvin. 'How dedicated my colleagues are. While I, I'm ashamed to say, have been sitting at home in domestic tranquillity. I'm afraid the meeting this afternoon tired me badly. And worried me.' 'I can imagine,' says Howard. 'But I'm not ringing about that,' says Marvin, 'I must bear my woes. No, guess what I did to pass my time this evening.' 'I can't imagine,' says Howard. 'I picked up Carmody's essays,' says Marvin. 'Hardly the most exciting way of passing the time,' says Howard. 'No,' says Marvin, 'a dull and tedious experience. The trouble is, and this is why I rang you, it's also a worrying one.' 'Why did it worry you?' asks Howard.

'Well,' says Marvin, 'have you ever thought what a difficult and strange business our practice of assessing students is?' 'I've often condemned it as completely artificial,' says Howard, 'but it happens to be our practice.' 'Trying to place a man on a scale of virtue, saying whether we deem him to pass or fail, trying to reach an objective standard.' 'Though all judgments are in fact ideologically subjective,' says Howard. 'Yet we agree to try,' says Marvin, 'we agree we can reach a consensus of judgment.' 'Not all of us,' says Howard. 'Do I take it that you're questioning the marks I've given Carmody?' 'Let me put it like this,' says Marvin, 'I wonder if, quite informally and out of hours, we might discuss them.' 'You mean you think Carmody's essays are *good*?' asks Howard. 'No,' says Marvin, 'they're bad and problematic. The trouble is they're evasive, they don't meet the tests you've set the man. But they also have intelligence, shrewdness, and cultural insight. The problem is to assess the level of the badness and the failure.' 'I see no problem,' says Howard, 'they're outright, failing bad.' 'I've read each one three times, Howard,' says Marvin. 'Now markers frequently disagree, and have learned ways of resolving their disagreements. My impression is simply that you're not using our elegant marking scale, with its plusses and minusses and query plus minusses, with quite the delicacy you might. So I found, reading them, that I often had here the sense of a C, there an intimation even of lower B, where you go for the full punitive weight of the outright and explicit F.' 'I see,' says Howard, 'and how did you come to be a marker of Carmody's essays?' 'Oh, by right, Howard,' says Marvin, 'you see, as I'm sure you know, marks here aren't finally awarded by individuals, but by the university. In practice the university is a board of appointed examiners. We're both examiners.' 'I don't agree,' says Howard, 'so I won't discuss Carmody's marks with you. Those marks can only be judged against his entire performance in my classes, which no one else can see and estimate. I've judged him, as his teacher, and you have to trust me, right or wrong.'

There is a pause at the other end, and then Marvin says, 'So my informal solution doesn't appeal to you.' 'Not a bit,' says Howard, 'I don't propose to look at Carmody's essays again. I don't propose to look at Carmody again, or have him in my classes.' 'Oh, dear,' says Marvin. 'Oh, dear, dear. A failing person? Is he really a failing person? We require a very high standard of nothingness for that.' 'I think Carmody meets all the criteria of nothingness you can devise,' says Howard. 'Then I'm afraid I shall have to register my formal dissent from you, Howard,' says Marvin. 'Now, naturally, I've done a bit of homework on this, and there is a university procedure when examiners disagree. We refer the matter to other examiners, and that I propose to do. I shall have Carmody's essays photocopied, and get all your marks and comments deleted, a not inconsiderable secretarial task, but one necessary to ensure justice. I hope that seems fair to you.' 'No,' says Howard, 'not at all. You're not marking Carmody, you're marking me. You're challenging my competence as a teacher, and I question your right to do it.' 'You, er, feel still that we can't settle this informally,' asks Marvin. 'No,' says Howard, 'I think you've got yourself a real bone of contention.' 'Well, excuse me for disturbing you at home,' says Marvin, 'I strongly disapprove of disturbing my colleagues in their leisure hours, but it seemed worth the try. How's Barbara?' 'Well,' says Howard. 'Good,' says Marvin. 'Goodbye, Howard.' 'Goodnight,' says Howard, and puts down the red telephone.

For a moment he sits at the desk; then he hears, and identifies, a small noise from upstairs. He gets to his feet, and goes up into the hall. The hall is darkened; but there, in bare feet, in the butcher's apron, is Felicity, a few feet from the telephone, looking at him. 'You were listening,' he says. 'That was private, Felicity.' Felicity smiles at him, appearing not to grasp the point. 'Oh, Howard, darling, what's private?' she asks. 'Private is doing business in my own house without it being interfered with,' says Howard. 'Isn't that rather a bourgeois attitude?' asks Felicity. 'Get ready,' says Howard, 'I'm taking you back to your flat.' Felicity puts her back against the wall; she says, 'I'm not going.' 'Oh, you are,' says Howard. Felicity's eyes brim with tears. 'Look at all the work I did for you,' she says, 'wasn't that good? Let me stay here.' 'It's an impossible situation, Felicity,' says Howard. 'Now come on to the car.' He takes her arm; they move down the hall. 'No,' says Felicity, pulling her arm free, 'you're being very silly.' 'Why am I being silly?' asks Howard. 'You need me so much now,' says Felicity, 'Suppose they ask your class about George Carmody?' 'I don't think anyone is going to bother asking my class about George,' says Howard. 'I think George has reached the end of the line.' 'But don't you see what that phone call means?' asks Felicity. 'The liberal reactionaries are ganging up against you. They'll support him. But if we supported you, the students in that class, if we said how terrible he'd been, they'd not be able to touch you. I think you'd be very silly to turn me out now.' 'Would I?' asks Howard. 'I'm not out to harm you, Howard,' says Felicity, 'I only want to have a useful part in your life.' In the dark hall they stand and look at each other; as they stand, the doorbell rings loudly over them. 'I'll be ever so good if you keep me,' says Felicity. Howard moves past her, down the hall to the front door. He opens it; on the steps stands someone in a cossack coat and high boots, holding a suitcase and a birdcage. 'Myra,' says Howard. Myra steps into the open door. She sees

Felicity down the hall; she looks at Howard. 'Oh, Howard,' she says, 'I've left Henry. I've got nowhere to go.' 'You've walked out on him?' asks Howard. 'Yes,' says Myra, putting down the birdcage, 'I've done it now. You will let me stay here, won't you?'

XII

On Saturday 7 October the sun shines, there is a light mist off
the sea, and Barbara gets ready to go to London. There is
bread in the house, food in the refrigerator; the guest-room
window has been mended, the dishes are washed, the glasses
have gone back to the wineshop, and all is fit to leave. Just
before nine o'clock, Howard, the helpful husband, goes up to
the square, and fetches the minivan; Felicity Phee, the helpful
help, takes the children outside, and lifts them, giggling and
full of enjoyment, into the back. Barbara is smart in a furry
coat, and high boots; she runs down the steps, carrying a small
striped suitcase, and puts it in the back, and shuts the doors,
and gets into the van beside Howard. Felicity waves from the
steps. 'Have a good time,' she shouts, 'I'll take care of all of
them.' Things are well arranged; Barbara smiles, the van
starts. The bright sun glares into the van windows as they drive
up the hill, through the traffic, and pull into the station yard.
'Weekend in London', say the posters under the covered
arcade where the van has stopped; Barbara will. She leans
across to her helpful husband; she kisses him on the cheek. She
kneels up on the seat, and kisses the children in the back. 'Be
good,' she says, 'all of you.' Then she lifts out her case, and
walks into the bustle of the concourse. They can see her from
the van; she stops and waves; she goes through the glass doors
into the bright ticket hall. She stands in the queue, and buys a
weekend ticket, waiting in front of the counter while the

192

booking clerk prints the ticket on a large console. Her coat is smart, her hair is frizzed and pretty; the people in the line look at her. She is still in good time for the train, so she goes to the news-stand at the end of the platform, and looks through the magazine display: the bright photography of faces, clothes and breasts, the clean modern graphics. She browses a while; then she picks out a glossy magazine designed for today's sophisticated woman, advertising articles about Twiggy, and living together, and the controversy about the vaginal versus the clitoral orgasm, and pays for it.

The train stands at the platform, a very convenient train, with a buffet. The day's travellers walk down beside it, past the orange curtains. Barbara joins them, passing the coaches until she finds the buffet; she gets in, finds a corner seat, and throws her magazine down on it. She looks around; the coach is not busy; the buffet counter is being arranged by the attendant. She puts her case on the rack; she hangs up her coat on the peg; she sits down, and places the magazine on her knee. She watches the people get onto the train. A young man in a denim suit, with a briefcase, comes and sits opposite her; he smiles at her, and she smiles back, but does not speak. The train whistle blows; the train pulls out of the domed shed of the station. With the magazine on her knee, she stares out at the freight-yards, the dumps of coal, the office blocks in the town-centre, the pillars of the motorway, the view, down through the shopping business of Watermouth, to the sea. The blind of the buffet rolls up; she gets to her feet, goes to the counter, and buys a cup of coffee, carrying it back in its plastic cup held in a brown plastic holder. The man smiles at her again as she sits; he says, 'Off for the weekend?' 'I'm a married woman,' says Barbara, and puts her head down, and reads an article about vasectomy. After a while she lifts her head and stares out of the window, at the fields and hedges. The day is bright; the sun shines and shimmers in her eyes; it is a red disk in her lashes. The man stares at her. At home the household arrangements are secure; Felicity will take the children for a walk on the beach this morning, and put out their lunch, ready in the refrigerator, and spend the afternoon with them at the fun-fair, and bath them before they go to bed. The man still looks at her; she puts her head down, and stares into the magazine, examining the fashion photographs in which, on some beach in Tunisia, nipples slip chancily into view out of loose silk, and female faces pout angrily, in the fashionable style, at the prodding camera. Her eyes are green; her cheeks are rubbed red; she sits comfortably in her seat, taking the man's gaze over her.

The train is convenient, the service to London fairly quick; that is one of the pleasures of Watermouth. It is a familiar journey. The cars stand in the car parks of London commuterland, and then there are the back gardens of London suburbia. The tenement area comes up; then they are following the Thames, and running down the platform at Waterloo under noisy loudspeakers. She rises from her seat, and puts on the furry coat. The man opposite rises, and lifts down her case. 'Have a good time,' he says. She smiles at him, thanks him, and goes and stands by the train door. When the train stops, the man walks beside her down the platform. He asks her name; she does not give it. She comes to the barrier, and there, waiting, waving, is Leon, in his much-worn leather motor-cycle jacket, his hair long. He pushes to her, puts his arm round her, kisses her. The man has gone. She puts down her case, and kisses him. 'Oh, you're here,' she says. Leon takes her case, and they go across to the station buffet, and sit talking busily over a cup of coffee. Her eyes are bright; she slips her coat down her shoulders. After a while they leave the buffet and walk across to the Underground entrance. They go through the busy concourse, take tickets, and wait on the platform for a Northern Line train. The train comes through the tunnel; they get in and stand close together, Leon's hand inside her coat, until the train reaches Charing Cross where they change to the Circle Line for Sloane Square. They leave the train there, hurry through the station, with Leon in front, laughing, and they come up into the street, among the traffic. Leon carries her bag; they make their way along, stopping frequently, staring into the windows of boutiques with their fancy display of fabric, their tactile colour-mixes, their strobe lights. They go in and out of shops, touch objects, look along racks of bright clothes. Music booms from speakers, and theft-detection cameras show their pictures on a screen, a smart couple.

They buy a pepper-mill; they look together at a sex magazine; they look through a rack of posters. Here and there

Barbara takes dresses off the racks, and shows them to the pretty shopgirls, and takes them to the fitting-rooms, trying them on, this style and that, in a crowd of girls in their underpants. Each dress she tries she shows to Leon, posing before him, showing him different selves, as he sits on a chair among the racks, or leans against the counter, talking to the assistants. Together, in due consideration, they pick two; they are put into high-coloured plastic bags, which she carries as they go on. Later they find a pub, and sit together drinking, and eat sandwiches from the bar. Afterwards they get on a bus, and go to a cinema; they watch a Hungarian film and lean lazily against each other, their hands feeling into each other. When the film is over they walk the shopping streets, walking and talking. There is a restaurant in Greek Street where actors go; they eat dinner there, and talk to acquaintances of Leon's. Then there is a pub where actors drink; they join a crowded table there, with actors and actresses, television-directors and writers, all talking in bright style about football. Girls kiss Leon; men kiss Barbara. Much later on, they go out, through the restaurants and strip-shows, to find a bus and go to Islington, where Leon's bedsitter is. They go past cracked stucco and antique shops and ethnic stores to the ramshackle house. They go up the stairs, unlock the door, light the gasfire. It is an untidy room, barely tenanted; there are posters on the walls, and photographs of sets, productions, many face shots. There are only two chairs, and a daybed, and a table, and an old brown carpet on the floor. There is a stereo; Leon switches it on, and noise booms. They then pull cushions off the daybed, onto the floor; they lie together in front of the gasfire, and reach out and undress each other, quickly; and then Barbara subsides backwards onto the cushions, and looks as Leon's face pushes towards her, his body comes over her. His hands stir pleasure into her, his body comes in.

It is pleasant to hold him inside, with the heat of the gasfire on the skin of her side, her leg. And later it is pleasant to make up the daybed, and get into it, and fold into each other again, to feel sensation, to let pieces of self come alive. It is pleasant, too, to wake in the night against flesh, to stir, to touch and press the adjoining body until it connects with yours once more. It is pleasant in the morning to lie in bed, while Leon goes out and fetches the *Observer*, and to read one section while he, undressed and back in bed, reads the other. It is pleasant to spend Sunday walking, looking at paintings in a gallery, lunching in a pub, going to look at the river. It is pleasant to walk along the shopping streets on a Sunday, past the bright displays, and the mirrors where you see yourself reflected, bright-looking yourself, with bright Leon, with his stark face and long hair, among all the other young people. It is pleasant to go back to the bed-sitter, and put the fire on once more, and begin again the touching and feeling and the delicate tactical motions that bring pleasure, which is pleasant, and to try on the dresses you've bought, and some of Leon's clothes and costumes, and smoke, and feel. It is only not pleasant to be told that Leon, who is busy with parts, will be busier; he is going off for five months on tour, with *Much Ado About Nothing*, to Australia and the United States. 'I don't know what I'll do when you're gone,' says Barbara. 'I'm not the only one like me,' says Leon, pulling her down. So it is depressing to wake up early on Monday morning, while Leon still sleeps, and let yourself out, and make your way with your case and your two dress bags to the bus, and the tube, and get to Waterloo for the busy morning train. It is hard to find a seat, and there is rain again, soaking the London suburbs, driving across the woods and fields. The magazine is open on Barbara's knee, but she does not look at it. She sits with her mouth open, her fur coat kept on, her face staring through the window. The train slides slowly down the platform at Watermouth. When it stops, she picks up her luggage and gets out. Howard is waiting in the concourse, in his leather jacket, a neat, new, brown jacket, the car keys in his hand. He kisses her lightly, and takes her bag. 'Did you have a good time?' he asks. 'Yes,' she says, 'quite good. I bought two dresses.'

They go outside, and get in the minivan; the wipers move backwards and forwards in front of them. 'How are the kids?' asks Barbara. 'Fine,' says Howard. 'They've gone to school?' says Barbara. 'Yes, I took them,' says Howard. 'Was Felicity all right?' 'She seems to get on very well with them,' says Howard. 'I think she likes them,' says Barbara, 'they like her. She takes an interest.' 'Yes,' says Howard. 'Did Myra get off?' asks Barbara. 'Yes,' says Howard, 'she's gone back to the farmhouse.' 'To Henry?' asks Barbara. 'No,' says Howard, 'Henry's not there. He's staying with Flora Beniform.' 'She should have kept him,' says Barbara. 'She may come to think that,' says Howard, 'since she doesn't know what to do with herself.' 'What did you do with yourself?' asks Barbara. 'I worked,' says Howard. 'No fires, no accidents?' asks Barbara. 'No,' says Howard. They are driving down the hill; they can see the turn into the terrace; the cranes on the building sites turn and creak. 'I'll put my dresses on for you,' says Barbara. 'Tonight,' says Howard, 'I've got to go straight up to the university. Your train was late.' 'Is anything happening?' asks Barbara. 'No,' says Howard, 'just usual. I have two funny little girls coming in to read me an essay.' They turn into the rainwashed terrace; Howard stops the van. He reaches in the back and lifts out the case. Barbara carries her two plastic bags to the front door; she gets out her key and unlocks it. The house smells dry and flat. 'Hello, Barbara,' says Felicity, coming out of the kitchen, wearing a butcher's apron, 'did you have a good shopping trip?' 'Yes,' says Barbara. 'Let me get you a cup of coffee,' says Felicity. 'No,' says Howard, putting down the case in the hall, 'if you want a lift up to the university, you'll have to come now.' 'Sorry, Barbara,' says Felicity, taking off the apron, 'but I've been very good. I've done lots of tidying up.' 'That's great,' says Barbara, 'Were the kids good?' 'Oh,' says Felicity, 'they're the sweetest kids ever. I'm really hooked on those kids. Do you want me to come back tonight?' 'Why not?' asks Barbara. 'I'd love to stay,' says Felicity, 'and I'm sure I'm useful.' 'Okay,' says Barbara, putting the dress bags down onto a chair. 'Stay a while. Do, that helps me. I can't do this place by myself.' 'Oh, good,' says Felicity, 'I love it here.' She casts a look at Howard, and goes out into the hall, to get her coat. 'Welcome back,' says Howard, pecking Barbara on the cheek. 'Bye now.'

Barbara stands in the hall as they go outside to the minivan. They get into it, and drive away, round the corner, up the hill. 'Isn't Barbara good?' says Felicity. 'Yes,' says Howard. 'You're angry,' says Felicity. 'No,' says Howard. They say nothing more until they have crossed town and are out on the dualled road, with the university coming into sight on the right. Then Felicity says: 'I thought she looked sad.' 'I didn't think so,' says Howard, 'she enjoys her weekends.' 'Did you enjoy yours?' asks Felicity.

'It had its pleasures,' says Howard. 'I don't really turn you on, do I?' asks Felicity. 'You don't appreciate me. You don't know how much I'm doing for you.' 'What are you doing for me?' asks Howard, stopping the van in the car park. 'A lot,' says Felicity, 'you'll see.' 'I can look after myself,' says Howard. 'You need support,' says Felicity, 'you're my cause.' Felicity gets out of the van, and walks toward the Student Union building; Howard gets out, locks it, and moves in another direction, toward Social Science. The students mill in the foyer; he gets into the lift. The lift doors open at the fifth floor; he gets out. He notices, on the information blackboard that faces the lift, a message has been scrawled in chalk, by one of the secretaries. He pauses to read it: it says, 'Dr Beamish has a snakebite and regrets he cannot meet his classes today.' He turns, and goes down the corridor towards his room. He can see, down the corridor, waiting for him, sitting on the floor, with their knees up, the two first-year students who came to him the previous Monday: the bright, bra-less girl, the fat, long-skirted one. They stand up as they see him coming, and pick up their books. 'Come on in,' he says amiably; the girls follow him into the room, and wait while he hangs up his coat behind the door. Then he sits them down, putting the fatter girl in the grey chair, for she is the one who will read her essay. He sits down in his own chair, and looks at them. The bright, bra-less girl, on the plastic chair, says: 'Dr Kirk, are you really a radical?' 'I am,' says Howard, 'but why?' The girls look at each other. 'There's a rumour around that they're trying to fire you,' says the bra-less girl, 'because you're such a radical.'

'Is there?' says Howard. 'Well, as it happens, they can't fire me for that. Only for gross moral turpitude.' The girls giggle and say, 'What's that?' 'Who knows, nowadays?' asks Howard. 'One story has it that it's raping large numbers of nuns.' 'Well,' says the fat girl, 'if they try, we'll stand by you.' 'That's very good of you,' says Howard. 'Have you found out who Hegel is yet?' 'Oh, yes,' says the bra-less girl, 'Do you want to hear about him?' 'I think we'd better stick to business and hear the essay,' says Howard. 'All right,' says the fat girl, 'but people say you're very nasty to students reading their essays to you.' 'You seem to be hearing a great deal about me,' says Howard, 'most of it hardly true. You read it, and see.' The girl pulls out an essay from between her books, and says, 'Well, you asked me to write on the social structure of imperialism.' She puts down her head, and starts reading; Howard, the serious teacher, sits in his chair as she reads, interrupting now and then with a comment, an amplification. 'Was that so nasty?' he says afterwards, when the discussion has finished. 'Not at all,' says the fat girl. 'Well,' says Howard, 'it was a reasonable essay.' 'What you wanted,' says the girl. 'I hope what you wanted too,' says Howard. He continues teaching through the morning; at lunchtime he finds it necessary to go and seek out Peter Madden, and sit in a corner of the cafeteria with him; they eat salad plate together amid the noise, and discuss. The discussion is long, and it is just before two o'clock when Howard gets back to his room. As he unlocks his door, the telephone on his desk starts to ring. He takes off his coat, sits down in his chair, and picks up the phone. 'This is Minnehaha Ho,' says a voice, 'Professor Marvin wishes you.' 'Hello, Minnie,' says Howard, 'Professor Marvin wishes me what?' 'He wants you to come and see him now, in his room,' says Miss Ho. 'Well, just a moment,' says Howard, 'I have to check whether I'm teaching.' 'It's urgent,' says Miss Ho, 'also you are not teaching. Professor Marvin checked already.' 'Oh, did he?' says Howard, 'very well. I'll be along in a moment.'

Howard gets up from the desk, locks his door, and goes along the corridor to the Department Office. The secretaries, just back from their lunch-hour, during which they have been shopping with string bags, are sitting at their desks. Professor Marvin's room is a sanctum beyond the department office, its entrance guarded by Miss Ho. 'Hello, Minnie,' says Howard, 'what does he want me for?' Miss Ho does not look up from the letter she has in her typewriter; she says, 'I don't know. He'll tell you.' Just then the door of Marvin's office flies open; Marvin himself stands in the doorway, very little, the familiar row of pens sported in the top pocket of his worn suit. The spirit of the age has tempted him into wearing his facial hair down to the level of the bottom of his ears; this provides him with a solemn expression. 'Ah, Howard,' he says, 'come on in.' Marvin's room is more spacious than those of the rest of his colleagues, for he is a man of many affairs; it has a thick carpet, and fitted mahogany bookcases, and a small xerox copier, and its own pencil sharpener, and a very large desk, big enough to hold a coffin, on which stands a dictaphone and three telephones. Small Arabic and Oriental features are included in the decor; there are framed wall tiles inscribed in Arabic script, and pictures of Istanbul and Trebizond and Shiraz, and a photograph of Marvin, taken when younger, riding very high on a camel, in Arab headdress. 'Do have a seat, Howard,' says Marvin, putting himself behind his desk, against the light, 'You know I hate to interrupt my colleagues when they have better things to do. But I've a problem on my plate, and I thought we needed a word.' 'About Carmody?' asks Howard, not sitting. 'Yes,' says Marvin, seating himself, 'that little bone of contention.' 'Then I think we do,' says Howard, 'I gather you've consulted my colleagues about his essays, despite my protest. I formally object.' 'I had to, Howard,' says Marvin, 'there is an official procedure. I gather you've also objected informally, by talking to them about it.' 'I found that necessary, yes,' says Howard. 'Of course that may explain why my little exercise turned out something of a failure,' says Marvin. 'I warned you it would,' says Howard.

'Well, you might like to know what happened,' says Marvin, 'if you don't already. The essays were seen by six examiners. Three mark him at passing level, with small variations, but mostly around high C or low B. Roughly in accord with my own judgment, in short. Two gave him Fs, much as you had, and one refused to mark altogether, saying you had told him this was interference with a colleague's teaching.' 'It seems to me a very instructive result,' says Howard. 'As I told you, marking is not an innocent occupation. It's ideologically conditioned.' 'In all my examining experience I've never had such a pattern of discrepancy,' says Marvin, 'so I think there might be a lower explanation. But I don't propose to go into those murky waters.' 'I'm sorry,' says Howard, 'but I'm afraid I feel my point's established. There's no such thing as objective marking.' 'It may be hard,' says Marvin, 'but in my view it's the task of a university to try for it. And if we can't manage that kind of disinterestedness, then I'm damned if I know what justification there is for our existence.' 'That's because you live in a liberal fantasy,' says Howard. 'Well, what do you propose to do about Carmody now?' 'Well, I've spent a somewhat painful weekend thinking over the situation,' says Marvin. 'And then I saw Carmody and his adviser this morning, and told them I could see no way of improving his situation. I also informed them that you had made a complaint against him.' 'In short,' says Howard, 'you told him that he'd made a malicious and unfounded assertion.' 'I could hardly say that,' says Marvin. 'After all, you've been instructing me in the fact that there's no disinterested marking. I had to ask him if he wished to take the matter further. He then became hysterical, said that he did, and then proceeded, in what I fear was a most unfortunate way, to make further accusations.' Howard stares at Marvin; he says, 'What sort of accusations?'

'Well, I'm afraid of a most gossipy character,' says Marvin, 'of a kind that in normal circumstances I would not have listened to. But I can't feel these are quite normal circumstances, in view of the specific challenge that's involved to our conventions and expectations of marking. Briefly, what his point boiled down to is that your marking, which disfavours him, favours others.' 'I see,' says Howard, 'which others?' 'The case he mentioned was that of a Miss Phee, who has, I see from the mark-sheets, been getting good marks in your course,' says Marvin. 'She's a good student,' says Howard. 'Why am I supposed to have favoured her?' 'Well, the point was partly abstract and political,' says Marvin, 'but I'm afraid it was also concrete and, so to speak, physical.' 'I don't quite understand,' says Howard. 'Carmody's way of putting it was crude but terse,' says Marvin. 'He said he could have done as well in your seminar if he'd had a left-wing head and, er, female genitals.' 'And what did you take that to mean?' asks Howard. 'He said you were having an affair with her,' says Marvin. 'There's one thing I agree with you about. He's a somewhat nasty man.' 'It's hardly your business, is it?' asks Howard, 'Even if it were true.' 'Precisely,' says Marvin, 'that's just what I told him.' 'Good,' says Howard. 'Yes,' says Marvin, 'I told him I felt the matter was becoming more moral than pedagogic. And hence that I could not listen to it.' 'I'm glad to hear it,' says Howard. 'And that the only person competent to deal with such questions was the Vice-Chancellor,' says Marvin. 'You sent him to see the Vice-Chancellor?' says Howard, looking at Marvin. 'No,' says Marvin, 'I simply told him what his options were. I pointed out that the charges were very serious, and if they were false he would find himself in the severest trouble. Indeed I advised him strongly to withdraw them, and go no further.' 'And did he agree?' asks Howard. 'No,' says Marvin, 'he said he felt his evidence made the accusation quite watertight.' 'His evidence?' asks Howard. 'Sit down, Howard,' says Marvin, 'I can't tell you how much I've detested all this. But it's as if you wanted it to expand like this.' 'What is his evidence?' asks Howard. 'One has to say this much for Carmody,' says Marvin, 'he has a certain capacity for research. If only he could have harnessed it to better use.' 'You mean he's been doing research into *me*?' asks Howard. 'That's it,' says Marvin. 'He's been taking great interest in your recent movements.' 'You mean he's been following me around?' asks Howard.

'You know,' says Marvin, leaning forward over the desk, 'I've always thought of myself as a very busy man, with a full diary of engagements. But if what he says is true, what your diary's been like lately I can't imagine. I don't know when you've had time to wash and shave.' 'And what have I been busy doing?' asks Howard. 'Well, you know that, Howard,' says Marvin, 'I hardly like to repeat these things.' 'I should like to know what Mr Carmody believes he's found out about me,' says Howard. 'Since you think they're matters important enough for the Vice-Chancellor to consider.' 'He claims to have a record of promiscuous sexual intimacy,' says Marvin. 'A rather circumstantial record.' 'Can I have some details of this record?' asks Howard. 'Well, it begins on Monday,' says Marvin, 'You had I gather, a party; in the late evening you were in your downstairs room, and according to Carmody an intimacy took place, on the floor, with Miss Phee.' 'Did I?' asks Howard. 'On Tuesday you had recourse in a different direction, to the flat of one of our mutual colleagues. It was an upstairs flat, but with diaphanous curtains, and again Carmody surmised intimacy.' 'Is that a matter for the Vice-Chancellor?' asks Howard. 'I should hardly think so,' says Marvin, 'but the evening continues. You returned home, your wife was out, and Miss Phee was in.' 'Did you know Mrs Beamish was also there?' asks Howard. 'I gather there was a significant time-lapse between your arrival home and Mrs Beamish's coming,' says Marvin. 'It was largely occupied with an extended telephone conversation with you,' says Howard. 'I shall ask you to testify to that if necessary.' 'Ah, what a web it is,' says Marvin. 'Of course I shall tell all I know.' 'And on Wednesday?' 'On Wednesday you stayed in,' says Marvin, 'I gather a fruitless evening for the outside observer.' 'I must have been recouping my strength,' says Howard. 'Is there more?' 'On Thursday you had dinner in a small French restaurant with Carmody's own adviser. The lady was present, so that we were all able to agree on the innocence of that occasion.' 'The evidence is beginning to look rather thin, isn't it?' asks Howard. 'Ah,' says Marvin, 'until the weekend. I gather your wife was away for the weekend, and Miss Phee came and stayed in the house over this period, and is presumably still there. According to Mr Carmody, it's been rather a lively weekend. Indoors and out, so to speak.' 'Did Mr Carmody also tell you that there were two children there, most of the time, and that Miss Phee was there to look after them?' 'He claimed they were no barrier,' says Marvin.

'Well,' says Howard, 'thank you for telling me this. I think it completely clinches my case. I told you the man was a blackmailer. You failed to be convinced. Now he's exposed himself totally.' 'He's certainly shown himself as vilely unpleasant,' says Marvin. 'And of course it will save time if he goes to see the Vice-Chancellor. After all, he's the person to deal with this sort of illegality. Unless, of course, it's the courts. I'm only surprised, and I expect the Vice-Chancellor will be, that you've treated him as if he had some sort of case.' 'Howard,' says Marvin, 'I should like you to understand I have not taken Carmody's side. But I did warn you not to let this become a bone of contention, and you have. I have to look at it all objectively. The trouble is he believes himself to be the victim of an injustice, conducting inquiries to prove his innocence.' 'I'm the victim of an injustice,' says Howard. 'Perhaps you might now see that. I can answer these charges and show the corrupt motives behind them.' 'Oh, that's good, then, Howard,' says Marvin. 'I mean, I think you will need to explain yourself a little to the Vice-Chancellor. Once he sees the photographs.' 'Carmody took photographs?' asks Howard. 'Didn't I say?' asks Marvin. 'He's obviously quite an adept with a camera. Of course the night shots are terribly unconvincing, pictures of shadows on closed curtains, and the like. Your problem will really be with the daytime pictures. I fear it is indubitably you and Miss Phee together in that ravine. And kissing in the dodgems.' 'It's obscene,' says Howard. 'All the apparatus of blackmail.' 'I find it all awfully distressing, Howard,' says Marvin, 'and I'm sure the Vice-Chancellor will too.' Marvin gets up; he walks round his desk, and pats Howard on the arm. 'I do wish you'd listened to me,' he says. 'Avoid bones of contention.' 'I think when you've heard Miss Phee's evidence . . .' says Howard. 'Oh, I shan't hear it,' says Marvin, walking Howard toward the door. 'Happily that's the Vice-Chancellor's problem. It's all passed beyond me, I'm very glad to say. You know, this is one of those bleak moments when I'm actually pleased to think I lead an utterly boring and empty life.'

Marvin holds open the door of his room, and stands there as Howard walks out. In the department office beyond, Miss Ho types furiously, not looking up, as Howard passes through. He steps out into the corridor, and walks along it to the lift. He goes down, out through the foyer, across the Piazza. On the far side of the Piazza stands the Humanities Building, a different affair altogether from Social Sciences, a place not of height, mass and dark, but of length, light and air. There are corridors here lit by long windows, with bushes growing against them; there are noticeboards on the walls speaking of theatrical productions, poetry readings, lectures followed by wine. Child art, for some reason, is displayed along the passages; students sit on benches and talk. The doors have bright nameplates; Howard inspects them as he walks. Then, before one labelled 'Miss A. Callendar' he stops, he knocks. There is no response, so he knocks and waits again. The door of a room adjoining opens a little; a dark, tousled-haired head, with a sad visage, peers through, looks at Howard for a little, and then retreats. The face has a vague familiarity; Howard recalls that this depressed-looking figure is a lecturer in the English department, a man who, ten years earlier, had produced two tolerably well-known and acceptably reviewed novels, filled, as novels then were, with moral scruple and concern. Since then there has been silence, as if, under the pressure of contemporary change, there was no more moral scruple and concern, no new substance to be spun. The man alone persists; he passes nervously through the campus, he

teaches, sadly, he avoids strangers. Howard knocks on this
man's door; hearing no reply, he opens it. The novelist is not
immediately visible; he sits out of the light, in the furthest
corner, hunched over a typewriter, looking doubtfully up at his
visitor. 'I'm sorry to disturb you,' says Howard, 'but I'm
looking for Miss Callendar. Do you know where she is?' 'I don't
think I do,' says the man. 'You've no idea?' asks Howard.
'Well, I thought she'd better go home,' says the man, 'she's in
a very upset state.' 'Well, this is a very urgent matter,' says
Howard, 'I wonder whether you'd give me her address.' 'I'm
afraid I can't,' says the man. 'It's very important,' says Howard.
'Miss Callendar's not easy to find out about,' says the novelist,
'she's a very private person.' 'Do you know her address?' asks
Howard. 'No,' says the man, 'no, I don't.' 'Ah, well,' says
Howard, 'if you want to find things out about people, you
always can, with a little research. A little curiosity.' 'It's
sometimes better not to,' says the man. 'Never mind,' says
Howard, 'I'll find it.' 'I wish you wouldn't,' says the novelist.
'I will,' says Howard, going out of the room, and shutting the
door.

He goes from the light and air of Humanities to the dark
and mass of Social Science; he sits at his desk and goes through
the faculty address book, the Watermouth telephone directory.
He rings the Registry, where these matters are supposed to be
on record; it is not held there. He rings the English department
secretary; he rings the Professor of English. He rings the
Accommodation Officer; he rings the university library. He
rings the university bookshop; 'Yes,' says the manager, 'we
require a home address for an account. I'll look and ring back.'
Howard puts on his coat and his hat, and sits at the desk,
waiting for the telephone to ring. 'Glad to help,' says the
manager, 'here it is.' Howard writes down the address, goes to
the car park, gets in the van, drives, through the bleak and
wintry day, into town. The address is as hard to discover in
reality as it is in record, being in a part of town that Howard
rarely enters, the quaint and holiday town. Castle Mount is
banned to cars; it is a bendy, cobbled, Victorian street over-
looking the harbour. You find the house by walking up the
steep hill towards the castle bailey; here you ask at a newsagents
shop, selling souvenirs, which will misdirect you, and then at a

café, which will set you right again. Spirals of mist come off the harbour; there are little hoots from fishing boats. At a house in a line of ornate Victorian properties, there is a bellpush marked 3A, with no name against it; it is so clearly the destination that he pushes it. He stands in the mist; after a while steps occur in the house, descending a staircase. The door opens, and there is Miss Callendar, in the ornate doorway, in a black trouser suit, with a suspicious, dark expression. 'Oh, it's you,' says Miss Callendar, 'how did you find out where I live?' 'It wasn't easy,' says Howard. 'It's not supposed to be easy,' says Miss Callendar. 'No disrespect, Dr Kirk, but I hoped it was impossible.' 'But why?' asks Howard. 'I told you,' says Miss Callendar, 'I don't want just any old Christian existentialist or Leavisite or Sociologist dropping by, just on the offchance.' 'But we can all be found,' says Howard. 'How?' asks Miss Callendar. 'Let me in, and I'll tell you,' says Howard. 'It's very much against my principles,' says Miss Callendar. 'I haven't come to accuse you or seduce you or convert you,' says Howard, 'I just want to tell you a story.' 'A story,' says Miss Callendar. 'It's very cold here,' says Howard. 'Very well, then,' says Miss Callendar, 'Come up.'

The big Victorian house has a faint smell of must. Howard follows Miss Callendar's velvet bottom up the stairs; then up more stairs, and more, until they are at the top of the house. A dark brown door leads off the landing; Miss Callendar opens it, and leads him in. 'There we are,' says Miss Callendar, 'my very convenient flat.' 'Yes, you told me about it,' says Howard. The flat is quite small; it has twisted walls, with water-stained Victorian prints on them, and a burning gas fire, a ragged red Afghan carpet, a standard lamp with a fringed and flowered lampshade, two armchairs and a sofa done out with chintz loose-covers. 'How did you?' asks Miss Callendar, standing in front of the gasfire. 'You're not in the telephone book,' says Howard. 'Owning no phone,' says Miss Callendar. 'And you're not on the electoral register,' says Howard. 'Owning no vote,' says Miss Callendar. 'But you are on the list at the bookshop, because they need a home address to open an account,' says Howard. 'Ah, well,' says Miss Callendar, 'it's a lot of trouble to go to, just to come and tell me a story.' 'You did hear his version,' says Howard, 'don't you think you ought to hear mine?' 'I'm very fair-minded,' says Miss Callendar, 'but everyone seems to be treating me as if I'm some kind of expert in stories. Which I'm not.' 'I thought it was your field,' says Howard, taking off his coat. 'Oh, no,' says Miss Callendar, 'we live in an era of high specialization. My expertise is in the lyric poem, a very different kettle of fish.' 'What's the difference?' asks Howard. 'Would you like a cup of tea?' asks Miss Callendar, 'I find stories very thirsty.' 'Thank you,' says Howard. Miss Callendar goes through another brown door, and there is the clank of a kettle. 'You didn't explain the difference,' calls Howard. 'Oh, a great difference,' says Miss Callendar, 'if there was a logical difference between form and content, which of course we're agreed there isn't, then stories would be very given to content and lyric poems very given to form.' 'I see,' says Howard. 'You see, my devotion, Dr Kirk, is to form. I'm afraid I find stories very lax and contingent.'

'I see,' says Howard, peering through a third brown door. It is another room Miss Callendar had described to him; the bedroom, with the bed in it. 'I'm glad you were hungry the other night,' he calls into the kitchen. 'I relished the scampi,' says Miss Callendar. 'I thought you'd bring me here then,' says Howard. 'I know you did,' says Miss Callendar, 'but as I explained then, there are limits to my appetite. Clearly very fortunately.' 'Why fortunately?' asks Howard. 'Well, I don't think I'd really have liked to end up in the record, with all the others.' 'Would it have been so bad?' asks Howard. 'Ah,' says Miss Callendar, coming back into the room, carrying a tray with a small brown teapot on it, 'you think it's an honourable roster. A roll of souls redeemed. Is that the gist of your story?' Howard stands in front of the window, which has a view across to the castle, and the wintry sea beyond; he says, 'At least I hope you don't believe Mr Carmody's version.' 'I listen to all stories with a certain healthy scepticism,' says Miss Callendar. 'Do you take milk?' 'Thank you,' says Howard, coming and sitting down on the sofa. 'Well,' says Miss Callendar, 'a tale of sexual heroism. Do go on.' 'I gather you know that I'm being accused of giving good marks to Miss Phee in exchange for her sexual favours?' says Howard. 'Yes,' says Miss Callendar, 'sugar?' 'And of general moral corruption,' says Howard, 'with political overtones. No, thanks.' 'I think you're basically being accused of intellectual persecution,' says Miss Callendar. 'Fig biscuit?' 'Thank you,' says Howard, 'but the key question is now my relationship with Miss Phee. You remember Miss Phee?' 'Do I?' says Miss Callendar. 'Yes,' says Howard, 'you saw me with her in my downstairs study, when you were leaving the party.' 'Then that was one of your episodes,' says Miss Callendar, 'I did rather think so.' 'It's a pity you don't know her better,' says Howard, 'then perhaps, instead of supporting Carmody's crazy story, you'd understand what repressed, evil nonsense it is.' 'I don't support his story,' says Miss Callendar, 'I don't know whether his interpretation of what he saw is right at all. I just have some reason, don't I, for thinking he saw what he saw.'

'But he saw nothing,' says Howard, 'he just looked in on me from outside and made corrupt deductions. Miss Phee's one of my advisees. She's a very sad creature. She's been through everything. Boy trouble, girl trouble, an abortion, the identity crisis, a breakdown . . .' 'The menopause,' says Miss Callendar. 'Not yet,' says Howard. 'Well, you've something to come,' says Miss Callendar. 'A scone? I made them myself.' 'Thanks,' says Howard. 'She had a crisis that night. A lesbian affair she was having was breaking up.' 'Isn't she rather hogging the problems?' asks Miss Callendar. 'She was in trouble,' says Howard, 'she went down there into my study, and started raking through my papers. She wanted to be caught, I think; anyway, I caught her.' 'The instinct of curiosity,' says Miss Callendar, 'Mr Carmody has that too.' 'Of course I was angry. But the meaning of the situation was obvious. She was crying out for attention.' 'So you laid her down and gave her some,' says Miss Callendar. 'No,' says Howard, 'it was very much the other way around.' 'Oh God, how awful,' says Miss Callendar, 'did she attack you? Were you hurt?' 'I'm explaining to you that she has no attraction for me,' says Howard, 'I didn't want her at all. I wanted someone else. In fact, you. Out there beyond the window.' 'But in my absence you settled for her instead,' says Miss Callendar, picking up, from a table at the side of her chair, a mysterious ravel of knitting, with needles sticking through it, and beginning to work on it, 'I see.' 'I want you to see that this situation isn't as Carmody described it,' says Howard, 'I want you to see it humanly.' 'My Carmody wanted you to see him humanly,' says Miss Callander. 'Miss Phee needed help,' says Howard, 'that's why I took her into my house. That's why she was there over the weekend while my wife was away.' 'Did your wife go far?' asks Miss Callendar. 'London,' says Howard. 'You did tell me about her trips to London,' says Miss Callander, 'she goes her way, you go yours. No doubt you were able to give her much more attention and help while she was away.' 'She was there,' says Howard, 'to look after the children. We looked after them together. We took them to the fun-fair, walked in the country with them.' 'But you did give her some help,' says Miss Callendar, 'there were photographs of the help.' 'Exactly,' says Howard. 'This was the situation that Carmody spied on and photographed and distorted into a blackmailing accusation, without knowing anything at all about it.'

Miss Callendar, sitting in her armchair, turns a row of her knitting. 'I see,' she says, 'and that's the story.' 'That's the essence of it,' says Howard. 'Do you mind if I criticize,' asks Miss Callender, 'with my imperfect expertise?' 'Do,' says Howard, 'Well, it's a tale of fine feeling,' says Miss Callendar, 'it's certainly got more psychology than Mr Carmody's. It's less ironic and detached, more a piece of late nineteenth-century realism. But his has more plot and event. I mean, in his, Miss Phee needs help quite frequently. And then you have to nip off one evening and help Dr Beniform, and then there's the little episode with me, not treated in your version at all, though I found it quite significant.' 'It's hardly relevant,' says Howard. 'That's not very kind,' says Miss Callendar, 'one hates not to be of the essence. Relegated to a minor sub-plot. In his version I'm quite a rounded character.' 'I'm not sure where you fit,' says Howard, 'since I thought the point of his story was that I'm giving good marks to Miss Phee for corrupt reasons.' 'That's right,' says Miss Callendar, 'his story does have an ending. Where you hand out the As and Bs. For her overall performance, as they say.' 'Whereas the point of my story is that if I did grade Miss Phee for her performance it wouldn't be As and Bs.' 'Yes,' says Miss Callendar, 'I see that. Well, there we are. It shows how different a story can be if you change the *point d'appui*, the angle of vision.' 'Angle of vision!' says Howard, 'That man's followed me everywhere, tracked my movements, photographed me through curtains, and then built a lie out of it. He's a fine angle of vision.' 'An outside eye's sometimes illuminating,' says Miss Callendar, 'and of course, as Henry James says, the house of fiction has many windows. Your trouble is you seem to have stood in front of most of them.'

'Look, Miss Callendar,' says Howard, 'these aren't just two little stories, for your bright critical intelligence to play with.' 'No,' says Miss Callendar, 'there's more at stake. But the trouble is I don't find your story's complete. I don't think you're telling me everything. I don't know what you want of Carmody, I don't know what you want of me. There's a plot you haven't given.' 'I don't know whether you know how much is at stake,' says Howard. 'You realize that Carmody's spied on me every day, and made up a story out of what he's seen that could cost me my job?' 'You could say he was trying to make sense of you,' says Miss Callendar. 'For God's sake,' says Howard, 'he's probably outside there right now, on a ladder, making up a story about me taking your clothes off.' 'Does he lie?' asks Miss Callendar, 'Isn't there some truth?' 'I'm not taking your clothes off,' says Howard. 'He's not out there,' says Miss Callendar, putting down her knitting on the table, and staring at him with wet eyes. 'He's got an appointment now. He's seeing the Vice-Chancellor.' 'Giving him his angle of vision,' says Howard. 'Yes,' says Miss Callendar, 'I'm sorry, I really am. Is it true that you could lose your job? All he wants is a chance.' 'There's a thing called gross moral turpitude,' says Howard, 'it's a very vague concept, especially these days. But I have political enemies who'd pin anything onto me they could.' 'Oh, God,' says Miss Callendar, 'this is why I came home. I just couldn't stand it. That awful, prying meeting this morning. I've been so worried about both of you.' 'About him?' asks Howard. 'He's a blackmailer and a fascist. You worried about him?' 'He's not a fascist, he's a person,' says Miss Callendar, 'he's a boy, and he's silly and frightened, because you frightened him. He's behaved wickedly and ridiculously. I've told him, I've attacked him. But he thinks you're out to destroy him, just because he is what he is, and he's struggling for his survival.' 'That's right,' says Howard. 'In other words, the classic fascist psychology. When everything's going in your favour, you claim belief in the values of decency and convention. But when your position's challenged, to hell with all that. Fight for self-interest with everything you can lay your hands on.' 'But what have you been doing with him?' asks Miss Callendar. 'You boxed him in a corner, and wouldn't let him out. You said on Thursday you might teach him again. Why did you say that?' 'You know why,' says Howard. 'You were playing with him to reach me,' says Miss Callendar. 'Look,' says Howard, 'while we were talking, he was spying. He's not worth your compassion.' 'He's a sad case,' says Miss Callendar, 'appealing for assistance. Like your Miss Phee. But one you bed and one you punish.' 'One's a person, and one's not,' says Howard. 'You're dangerously misdirecting your compassion. Look at him. Inspect his cropped little haircut, his polished shoes. Think about that arrogant, imperial manner. He expects the world to dance to his tune. If it doesn't, he smashes out. He can't face life or reality. He feels nothing except terror at being threatened by those who are actually doing some living. That's the meaning of his story. That's the person you're supporting.' 'I've done no more than I should, as his adviser,' says Miss Callendar, 'and rather less than you've done for Miss Phee.' 'No,' says Howard, 'you've believed him. You told me that. He offered an explanation of what you couldn't understand.' 'I haven't accepted his charge,' says Miss Callendar, 'I have believed what he saw to be true.' 'You haven't also helped him see it?' asks Howard. Miss Callendar looks at Howard; she says, 'What do you mean?' Howard says, 'It was on Tuesday Carmody and I had our fight. But he knows all about Monday night. About Felicity Phee and me in the basement. He must have been standing just about where you were standing, at exactly the same time, to know that.' 'You think I told him?' asks Miss Callendar, 'I didn't.' 'Did you see him that night, when you left?' asks Howard. 'Where was he?' 'I don't know,' says Miss Callendar, 'but I didn't tell him.' 'How do I know?' asks Howard. 'You don't,' says Miss Callendar. 'No,' says Howard.

Miss Callendar gets up out of her chair. She stands in front of the fire; she picks up a glass globe from the mantelpiece. There is a tiny village scene inside the globe; when she picks it up, snowflakes start to foam within the glass. Howard gets up too; he says, 'Do you understand what I'm saying to you?' Miss

Callendar looks up; she says, 'Why do you blame me?' 'You've got to make your choice,' says Howard. 'Where you are. Who you're with. Whose story you accept.' 'I like to be fair,' says Miss Callendar. 'You can't be,' says Howard. 'Do you know where you're going? You're going his way. You'll end up just like him.' 'What do you mean?' says Miss Callendar. 'Look at this room you've shut yourself up in,' says Howard. 'It speaks what you are.' Miss Callendar looks round her room, at the chintz armchairs, the standard lamp, the prints on the walls. 'It's a very convenient room,' she says. 'It's a faded place,' says Howard, 'somewhere where you can hide, and protect yourself against anything that's growing now. Life and sexuality and love. Don't you hide?' 'I like to be a little elusive,' says Miss Callendar. 'He's destroyed himself, and you will too,' says Howard. 'You'll dry up, you'll wither, you'll hate and grudge, in ten years you'll be nothing, a neurotic little old lady.' 'It's a very nice room,' says Miss Callendar. Howard says: 'Freud once gave a very economical definition of neurosis. He said it was an abnormal attachment to the past.' Miss Callendar's face is very white; her dark eyes stare out of it. 'I don't want this,' she says, 'I can't bear this.' 'You've got to forget him,' says Howard, putting his hand over the hand that holds the little glass snowstorm, 'You've got to be with me.' 'I shouldn't have let you in,' says Miss Callendar. 'What did you do to him?' 'I'm not interested in him,' says Howard, 'I'm interested in you. I have been all along.' 'I don't want you to be,' says Miss Callendar. 'Is that your bedroom in there?' asks Howard. 'Why?' asks Miss Callendar, lifting a sad, crying face. 'Come in there with me,' says Howard. 'I don't want to,' says Miss Callendar. 'It's all right,' says Howard. 'He's not there. He's gone to see the Vice-Chancellor.' 'I don't want it,' says Miss Callendar. 'Another Miss Phee, getting the help.' 'Oh, you're more than that,' says Howard. 'Not a sub-plot,' says Miss Callendar. 'The thing it's all been about,' says Howard. 'Come on.'

He puts his hand on her arm. Miss Callendar turns, her dark head down. 'Yes,' says Howard. Miss Callendar moves toward the brown-stained bedroom door; she pushes it open and walks into the room. It is a small room, with, against one wall, a very large wardrobe; the bed is bulky and high, and has a wooden head and foot. On it is a patchwork quilt; Miss Callendar straightens it. Outside the window is a little garden, on the slope; Miss Callendar goes to this window, and pulls across the heavy plush curtains. The room now is nearly dark. Still standing by the curtains, away from him on the other side of the bed, she begins, clumsily, to remove the trouser suit; he hears the whisper of cloth as she takes things off. 'Can I put the light on?' asks Howard. 'No, don't, you mustn't,' says Miss Callendar. The clothes fall off onto the floor; her body is white in the faint light. She moves from her place; the bed creaks; she is lying on top of the quilt. His own clothes are around his feet. He climbs onto the bed, and touches with his hand the very faintly roughened softness of her skin. He feels the coldness of his hand on her, and a little pulling shudder, a revulsion, in the flesh. His hand has found the centre of her body, the navel; he slides it upward, to her small round breast, and then down, to her thighs. He feels the springs of response, tiny springs; the stir of the nipple, the warmth of the mucus. But she scarcely moves; she neglects to feel what she feels. 'Have you done this before?' he whispers. 'Hardly ever,' she whispers. 'You don't like it,' he says. 'Aren't you here to make me?' she asks. He kneads and presses her body. He lies over her, against her breast, and can feel the rapid knocking of her heart. In the dark he moves and feels the busy, energetic flesh of himself wriggling into her, like a formless proliferating thing, hot and growing and spreading. Unmitigated, inhuman, it explodes; the sweat of flesh, of two fleshes, is in the air of the dark room; their bodies break away from each other.

Miss Callendar lies with her face away from him; he can smell the scent of her healthy shampoo close to his face. 'I shouldn't have let you, it's wrong,' she whispers. 'It's not wrong,' he says. How can he have thought her quite old, when he met her first? Her body against him feels very, very young. He whispers, as to a child, 'Promise me you'll not think about him again, act for him again.' Miss Callendar keeps her head turned away; she says, 'That's what it was for.' 'It's for your good,' says Howard. 'Those things you said,' says Miss Callendar. 'What about them?' asks Howard. 'You said them just to get inside me.' 'I think you'd have let me, in any case,' says Howard. 'It was bound to happen.' 'Historical inevitability,' says Miss

Callendar. 'There was an ending. I was it.' 'That's right,' says Howard. 'Marx arranged it.' After a moment, Miss Callendar turns her head; she says, 'Marx said history is bunk.' 'That was Henry Ford,' says Howard. 'No, Marx,' says Miss Callendar. 'Oh, yes?' asks Howard, 'where?' 'A late insight,' says Miss Callendar, turning her body over to face him. 'It's my field,' says Howard. 'Blake for you, and Marx for me.' 'I'm right,' says Miss Callendar, 'it's a critical ambiguity.' 'If you want,' says Howard. 'Was I awful at it?' asks Miss Callendar. 'It's like golf, you need plenty of practice,' says Howard. 'We can arrange it.' 'You're so busy,' says Miss Callendar, 'and George will be on duty again.' 'Oh, I don't think so,' says Howard, 'I think we can deal with him.'

XIII

And now it is the winter again; the people, having come back, are going away again. The autumn, in which the passions rise, the tensions mount, the strikes accumulate, the newspapers fill with disaster, is over. Christmas is coming; the goose is getting fat, and the papers getting thin; things are stopping happening. In the drives the cars are being packed, and the people are ready, in relief, to be off, to Positano or the Public Record Office, Moscow or mother, for the lapse of the festive season. There are coloured lights along the promenade, now on, now off, according to the rhythm of the power strikes; Nixon is back in office for a second term, and there is talk of seasonal truce in Ulster. Mock fir trees decked with empty tinsel packages stand in the pedestrian precincts where the shoppers crowd and generate minor economic boom among consumables; there are train crashes and plane crashes, as there always seem to be over this season. Snow flurries over the sea; people assume cheeriness; telephones ring to transmit Yuletide compliments. The Kirks, that well-known couple, catch the mood and decide to have a party. They have, actually, had a party at this point in time, the end of the autumn term, the first term of the year up at the new university spreading on the hill, for the past two winters. But it is hardly a tradition with them, and can hardly be, for who can predict ahead of time the strifes and dissentions, the fallings out and the fallings in, that will come upon a group of intelligent people like this when they get together to generate the onward march of mind, the onward process of history. In any case the Kirks are, of course, enormously busy people, with two full lives, and two separate diaries; they are not in the house together very much; there is little space for planning and conversation, with so much in the world to do. But as it happens they do find themselves in the house together, in that last week of term; and though the strife has been considerable, the term wearing, and their own relationship uncertain, for when one is up the other is down, yet some atavistic instinct manages to seize them. They look at each other, with natural suspicion; they examine the mood and the milieu; they say, but not very certainly, 'Yes.' And then they fetch the common household diary—Howard had fetched it last time, so Barbara fetches it this—and they sit down together with it, in the pine kitchen, and inspect the busy pages. There is a free date that suits them both quite equally, and does not affect their separate plans. They seize it; the date is Friday 15 December, the last day of the term.

After the instinct about the party has come to them, an instinct so tentative and uncertain that neither is quite sure whom to blame for it, the Kirks go together into their living-room and pour themselves out a glass of beer each, and they begin to plan it. It is a small inspection of their present relationships; and it becomes quickly clear that it will be a thinner, smaller party than their last one, held at the beginning of this same term, when the prospects were pleasing and the future full of options. For wear and tear have overtaken the Kirks, and their friendships, and their friends. There have been splits and dissensions, and changes of partner and changes of alliance; new divorces pend, new political associations burgeon. He no longer speaks to her; they no longer speak to them; it is not easy to plan a party, unless one is very *au courant* with movement and mood, but the Kirks have a way of being that, and they build up their list accordingly. There are people who, it can be taken, will not now come when summoned by the Kirks; there are people the Kirks will not now summon under any circumstances. The people are already in the process of leaving, for the final week of term is a reading week, and many students have surreptitiously disappeared, and some faculty; there are many with other commitments, caucuses, or affairs.

There will be, therefore, no ministrations from Flora Beniform, for she has been absent for the last three weeks; fieldwork in West Bromwich, where there has been a significant outbreak of troilism, has called her away. There will be no Roger Fundy, for he is committed in London that day, appearing before magistrates on a charge of assaulting the police, a consequence of a recent Grosvenor Square demonstration against Cambodian policy. There will be no Leon, for Leon is touring with *Much Ado About Nothing* in Australia, and no avant-gardists from the local theatre, for the cast of *Puss in Boots* is not Kirk company. But there are others, a bouncing if battered crew of survivors, for the radical cause at Watermouth this term has had its victories, and there is every reason to appear in good humour. So the wind beats on the windows, and the night comes in fast; the lights flicker in the broken houses across the streets; the Kirks sit in their corduroy Habitat chairs, and name names and plan delights; the party takes on its modest shape.

After a while, Barbara rises, and goes to the door of the living-room. 'Felicity,' she shouts into the complex acoustics of the hall, 'Howard and I are busy planning this party. I wonder whether you'd mind bathing the children tonight?' 'Yes, I do mind,' shouts Felicity from somewhere, probably the lavatory, where she spends much time, 'I'm tired of being exploited.' 'I don't know what's the matter with Felicity,' says Barbara, sitting down again in the corduroy chair. 'Never mind,' says Howard, 'I think she's in another crisis.' 'I expect you stopped laying her,' says Barbara, 'you might have thought of me.' 'I try to do my best,' says Howard, 'but there's so much.' 'Yes, we gathered,' says Barbara, 'from Carmody's camera.' 'What about the Beamishes?' asks Howard. 'Or is it Beamish and Beamish?' 'They're together,' says Barbara, 'they have been ever since Dr Beniform went away. But would they come if you invited them?' 'Henry's a friend of mine,' says Howard. 'Still?' asks Barbara. 'After Mangel? I can't imagine he ever wants to see you again.' 'Oh, Henry sees the other point of view,' says Howard. But there is good reason to wonder, for, if the high point of radical success in the term was the occasion of the Mangel lecture, it did not go exactly well for Henry. For the department did issue its invitation to Mangel, and there was much dissent among the faculty, and much resentment, and the news penetrated with great and mysterious speed to the radical student groups on campus who, having already managed two sit-ins, felt in great strength and in a mood of unprecedented cooperativeness one with another. They put up many posters, and held many meetings, some addressed by Howard, that martyr of Carmodian persecution; on the day of the lecture a great crowd gathered, outside the Beatrice Webb Lecture Theatre, where the event was to take place, chanting and angry. Professor Mangel had indicated in advance that his topic would be 'Do Rats Have "Families"?', but this was found a typical liberal evasion, and indignation ran the higher, and many bodies lay down and obstructed all the entrances to the room, while massive and hostile forces assembled inside, making the radical point with roars and posters.

'It was Henry's own fault,' says Howard, recalling the famous victory. 'He was determined to be provocative. Henry makes accidents.' 'There are people who feel he was the only one who behaved decently,' says Barbara. 'Christ, Barbara,' asks Howard, 'are you going soft in your old age?' 'I didn't like it,' says Barbara. The unfortunate thing was that the task of introduction had fallen to Henry; it should more properly have gone to Professor Marvin, but he had suddenly confessed himself afflicted by an alternative engagement, in Edinburgh, giving a lecture on messianism, or failing that to Mangel's old pupil, Dr Beniform, but she had been claimed by the demanding affairs of West Bromwich. In the event, it was Henry, who, that day, had stepped carefully through the bodies, and entered the forbidden space of the Lecture Theatre. 'Why didn't he just tell them what had happened?' asks Howard. 'Oh, you'd have been disappointed if he had,' says Barbara. For Henry had stood at the podium, stark with his bandaged arm; he had said, politely, 'I ask you all to disperse.' Peter Madden had pushed in front of Henry; he had announced to the audience, 'This lecture is forbidden by radical opinion.' The audience had roared its assent, 'Forbidden, forbidden,' and 'Fascist, fascist,' and then Henry had been unwise. He had pushed Peter Madden aside with his good arm; he had waved his bad one; he had shouted, 'You're the fascists; this is a crime against free speech.' Then the crowd had pushed and jostled;

Melissa Todoroff, noticeable in the audience for her poster 'Hysterectomiże Mangel', had thrown a bread bun at Henry; this had unleashed the forces, who surged onto the podium, and knocked Henry's unsteady body down, and somehow, in the mêlée, trampled him underfoot. In their anger they had then rushed to his office, left unlocked; they had pulled open the filing cabinets, and tipped out or stolen the papers; they had broken the silver-framed mirror; they had poured tea out of the Teasmaid over the Norwegian rugs, and then smashed the Teasmaid; they had tossed his research notes into the mess.

'He needn't have been provocative,' says Howard, 'he could simply have told them about Mangel.' 'Myra says he was afraid they might cheer,' says Barbara, 'and that he couldn't have borne.' In fact it was not until the next day, when Henry was in hospital, that the news about Mangel became known; of the many there that day, only Mangel had neglected to come, having died, the evening previous to the lecture, of a heart attack, in his London apartment. 'Let's ask him, anyway,' says Howard, 'it will give him a chance to make his peace.' 'The more we go into this,' says Barbara, 'the more I feel the last thing we need is a party. I think it's a very doubtful celebration.' 'You thought that last time,' says Howard, 'and it cheered you up.' 'My God, Howard,' says Barbara, 'what in hell do you know about my cheerfulness or my misery? What access do you have to any of my feelings? What do you know about me now?' 'You're fine,' says Howard. 'I'm appallingly miserable,' says Barbara. 'Tell me why?' asks Howard. 'I prefer not to,' says Barbara. 'Okay,' says Howard, 'you need a party.' 'My God,' says Barbara, but they go on planning, and talking. A bit later on they go out into the hall, and one stands by and the other makes calls, and then they reverse roles, for the Kirks do everything together and in fairness. Sometimes the telephone is not answered, and sometimes the answer is a refusal; but there is, as they surmise, the human stuff ready and available to be a party, a seasonal, Christmassy party. 'It'll be fine,' says Howard. Afterwards they eat, and later they go to bed, and lie on each other. 'What you need is a break,' says Howard afterwards, 'there's just been too much happening.' 'To you,' says Barbara, 'not to me. Name one thing that in any good sense has lately happened to me?' 'Go up to London and shop,' says Howard. 'Buy presents.' 'There's nothing there,' says Barbara, 'nothing at all there.'

And the days go by, and Howard tidies up at the university, setting vacation essays, inviting the students who still manage, somehow, to be about to his party, and then it is the morning of Friday 15 December. The Kirks rise, early and together, they go down the stairs and into the kitchen. Felicity Phee, who still sleeps in their guest bedroom, is sitting at the pine table, dark-eyed, in her drawstring top and long skirt, eating toast; the children are somewhere, she does not know where. 'It's a pretty busy day,' says Barbara, 'I hope you can give me a hand.' 'Actually I'm packing,' says Felicity, 'I think you've had all the help from me you want.' 'But how will I manage tomorrow?' asks Barbara. 'Tomorrow will sort itself, Barbara,' says Felicity, 'you'll manage. I'm sure there's always someone who'll do all those jobs just so they can have the marvellous company of the Kirks.' 'Have we upset you, Felicity?' asks Barbara. 'Well,' says Felicity, 'I suppose a person always has to keep moving on. I'm just into something else. I'm joining a Hare Krishna community.' 'Oh, Felicity, that's not you,' says Barbara. 'I don't think too much is known around here about what's me,' says Felicity, 'I've done a lot for you both. I mean, I have, haven't I, Howard?' 'Yes,' says Howard, 'a great deal.' 'Well, you sort of hope to get something out of that, and if it doesn't work out, well, you have to keep moving. That's Dr Kirk's advice. He likes people to keep moving.' 'Oh, good,' says Barbara, 'you've discussed it.' 'I mean, I don't say there's so much that's smart about his advice,' says Felicity, 'but that's his job, and I suppose he sort of knows something about it. Maybe.' 'You're angry with us, I'm sorry,' says Barbara. 'It's all right,' says Felicity, 'you're just not my kind of scene any more.' 'Anyway, stay for the party,' says Howard. 'Maybe I will,' says Felicity, 'if you mean just be around. I mean, not work. Just enjoying myself.' 'That's right,' says Howard.

Howard goes and fetches the van; the Kirks get in. 'I think you exploited her,' says Barbara, as they drive up the hill toward the shopping precincts. 'Still, as you always say, everybody exploits somebody. I'll get the food, you get the wine.' The Kirks move through the precinct, with its artificial fir trees, its massed crowds, its abundance of shiny goods. Then they drive back down to the damaged terrace; there is just time to get the children off to school. 'Last day, last day,' shout the children, as they get into the van. Howard, along with the other mothers, drops them and then goes into the university, to dictate letters, say goodbyes. The trunks are piled up for collection by British Rail outside Toynbee and Spengler; buses are taking students down to the station. From the administration building still hang tattered remnants from the sit-ins of the term; a red banner saying 'Come on in, it's living' and another saying 'Fight repression'. A small burn mark on the concrete indicates the area where a radical faction tried to advance the protest further by starting a fire. The campus, emptying, looks like a deserted battlefield; inside there are dark corridors and cold rooms where fuel economies amount to social disfunction. Everywhere is the worn, public look of a place that has seen much, and is used by everybody, and belongs to nobody. Howard sits there, in the purity of his anonymous room; he works and he telephones; he looks with pleasure over the landscape of his late victories. In mid-afternoon, he goes through the littered Piazza to his van, and drives into town, to pick up the children from school. The schoolyard is buoyant with farewells, crowded with parents; Martin and Celia run to the van bearing toilet-roll Santas, and child art calendars, and an attempt, on Martin's part, at a crib. Martin has a black eye; Celia's boutique dress is torn. 'What happened to you?' asks Howard, as they get in. 'Oh,' says Celia, 'we had a party.'

Howard drives back toward the stage and scene of his own. In the kitchen, Barbara is absent; he hears water running in the bathroom. He sets to, and opens bottles; he walks about the house, arranging furniture, setting out spaces and counterspaces. The darkness is down already; he stands in his bedroom, while glow lights the battered houses opposite, and fixes lights. Barbara comes out of the bathroom, and he goes in. He strips and takes a bath, powders himself, and goes through into the bedroom to dress. Barbara is in there, putting on a bright silvery dress. 'Is it all right?' she says. 'Where did you get it?' asks Howard. 'I bought it in London,' says Barbara. 'You never tried it on for me,' he says. 'No,' says Barbara, 'I offered, but you'd not got time.' 'It's nice,' says Howard. 'Yes,' says Barbara, 'he had very good taste.' Barbara goes out of the bedroom; Howard begins to dress himself, smartly, neatly, for the fray. The children come in, and run around. 'Will the people make as much mess as they did last time?' asks Martin. 'I don't think so,' says Howard, 'not so many of them.' 'I hope nobody jumps out of the window again,' says Celia. 'Nobody jumped out of the window,' says Howard. 'Someone just hurt himself a bit.' 'Uncle Henry,' says Martin. 'Is he coming?' 'I don't know,' says Howard, 'I'm not sure who's coming.' 'Supposing nobody comes,' says Celia, 'who'll eat all that cheese?' 'Not me,' says Martin. 'Oh, lots of people will come,' says Howard, 'you'll see.'

And lots of people do come. The cars roar in the terrace. Howard goes to the front door to open it for the first guests; the bright lights from the house fall across the damaged pavements, and shine on the debris and demolition of the street. The guests walk into the glow, towards the step; here is Moira Millikin, carrying her baby, and behind her the Macintoshes, each of them bearing a baby in a carrycot; Mrs Macintosh, when she did deliver, delivered in bulk, and had twins. Barbara comes down the hall, wearing her silvery showpiece and a large Russian necklace, her hair done in a social bun. 'Your lovely parties,' says Moira, coming inside, taking off her cape, showing her pregnant bulge, 'Can we stick this one somewhere?' 'And these,' says Mrs Macintosh, looking very thin, with just a small loose bounce at the stomach where not all fitness is back. 'Hello, Kirks,' says Macintosh, taking off his macintosh, 'Are we the first ones again?' 'Great to see you, come inside,' say the hospitable Kirks, a welcoming couple, both at once. No sooner are the first arrivals in the living-room, with drinks, talking breastfeeding, when more guests arrive. The room fills. There are students in quantities; bearded Jesus youths in combat-wear, wet-look plastic, loon-pants, flared jeans, Afghan yak; girls, in caftans and big boots, with plum-coloured mouths. There are young faculty, serious, solemn examiners of matrimony and its radical alternatives; there are strangers from the Kirks' general acquaintance—a radical vicar, an Argentinian with obscure guerrilla associations, an actor in moleskin trousers who has touched Glenda Jackson in a Ken Russell film. Minnehaha Ho has come, in a cheongsam; Anita Dollfuss, with her big brown dog on a string, is here, fresh from months of sleeping through seminar after seminar. Barbara, in her bright green eye-shadow, her silvery dress, appears here and there, with her plates of food: 'Eat,' she says, 'it's sociable.' Howard goes about, a big two-litre bottle hanging on the loop from his finger, the impresario of the event, feeling the buoyant pleasure of having these young people round him, patched, harlequinned, embroidered, self-gratifying, classless, citizens of a world of expectation, a world beyond norms and forms. He pours wine, seeing the bubbles move inside the glass of the bottle in the changing lights of his rooms. The party booms; a jet out of Heathrow roars over the top of the town; a police-car heehaws away on the urban motorway; in the abandoned houses opposite the little lights flicker, and behind them the expanding urban waste.

Inside the party grows, thickens, becomes fissiparous. Space fills up; activity is forced back through the premises, into new rooms with new colours on the walls and hence new psychic possibilities, rooms with new tests to perform, for there is food spread on a table in the dining-room, and a space for dancing in the Victorian conservatory, and recesses of intimacy and silence upstairs. Somewhere someone has found a record-player and set it going; somewhere else in the house a guitar is playing. 'Hi,' says Melissa Todoroff, arriving in a tartan dress, 'I salute the radical hero. I think you're wonderful, I think you're tops.' 'Let me take your coat,' says Howard. 'Thanks,' says Melissa. 'Now. Where do I go to get laid?' In the hall the bra-less girl from Howard's seminar, still bra-less, is explaining the philosophy of Hegel in detail to the actor who has laid hand on Glenda Jackson, and has now laid hand on the bra-lessness. 'It's eminently a dialectical portrait,' says the girl. 'Don't pinch.' In the living-room, the familiar group or coterie from the Radical Student Alliance stand together in a corner, solemn, looking a little like the scene at the Last Supper after the guests have risen. They are being accosted by Miss Callendar, who wears a bright thin caftan, and has let loose her hair, and is saying, 'Hello, what have you all come as?' In the Victorian conservatory, where the dancing is desultory, Barbara stands in silver, talking to Minnehaha Ho, who is wide-eyed and solitary against the wall. 'What kind of contra-ceptive do you use?' Barbara is asking, in her sociable concern.

On the landing Felicity Phee, in her same long skirt, is talking to Dr Macintosh. 'The awful thing is,' says Felicity, 'I thought I'd found out where I was and now I'm there it's not where I am at all. If you see what I mean.' 'I do,' says Dr Macintosh sagely, 'that's it, isn't it? Existence never stops. The self keeps going on, endlessly.' 'Oh, I *know*, Dr Macintosh,' says Felicity, 'you're so right.' In one of the rooms off the upstairs landing, a mattress that Howard has thoughtfully laid out beforehand is squeaking in one of the familiar rhythms of the universe.

There is turmoil in the hall; Anita Dollfuss's dog has bitten the radical vicar, and compassionate persons take him away upstairs for treatment. 'I'm sorry, Howard,' says Anita, 'you'll stop inviting me. He tried to pat him. He should have patted me.' The dog pants happily at Howard, who says: 'That reminds me, you've not seen Dr Beamish, have you?' 'No, I haven't,' says Anita Dollfuss, in her long long dress, her hair in its Alice headband, 'I don't think he's here.' He walks about with his bottle, upstairs, downstairs; Henry has clearly neglected to come. An uneasy instinct takes him to the closed door of the guest bedroom. He taps; there is no answer. He opens the door; the room is dark. The window is in place. 'Do you mind, please?' says the voice of Dr Macintosh, 'I'm afraid this is occupied.' 'I'm sorry,' says Howard. 'It's Howard,' says Felicity. 'We don't want you, Howard. Why don't you find your Miss Callendar?' He goes downstairs again into the party. There is no Henry, there is no Flora, and now, it seems, there is no Barbara; the spread of food is devastated, and the hands that tend it seem to have found other, better pastures. With hostly compunction, Howard goes into the kitchen. He stands in front of the wallpaper celebrating the lines of onions and garlics; he stands in front of the pine shelves, with their scatter of selected objects: the French casseroles, the row of handthrown pottery mugs in light brown, the two pepper-mills, the line of deep blue Spanish glasses from Casa Pupo, the dark brown pot saying *Sel*. In front of him, in a rush basket, lie ten long French loaves; Howard stands at the pine table, and neatly, crisply he slices the crusty bread. The room is his, but then the door opens. Myra Beamish stands there, wearing a dress that looks as if it has been made from sacking. 'There you are,' she says, coming in, 'you look like an extremely trendy peasant. Where's

Barbara?' 'I don't know,' says Howard, 'she seems to have disappeared, so I'm doing this.' 'Oh, ho,' says Myra, sitting down on the edge of the table in her sacking dress. 'Well, never mind, you seem to be doing a great job. Do you cook too?' 'I have a few specialities,' says Howard. 'Well, Howard, I must try them sometime,' says Myra.

'Has Henry come?' asks Howard. 'No, Henry's not coming,' says Myra, 'he's sitting at home very depressed because he can't get on with his book.' 'I thought he saved most of his notes,' says Howard. 'He may have saved them,' says Myra, 'but with one arm in a sling and the other broken and in plaster he can't really write very well.' 'I suppose not,' says Howard, 'but he could come to a party.' 'Well, Howard,' says Myra, 'he doesn't want to see you. He does blame you, you know. You did encourage them.' 'But he's usually so good at seeing the other point of view,' says Howard, 'and politics isn't a bloodless business.' 'I thought it was horrible,' says Myra, 'all those screaming people. I panicked, I ran out.' 'Any sensible person would have panicked,' says Howard. 'You're teasing,' says Myra, 'you know I'm very bad about these things. I know I'm very square.' 'But anyway you came, Myra,' says Howard. 'Well, I don't do all that Henry wants me to do,' says Myra, 'in fact, I rather do what he doesn't want me to do. I felt like seeing you, you lovely man.' There is a stir on the table; Myra suddenly leans forward and kisses Howard, catching him obliquely on the nose. 'That's to say Merry Christmas,' she says. 'Ah,' says Howard, 'Merry Christmas to you.' Myra bends seriously over her black handbag, and dips down into it. 'I don't suppose,' she says, taking something from the bag, 'I don't suppose you still remember that time in my bedroom.' Howard looks at her; she has taken out a mirror, and, her head down, her nose shining under the overhead light, she is inspecting her lipstick, her mouth open in an O. 'A very long time ago, Myra,' says Howard. 'I know you've been everywhere since then,' says Myra, 'toured the parish. But come again sometime, won't you? It would be different. I was silly then. I'm not so bloody bourgeois now. I know what I missed.' 'But what about you and Henry?' asks Howard, 'I thought you were back together again.' 'You and Barbara are back together again,' says Myra, 'but you have an advanced marriage. It doesn't keep you on a very tight rein, does it? We did hear all the rumours about what Mr Carmody found out.' 'Don't believe all that,' says Howard. 'No, Barbara and I have learned to accept each other's lifestyles.' 'You mean Barbara's learned to accept yours,' says Myra, 'or has to, for want of a better.' 'It works both ways,' says Howard. 'Anyway,' says Myra, 'Henry's got to accept mine. We're back together, Howard. But on my terms, Howard boy, on my terms. It's one of those intelligent marriages, now.'

'But what does Henry get from it?' asks Howard. 'Is it fair to Henry?' 'I don't understand you, Howard,' says Myra, 'this unwonted concern. Henry had Flora Beniform. So I can do what *I* like. Isn't that right?' 'Oh, Flora is primarily therapy,' says Howard. 'Oh, I know you've been round there, too,' says Myra, 'Flora is primarily the classic bitch done up in modern dress. But I'm sure you are too, Howard.' 'A bitch?' asks Howard. 'No,' says Myra, 'therapy. And we all need treatment. It's the age of treatment. I'm asking for some.' 'But I can't help thinking about Henry,' says Howard, 'how is he? He's depressed, he's helpless, doesn't he need you?' 'This isn't like you, Howard,' says Myra. 'I'm concerned for Henry,' says Howard. 'You hold him in contempt,' says Myra, 'you and your cohorts break his arm and smash his nose, when he's trying to do something moderately decent. You despise his mores. And then, when nobody needs it, you express concern for him. He'd rather be without it, Howard. Devote it to me.' 'Yoo-hoo, baby,' says Melissa Todoroff, standing a little unsteadily in the doorway in her tartan dress, 'how about splashing some of that wine you're hiding into my glass?' 'I'm sorry, Melissa,' says Howard, picking up a bottle. 'Or maybe you should just pour it, right, down, my, little throat,' says Melissa Todoroff, coming into the room. 'Am I neglecting you?' asks Howard, pouring wine. 'You sure are,' says Melissa, putting an arm through his, 'you haven't come near me for ages.' 'How's the party?' asks Howard. 'There are things going on out there,' says Melissa, 'that would make your nipples pucker. Well, hi there, Myra. How's it going?' 'I'm just going,' says Myra, picking up her bag, 'I'd better go back to Henry, hadn't I?' 'Uh-huh, uh-huh,' says Melissa, watching as Myra walks out of the door, in her sacklike dress, 'did I do something?' 'I don't know,' says Howard, detaching his arm, and beginning to slice bread again, 'of course you did once throw a bread bun at Henry.' 'Oh, God, I did, that's right,' says Melissa Todoroff, with a gay, hacking chuckle, 'and then we trampled him underfoot. Is she sore?' 'I don't know whether Myra's sore,' says Howard, 'but . . .' 'But Henry sure is sore,' says Melissa, 'he has a sore face and a sore arm and a sore ass and he's sore.'

'That's right,' says Howard. 'Well, he got in the way of justice,' says Melissa, 'you know what they say, if you don't like the heat, get out of the kitchen. Maybe that's why she got out of the kitchen.' 'Maybe,' says Howard. 'Oh, boy, wasn't that a day?' says Melissa Todoroff, reminiscent, 'I really blew my mind. What a trip. Freedom and liberation seemed really real. The people chanting, the crowds roaring, all crying for goodness. It was Berkeley, Columbia, Vincennes. We were all so beautiful. Then, zap, with the bread bun. Things were so wide open and easy. Will we ever be like that again?' 'It was only a couple of weeks ago, Melissa,' says Howard. 'You know what they say,' says Melissa, 'a week's a long time in politics. Fantastic. There was action then. People really felt something. But what happened to it?' 'It's around,' says Howard. 'You know what's the matter with people now?' says Melissa, very seriously, 'They just don't feel any more.' 'Not the way they did last week,' says Howard. 'They sure don't feel *me* any more,' says Melissa. 'The night's young,' says Howard. 'Not as young as it used to be,' says Melissa. 'But I mean, seriously, who, anywhere, now, is getting down to the real, root, radical problems of the age?' 'Who?' asks Howard. 'I'll tell you whom,' says Melissa, 'nobody, that's whom. Who's authentic any more?' 'You seem pretty authentic,' says Howard, slicing bread. 'Oh, God, no, Christ, really, do I?' says Melissa Todoroff, agonizing. 'Do I really seem like that to you? I'm not, How, it's just a front. I'm more authentic than these other bastards, but I'm not authentic the way I mean authentic.' 'You are, Melissa,' says Howard. 'You're giving me shit,' says Melissa Todoroff, 'you're a good guy but you're giving me shit.' Melissa Todoroff walks towards the door, precariously carrying her glass of wine; she says, 'I'm going right back there into that party and then, wow, watch out.' At the door she stops. 'I don't care what your friends say about you, you're a good guy,' she

227

says, 'a radical's radical. And if you really work at it, you could be a radical's radical's radical.'

Howard stands for a while longer, in the kitchen, slicing his hostly bread; then, the chore done, he walks back into his own party. It has changed, grown weak at the centre, active at the circumference. In the living-room, where the main illumination is the flashing string of lights on the children's Christmas tree, there is torpor; a few people lie about, chatting, in varieties of intimacy. In the Victorian conservatory, there is desultory rhythmic dancing; junior members of faculty bounce and rock in the near-darkness. In the dining-room, the piles of bread and cheese stand in a state of neglect; Howard's dutiful ministrations are no longer needed. The party's momentum is clearly elsewhere, in nooks here and there, in the upper parts of the house, in the garden, perhaps even in the waste land beyond. A few people are going, in the hall; there in the hall stands a figure wearing an anorak and a large orange backpack, from which protrude various large objects. 'I'm off now, Howard,' says Felicity Phee. 'Someone's giving me a ride to London. I've cleared out all my stuff.' 'I'll see you next term,' says Howard. 'I don't know whether you will see me next term,' says Felicity. 'Haven't you sort of passed me up?' 'Well, we'll meet in class,' says Howard. 'I doubt it,' says Felicity. 'I went to see Professor Marvin today, and asked him to find me a new teacher.' 'Oh, I don't think he'll do that,' says Howard, 'after the trouble with George Carmody.' Felicity looks at him; she says, 'I really don't think you'd better stand in my way. I mean, I know as much as anyone about what happened with George Carmody. Do you plan to get rid of me too?' 'Of course not,' says Howard. 'Of course not,' says Felicity, 'I know everything about you.' 'What does that mean?' asks Howard. 'I wanted to help you,' says Felicity. 'I wanted you to recognize me.' 'You did help me,' says Howard. 'Okay, well, it didn't do me any good, did it?' asks Felicity. 'You won and I didn't. So now just leave me alone.' 'I will,' says Howard. 'Well, do,' says Felicity. 'Say goodbye to Barbara for me. If you can find her.'

The party can spare its host now, having become entirely self-made, as good parties must; a little later, Howard goes downstairs, into his basement study. The sodium light shines over the tops of the broken houses, penetrating stark orange designs onto the walls, the bookcases, the African masks. The street is empty of people; Howard draws the curtains. 'So this is the scene of your many triumphs,' says someone coming down the stairs. 'It's all right, Annie,' says Howard, 'no one can see us. He's not there any more.' 'I rather wish he was,' says Annie Callendar, coming into the study. 'The critical eye.' 'Is it strange to be on the inside?' asks Howard. 'Yes,' says Annie, 'I suppose I ought to be raking through your book.' 'It's gone,' says Howard, 'it's being printed.' Later on, under Howard on the cushions, Annie Callendar says: 'I can't help thinking about him out there.' 'He's gone, he's gone,' says Howard; and indeed Carmody has, fled weeks ago after a brief student sit-in—the banners said 'Preserve academic freedom' and 'Work for Kirk' —had demanded his expulsion, after the story of his campaign against Howard had become widely known. 'I never knew whether you believed me, Howard,' says Annie Callendar. 'I really didn't tell him.' 'Tell him what?' asks Howard lazily. 'You didn't tell him what?' 'I didn't tell him what I saw that night,' says Annie. 'You down here laying little Miss Phee.' 'Of course I believed you,' says Howard. 'Did you?' asks Annie. 'Why?' 'I know who did tell him,' says Howard. Annie stirs under him; she says, 'Who did? Who'd do that?' Howard laughs and says, 'Who do you think? Who else knew?' 'Little Miss Phee?' says Annie Callendar. 'That's it,' says Howard. 'You're smart.' 'But why should she?' asks Annie. 'Why get you into trouble?' 'You see, she wanted to help,' says Howard. 'It's an odd way to help you,' says Annie. 'I shan't help you like that.' 'She thought like that,' says Howard. 'What she said was, she wanted to defend me against the attacks of the liberal reactionary forces, and they needed something to attack me with so that she could defend me properly.'

'It sounds a little crazy,' says Miss Callendar. 'She is a little crazy,' says Howard. The party noise booms above their heads. Annie Callendar says, 'When did you find out?' 'Oh, I don't know,' says Howard. 'Before he went?' 'Yes, it was,' says Howard. 'On the strength of that, you got rid of him,' says Annie Callendar. 'Rose to your present radical fame on campus.' 'He was an historical irrelevance,' says Howard. 'Did you know before you came to see me that afternoon?' asks Annie Callendar. 'I can't remember,' says Howard. 'Of course you can remember,' says Annie, 'you did.' 'I may have done,' says Howard. 'Did you plan it with her?' asks Annie. 'Did you know all along?' 'I think we discussed it,' says Howard. 'But what was it for?' asks Annie. 'I wanted you,' says Howard, 'I just had to find a way to you.' 'No,' says Annie, 'that wasn't all. It was all a plot.' 'I thought you liked plots,' says Howard. 'In any case, it's the plot of history. It was simply inevitable.' 'But you helped inevitability along a little,' says Annie. 'There's a process,' says Howard. 'It charges everyone a price for the place they occupy, the stands they take.' 'You seem to travel free,' says Miss Callendar. 'Some travel free,' says Howard, 'some pay nice prices. You enjoy your price, don't you?' 'Going to bed with you?' asks Miss Callendar. 'Which was the real end in view,' says Howard. 'No,' says Miss Callendar. 'Ssshhh,' says Howard, 'of course it was.' Up above, the party noise vibrates. A small trouble is taking place in the hall; Mrs Macintosh, holding one carrycot, stands facing Dr Macintosh, holding another. 'You slipped upstairs with her,' she says, 'and I was breastfeeding.' 'The girl was crying,' says Dr Macintosh, 'she was very upset.' 'Right,' says Mrs Macintosh, 'this is the last party you come to.'

But it is a small altercation, and down in the basement they do not hear it. Nor do they hear when, higher in the house, in a guest bedroom empty of Felicity's things, a window smashes. The cause is Barbara who, bright in her silvery dress, has put her right arm through and down, savagely slicing it on the glass. In fact no one hears; as always at the Kirks' parties, which are famous for their happenings, for being like a happening, there is a lot that is, indeed, happening, and all the people are fully occupied.